Personal Experiences

Blood, Sweat —

Tracy Lee

Never
Tears! ♡

Tracy

PERSONAL EXPERIENCES

Published by: Tracy Lee

including infringement without monetary gain, is investigated by the FBI and is punishable by up to 5 years in Federal prison and a fine of up to $250,000.

Cover Art Design: Sprinkles On Top Studios
Cover Art Illustrations: Sprinkles on Top Studios
Format/Page building/Conversion: Princess SO/ Beastie
BOOKS

ISBN: 978-1492711971

PRODUCED IN THE UNITED STATES OF AMERICA

10 9 8 7 6 5 4 3 2 1

Content Warning

This book contains adult language and may be considered offensive to some readers. And are intended for sale to adults ONLY, as defined by the laws of the country in which you made your purchase. Please store your files wisely, where they cannot be accessed by under-aged readers.

Please be advised as part of this story the main character endures misuse before escaping and setting off into a new life and grows to overcome her past. Some scenes contain some scenes that are not for the light-hearted. Reader's discretion advised. (Contains: Adult language, sexual MF participation, and explicit scenes of arousal).

Acknowledgements

I just have to take a moment and thank everyone that has contributed something, whether it be reading and editing my crappy commas or if it was the 6:30 am phone call when I had an idea and needed someone to run it by. (I bow with my hand over my chest) Thank you from the bottom of my heart!

To my husband and our children…all 6 of them who have eaten shitty dinners and walked around a "lived in" home until this book was complete. You know mommy's not a good multitasker. I love you all bigger than the sky!

To my Trina-Bean…if it wasn't for your words of encouragement and your sleight of hand on my ass keeping me full steam ahead, I don't even think I would've ever published this. Keep up the "get it done!" for the next one.

To my Kay-Kay…I swear to god, I will never call it a restroom again! Heheh. I love you with all my heart and since I've known you since we were kids you have earned the right to be that judgmental Bitch that you are when it comes to my work. You hold my heart!

To my Rachel (AKA Nikki) to my Lilly (AKA Jeni) - Thank you both for giving me the friendship of a lifetime! The memories that I have made with the two of you demand to be lived in for eternity. From the cruising back and forth between mud holes and Regency in the Blue t-bird scaring the shit outta each other with the beginning of Ozzy singing "Crazy Train" to sitting at the house playing Asshole and drinking Jim Beam and Mt. Dew (still my favorite!). I feel blessed that I was able to have something so special not just with one of you but with both of you! You both make my soul complete! Love you girls! Nik, no matter how far apart we are or how young we turn (we're so not that age) you're always my sister from another mister, there will always be thoughts of us in the mustang with "horny toad" "Night at the Roxbury" dancing and C and C Music Factory on the tape player! Hehehe. And we always have McDill and Germany! My years with you attached at the hip were tragically too short; I wish we had a lifetime of being teenagers. Your encouragement and love when I thought I sucked at something showed me that I can do anything I wanted to. Jen, Your faithfulness and dependability as a friend is never ending. Never have I met another soul that would be so loyal. May you and your beautiful angels be richly blessed with infinite amounts of love, joy and prosperity for all you have given of yourself. I also some of the greatest memories of all time that have been provided by you; my eighteenth birthday party for one! Muddin' and ALWAYS remember never to use a Jim Beam bottle to try and hurt a burglar. Hahaha! "There's always ghosts in the sofer"

To my Trevor…you will always be the greatest regret I can't take back…you're "I told you so" would be music to my ears! Glad you found your happiness.

I need to give a great big hug to Amy Hutchins for all her great advice, encouragement and support. I still owe you a beer, girl!

A HUGE Thank you to Sarah over at Sprinkles On Top Studios for putting my kickass cover together; you did an amazing job and I greatly appreciate it!

A Tremendous Thank you to my beta readers; Amy, Becky, Jennifer, Rebekkah!! Love you guys! You're amazing and I'm thrilled you were the ones who got to experience "my first time" along with me. I look forward to many more years AND BOOKS with ya'll.

And To All My Readers!

You are the ones who make this worthwhile. To allow me to touch your lives with what is rambling around in my head overwhelms me heart and soul! I feel so blessed to have you believe in me!

Dedication

This book is dedicated to my children who are the rulers of my universe!

May you find all the joys that this life has to offer; May you avoid a great deal of the misery life attempts to envelop us in. May you find the one that gives you breath and treats you as though you are theirs' as well. May you always have unrelenting strength to hold yourselves up higher than the rest; to be what you have been made to be.

Kyleigh, Kolton, Katheryn and Kenna'D;
Mommy loves you as much as the sky and always remember: they can have your blood, they can have your sweat but never let them have your tears!

Table of Content

Prologue

May 1979

Recess was always my favorite part of the day, when school was in session, that is. Spring made it even better. The coolness from winter was still in the Georgia air but you could feel the warmth summer sprinkling on you as it forced its way closer, which made it just the right time for a good game of tag. The game was always boys against the girls in our little group and it always seemed that the boys were always chasing the girls, never the other way around. Having two best friends didn't seem weird to me at all. Some people would swear that only one could really be your best friend, but that wasn't the case. It was always Lilly, Rachel, and me, Elleny—Elle, for short. There wasn't any jealousy between us. We were more like sisters than best friends. Growing up in a small town where you lived in the same neighborhood or within walking distance made it so that we were close… sister's close. The boys, now that was a different story.

"Stop pulling my braid, TJ!" I shouted at the top of my lungs while I pouted, knowing I was out of the game. Rachel yelled as she touched the back of TJ's shirt. "Tagged him back for ya, Ellie!" I ran over to the sand sideline that bordered what used to be the old high school soccer field while TJ squatted down, catching his breath. "Once this game is over, we're playin' telephone. Bear, you'd better tag Rach or else I'm gonna tell'er how much you love her," TJ said, antagonizing him. "I'm gonna get her." He got close enough to

15

grab the bottom of Rachel's dress. "Hey!" Rachel screeched as she came to a complete stop in front of Bear. She raised her index finger right up to the tip of his nose and waved it from side to side. "No fair, you're not being very nice grabbin' at a lady's dress like that, Bear!" He took a step back and replied in his best southern gentlemen accent a second grader could muster. "Aw, come on, Rach, I didn't mean a thing by it… promise."

I was sitting in the sand listening to them bicker while picking up the handfuls of grit and letting it run through my fingers. I needed to decide on what phrase to use for our first game of telephone. Hearing Lilly shriek in that high pitched scream only dogs could hear, made me jerk back to reality as she came to a landing right next to me. "Yuck, if Curtis Noland touches me one more time, there won't be enough medicine in my next cootie shot to make him go away." Curtis dropped down beside her. His eyebrows were raised, his eyes were as big as small planets, and his face was covered in obsession– second grade love. He smiled. "Wanna play house, Lilly?" Lilly's contorted face turned and looked right at Curtis. Seeing all that boy's emotions right there in his bulging eyes, she grabbed fists full of sand and threw them right in his face. Quickly, Lilly jumped to her feet and ran as fast as she could go in the direction of our teacher Ms. Wilde. Wiping the miniscule grit from his face, his expression never changed, even his smile. Curtis blew and spit the sand from his mouth, stood up, and continued chasing her.

My eyes focused back on the field where our game of tag had obviously come to an end, seeing as how Rachel was skipping her way toward me with a wide grin on her face as she repeated, "I tagged him, I tagged him" in a nanny-nanny, boo-boo tune. Just then, she turned and screamed at Lilly to come back over to where I was sitting and all six of us sat in a perfect circle, Indian style, with hands in our laps. "I'm going first!" I declared to the circle. I got up on my knees and leaned into Rachel to whisper my secret like it was the most important words I would ever speak. One by one, the others discovered my secret. While smiles on each face got bigger and bigger, the secret continued around. Reaching the last person, Curtis yelled out, "I have a behind and I think it's funny!" Everyone in the group laughed and looked at each other, pointing, trying to figure out where and who changed what words and why. TJ looked at me and noticed I was the only one not laughing. My eyes were wide and my lips were tight with just a little shake. I felt like I didn't know whether to cry or scream. At that precise moment is when I lost it. I screamed at the top of my lungs "That is not what I said! I said bees live in hives and I like to eat honey! I don't understand what is so funny about I have a behind and I think it is funny, it makes no sense!"

We are from the south. We ladies are southern belles with southern charm. We fan ourselves, so as not to drip one drop of sweat from our beautiful bosoms even though we have to wear four hundred pounds of girdle and dress. Oh, and don't forget about the men, they are gentlemen. They sit on their front porch in their white suit pants, long-sleeve pinstriped, tailored shirts, and pastel colored bowties with a sweet tea on their knee as they bask in the hot Georgia sun.

My daddy taught me that.

TJ suppressed his laughter as he spun around to Curtis, whispering low in his ear. Curtis' eyes got big and his smile grew wide, as he echoed to Lilly what TJ had said. Lilly's eyes grew even wider as she repeated the phrase to Bear. As the classified information made its way around the circle, my anticipation grew. What could create this expression on everyone's face? Eyes bulged out of heads as though they were about to explode. As the anticipation grew, Rachel closed in on my ear to whisper the secret that had everyone stunned and giggling incessantly. I listened as though my life depended on this information. It took a second, but then the words finally sunk in. Arching my shoulders up as the rest of my body tightened, I screeched, "I am not saying that, Trevor!"

17

"Yes you are! Those are the rules and don't call me Trevor!"

"No…I am not!"

I noticed TJ had moved up to his knees and was leaning across the circle at me. "Yes… You… Are!" TJ hissed.

Looking through deadly eyes, I could feel my anger growing. Knowing I was going to have to repeat this horrid secret, I finally murmured, "When I grow up, I'm gonna marry Trevor Jordan McHale." At this announcement, the whole circle erupted in laughter and started chanting, "Ellie and TJ sitting in a tree, K-I-S-S-I-N-G." In a bluster, I got up to leave the group when Bear stood with me and informed the whole group, "That's okay, Ellie. I'm gonna be marryin' Rachel Elizabeth Locke." Bear leaned in quickly, planting his lips on Rachel's cheek. Disgusted, Rachel got up and ran away singing, "Circle, circle, dot, dot, now I have my cooties shot."

As Lilly, Rachel, and I were dashing toward the swings, Ms. Wilde blew the whistle and hollered for her second grade class. We embarked on what seemed like a long trek, but really the building was just on the other side of the field. TJ ran by us and upheld his stance. "Oh, it'll happen, Elleny Jean Barker. I can promise you that."

"Not in a gazillion years, TJ! I won't marry you, tha…that's just gross!!"

"Then I guess I'm never gonna be getting married then."

Chapter 1

June 1992

"I can't believe we made it. Finally! If Bear stopped one more time, for one more thing, I was gonna scream," Rachel informed us as she pulled down the lawn chairs from the back of the truck to hand down to me. Senior skip day had become a yearly tradition for seniors at Richland High. The six of us decided to make a weekend out of it; going to the lake, camping, swimming, rolling the trucks in the mud. I may have been a pink princess, but I wasn't too good for a mud bog at the local mud hole.

As I stood there in my daisy duke jean shorts, pink tank top, and flashy bikini on underneath, I made sure to get those chairs planted firmly on the water's shore. A song about being down by the Chattahoochee blared from the radio as I grabbed a long neck and stashed it in the front pocket of my shorts. I grabbed Lilly and Rachel's hands and dragged them down to the lake's edge. Stopping abruptly, Rachel, in her sweet Georgia girl accent screeched, "Wait, we need more beer than that! Once I'm in that chair, I ain't movin' for nothin'."

Coming back up to the camp area, I noticed that there were five coolers sitting by the tents. I looked in the first cooler and saw all of the meat we would be grilled for our dinners. I looked in the second one expecting to find beer and found all of the snacks and side items to go along with the meats instead. "Where's the beer? Did the boys drink them all?" I was getting frustrated that I wouldn't find any beer at all when I opened the third one. "Aha, I found it!" I attempted to pick up the beer cooler myself and found that it was way heavier than it appeared. I called for Lilly to grab the other side.

I grabbed one side and handed my beer to Rachel asking her to hold it for me. Looking up from the ground, I heard a *swish* of the bottle being opened. "Sweetie, I asked you to hold it, not swipe it," I sweetly expressed while glaring at Rachel.

Laughing a deep laugh, she knew what I was saying to her. "Keep your panties on, there's more in there." Rachel teased as she sauntered in front of us back down to the water. "Trust me… I know. We stopped at every fuckin' curb store between Richland and here to clean 'em out of beer. Bear took Bubba's fake ID, he's gonna be pissed when he goes to use it this weekend. Serves 'em right for not carryin' his wallet twenty-four seven."

Bubba is Bear's older brother, he's twenty. They moved here from Louisiana to live with their grandparents so that their piece of shit parents could go sell peaches on the side of every interstate they came in contact with. They turned out to be even shittier parents by naming them Ernest and Willie. So, when we met them, we gave them nicknames. Ernest is Bubba and Willie is Bear. We called him Bear because when he was young he liked to give and receive hugs since he wasn't getting any at home. But, not anymore. If you valued your life, you wouldn't try to hug him. Both Bear and Bubba liked to fight. No one ever called them by their real names… ever. No scratch that, one time at a bar, a guy who worked with Bubba thought he'd be a smartass and called him Ernie, which landed him in the hospital and Bubba in jail and jobless.

Speaking of Bear, Rachel and he had been together for years now. At first, it seemed strange, considering they're complete opposites. I think Rachel was with him just to piss her daddy off, since he thought his debutant daughter should be with a "good, decent, and wealthy young man." Rachel, TJ's cousin, is not only lavishly well-off, thanks to her daddy's money, but she wass absolutely gorgeous. Brownish, blonde curly hair that came down to her shoulders, cute figure, big boobs– thanks to the most prominent plastic surgeon in the Atlanta area– and a smile that four years of braces made breathtaking. She was around five-eleven but didn't weigh one hundred and twenty pounds soaking wet. Bear was just what you would think someone named Bear would look like. Six-three, two hundred and fifty pounds, longer brown hair in the back and a full beard. That's right, at eighteen he had a full beard. His eyes were so brown they were black. He had a scar above his right eye that was probably put there by some drunk down at Sheila Kay's, a bar on the outskirts of town and home to every piece of scum and white trash known throughout McIntosh county. He dipped and continuously had a pinch in between his gums. I don't ever remember a time when I didn't see him without carrying two beer cans with him, one as a spit can. I personally never wanted to find out which was the beer.

Lilly and Curt were two peas in a pod and totally made for each other. Both attractive, Lilly was petite, thin, and curvy. She barely hit five-six. Her hair was long, wavy brown with a hint of red that touched the middle of her back and she had the most alluring brown eyes you would ever come across. Lilly had a great personality, outgoing and witty, but, bless her heart, she had the attention span of a gnat to go along with her hyperactivity. If she wasn't doing, she was talking. If she wasn't talking, she was thinking of what she should be doing or talking about. Curtis was so crazy in love with her, he'd follow every moment of every activity right alongside of her.

Curt was blonde with gorgeous blue eyes. His hair was short, but having been a swimmer in school he was hairless. You could not find one single hair on his body. Well, what wasn't covered up anyway. As for the rest, we didn't want to know. It would be like asking about your brother. He was built, but not as big as Bear. He was more on the skinny side. Standing six-one, he was tall and muscular.

Curtis was going to be lost when Lils left for school. She was accepted to Texas University where she was going to be living with her aunt and uncle off campus. Curtis had been working with Bear as a pipefitter and was going to wait back in Georgia for her. Of course he would go visit, but he accepted her decision and stood behind her on it.

TJ and I were perfect together, so everyone thought. I, on the other hand, always felt like I was never good enough physically for him. No words could describe how beautiful he was, while I'm just me.

Six-three, brown hair longer in the back with blondish natural curls hanging on his neck from outside his backwards baseball cap. He had beautiful hazel eyes that had much more green than brown, and a little dimple right below his left eye that was so cute. I called it his angel kiss. His nose was crooked, but that was from the seventh grade when Skeeter ended up catching him off guard and socked him right in the nose. Personally, I always thought he got the better end of the deal. When Skeeter came out of that fight, he looked horrible.

TJ was a country boy, through and through. Worked summers and weekends at his granddaddy's farm fixing fences, rounding up horses, and fixing anything mechanical. He amazed me—straight A student and fullback of the Richland High Eagles football team. They even retired his jersey at the end of this past season. Now, number four will never be seen on another jersey again. That was his number. He was offered a full football scholarship to Georgia State and I couldn't be happier for him.

Yet, here I was, five-nine and a so-so body. I'm a curvy girl with a nice rack, but more junk in my trunk and a pooch I just can't seem to lose no matter how much I exercise. Having straight brown hair with purchased highlights, I just feel plain. Cute, but not Rachel pretty. I may not have been kissed by the glamor fairy, but I was definitely tackled by the wisdom wizard. I applied to seven different colleges and was accepted to each and every one. Since Rachel was accepted into the University of Florida as well, I decided to accept their admission. Getting an off campus apartment, we were ready to spread our wings and fly.

I felt warm hands come around from behind me and touch my cheeks, breaking me from my thoughts. I looked up to see TJ's face approaching to kiss me. "Hey, darling," I heard right before his lips touched mine. "Hey, babe," I answered, wrapping my arms around his neck to deepen the sweet kiss to something more sensual. As he broke the kiss, he pulled away slightly and whispered, "Why is it that you're sitting that sweet ass in this here chair instead of in that lake, wrapped around me?"

I looked beside me at Rachel and Lilly who were trying desperately to hide their smiles. I, being embarrassed and rendered speechless, mumbled, "Um..."

He grabbed my hand to pull me up from my chair. Just as I started walking, he dipped down, put his shoulder in my stomach, and lifted me up, carrying me the rest of the way down.

"Trevor Jordan McHale, put me down!" I screamed.

All I heard was laughter. Somewhere behind me, Lilly was stating that I was in some deep shit. Once we were in the water, Trevor slowly lowered me down as my legs wrapped around his waist. He laid a sweet, tender kiss on the inside of my neck.

"I am lovin' the new suit, babe."

Timidly, I looked down at my chest and felt TJ's eyes as he scrutinized every inch of me "Oh yeah? It's pink and silver, my favorite colors."

He knew compliments made me blush and he always thought it was cute when I did. Therefore, he always went out of his way to pay me kudos. "Ellie-bean, I know what your favorite colors are." He waded out further as my legs stayed securely around his waist, affectionately rubbing his fingers up and down my sides and across my ribs.

23

"Sweetie, we're eighteen, you can quit calling me Ellie-bean." He had given me that nickname when I was eleven. I thought it was sweet at first, but being older now, it was well-worn.

"I don't care if your eighteen or ninety-eight, Ellie-bean, I will always call you that." Leaning back, I glared and a small smile broke out on his face.

I giggled, "Ninety-eight, seriously? I think you're being a little ridiculous." I held my thumb and index finger close demonstrating a little. "I wouldn't make plans that far ahead there, Mr. Fullback for Georgia State. You never know what might happen."

"What did I tell you when we were in second grade, darlin'? I meant what I said." He pulled his hand up from the water and tracked it across my cheek. I threw my arms around his neck and hugged him tightly, laying my chin on his shoulder. My mind drifted into the peacefulness that surrounded us and the sound of water splashing against TJ's body as he stepped farther and farther away from our friends and the shoe. Trevor pushed his shoulder up to get my attention and I raised my head, my eyes meeting his.

"So beautiful, babe."

"TJ," I whispered.

I knew where this was going and I didn't want to talk about it. He always brought it up when we had a moment to ourselves and I wasn't in the mood to discuss getting engaged. It's not that I didn't want to spend the rest of my life with him—I planned on it—I just wasn't one for marriage.

What was a piece of paper going to do to make your love for someone grow stronger? I had lived with my daddy during his marriage to Mona and that piece of paper did not strengthen that bond whatsoever. I was totally happy with the way things were and would continue to be happy as long as I was with TJ. But, right now, we had to concentrate on school. I didn't want anything to come between our goals and that's where this conversation was headed—straight down the middle.

"Damn, baby, how am I going to live with just seeing you on holidays? It's gonna be a bitch! I can't stand the thought of it."

I knew it!

Tensing up my spine, I wanted this to be over before it began.

"TJ, stop."

"Elle, we have to talk about it sometime."

I started to feel frustration rise up from inside of me. I unhooked my legs from around him and attempted to touch the lake's sandy floor. I wasn't even close.

"Not now, we still have time before Rachel and I have to leave and I don't want this weekend ruined."

"Elle, it's not like I'm saying let's run off and get married, I'm just thinkin' of an engagement."

"Trevor, you know how I feel about this and I'm not talking about it right now." I shook my head vehemently. "First off, I'm don't want either of us tied down to something that may eventually fail. Second, we're only eighteen. We need to concentrate on attaining what we want, our goals. I need to concentrate on medical school and you need to become a corporate raider."

He had opportunities that had been presented to him on a silver platter. The time for him engaged and tied down to a girl was not now. No matter how much we fought over it, I would not change my mind on this subject. He didn't know what the future held for him; he could have a national scout come to one of his games and potentially end up playing for the NFL. I was not about to hold him back in any way.

I heard his aggravated breath and knew he was trying to keep his composure.

"Okay, first off, it's an investor, not a corporate raider. Second, it won't fa—"

25

Waving my hand in a circular motion, I interrupted what I knew was a statement he couldn't be positively sure of.

"Tomato, to-mah-to, same thing. Personal experience has taught me to not to change a good thing, ya know?"

"Elle—"

Losing patience, I began to speak louder.

"No, Trevor! We're good. Solid, right? Bendable, not breakable."

"Babe!"

Grabbing his face, I held his cheeks in my hands. I wanted eye contact so he would see that I was not budging on this. "Please, sweetie. Please? Not now. Let's enjoy this weekend. We're together, let's be together."

"Shit!" I knew I had won this battle, but the war was far from over. If only he could see things my way. "Okay, fine. But, this discussion is far from finished."

I didn't want to agree or disagree, so I ignored his statement. I turned toward him, resumed my position around his waist, and told him what always made everything better.

"Love you, baby."

Smiling, he replied, "Love you, too."

TJ touched his lips to mine. His tongue touched the crease of my lips in an attempt to deepen the kiss. I allowed him access and he proceeded to explore every crevice of my mouth with his tantalizing tongue. Tasting TJ on my tongue was exhilarating, like tasting sugar straight from the cane. Feeling his arms tighten around me rendered me defenseless, yet I'd never felt more loved; safe from everything and everyone. As his arms squeezed, my legs tightened. I heard a low moan deep in his chest.

I continued with my actions to see if I could achieve more of those impulsive sounds. I loved hearing him moan and breathe my name. Slowly, I lowered my hands from around his neck, sliding them gently over his back. I felt every muscle flex as I ran tips of my fingers, ever so slowly, down to the top of his swim trunks and over his rigid backside. Squeezing slightly, I received my reward in a much deeper groan.

His hands explored my breasts through the thin bikini top. Slowly sliding one triangle of material to the side, he slid his thumb over my nipple. I couldn't help the moan that forced its way past my lips, goose flesh raising on my skin as my nipple tightened in anticipation.

"Damn, get a fuckin' room, ya'll! Them fish are runnin' for cover! Ain't no one wanna see live porn at the lake!" Bear squawked.

I lowered my face down into the crook of TJ's neck, knowing I must've turned ten shades of red.

Lilly and Curt began to laugh and whoop, like they were appreciating every minute of the show we inadvertently put on. Gazing up slightly, I saw Rachel raise her hands and cup them around her mouth, creating a make-shift megaphone. "That's fuckin' gross, Elle! I don't wanna talk about my cousin's sex life, let alone watch it!" she hollered, disgust clear in her tone.

I felt TJ's chest vibrating in silent laughter. I imagined him rolling his eyes as he started back toward the shore.

"I'm glad we stopped. I'm gonna have a hard time getting out of this water without embarrassin' myself," he whispered, his breathing rapid.

Snickering, I grabbed the front of his trunks. Feeling how hard he was, I smiled in agreement. Then, I unwrapped myself from his delicious body and swam back to the shore. As I felt my toes finally touching the sand, I replied to Bear since he decided to fuck up my moment.

"Don't be jealous you ain't getting none of this!" I took my hands and ran them down the curves of my body, my eyes following the movement. I peeked up from under my lashes and watched Bear's eyes get rather large as I moved my hand lower, acting like I was going to put my fingers down the front of my bottoms. Quickly, I pulled my hand back up and

27

flipped him the bird. Everyone on the shore busted out in laughter as I began walking again.

"The fuck she say to me?" he mumbled. "I'll have you know, Elleny Jean, I don't need none of that." His arm flew up through the air and pointed at me. "I knock the bottom out of it daily," he replied, thrusting his hips back and forth.

Walking out of the water, TJ laughed. "Well, now there's something I could've gone through life without seein'." I broke out laughing hysterically.

Rachel gasped as she removed her sunglasses. Mouth gaping open, she laid into him, "Willie Bob Jackson, I can't believe you just said that out loud." Curling up her top lip, she got a repulsed look on her face. "And, what the hell was that humpin' thing you were doin'? I mean…for fuck's sake!"

"Rach, if he fucks like he humps air, I know why you like your toys," Curtis said, finally catching his breath. He must've been pretty shit-faced since usually he didn't join in on the ruckus.

As a matter of fact, I think his shit-faced was shit-faced for him to come up with that one. The air around the shore became so thick, you couldn't see four feet in front of you. Silence had built a fence around us and no one knew where to find the gate to get out. Bear's face turned to stone. Rachel's turned pale before shimmering in what I thought was the prettiest shade of red. Lilly broke the silence by screeching Curtis' name.

Rachel glared at Lilly through eyes that could have committed murder. "I can't believe you told him, Lilly. I told you that in secret."

Bear yelped in horror. "What the fuck, Rach!"

Rachel stood from her seat and swiftly materialized in front of Bear, struggling to get her arms to wrap around him. Her voice had now changed from demonic to an obnoxious whiny beg, like a child who walked past a toy store and pleaded to go in. "Bear…baby, come here." I rolled my eyes and thought to myself, *oh god, here we go.*

"You told her about our…our…private life?"

All you could hear was the muffling of snorts as we tried our hardest to withhold our laughter, all except for Curtis, who was laughing his ass off.

"Bear, honey…" Rachel said struggling to pacify him. Pointing back at Lilly, she continued, "I told her in confidence, like a sister…" Rachel gnashed her teeth. "A sister I'm gonna strangle."

He knew we talked. I mean, come on, we are girls and best friends; we talked about everything. All three of us discussed our sex life. We all had toys and we chatted about using them. We didn't go into detail, but we talked. Hell, we drove an hour to another town together just to purchase our vibrators so we didn't run into anyone we knew. We gossiped about shit like this to find out which of our men were more adventurous in bed. Finding out that Bear and Rachel used toys together—which she did not ever mention to us—I had a feeling her man was the winner.

Finally, I'd had enough. "Bear, it's okay. It's no big deal, darlin'," I said, trying to make an effort to calm Bear down. He was quickly pacing back and forth, either trying to talk himself down or just talking to himself. I had no fucking clue, but it seemed to be the latter. "No, it's not fine. That's private…intimate…between the two of us, no one else."

"Baby, I'm sorry, come here…" Grabbing a hold of him around the waist, Rachel pulled as best as she could since he weighed so much more than her. She began giving him short tender kisses.

"I can't believe you told 'em that shit, Rach," Bear whispered.

"Baby, I'm sorry. If I could do it over, trust me…" Rachel turned to glare a "go to hell" look at Lilly, "I would."

Lilly just raised her eyebrows and mouthed, "Okay" to herself as she went back to reading her article on the New Kids on the Block.

Bear grabbed Rachel in a hug and began kissing her fervently. She jumped up and wrapped her legs around him as he began walking them to their tent. You could still hear him complaining and Rachel trying to make it better.

"Oh my god, ya'll, Rachel's gettin' knocked up tonight. Make up sex is going to be her downfall," Lilly stated.

"Fuck off!" We heard yelled in unison from the tent.

Looking back at the group that was now minus two, I saw TJ's face. He didn't look happy.

"Lils, what the hell!" TJ exclaimed.

"It wasn't me, it was Curt."

"Okay, it's over," I said, attempting to squash the whole situation. Having had enough, I walked over to the truck, jumped inside, and went directly to the radio. Pushing the seek button, song after song flashed by.

Hearing Ann Wilson of Heart belting out, "How do I get you alone…" I stopped. I loved that song! TJ's hand wrapped around mine as he began gently tugging me out from the cab. I pulled away, flirtatiously looking at him. I knew he could see the lust in my eyes.

"Now, now, darlin', I just wanna dance." I slowly molded my body into him. Wrapped tight in his arms, a warm sensation arose throughout my body, yet dread began to settle in. Question after question popped into my head. What was going to happen when we were apart at school? How would we survive? Not wanting to appear distraught, I pulled him closer to me.

"You okay?"

I slapped a fake smile on my face and answered him honestly.

"Fine, just feels good, here with you, I'm going to miss this."

We stopped dancing and stood there a minute, our eyes connected, like they were carrying on a conversation themselves. I could see what his mind was telling me, but I also saw what his body was saying. The desire that was burning in him told me I was in for it. He wanted me… and he wanted it slow, taking his time to encounter every inch of me; relish every second that he was touching, tasting, watching, and hearing me. He seemed like he was a man dying of thirst and I was his water. Sensing TJ pull away, I knew it was time and I was up to date with what was on the agenda. Slowly, we walked hand in hand to our tent.

Inside, TJ immediately turned and zipped up the doorway. Hearing the music still blaring in the background, nothing else mattered. Not Bear and Rachel, not leaving for school, nothing. Just he and I, our hearts secured to each other.

"TJ."

"Shh."

He went to his bag, reached down in it, and grabbed something.

"Whatch'a got?"

Walking closer to me, he began speaking. "You know that my day begins and ends picturing your beautiful face?"

"Baby," I whispered.

Reaching me, he laid his palm up against the back of my neck and ran his thumb over my eyebrow and down my cheek. I slowly closed my eyes, memorizing the feel of his touch.

"Open your eyes, babe," he whispered softly as he leaned down, touched his nose to mine, and looked into my eyes. "It'll never be enough."

"What won't ever be enough?" I murmured just as soft.

"Touching every part of you, for the rest of my life."

As he was talking, he grasped my left hand. With his other hand opened, I saw the little black box.

I began to panic.

"TJ!"

Shaking his head, he could see the panic on my face.

"It's not what you think."

Exhaling the breath I was holding, I calmed down a bit. He opened the box and I pulled back the breath I just exhaled.

"TJ…it…it's beautiful."

"You like it?"

Tearing up, I couldn't talk. I just nodded my head. Inside was a fourteen karat white gold ring. The band was so thin and delicate. It attached to an elegant small anchor and right in the middle of the bar that came across the top of the anchor was a small diamond.

He slipped the ring on my finger and stared into my eyes as he promised, "I will be anchored to you forever and always." Hearing him say those words, rendered me speechless. Tears were spilling down my cheeks and no matter how hard I tried, I couldn't get them to stop. Not being able to take anymore, I got up on my tip toes and brought my mouth to his. Barely touching lips, I breathed, "I will remind you of that when I'm ninety-eight." I laughed apprehensively. "I love you, TJ. I will spend the rest of my life proving to you how much I do."

Before he had a chance to reply, I put my mouth to his. Leisurely, I caressed his lower lip with my tongue. Feeling his tongue slip out trying to touch mine, I pulled back. Doing it again, I opened my eyes to see him. His brows were pulled tight and his eyes were beaming at me. I smiled under his lips and opened to allow him access. He didn't miss his chance and entered my mouth on a soft moan like he had returned home after a long trip.

Beginning to explore my mouth, he took over the kiss. He tilted his head to the side to meld closer to me and I allowed him. As warmth started to build in my belly, I let out a small whimper. This was his permission to continue. His hands began traveling from my neck to my shoulder and down my back. My bikini strings were untied, hanging down my sides. Reaching around to my front, he caressed my breasts with his large hands.

"Oh God, Elle."

"Don't stop."

Pulling away from my mouth, his kisses became faster down my neck, then my chest until he reached my breast. Continuing to work my right one with his hand, he gently covered my left one with his lips, sucking, licking, and pulling firmly. I bowed into him for more. Feeling the wetness that began to build between my legs, we found a rhythm that we both couldn't say no to. As he made his way to my other breast, he lifted his head and watched as he pinched my nipple between his fingers.

"God, look at you. Your breasts are so beautiful, and your nipples get as hard as I do when I touch them."

"Don't talk like that, you're gonna have me coming before you even get in me."

"Well, let's not waste any more time."

He continued to kneed and pinch my breasts, while his other hand slowly and gently continued lower, past my belly button down to my bikini bottoms. Reaching inside, he ran his finger up and down, feeling the wetness that continued to build only for him.

"Elle, I need you so bad."

"Don't stop."

He gave my breasts one more tender kiss, then worked his way lower, laying kisses as he went. When he was right above my belly button, he laid us back on the sleeping bags.

"What are you doing?"

"I wanna do this, Elle."

"You really want to?"

"Elle, you've never let me do it, please... I need to taste you."

I really didn't have a problem with him going down on me, other than I heard that Becky Stanfield had let Hopper Lewis go down on her at Stacey Roger's sixteenth birthday party. Monday morning, rumors started flying that she was a "Mary Rotten Crotch" and that kind of ruined it for me.

"Just remember, I was in that dirty lake."

"Elle…seriously? Just lay back and enjoy it."

Feeling his warm breath on my thighs made goose bumps raise on my skin as my breathing accelerate. The anticipation was overwhelming. I knew what was going to happen, but I didn't know what to expect. My mind wouldn't stop, it was like a whirlwind of thoughts and a sinking feeling of being overly self-conscious. I was so glad I made that waxing appointment right before this trip. Just as nudging thoughts of self-doubt ran through my mind, I felt the first touch of his tongue. It was like nothing I had ever felt before in my life. It was heaven. No—it was a chocolate covered heaven.

"Oh…my…God, Elle."

Jumping up nervously, those nudging comments slammed into the front of my head. "Oh my God" was not something you wanted to hear when a man was between your legs.

"'Oh my God', what?" I retorted apprehensively. I looked up at him with nine shades of embarrassment all over my face.

"You are the best thing I have ever tasted. It's like the juiciest peach I have ever eaten."

Trying quickly to get back in the mood, I rolled my eyes and attempted to calm myself. I thought if I said something it would help, so I said a monotone, "Yeah, me too…don't stop."

He continued to lick, suck, tickle, and tease until I began to relax. The sounds that came from him were intensely erotic. It made me even wetter until I felt the wave of ecstasy building and it was a big one.

"Oh yeah, don't stop, TJ. I'm almost there. Oh my god, baby, this is so amazing!" I began to roll my hips against his mouth.

"Oh yeah, Elle, that's it, work yourself against my mouth. God, you're so beautiful moving like that. Fuck, I'm gonna come so hard."

Before I even had time to come down from the orgasmic wave that had taken over, TJ was opening my legs and rubbing his thick, rock hard length against my core.

"God, baby, you're soakin' wet."

"Well yeah, what did you expect? That was amaz—"

Slowly, he pushed himself into me, interrupting all thoughts. Pushing my hair out of my face, he whispered loving endearments as I was wrapped around him in the most intimate way possible. Fully seated within me, he stopped moving. We laid joined together, staring at each other.

"TJ."

"Shit, Elle," was the only response I got from him as he buried his face in my neck.

"Kiss me, baby," I whispered as I reached down to bring his head back up to me. I kissed him tenderly as he began slowly moving out then in again. The circling of his tongue was following the same motions as his hips. I sucked his tongue into my mouth earning me a long, deep groan of pleasure from within his chest.

"Elle, babe, you with me?" TJ whispered softly in my ear.

"Yes, don't stop!"

Feeling my release building again, I wrapped my legs around his back as tight as I could and began to roll my hips that followed his tempo, making it build even faster.

"Oh shit, baby, I'm not gonna be able to hold off if you keep grippin' me like that. Come with me. I can feel it, you're so close, baby. Yeah, that's it!"

As I felt my orgasm building and filling me from the bottom of my toes to the top of my head, I knew we were going to come together. It was the most perfect ending to the best sex I think we had up until then.

While still joined, TJ laid on top of me. I loved to feel his weight on me after we made love. It felt like it was his way of telling me we were not only one during, but after as well.

"You with me, babe?"

35

He always asked me this question after and I always answered the same way.

"Always. Anchored to ya. "

This was the time that we would spend enjoying each other, chatting about anything that was on our minds, but most of the time we would be discussing what we had just done. The new things we tried, whether we liked them…or not. It was so comforting to me, it felt as if we were on the same page.

Laying there in our tent on a pile of sleeping bags with TJ rubbing circles on my stomach right above my belly button, I blurted out a question that just popped into my head.

"TJ, if we were to have a baby, I mean…when we are older…much, much older, what would you wanna name it?"

He stopped is hand from rubbing and looked at me quizzically, yet smiled as though he liked the idea of me being heavy with his child.

"If I had a girl, I'd name her Layla."

"Layla?" I chuckled. "I think of a girl all spread out on top of a jaguar in a Whitesnake video when I hear the name Layla."

Laughing, he replied "I got it from that Eric Clapton song. That's such a great song."

"Okay, okay…what about a boy?"

Looking off over my shoulder, he thought for a moment before blurting, "Dylan Lucas."

Shocked by this information—that really was a beautiful name—I got the feeling he had thought about that name long and hard. Feeling that we were getting way too deep into this conversation, I quickly changed the subject to something I knew would definitely not bring it back up.

"Wanna get a shower?"

It was there, in that very moment, that I realized my life; everything was going flawlessly for me. I had the perfect boyfriend, I was going to the perfect college, I was going to be the perfect doctor, settle down and have the perfect kids—minus the name Layla—the perfect house and I definitely would be out of Richland, which made the whole scenario perfect. There was no way my life could get any better than what I had.

Needless to say, never in a million years would I have thought that my life would be changed and not for the better. Nothing would ever be the same again after this weekend.

Tracy Lee

Chapter 2

Present Day 2010

Feeling TJ's touch early in the morning was priceless to me. The way he slid his fingers gradually down the side of my torso, tracing the lines of my hip bones, I knew what he had on his mind. He started slowly kissing where his fingers had just been, making his way to my thigh where he tenderly turned me to my back so that he had better access.

"Good mornin', Ellie-bean" he said in his slow Georgia accent. "I love waking up to you in my arms."

"Mornin', darlin'," I breathed in my sleepy tone as I stretched to meet the new day.

"And what do we have here?" he hissed as he ran his fingers down to the top of my leg. "This is where my heaven is found." His fingers teasingly stroked the entrance to my innermost core. "Right here…" I moaned in pleasure from his touch.

He began to rub his fingers up, down, and inside of me. At first he was slow, leisurely, then he became faster, more persistent in his ministrations. I began to feel like I was reaching for the peak of a tall mountain; so close…so very, very close.

"Oh yes… don't stop, TJ. Oh my God, that feels so good!"

As I commenced climbing over the mountain's summit, I heard a mosquito buzzing around my head. Quickly, I opened my eyes to shoo the thing away. There was no mosquito. I heard it again, getting louder. I looked around for it, following the buzzing.

"Get up! Turn it off, Ellie. Turn off the goddamn alarm!" I jumped awake, surprised by the loud roar.

I had it again! I was going to kill Rachel. I told her that tea wasn't gonna work.

"What the fuck, Ellie!" The loud shriek pierced my eardrums, bringing me from my mental murdering of Rachel Locke-Harrington.

"It's six-fifteen, goddammit! You let me over sleep! Now I'm gonna have to hear Slade's bullshit on why I wasn't there at six-thirty to pick him up and blah-sucking-blah! I don't think I ask a lot of you and what I do ask, you always seem to fuck up! Can't you do one thing right? I mean, come on, it's not like I'm asking you to do major surgery here! I'm asking you to wake me the fuck up! Fucking woman, you have a brain the size of an ant."

I was barely awake, my response was scripted since according to *him*, I'm the one who is the screw-up. Apology, short excuse, and change of subject. *Don't argue, Elleny.*

"Look, I'm sorry. I was up late last night working on the bake sale items for Luc's football boosters. Are you going to be able to take JoJo to her thing tonight? She has two more nights of court ordered volunteering."

"Are you shittin' me?" He laughed as he threw on a t-shirt. "Ellie, you expect me to work all day, probably since you've overslept you ain't gonna have time to make me a lunch, so I'll go all day without eatin'. Then, you expect me to come home, grab JoJo, and take her to that shithole where those people are as capable of working as I am? Then, go to the football field for practice tonight? Who do I look like…Super-fuckin-man?"

Always the screw up!

Did he just hear what I said? It wasn't like I was out with the girls, drinking and throwing money in another man's G-string until four in the morning, for Christ sake. I looked my husband straight in the eyes and wondered if he had lost his mind. It took all that was within me not to slowly walk over to him, gradually, yet scandalously, bend down to look at him with a sensual smile on my face and scream "FUCK YOU!" as loud as my lungs would let me. Instead, I just grabbed my skirt and shirt and headed for the bathroom to begin my day.

Mornings were never easy in my house, getting three stubborn teenagers ready for the day was always overwhelming. Breakfast couldn't be just cereal and toast, it had to be a full-on southern-style breakfast—eggs, sausage, bacon, grits, coffee, and juice—and no one ever ate the same thing. "I have three wonderful, beautiful kids," I began chanting out loud as though I was talking myself out of becoming animalistic and killing my young.

"Stop it!"

"No, you stop it!"

"Touch my plate again, douchebag, and I swear to God…"

"Harlee!"

"What! Bieber wanna-be over here keeps touching my food."

Flipping over an egg one more time in the pan, I rolled my eyes at my one and only son. "Luc, come on. Just eat, sweetie. Can't you act your age? Where's JoJo? Did you knock on her door to wake her up?"

"I tried, Momma, but you know her. I'm not sacrificing myself just so she will get out of bed!"

I took my hands out of the warm, soapy dishwater, grabbed a towel, and wiped off the soap suds while I walked to the bottom of the stairs that led to the bedrooms.

"JoJo, you have ten minutes until I leave. If you don't want to ride the bus to school, I suggest you get down here."

JoJo miraculously appeared the moment I walked back to the ever-growing mound of dishes.

"Toast—two pieces, just butter. Thanks, Momma," JoJo ordered, as though I was a short order cook.

"JoJo, you know you have that thing tonight."

"I know, you don't have to keep reminding me."

"This means you have to tell Sandy…I mean, Coach Johnson you won't be there for cheer practice."

I pushed the bread down into the toaster and grabbed the items I was going to need to make a lunch for my husband. I quickly threw together two olive loaf sandwiches and tossed three bags of chips and two pudding cups into his lunchbox. Done. Finished. Just as I finished up, JoJo's toast popped up. I buttered the toast and handed off her breakfast.

"I know, Momma. Already taken care of."

"I just want to make sure. You really should've thought about the repercussions of what you did so you wouldn't have to do that thing tonight."

"Momma!" She rolled her eyes and threw her toast back down on the plate. "They're not idiots, they know. You don't have to talk in code like their five year olds, they're seventeen and fourteen!"

Out of the breakfast nook, I heard Harlee's voice echo, "Yeah, Momma. I'm fourteen."

"Whatever, Harlee. Eat, we have to go," I replied as I attempted to start the dishes again. I took a deep breath and repeated the mantra in my head, yet again. As I began to calm down, I started to remember who was in charge here.

"Hurry up, ya'll. I have to get to work. We have a new client comin' in today with a huge job and Mr. Stevens is gonna need my help. I won't be home until six, so, JoJo, you'd better be ready to go when I get home."

"Well, if it ain't the fucking Cleaver family." The kitchen grew quiet almost instantaneously. I was facing the sink when I heard and felt a *whap* on my backside.

"Shew-wee!! Look at that ass jiggle. Baby got back, but daddy no like. Luc, look here at your momma's ass, it was perfect until she had ya'll."

I closed my eyes. I was not going to fight with him this morning. If I just let him talk his shit he'd leave and go off to work. If I ended up arguing with him, he'd stick around for another hour or so and then I'd really be getting it.

I looked at Luc and JoJo and told them to take Harlee upstairs to get her school things while I finished cleaning up breakfast.

Going back to the sink, I stuck my hands in the water to find another plate to wash when I heard my husband in my ear.

"I swear, baby, if you'd be a better wife and pay more attention to your husband, ya might find yourself in a better mood, 'cause you'd end up getting fucked more often." He finished by wrapping his hands around both my breasts and squeezing roughly. I winced to myself but didn't say a word, nor did I pull my hands from the water.

"Shit, Ellie, your tits sag as bad as a nasty homeless bitch. You might wanna think about getting those fixed," he trailed off as I heard the door to the garage slam.

Yeah, okay, that's what I want—not!

I closed my eyes and thought about what he had said. No matter how hard I tried, his trash talking always cut me to the bone. How could someone talk that way to another person, especially the person you vowed to love and cherish for the rest of your life? I wanted to break down, but I couldn't. I had to be strong for myself and for my kids. He had gotten too many of my silent tears in the past, he wouldn't be gettin' anymore if I could help it. There was never love between the two of us, not that I wouldn't have wanted it. I tried—way back when we first got together—but I just couldn't do it. Now, I didn't feel shit for him other than extreme loathing and disgust. According to him, he felt the same way toward me.

Exhaling, I looked around the kitchen. I began putting things back in the fridge and taking more dishes to the sink. If I didn't want to come home to wash dishes before starting dinner, then I'd better hurry up and get them done. I grabbed my iPod and ear buds and blasted my music until I was taken away…

No one was allowed here but me. This place was peaceful, happy, and safe. This place was mine and mine alone. I came here whenever I had a bad day, am overwhelmed by life, or if the worst happens–*he* came home drunk. Sometimes, he came home pissed off and ended up taking it out on me.

This place, however, was wherever I wanted it to be, but it would always be with the same person. Today, I was riding in the truck singing the chorus to Boston's "More Than a Feeling" while head banging. I stopped for a moment to look over at TJ as he smiled a beautiful beaming smile, eyes flicking from me to the highway while he played air guitar. He always made me laugh hysterically. I had every detail I needed and the long road out in front, leading us anywhere we wanted to go. I could smell the leather of the seats mixed with his cologne. My pink bandana hung from the rearview mirror, drenched in my perfume.

Every day here was sunny and the windows were always rolled down, the wind blowing in my hair. God, this was where I loved to be; no worries, no stress. I would think back to the nights spent with him, making loving and enjoying everything about each other's bodies.

He was my first and the last in my eyes. Yes, my husband gave me my beautiful child, but that's it. He was and is an opportunity.

Hearing the song come to an end, I was pulled back to reality. I looked at the clock.

"Shit, we gotta go! Kids, get in the car!"

Growing up in Richland, I couldn't wait to get out. Never would I have thought I would be raising a family here. Having my children go to the same schools I attended when I was their age made it even worse. I could feel the freak out erupting inside of me over this subject. The only thing that made me feel any better was that I encouraged my children to not stay in this god-forsaken town. Go to college, travel…see the world. Something I knew I wouldn't have the chance to do again until after Harlee turned eighteen.

I drove to two different schools, hurried the kids out of my Expedition, and started my drive through town to work. Hitting the button on the dash, the ringing tone of Rachel's phone blasted throughout my truck. I hoped and prayed I would have the privilege of waking her ass up.

"What's up, biatch?"

Damn. She was already awake.

"Rach, you aren't a teenager anymore. Hearing you say that makes me think of a senior citizen laying it on thick to a twenty year old."

"Okay then…what's up, bitch!"

"I had the dream again."

I heard the loud thud of her coffee cup as she slammed it down.

"Shut up!"

"No, seriously, last night."

"Did you drink the tea?"

"Yes, I drank the tea," I replied facetiously.

"Did you follow the directions explicitly? And, don't be a smartass!"

"Fine and yes. I followed the directions to a tee, no pun intended."

I giggled at my unintentional joke.

"Shut the fuck up, Elle!"

I laughed louder. "I drank the tea two hours after dinner, but an hour before I went to bed. I didn't watch TV, I didn't listen to my iPod, and I *still* had the dream."

"Oh no, Elle, this is worse than I thought."

"What…" the smile left my face as I became serious in an instant. "What the hell does that mean, Rach?"

"It means I'm gonna have to do a little more digging to find out what your subconscious is trying to tell ya."

"Well, if I oversleep again because I'm having a wet dream about another man next to my not so loving husband, I think I'm gonna have to either kill him for yelling at me or kill you for not helping me with this problem."

"He didn't…"

"He did…"

"Hey, Elle, I have a question that I want you to answer honestly." A long pause followed. Just as I thought maybe I had lost her, she continued, "Have you tried to make contact with him?"

"Hell no," I replied immediately. "And you know why. You also know that his name is not allowed to be spoken, written, or googled in my household."

"I know, honey. Calm down. I just wanted to make sure. He is on your mind whether you want him to be there or not, and we need to find out why."

"Well, we will have to work on it later. I'm at work and JoJo has her thing tonight, maybe next time she will think twice before toilet papering Sheriff Corder's house."

Yes, that's right, my angel daughter decided that since Sheriff Corder pulled her and her friend Ashlee over for going eight miles over the speed limit, then proceeded to write her a ticket, she and Ashlee would take matters into their own hands and toilet paper his house. They probably would've gotten away with it if he hadn't gotten an emergency call in the middle of the night where he had to go into the station. He walked out and there they were, throwing rolls of paper into the tree in front of his house.

I had to go and pick her up from the station at three-thirty in the morning.

She got that from her daddy.

"Hey, you need to get off her case. The only difference between her and us was Sheriff Watson was just too old to catch us."

"I know, but I can't afford to have more rumors floating around town. We're not the most popular family as it is."

"Who fuckin' cares, Elle. You have the ones who love you and those kids, that's all that matters. The rest can go fuck themselves. Hey, wanna do lunch this week?"

This is why she is my rock.

"Sure …Thursday okay?"

"Sounds perfect, see you then. I love you, Ellie-bean."

I rolled my eyes at her saying my nickname that TJ gave me. It always made me feel a stabbing pain in my heart, especially after what happened.

"Love you, too, Rach."

Walking up to the front doors of the Richards, Klein, and Daugherty Law Group, I did my normal personal inspection routine. Matching shoes? Check. Hair half decent, makeup in place? Check. Put on bra and panties? Check. Deodorant? Check.

Good God, I am a complete woman! I mentally congratulated myself.

Richards, Klein and Daugherty was a law firm that dealt mostly with corporations and investors that bought and sold companies back and forth to each other. I was Loren Stevens' administrative assistant, and had been for the last fifteen years. I prepared all of the contracts and forms, and preformed minimum research for potential clients. This new purchaser was not someone we had dealt with before.

The Mac-Gentry Firm was headquartered in Burlington, Vermont. To me, this seemed very incongruous since they were interested in purchasing here, in small town Richland. The company they would be obtaining hadn't been a prosperous one in several years. Richland Manufacturing was a company that most of the men in town worked for. Always having the same owners, it was a welding company that built rigs for off-shore drilling.

Whether this deal was a little unorthodox or not, I had to be in on it. It was personal seeing as my husband was a foreman there.

Not knowing what the future would hold for Richland Manufacturing, everyone around town had been walking on eggshells. The town wasn't flourishing financially because no one knew what the outcome of this purchase would be.

Were the new owners going to close it down? Would they keep the same employees or would they outsource? All information concerning the company was being withheld, even Mr. Stevens didn't know.

Reaching the elevators, something felt....off. The hair on the back of my neck was standing straight up and I felt... well, weird. I completely blamed it on my morning: waking up late, dealing with *him*, then dealing with the kids. Staying up until three in the morning cooking didn't help either. As I rode up the twelve floors, I attempted to shake off the eeriness. I took a deep breath as the elevator doors opened. Mr. Stevens paced quickly in front of me.

"Elle, thank God you're here," he exhaled, panic in his voice.

"Loren, I told you I was going to be in early. It wasn't as early as I wanted to be here, but I had a crap morning."

"It's okay. You got the contracts in order, right?"

"Yes, sir," I reassured him as I briskly walked to my desk. "They're on my desk. All I have to do is put the packets together. I'm going to go work on them right now. I set up the power-point last night and everything is ready to go."

Loren Stevens was in his early forties. His strong country accent would make Gomer Pyle laugh. He tried with all his heart to hide it, but being from the south, you'd find that much of a drawl nearly impossible to disguise. He was six feet tall and held a little more weight than the average man of that stature, but it didn't take away from his attractiveness. Clean shaven, his salt and peppered hair was always well kept. Loren married a sweet woman named Leeza. They didn't have any kids, so he spoiled her rotten. They had been together since college and I always found myself a bit envious of their loving relationship. Loren had been working to become a full partner within this law group and this deal was the one that was going to get him that position.

Sitting down at my desk, I flipped my computer on and opened up my email. Fifty-five new emails. Scrolling through them swiftly, I wanted to ensure there was nothing that couldn't wait until after this morning's meeting.

Noticing an email from Rachel, I immediately opened it. It was an e-card that read: "Just thinking of you". A small smile touched my lips as I pictured Rachel sitting in front of her computer, wearing her silk night-gown that fanned out across the floor. Her very expensive long blonde hair laying over her shoulder, a cigarette in one hand and a mimosa in the other, typing her own loving message, with one finger of course.

"Just because he's on your mind doesn't mean you can't be on mine...biatch!"

I laughed softly thinking back to this morning's conversation. She must've went straight into her study right after she hung up with me and sent this card. Which reminded me, Lilly would be getting a call from me tonight to let her know about our lunch date on Thursday.

Realizing I needed to get back to work, I pulled out the packet folders with the company's initials imprinted in gold calligraphy on the front and filled them with forms, information sheets, and the final contract that would be signed by the CEO's or owners that would be attending.

Finishing up, I called out to the main receptionist, Laurie, and informed her that we would be conducting a contract signing in Conference Room B at ten forty-five. I asked if she would tend to the refreshments and she gladly obliged. I hung up the phone and looked to the clock, perfect timing.

I headed to the conference room to start setting up. The enormous room could seat twenty-five to thirty people. It's thick, rich, burnt red painted walls lined with a dark chair rail put off the old southern country feel. It was decorated by the most prominent interior designer in Marietta; dark mahogany wood with a hint of gold adornments. The partners of Richards, Klein, and Daugherty always wanted to exude the "old money" feel. God knows they will be taking enough "new money" from these companies. I walked to the enormous wooden table that had been polished so that it reflected the sun coming in from the large windows overlooking the city. Around the table were the very masculine chairs, which were all dark leather and tufted with large gold buttons. I thought that maybe one day I'd walk in here and see Hugh Hefner sitting in one wearing a red velvet robe with a cigar in one hand and a glass of whisky in the other.

I released the folders that almost plummeted to the floor—twice. Looking around, I realized, this was it…this was my life. No hospital, no doctor's office. I didn't do the college thing. I gave it up for one weekend that was life changing. "Was it worth it, Elleny?" I asked myself out loud "Was it worth what you've become?"

"Who are you talking to, Elle?" Laurie whispered in her already quiet voice, afraid that she was disrupting a conversation. She looked around for a moment, trying to find whoever I was carrying on with.

"I'm sorry. Just talking to myself. You know, just having a moment," I admitted as I felt my cheeks turn red from realizing she was listening to me drown in my own self-pity.

"Well, just so you know, Mr. Stevens' clients were stepping off the elevator as I was coming in here, so you better wrap up the pep talk."

Smiling a smile that broke through my still red cheeks, I graciously thanked her for helping with the set up as I left the room to go finish getting everything we needed for this meeting.

Heading down the hallway, I heard Mr. Stevens welcoming the clients out in the reception area. The older gentleman was introducing himself to Mr. Stevens, but I wasn't really paying attention. I did, however, catch him asking for directions to the restroom. I quickly grabbed my memory stick with the power-point presentation on it and headed back to the conference room.

I walked the hallway, seeking Loren out. Since the clients had gone to the restroom, I needed to confirm whether he needed the packets passed out now or if he wanted me to wait until after the presentation. "Loren, do you want the—"

Like I had walked right into fast setting concrete, I abruptly stopped. Sitting down in the head chair, looking right at me, was not Hugh Hefner in a red velvet robe.

It was the man whose name I vowed never to speak again. The man I never wanted to see again.

Oh please, God no… oh fuck … no, no, no, no!

Sitting there, not even ten feet away from me, in his fifteen hundred dollar suit, was Trevor McHale. His hair was cut short, all the blonde curls were gone, but it was the same brown. Those hazel eyes that still had more green than brown shined as if they were lighting the room. I missed staring into those eyes. The small little dimple right below his left eye was still there, but his nose was different. He had it fixed. It was straight and the bump was gone. Nevertheless, you could tell it was him. TJ, here in the flesh. He was still so gorgeous. He was older but he still had that beautiful face, the one I held in my hands time and time again to look deep into eyes that held my future. Everything that was my happiness since second grade was sitting right across the room from me and I couldn't do anything about it.

Every memory containing TJ McHale flashed through my mind in seconds. All the dreams I'd been having for the past few months came back to me in a flood of emotions. Every touch I had felt on my body, every space of skin I'd touched on his. Places I'd kissed. The way his muscles would tense as I'd gently run my fingers over them.

I didn't know whether to run out in a panic, stay where I was, or scream and cry like a two year old. I mentally grabbed ahold of my shoulders, shook them, and assured myself he wouldn't say a thing. Just keep calm and walk. *Damn it, Ellen, cowgirl the fuck up!*

51

"Elleny, I would like to introduce you to Mr. Trevor McHale of the Mac-Gentry Firm. Mr. McHale, this is Elleny Harper-Jackson, my assistant."

I told myself to smile. "It's a pleasure to meet you, Mr. McHale. Please, call me Elle," I articulated, how…I have no clue. I don't even remember moving my mouth. I realized my hand was sticking straight out in front of me. Once again, I had no recollection of telling my body to do this.

As his eyes hit mine, he clasped a gentle but very firm hand over mine. At that moment, a stillness I haven't felt in a long time washed over me and I found serenity. Nothing mattered—no kids fighting, no asshole husband, no bill collectors breathing down my back—everything was gone. I was now in my place. In the cab of that truck, wind blowing my hair around, the smell of this man filling my nostrils and the taste of him on my tongue. The baffling thought of how I had let this man go long enough for him to drive us somewhere was filling my mind. I wanted him so bad. This was in my place, in my mind—no, wait. He was here, right in front of me, holding onto my hand; the man who was supposed to be mine. My world, my one and only, the man I swore I would be anchored to throughout this life; the man I told to fuck off, that I never wanted to see him again.

Mine!

I quickly pulled my hand back and turned to leave when I heard Loren's concerned voice.

"Elle, you alright? You look pale, like you've seen a ghost."

You have no idea, but you're pretty damn close, Loren.

"Actually, Lor…um, Mr. Stevens, I'm not feeling so well. I think I'm going to take a minute in the powder room. If you gentlemen will excuse me. Mr. Stevens, everything you need is right there. I will send Ginger in to help you with the presentation."

I quickly and professionally dashed out of Conference Room B. On my way to the restroom, I grabbed my purse and surged toward Ginger's desk to beg her to take my place in the meeting. She had no issue with that and sauntered in there as though the world was peachy-perfect.

I made it to the restroom and opened my bag with shaky hands. Grabbing my phone, I pushed the number five on my speed dial. If I had to dial Rachel's number, I didn't think I could do it.

"What's up, bia—"

"I know what my subconscious was trying to tell me."

"You do? What? And, why are you calling me on your cell, aren't you at work?"

"I'm in the bathroom, Rach. It was trying to tell me to get ready, to put my guard up."

Rachel giggled. "Get ready for what? Why would you need to guard yourself? Jesus, Elle, did you smoke something in that bathroom? "

"Rachel, would you fucking listen to me? It was trying to warn me."

"Okay, Elle, I'll bite. Warn you about what?"

"My run in with TJ."

The line got quiet for a moment, like Rachel's mind was churning. Either that or she was struggling not to panic.

"You're what? What the fuck are you talking about, Elle?"

"He's here, Rachel, in my office. Conference room B, to be exact. As a matter of fact, he's sitting down with my boss signing a contract to purchase Richland Manufacturing. He's coming back to Richland."

I heard Rachel gasp.

"Shut the fuck up!"

Tracy Lee

Chapter 3

August 1992

Looking at the mess I called a bedroom, not only did I feel sick to my stomach, I felt overwhelmed. Packing up everything that you have lived with for the last eighteen years was not an easy chore. I had collected a lot of crap and everything I had belonged in one of three boxes: decorations for my new apartment used only as a deterrent of home sickness, Daddy's storage unit where everything of worth was kept, or in the trash.

I could not believe that by this time next week Rachel and I would be in our new apartment getting ready to begin our first day of college. Sitting on the edge of my bed, I waited for my stomach to calm down. I talked myself out of being sick by convincing myself I was stressed out and needed to eat something light.

That night was the gang's going away party. Since Rachel's parents were cruising around Mexico or the Bahamas, we decided to use their house. It wasn't like they didn't have the space to hold two hundred of our closest friends. Their house could've been used in the remake of *Gone with the Wind.* Set on what looked like a plantation of twenty-five acres, it was an eighty-five hundred square foot home with nine bedrooms, twelve bathrooms, an indoor-outdoor pool, and a theater room that sat fifteen people. But, that wasn't the point since we really didn't have two hundred close friends. Rachel,

Lilly, and I told someone who told someone and word of mouth caught on quickly.

I finally called it quits on the packing around four and decided I'd go downstairs and make a sandwich. I was still feeling nauseous and knew I had to have a little something on my stomach so I could last more than an hour of drinking without passing out.

Standing on a dining room chair shaped like a small throne in the middle of the large living area, I slurred, holding a shot of tequila above my head.

"Come on, my bitches...just one more shot. To college! May we become more experienced—life wise, that is," I said quickly, looking at TJ and winking. "And, may we become wiser, since this is costing our parents a shitload of money!" I screamed as I heard two hundred voices simultaneously chiming together, "Here, here!" I cheered the air and tossed the shot back.

TJ grabbed my hips and gently lowered me down as I laughed hysterically at nothing. Shouting over Def Leopard's *Pour Some Sugar on Me*, I asked Lilly to go and grab a bottle of tequila so that we could refill our shot glasses for another toast. TJ, with beer in hand, yelled for her to grab another beer for him as well.

"Baby, this is the best night of my life!" I screamed as I wrapped my arms around his neck, listening to the pandemonium around me.

"Yeah, you said that last weekend too," TJ said as he laughed.

"God, baby do you hear that? The lead singer of Def Leopard sounds like he got kicked in the balls!"

TJ exploded into laughter. "Darlin', I am just about ready to cut you off! Those are the dumb fucks behind us sucking on helium and singing with the music."

I looked behind me and exhaled. "Oh shit, that scared me!" I exclaimed, riotously laughing as I swayed back and forth while grasping onto TJ's neck.

I stopped swaying, looked TJ in the eyes, and whispered right up next to his ear, "Kiss me, baby, and then take me into your auntie's room and ravage me."

"Seriously, Elle-bean, I think the moment you hit that bed you are gonna pass out."

"No, I won't," I argued.

"Yes, you will, Elle. You're pretty drunk."

"Trevor McHale, are you gonna take me into your auntie's bedroom and have your way with me or what?"

"You think you can handle that?"

"Hell yeah I can! I can handle anything you throw at me."

"Okay, then…you're on!"

As the music changed to Garth Brooks people jumped up around us and started slow dancing. TJ grabbed my hand.

"Wait up a minute, darlin'. I wanna dance with you."

I clasped my hands together around his neck, laid my head against his chest, and felt the vibration that was booming in his chest as he hummed along with the song. As he began to sing , I raised my head and looked into his eyes. Listening to him sing the song to only me, his beautiful voice shot straight to my heart. I lifted my hand to his cheek and he turned so that his mouth was against my palm, gently kissing it.

Sobering up, I could feel the lyrics. I would never have to question how much this man loved me, anyone could see it ran as deep and whole heartily as mine ran for him. Never would another be able to hold our hearts; they belonged solely to each other.

At this very moment, I felt like I couldn't physically get close enough to him. He permeated every inch of me. Feeling my stomach getting nauseous again, my emotions overwhelmed me. I needed to get out of this room. The walls seemed to be closing in all around me. Quickly and harshly, I pulled away from TJ.

"Ellie-bean?"

"I have to go to the bathroom."

"What's the matter, you feeling alright?"

"No, I've just got to…I need some air."

"Okay, you wanna step outside?"

"Sure."

Already on my way to the door, I looked around. Bear and Rachel were sitting at the dining room table playing a game of Quarters, and Lilly and Curt were sitting on the couch laughing at a game of Asshole. I relaxed a bit and opened the front door. The cold autumn Georgia night air hit me like a slap to the face and I closed my eyes, taking a deep cleansing breath.

"Much better."

We walked around for a few minutes coming to rest in front of a large oak tree on the side of the house just outside of the front flood lights reach. I slid down to sit and crossed my arms over my knees, resting my forehead on top.

"Elle, what happened in there?"

Raising my head and watching for a moment, his face was scrutinizing. I considered lying, but the truth inherently came out.

"TJ, do you sometimes feel like we need this break?"

Shaken, he got to his feet and defensively bowed up his back as if putting himself in self-defense mode.

"What the fuck are you trying to say, Elleny?"

"Baby, sit down. We're just talking," I said, trying to calm him.

"No, I wanna know right now. What the hell is behind this?"

I took another deep breath to clear my head and began my confession.

"I love you, TJ. So much. There is no way you could even begin to comprehend how much."

As he took a step closer to me, I heard him take a breath. Whether he was calming himself or showing me he was taking in what I had just confessed, I wasn't sure. He knelt down so that he could look into my eyes.

"Babe, are you with me?"

"What?"

"Are you with me?"

"Didn't you just hear what I said to you?"

"Yeah, I did. Now, are...you...with...me?"

I knew what he was looking for, striving for. He needed my reassurance. Even though I just told him that he was my complete world—my day, my night, my heart, my soul—he still needed to hear those four little words.

"Anchored to you, baby," I muttered through watery eyes and a throat that didn't want to work. I grabbed a hold of the top of his shirt and pulled him down until we were mouth to mouth.

That's when he said the words that tore my world apart.

"Can't go a day without breathing and since you're my breath."

I slammed my mouth down onto his lips.

I opened my mouth to give him the access I was craving. With the way he devoured me, it was like he couldn't get close enough, deep enough to me as well. I tried following his lead, to bring him in closer, but it didn't work. I briskly turned my head to the side, then to the other, but it still wasn't deep enough. Abruptly, he pulled away.

"Wha...what are you doing?" I asked, winded.

"Take your clothes off now. Lay them on the ground."

"What...TJ, are you crazy? It must be fifty degrees out here. We'll catch a cold."

"Do it," he demanded.

I knew something wasn't right when I looked at him. His veins were bulging on the side of his temple and his jaw was clenching and releasing in quick recession. He was acting like he was a drug addict and right in front of him laid his drug of choice, the drug he couldn't get to fast enough.

"Baby…what's wrong?" I whimpered.

TJ came face to face with me, his eyes never leaving mine. Beginning to unbutton my blouse, I could see his hands were shaking. I wasn't sure he would be able to undo many more of the small buttons.

Not caring by this time, my clothes went flying. Why he was acting like this, I had no clue. All I knew was that he had to have me.

"Hurry, Elle! God, baby, I ache for you. I need this pain to go away." I couldn't stop the tears that came out of frustration and overwhelming emotion. I couldn't figure out for the life of me why he was acting like this.

"I'm hurrying! Jesus Christ, what's wrong, baby?"

Completely naked, I laid down on top of my clothes. He wasn't even undressing. He grabbed my knees with his hands and gently opened my legs. I could tell he was trying to maintain control, but he was losing it and it was killing me. Sobbing, my tears mixed with my mascara as they both ran down my face. I felt him as he slowly wiped my cheeks.

"This right here, baby? This is what connects us. This is how I can get you as close to me as I need you to be."

He began running his fingers between my legs. I laid my head back, tears still flowing as I gasped for breath. I closed my eyes, anticipating his touch. The cold breeze was blowing against my naked body, but I didn't feel anything with the heat building between our bodies.

He plunged his fingers deep into me and slurred, "This right here is what anchors me to you, this is what will anchor me to you for the rest of my life."

He gradually bent down, put his head between my legs, and kissed tender, wet kisses on the inside of my thighs.

"This pussy right here, is something that no one will ever know but me. Isn't that right, baby?"

It took all the strength I had to mumble through the sobbing and blubbering, "Yes, baby. It's all yours."

I started breathing faster as he sucked my clit into his mouth. I began moving against him wildly as he penetrated me with his tongue. I moaned deeply. Hearing the heady moans coming from his mouth, I ran my fingers through his soft hair. I pushed against him harder, encouraging him not to stop.

"TJ, I'm going to come," I said on a gasp.

"Give it to me, Elle. It belongs to me, baby. Let me have it," he said as he began moving his tongue faster, determined.

I felt the first wave hit me like a ton of bricks. Then another and another. Trying to catch my breath, I felt him taking long, slow draws, lapping and sucking like a starving man who was receiving his first and last meal.

TJ dropped down beside me on the ground, threw his arm on top of his head, and stared at the sky above us.

I started grabbing for my clothes, when I heard him.

"What you're feeling, about loving me so much I wouldn't understand it? I feel it, Elle. But for the life of me, I feel like I'm just hanging onto you by a thread. Any minute now you're gonna cut me loose, then I won't know how to go on living."

I froze. Dropping my clothes, I began to feel the waves of nausea and panic rise again in my stomach. Not because of what just happened, but because he was in agony—physically and emotionally. I could see a tiny streak run down his cheek as he just stared up into the dark, cloudless sky. He had nothing to worry about when it came to other men. For me, there was no one other than him.

What bothered him—which he would never admit—was not knowing how to get on with his life. He wanted a life where there was a well-defined line between him and me and him and the world. That feeling wasn't exactly foreign to me since that was what I was feeling as well.

I knew he wanted to go to school. I knew he wanted to play ball—it was what he was good at. I knew he wanted to get a degree in business and work with investments—it was what he was even better at. He didn't think he could live that life without me. We were totally suffocating each other. What we thought was a beautiful romance was metaphorically killing us because we couldn't stand to be away from each other. No…we couldn't live without each other.

Can't go a day without breathing since you're my breath.

Something had to change. He knew I wasn't going to cross that line and he just proved to me that he wasn't willing to cross it either. I had to come up with something.

Little did I know that our answer was with us all along.

"Wake up, mother fuckers!" Bear screamed through a mouthful of god only knew what. Hearing his voice mixed with the squishing of the food he was feasting on made me want to sit front row to a concert that was being thrown in the porcelain god concert hall. Thanks to the alcohol intake of the night before, hearing him scream throughout the bedroom made my head throb and my stomach even queasier.

"Oh my God! Who is the one who will be taking an ass whooping for letting me drink so much," I gritted out through teeth that refused to stop clenching. If they did, all hell was going to come up.

I heard TJ groan next to me.

Rachel joined in on the conversation like someone had called a meeting in the bedroom. "And, who gave ya'll fucktards permission to sleep in my momma's bed?" Swinging her neck from side to side and snapping her fingers, she continued on with her little tirade. "You better not have gotten anything on those sheets because I'd really have to kick your asses. Plus, I don't feel like doin' sheets and the maid doesn't come in 'til Monday."

Suddenly, my stomach decided it was time to unclench my teeth. Running to the bathroom, I noticed TJ sat up quickly in bed. I made it to the toilet before all hell broke loose. *How could I possibly still have food in there after throwing up this much?*

I stopped heaving for a moment and reached over, slamming the door shut. Laying the tip of my forehead on the toilet seat, I prayed nothing else would come up. Too late, round two began. Ten minutes later, I began round four. This continued for an hour. Finally, a reprieve. I washed my hands, swished mouthwash in my mouth, and headed for the kitchen.

As I walked into the kitchen, all heads jerked my way. Everyone looked like zombies. Faces were pale, eyelids were rimmed with red, and each one looked as if they were moving in slow motion.

I grumbled, "Mornin', ya'll. Babe, can you take me home, I'm still not feeling well."

"Sure, just let me get my things," TJ mumbled back. I think he was still drunk.

"Rach…Lils, call me later. Love ya, Curt…Bear."

"Kay, babe…bye, Elle," Rach and Lilly said in unison.

"Love you, Elle. Feel better," Curt said.

"Bitch…" Bear groaned.

This was his normal greeting or farewell. If he didn't call you a bitch or a motherfucker, you weren't a friend of his.

I slept the whole way home. Hearing the truck door slam, I opened my eyes to see TJ smile a small smile in my direction. I heard the passenger door open then felt him wrap me up in his arms. I laid my head on his shoulder and closed my eyes again. Every step he took was torture. My stomach fluttered and my head spun even as I grasped ahold of the back of his shirt to keep my grounding. I moaned as TJ stepped up the front steps. Reaching behind me, I pushed the doorbell seeing how TJ's hands were tied up. My stepmom, Mona, opened the door.

My momma passed away when I was four. She was in a car accident and my daddy had never been the same. My momma and daddy shared a love that could never be replaced. She was lucky enough to move on and forget him, he didn't have that luxury. When my momma died, half of Daddy died, too. The other half belonged to me. He was the other love of my life. My daddy, Maxwell Winston Harper II, was a doctor and he loved what he did. Being the town's general practitioner, he had seen everything from the common cold to babies delivered. He had never practiced anywhere else.

When I was ten, Daddy thought I needed a female figure in my life. This is where Mona came in. Mona wasn't a female figure to me though, she's nothing but white trash dressed up in my daddy's money.

"Mornin', Trevor, I see my golden child has been up to her old ways." Mona knew me too well from past summer experiences, but one thing they didn't have to worry about was TJ McHale. They knew he would never do anything that would bring shame to the Harper name. My family was sixth generation Richland Harpers. This meant that we "Harpa's" had a reputation to uphold.

Mona was a trophy wife who hung out at the golf course, ate red meat, and drank red wine. Of course, she was sensible about it. She only got drunk behind closed doors. Mona was infamous for drinking all evening then picking fights with Daddy over why he didn't want to be around her anymore. She'd given him ultimatums; if he didn't want her, she'd find someone who did. He would remind her drunk ass that she was the one who signed the prenup, so if she decided to "go out and get it somewhere else" she'd lose everything. So, Mona would shut her mouth, grab another bottle of wine, and drink until she passed out. It was a never ending cycle. In public, they were the perfect Georgian husband and wife.

That's because they were Harper's. No one looked down on a Harper.

My step-momma reeked of her hatred for me; jealousy oozed out of every pore on her body. If my daddy wasn't at work, he was with me and that chapped her ass. She was waiting for the day when I wouldn't be around. Me leaving for college meant she would have my dad all to herself. But, what she didn't realize was that he still wasn't planning on wasting his time with her. No one was gonna pull the wool over Maxwell Winston Harper's eyes. He didn't love her, she was nothing to him aside from a companion to lay beside in bed.

TJ carried me to the bottom of the stairs that led up to my bedroom. My father was waiting at the top. Taking one look at me, he quickly became concerned.

"Trevor," my daddy greeted with a nod of his head.

"Mr. Harper." TJ nodded back.

With his left eyebrow raised, he inquired, "Elle, you feelin' okay?"

"I'm fine, Daddy. I just think I have a stomach flu on top of…well, I think I may have had one too many cocktails last night."

Knowing I was underage, Daddy ignored the last part of what I said. He always taught me to be honest, so he would know what he was dealing with if anything ever happened. I was never one to experiment with drugs, they always scared me, so that would never be an issue. Growing up with a doctor in the house, I had heard stories and that was all I needed to know on that subject. Besides, I had a strong head on my shoulders and knew what I wanted in life. I wasn't stupid enough to risk my future. I also was never one who gave into peer-pressure. I had to have some type of control when it came to situations and if I couldn't, I didn't participate or partake. My daddy knew this and trusted me to make the right decisions. He knew my friends and their families as well. He knew kids were gonna be kids and have a good time but he also appreciated that we knew when to draw the line.

"Sweetie, why don't you go upstairs and lie down. I will have Clara make you some chicken soup, something light on your stomach."

Clara was our full time cook. She would come in at six-thirty in the morning, make breakfast and then make some type of salad for lunch. She made the best chicken salad, it was to die for. Rotisserie chicken with cranberries, raisins, and diced up walnuts. Just enough mayo to wet it but you could still taste the spices. She would start dinner and be gone by five-thirty every day. Clara was as cute as a button. White shoulder-length hair that was always pulled back in a ponytail at the nape of her neck. She was short, five-foot at best, and a little stocky. Clara always dressed so professionally, you couldn't tell that she spent most of her time in a kitchen. She began working for us before my momma passed. Her stories about my momma and daddy would keep me enthralled all afternoon as she cooked our dinner. That's how I found out about how much they loved each other.

"Trevor, will you please help Elle up to her room while I go speak with Clara."

"Yes, Mr. Harper."

"Thank you, son."

Helping me up the stairs, I felt as though I was going to get sick again. I asked TJ to drop me off at the powder room that was attached to my bedroom and he could go on home. I didn't want him to hear or see me puking up whatever was left in my system.

Disappointed but understanding, he dropped me off at the restroom and went downstairs to leave. I had lost count on how many times I had gotten sick. I remembered crawling to my bed after being in the bathroom for what felt like forever and that's it.

After waking once and falling back asleep, I opened my eyes once again. I felt weak, very weak. I saw Daddy sitting over me with my wrist in my hand, taking my pulse. I asked him what time it was but don't remember him responding before I fell back to sleep.

Lying in bed, I heard what sounded like chimes ringing. Keeping my eyes closed I just listened to the sounds. Coming out of my sleep induced haze, it hit me that it was an alarm going off. Was it time to get up already? I reached around to shut off my alarm.

"Put your arm back down, sweetie."

Surprised at the bizarre voice, I peeked through barely opened slits. Glimpsing around concerned, I caught the sight of a tall African American nurse doing something with the IV pole standing next to me. She was light skinned with the most beautiful complexion I had ever seen. The sides of her hair were pulled back in a barrette on top of her head and her scrubs were aqua.

"I take it you don't know where you are?"

"Umm, a hospital?"

"Do you remember why you're here?"

"No," I replied, beginning to panic. Hearing the machine beeping, I took it she was also aware of my panic attack.

"It's okay…calm down. I'm gonna explain. First off, my name is Keisha. I'm your daytime nurse, I will be here 'til seven tonight. I was going over your notes when I noticed your bag of fluids was empty. So, I changed 'em and here we are. You were brought in because you couldn't keep a lick of anything down and were severely dehydrated. Honey, your daddy is a mess worryin' over you. It says in your chart that Dr. Robbins is your attending physician and he has ordered some more tests to be run. They are waiting on your blood work."

Grabbing my wrist, she looked at her watch while she counted. "Do you know what today is?"

Looking at Keisha, my mouth dropped opened and my eyes were as wide as they could be, which wasn't very far. I just shook my head while I listened to the machine beside me beep double time.

Resting my hand back under the sheets, she began tucking the hospital sheet in around me. "Today is Wednesday. Your parents brought you in on Sunday."

Thinking back to the party that was on Friday night, this meant I had been asleep for three...no, four days.

"Holy shit, what the hell is wrong with me?" I whispered out loud instead of in my head.

"Won't be long before we'll be findin' out, baby girl."

"My parents—"

"Are in the café. Your momma finally pulled your daddy away and forced him to eat something."

"That's not my momma. She's my stepmom," I quickly responded to Keisha's explanation.

"Oh," Keisha breathed, her lips forming the perfect "O".

"It's okay, you wouldn't have known. As a matter of fact, I have no clue what she's doing here."

"Well, to tell you the truth, before today, I had never seen her before."

There ya go, the truth had been set free. Even though she lined her lips and hid her crazy like the good Harper she acted to be, her neglect was her giveaway. I bet the Richland Gazette would be happy to run a whole article on it. I could see the byline now.

Saddened by the hospital admittance of her only step daughter, Elleny Harper, Mrs. Mona Harper had yet to step foot in her room to even deliver a bouquet of flowers.

"Well, well, my princess decided she needed lots of beauty sleep, did she? I seem to disagree with her on that subject."

I heard my daddy's cheery yet concerned voice coming into the hospital room before I saw him. As per his profession, he headed straight to my chart to check out any updated notes that were added while he was out. He set his coffee down and began reading intently as he went over the notes precisely.

"Can I eat?"

Daddy raised his head and looked at Keisha with one eyebrow raised. "And she's hungry? I'm flabbergasted!"

This got a tiny giggle out of Keisha as she set to leave the room. "It's your call, Doc."

"Toast and tea, un-sweet and bland."

"Daddy!"

"Don't 'daddy' me. I want to see if it will stay down before you start pigging out."

I rolled my eyes but mentally agreed. I really wasn't in the mood to hurl anymore.

Getting a little toast on my stomach had me feeling stronger, now we had to see if it stayed down. Having had eaten two hours ago, so far, so good. The nurse came into my room to offer me some Jell-O, and the doctor wasn't far behind her.

"Good Afternoon, Ms. Harper. I'm Dr. Robbins. I see you ate some solid food several hours ago and have kept that down so far. How are you feeling?"

I looked at Dr. Robbins and didn't know if I should answer him truthfully. *Actually, I feel like a John Deere ran me over, came back around, tied me to the bumper, dragged me twenty miles down the road, then left me for the wild hogs to find and finish me off.*

Instead, I just smiled and offered, "Better than I did."

The doctor walked to the side of my bed, pulled the chair up beside me with a manila folder in his hands, and began to flip through the pile of papers. "Well, we ran some tests and everything looks good. All your levels appear to be normal except for one. Ms. Harper, if you don't mind, I would like to ask you a personal question. Would you consider yourself an alcoholic?"

Baffled, I asked, "I'm sorry, could you repeat the question? I don't think I heard you correctly. I thought you just asked me if I was an alcoholic."

"Yes, I did. When your father brought you in on Sunday, he had given us a forty-eight hour history on your behavior: what you did, where you were, and who you were with. He disclosed that you had been at a party and had consumed an excessive amount of alcohol. For this reasoning, and for the safety of your baby, I need to know if we should really be contemplating getting you into a rehab program."

I didn't hear anything after the word "baby". The monitor next to me starting going triple the speed it normally should've been.

"I'm sorry, are ya'll giving me something that would affect my comprehension? I thought I just heard you say baby."

"Ms. Harper, I did say baby. You're pregnant, a little over eight weeks."

My whole life flashed before my eyes—no more parties, no more friends. Who would want to hang around someone with a kid? I sure as shit didn't want to and yet, here I was, finding out that I would be the one *with* the kid.

Somewhere in the back of my mind, I remembered my birth control pills. I began laughing hysterically and looked back at the doctor.

"I am so sorry, Dr. Robbins, but there's been a terrible mix up. Me being pregnant, it's not possible."

As he began flipping through the files, page after page looked like nothing but printed sheets of paper with scribbling besides graphs. He read the results and then checked out the name on the chart again.

His eyes came back up to me as he asked, "Oh, and how's that? If you'd like I can order a sonogram.

"Doctor, I am on birth control pills, have been since I was thirteen. I have had irregular periods all my life. Dr. Harper refills my prescription every six months and I NEVER miss a pill. That's how it is not possible".

"That's odd. Well, was there a chance you were on antibiotics anytime during the month of May or June?"

Thinking back through the times when I had been sick, which wasn't hard seeing I haven't been sick a lot, I did remember back at the beginning of June when I had a sinus infection and Daddy put me on antibiotics. Then the senior skip weekend at the lake popped in my head. *Holy shit on a stick!* I said to myself. That weekend was actually a week after I finished the last dose of medicine.

Noticing the smile leave my face gradually, Dr. Robbins knew that I was now comprehending everything he had said to me. I began realizing that my and TJ's lives were totally fucked. I pictured our futures. Me standing out in the back yard of our home, a run-down old shack, hanging hand-washed ratty clothes out to dry. I could see that I was barefoot and pregnant again, thanks to another cocktail of antibiotics and birth control pills. With a kid on my hip, three other kids fighting as they chased each other around me, TJ was sitting up on the back porch in overalls, cigarette hanging off his lip as he reached down into a red cooler pulling out another beer. His sluggish words tore through me as he admitted that I was the reason for all of this. I was the one who had screwed up his life and he wished he never met me.

This couldn't be happening to me. No, this was a bad dream. I was still sleeping and I was going to wake up any moment now and be back in my pink room which was messy because of all the boxes, clothes, and princess shit all over the floor. I would wake up and go back to packing for college.

That's when it hit me—college. I was supposed to be leaving for college in a week. I was getting the hell out of Richland and beginning my life. So was TJ. He had a scholarship, he couldn't turn that down. He had waited his

71

whole life and worked his ass off for this opportunity. Coaches from all over the United States were trying to recruit him. There was no way he was missing his chance, I wasn't going to let him.

"…Harper. Ms. Harper?" My name caught my attention and I turned to Dr. Robbins. "I see you have a lot to think about. If you have any questions, I'll be here all evening. Please let your nurse know and they can page me."

He knew what was going through my mind. "The state of Georgia prohibits abortion, unless the health of the mother is at risk or the fetus is not viable. I'm sorry."

I nodded my head with tears in my eyes and waited for him to leave so that I could succumb to my breakdown alone.

My mind was going a thousand miles a minute. What do I do? Where do I go? Do I keep it? Do I get rid of it? There were two questions that I already knew the answers to. One, no one was going to know about this. Two, TJ was definitely not finding out about this. He would not ruin his life because of my mess up. I didn't even realize the tears were still streaming down my face.

Staring at the wall, I was in a haze. I heard the door burst open as my father surged through only to come to a halt a second later. Lifting my head, I looked in his eyes and I knew he knew. I couldn't do anything. I couldn't cry anymore, I couldn't even speak. I just stared into his eyes. He slowly walked over to me like I had a knife to my throat and one false move meant the end of the line for me. He gently sat on the corner of the bed.

"Elle—"

"Don't!" I cried. Hearing the harshness in my tone, I cleared my throat, knowing I couldn't take this out on him. "Please, Daddy, don't. I know. Trust me…I know," I whispered.

"Oh, Elleny, my dear sweet baby, I wasn't going to say anything negative. Baby, we will work it out. Please, darlin', I can't lose the other half of my heart."

I grabbed my daddy by the lapel of his shirt, laid my head on his shoulder, and sobbed into his chest. I felt like I was nine again when I had fallen off my bike and scraped my knee. I would run straight to him and he would hug me so tight, telling me it was going to be okay. He'd then wash up my boo-boo, put a bandage on it, and everything would all be okay. My daddy knew what to do.

"I just cannot believe the shame this is going to bring on this family!"

I looked up to see Mona standing there in her cream colored chiffon blouse that was crocheted in the back but tied in the front, peach colored capris, and six-inch, gold, open-toed stiletto heeled sandals. Her blonde hair was teased big with a gold butterfly barrette on the right side of her head. Mona's six inch gold hoop earrings hung from her ears and the ten karat baguette diamond tennis bracelet Daddy gave her at her fortieth birthday party two years earlier dangled from her wrist.

"Do you know what you are going to put your father through for this little stunt, young lady? I told you, Maxwell, we should've put her in that boarding school years ago. She would've learned manners and respect there. I swear to that sweet, little baby Jesus in the manger that you have put your daddy through so much shit, he's probably on the verge of a heart attack. Is that what you want, little girl? You want your daddy buried right there next to your momma out in Oakland Heights Cemetery?"

"That's enough, Mona!" my father bellowed. "How dare you talk to her like that? I don't know what the hell you are thinking, but you better backtrack it real quick!"

Mona jolted back like she'd been hit by lightning. "I'm just thinkin' of you, sweetheart. I don't want you to over exert yourself. You know what stress can do to a body."

"Go home, Mona. I'll have one of the attending drop me off later."

"But, suga-britches…"

"Just go!"

73

"Maxwell," she whispered.

"See you at home, Mona!"

The combination of Mona's mumbling and her shoes clickety-clacking made me realize that what she said was all true. I had been an irresponsible brat that more than likely drove my daddy to the nuthouse, he just wouldn't get out of the car. I knew that whatever my decision was going to be, I was going to be alone and I would have to be okay with that.

"Daddy…" Closing my eyes and still resting my head against his chest, I could smell his cologne and it brought me back to when I was a kid again. I was still enjoying the feel of my dad pushing the hair out of my face.

"Yeah, darlin'?"

"We can't tell anyone about this, okay? You have to do whatever you have to do to make sure that Mona doesn't say a word."

"Baby, Trevor deserves to—"

"No! He deserves to go to school and do what he's planned to do. He does not find out about this!"

"Elleny!"

"I know what I have to do, Daddy."

Sitting up in the bed on the second floor of Richland Memorial hospital, I had made up my mind and I was sticking to it.

"You do? Well, let's hear it."

"It looks like I'm gonna be a momma."

Chapter 4

Present Day 2010

I finished my conversation with Rachel and exhaled, staring into the restroom mirror. Thinking of what my next move was going to be, I came to the resolution that I was going to be professional about this and not let him get to me this way. I was going back out to my desk since I couldn't leave anyway; we had two more appointments this afternoon.

"It's been seventeen years, Elleny. Let it go." I said to my reflection. "I'm sure he doesn't even give you a second thought. He's probably married and has moved on, which is what you've done. Let it go."

I examined my outfit, straightened out my skirt, and adjusted my blouse. My hair was pulled back in a chignon at the nape of my neck, so I fluffed my bangs and reached into my purse to grab some clear gloss. I wanted him to see that I was undisturbed by this cluster-fuck of a reunion. He was not going to get to me. No way, no how.

I threw everything back into my purse, took one more deep breath, and walked out of the restroom straight to my desk. I didn't look around and I didn't converse with anyone. I had to concentrate on what my objective was: showing him that he does not, nor has he ever crossed my mind.

Yeah, right.

I made it to my desk and began to go through my email when I heard Mr. Steven's voice.

"Gentlemen, we can't prolong this transaction any longer. The board of director's at Richland Manufacturing wants to close this deal as soon as possible."

"We understand that, Mr. Stevens," I heard the older gentlemen retort.

At this point, all three men were coming out of the conference room and were headed toward my desk as if they were going to go into Mr. Stevens' office. As soon as they walked past my desk, TJ's voice caught my attention.

"I'll tell you what, Stevens…" they stopped right in front of my desk and TJ turned to face me, "I know that you and Miss…Miss…I'm sorry, Miss, what was your name again?"

Trying not to grit my teeth, I smiled the biggest "fuck off" smile while chanting, "I hate this man" over and over again in my mind. Cynically, yet professionally, I decided to respond. "Mrs. Barker-Jackson, Mr. McHale. My name is Elleny Barker-Jackson".

"Ah, yes that's right. Again, my apologies. Loren, I know that you and Mrs. Barker-Jackson," he queried, as if he was looking for a correction if he was wrong, "have worked long hours on this arrangement. Let's you and I make us a little deal. Strictly off the record, of course. You give me forty-eight hours to go over this contract and on Thursday, Mrs. Barker-Jackson can meet me in my hotel's restaurant, twelve-thirty, where she can pick up these contracts, no stipulations."

Oh my god, what the hell was he doing?

I had to think of some excuse to get out of this and I had to think of it quick.

"Mr. McHale, I don't think—"

"You've got yourself a deal, McHale."

Whipping my head around from TJ to Loren, I know he had seen that my eyes were the size of dinner plates. Unbeknownst to him, my boss had just thrown me under the metaphorical bus. That's right, the one who would be receiving my letter of resignation first thing Friday morning. I had to get out of this and I had to get out of it now.

"Mr. Stevens, I'm sorry, but I think that this is highly unethical—"

"Elle, we will discuss this at a more suitable time."

Yes, we sure as shit would be discussing this just as soon as Trevor McHale, king of the douche lords, got the hell out of my face. The nerve of him! I wanted to kick him in the—

"Gentlemen," my asshole of a boss' voice brought me out of my morning mental ball crushing, "I want to thank you for coming in and I look forward to receiving the information Thursday afternoon."

As I looked back at TJ, I noticed his eyes never left me. He just stood there staring at me as though he knew exactly what was going on in my head. I stared back at him, this time through lethal eyes. He got my point, considering the large shit eating grin that had covered his face.

"Until Thursday, Mrs. Barker-Jackson. Loren, always a pleasure."

"Mr. McHale," was my only response.

I was already through with this whole morning. Tonight was going to be a dinner and wine kind of night where wine would be served as the main course.

Once again, Trevor had totally come in and out of my life like an F-5 tornado. I could not believe what just happened.

I saw Loren coming back to his office from walking both men down to the elevators. I met him inside.

"Loren, this meeting on Thursday is a mistake. I cannot go meet that man. If you want, I will send a messenger to pick up the contracts but this little agreement that you and McHale have come to is not going to happen."

"Elleny, how long have you been my assistant?"

I looked at him perplexed and answered quickly, "Fifteen years."

"And how many times have I asked you to do something that didn't have your best interest in mind?"

Knowing where this conversation was heading, I answered, "None."

"Do you know what this means when this merger goes through? Not only for me, but for you?"

Lowering my head and looking at the floor, I knew what this meant for the both of us. For him, it meant that he would be partner. For me, it meant a hefty raise plus bonuses. This meant, I wouldn't have to count on what little money *he* brought in and I could stash some away without him knowing.

"Loren, you know this meeting is bullshit. He's screwing with us and, to be quite honest, I don't have the time nor the patience to deal with him."

"Elle, at the most, thirty minutes. He probably wants to have a drink with you. Go, have a drink then take the rest of the day off."

I scoffed at the attempt to butter me up. "Are you serious? You expect me to accept that offer? "

His face turned serious and the gleam left his eyes. "Elle, I expect you to think about yourself and your kids."

The smile left my face and I began to pick up the stack of papers on his desk, busying my hands and trying to forget this conversation was even happening.

"Elle—"

"Don't, Loren!" I roared, throwing the papers straight back down to his desk. "You know I have no choice. Leaving is not an option for me. He's made it quite obvious that he will take my children and hide them. He has all that…that backwoods family who live in those swamps down in Louisiana. I would never see my children again. How dare you even think that I'm not considering my kids. Everything I do is for their benefit."

"I know, Elleny. Look, I'm sorry. I didn't mean it like that. I…it's just that I worry about you."

"Well, you have wasted your time! Worrying is not doing anyone any good. By the way, I will be taking that meeting on Thursday and the afternoon off just so this conversation will be over with."

I walked past him to leave his office and stopped. Closing my eyes, I felt remorseful for just ripping this poor man's head off when all he was just concerned.

Turning around, I lost my attitude. "Thank you for thinking about me, I appreciate it. You are like family to me, Loren, both you and Leeza, and I respect you immensely. Please don't take offense, I am just pissed off that McHale put both of us in this position and I feel like I have no other option."

"I understand. You know I would never put you in a situation where you felt uncomfortable or in danger, don't you?"

Exhaling hard, I didn't even have to think of that answer. "Yes, and I totally agree. This meeting is something we can't pass up so I will be leaving at noon on Thursday to pick up the contracts from McHale and then I will swing them by here so that you can get them filed. Then, I'm going shopping."

Laughing and rolling his eyes, he approved.

After lunch, the day from hell surprisingly flew by. I think it was due to the fact that we were crazy busy. The other two appointments went off without a hitch. Presentations went well, contracts were signed, champagne was popped and off they went on their merry way.

Now, I was actually leaving work fifteen minutes early. As I climbed into my truck and fastened my seat belt, I could hear my phone jingling in my purse. Reaching down on the floorboard of the passenger seat, I pulled my purse up and grabbed my phone. Looking at the caller ID, I could see it was

Lilly. I had a feeling I knew what this conversation was going to consist of. I started the car and let the air conditioning get cool as I answered.

"Hell—"

"Oh my God, Elle! Are you okay? Where are you? Do we need to come over for a girl's night? I can bring the tequila."

"First off, Lils...hi! Calm down, take a breath. I'm fine. I'm leaving work. No, I can't get together tonight, we have a shitload to do, but I will take a rain check on the liquor."

"Okay, honey, wanna get together tomorrow night? I know today was a big deal, I think it would be good if you talked about it."

No, she thinks it would be good if we talked about it because she's nosy and wants all the juicy details.

"That sounds great. Tomorrow night would be good, but I think it would be better if I didn't talk about it."

"That hard, huh?"

"Lils, I've always known in the back of my mind that this day would come, but I never really knew how I would react to seeing him again. Let me tell you, I wish I would've had a chance to brace myself."

"I'm so sorry, sweetie."

"I know, me too. Look, Lils, I have to run. I have to take JoJo to her thing tonight, take the baked goods to the football field, and I had a shit morning even before my run in with TJ because I had that dream again."

"Well, did you drink the tea?"

"Yes, I drank the goddamn tea! Look...shit, I have to go. Bear will have a fit if I'm late and since he tore me a new one this morning, I don't need to hear how I'm the biggest screw up ever born again tonight."

A moment of silence hovered over the line. The silence lingered so long I thought I got disconnected or hung up on.

"Lil—"

"You are not a screw up, Elleny Jean! I don't ever want to hear that come out of your mouth again." I could hear the shakiness in her voice, she was trying to hold it together. "You are a wonderful, loving mother and wife who has sacrificed everything for your family and friends and he's just a...well, he's a fucking asshole! Don't let him tear you down, Elle. Don't believe a word he says."

My other rock, right here.

As tears welled up in my eyes, I needed to hear that encouragement so much. Today was so much harder than I wanted to admit but I wouldn't let anyone know that. My girls have stood beside me through the worst in my life and have supported my decisions, even if they didn't agree with the choices I made. They knew I was doing what I had to do for my children and especially for TJ. They were aware of my secrets, they vowed to take them to the grave, and I knew they would.

"Thank you, Lilly. Thank you for being there. I love you so much."

I could hear her sniffling. "Elleny, you have no idea how fearless you are."

Harshly, I sneered and grumbled while I wiped the tear from my eyes. "I'm a coward, Lilly."

Speaking softly, Lilly blew me away. "Sweetie, you're a conqueror."

The tears began to fall faster and heavier. I knew that I couldn't take much more of this. "Love you, Lils."

"Love you too, babe. I'll talk with you soon, okay?"

"Okay, night."

"Night."

I pulled my truck to the main entrance of the building. Taking a minute, I popped in my Jimmy Buffett CD and pushed the number to my favorite song: number nine. Hearing the beginning of Margaritaville come over my speakers took me back.

Key West, summer of '91. Lying out on the beach with the girls while the boys tossed the football back and forth. Sitting up and looking out over the ocean water made my head clear. I walked to the water's edge and could feel the crest of the waves roll over the tops of my feet. I fought against the tickle that the bubbled foam left when the waves rolled back out. The warmth of two arms wrapped around me. I craved the feeling of his sweet, gentle kiss on the back of my neck. He slowly bent down as I heard a whispered, "Love ya, babe."

Why couldn't I stop thinking about him? What I would give to have him totally erased from my memories. I despised him for giving me these memories that I wanted so badly to be my reality. I hated him for a decision I made that he knew absolutely nothing about.

What was wrong with me?

I had absolutely lost my mind. How did any of this make sense? He had nothing to do with any of this, yet I hated him for choices that *I* had made.

At the time, I made the decisions that I thought were in his best interest. He didn't need to be tied down to a baby and married to a teenage mom that he would eventually come to resent for ruining his life. He was above that. He needed to do what he had to do—live his life. I had no claim to him, I wasn't his wife, nor would I ever be.

As I pulled into my neighborhood, I pushed all thoughts and memories of Trevor to the furthest corner of my mind and put up my defenses. I had a feeling the with the way my day was going, tonight wasn't going to be any different.

Turning the corner and seeing my house, Bear's truck wasn't in the driveway. *Maybe I'd be getting off easy*, I thought to myself. I pushed the garage door opener and pulled in. This wasn't going to be a long stay, just had to pick up the stuff for Luc and have JoJo jump in.

Walking in the house from the back door, I yelled, "JoJo, come on, darlin'. Gotta go!"

JoJo stumbled down the stairs. Her eyes were red and she was gasping like she'd been crying.

My body tensed as my face went blank. I quickly assessed the situation, thinking maybe something was wrong with one of the other kids.

"It's Daddy, Momma."

Shit on a stick, what had he done now?

"I think he stopped by Toppers."

Toppers was the bar that replaced Sheila Kay's ten years ago. A run down, trashy strip club on the outskirts of town. Bear kept that place in business. He would stay there all night drinking beer with the rest of his white trash friends while handing his paycheck over to the white trash dancers instead of bringing it home to his family.

What the shit!

He knew he had football practice tonight. Now, not only did I have to extinguish this fire, but I had to show up at football practice and lie my ass off as to why Bear wouldn't be showing up for practice. Again.

Why couldn't things be simple!

Holding my breath to calm myself, I braced against the stove top. I had to close my eyes to figure out what my best option was.

"First off, where's your sister?"

I began analyzing her up and down, looking for something that would answer me quicker than she was. "What did he do, hit you? Say something to you?"

"Momma, I think he's drunk. Real drunk this time."

Panic kicked in. Outwardly, I tried to stay calm for the sake of my daughter. Inwardly, I was stabbing that mother fucker to death. "JoJo, where's your sister? Did he take her somewhere?"

"I made her go next door to Mrs. Lewis' house. Momma, he was saying some awful things..." JoJo stopped talking so that she could wipe the tears from her face. Bear didn't talk to her this way, she was his princess. He always thought so much more of her than the other two. That's not to say that he didn't have his moments, but very rarely had she seen this side of him.

"How Luc and I were bastard kids and he should've let your ass sink itself, whatever that means. He said he wished we were never born, Momma, and how we were all fucking up his life."

Boiling inside, I kept telling myself to stay calm. I needed to diffuse this situation not add to it. My children didn't know anything about the deal I had made with Bear.

"JoJo, baby, look at me." Putting her cheeks in my hands, I guided her face toward mine so that her eyes made contact with mine.

"Baby, I'm sorry you had to see Daddy like that but I need you to take a deep breath. Calm down, pull your shit together, and answer some questions for me. When did he get home?"

"I don't know, Momma. He was here when Katelyn dropped me off."

"Ok, good girl. Now, was Harlee here when he went off on his rant?"

"She was watching television. He came down the stairs all dressed up with cologne on. I thought he was getting dressed to go out with you. He came into the living room talking about this house being a mess, I could hear him slurring his words so I went and snatched Harlee up and told her to run next door and stay there until I came and got her."

"Awesome, baby. I'm so proud of you, you did right. I'm sorry you had to see that, he can get kinda stupid when he's been drinking. He didn't mean what he said."

"What was he talking about...why would he say Luc and I were bastards?"

I did not want to tell the twins about TJ because of Bear's attitude. That story was mine to tell and I wanted it to be on my terms. We had talked about this. I made it clear to him that he could treat me like shit but he was not going to treat any of my children this way.

"Sweetie, that wasn't Daddy talking. It was the liquor, okay? Listen, I need for you to get your stuff. You have two more nights of community service, let's get through this. Go clean up your face so we can go. I'm gonna call Mrs. Walters and tell her we are on our way. Now, scooch."

Watching her run up the stairs, I walked over and grabbed the cordless phone. I had to think of what excuse to give my neighbor for why my kid ran over to her house and couldn't come home. I was getting really tired of making excuses for my asshole husband. I set the phone down for a minute to catch my breath, braced my head in my hands, and counted to ten. Then, I dialed my neighbor and asked her to send my daughter home.

Sitting there, attempting to collect my thoughts, the memory of another time Bear came home drunk came to mind. The twins were three and Harlee was just born. The twins were asleep but I was up because of Harlee. She had colic and cried a lot. It was after three in the morning and Bear still hadn't come home from wherever he was, which wasn't really a surprise.

Headlights shined through the window over the front door. I walked briskly over to the door and held it open as he stumbled up the front path. "Where the hell you been, Willie Jackson? It's after three in the morning and I have to work in the morning!"

Getting right up in my face, he slurred, "Who da fuck you think you talkin' to, bitch? Last time I checked, my momma done been buried out there in that cemetery under six feet of dirt!"

I could smell the mixture of alcohol and cheap perfume on him—it was strong. I closed my eyes at the whole situation.

"You don't think you owe me a phone call, at least to let me know you're alive?"

"If I recall, bitch," He was right up in my face, saliva flying in my eyes as he spoke, "You should be owin' somethin' to me seein' how I was the one who saved your ass from havin' a slut reputation. Although, now that I know you the way I know ya, I think maybe it would've suited ya."

Because he was drunk, his reflexes were slow. So he didn't react until several seconds after I slapped him. My hand stung from the impact of skin meeting skin. Quickly grabbing my wrist, he twisted my arm behind my back, shoving my hand up between my shoulder blades. I could feel the bones grinding together, attempting to move in a direction they weren't meant to be in. He bent me over forward and got down so his mouth was next to my ear.

"That was your freebie, bitch. Next time, I slap back and I guarantee you won't be getting up off that floor. Then, since it looks like you ain't a very good momma just fallin' asleep wherever ya land, I'll be takin' those bastard kids and findin' them a proper momma. I'll take all three of them to where you'll never see them again. You try to leave with them? I will find ya and I'll take 'em then, too. You wanna fuck with me, bitch? I ain't the cocksucker that gave you those bastards. I don't walk away empty handed. Don't ever lift a hand to me again and don't ever ask me where the fuck I been. It ain't any of your business!"

After that night, I learned quickly not to ask any questions or make any waves. If he was pissed off enough, I wouldn't put it past him to just take off with my kids out of spite. I believed him when he told me he would, so what he said went. No questions were asked and as long as I had my kids, that was all that mattered.

I shook off the memory and got my emotional shit together along with the things I had to take to the football field. As I was packing up, my baby girl ran in the house, straight to me. Her arms locked tight around my waist.

This was why I put up with his shit. This made all of the name calling and bruises worth it. I couldn't bear to lose my kids.

"Well, hey there, my sweet angel. How was school today?" I rubbed her back to reassure myself she was there.

"Good, Momma. Have you seen JoJo?" With fear in her eyes, she hesitantly looked around for Bear.

"Yes, she's fine. She's getting her stuff because we have to go. Daddy left. Here, grab a pan of brownies and let's take 'em out to the truck." I grabbed the other pans and headed for the garage. Turning, I screamed so JoJo could hear me.

"JoJo, come on! Harlee and I are in the truck waiting."

We walked through the garage to the truck. Getting into the car, Harlee fastened her seatbelt, grabbed her PSP, and started playing games. I looked up to see JoJo walk out and get into the back passenger seat. The click of the seatbelt told me she was settled and ready to go. I turned around and smiled at her. I couldn't help but just sit there for a moment and stare at my daughter. Seeing her smile at me filled me with the most beautiful pain. I looked into her hazel eyes; more green than they were brown with a little dimple right under her left eye. She was her father's daughter but my whole reason for existence.

"Okay?"

"Yes, Momma, I'm okay."

"Wonderful, sweetie. Love you, my sweet baby."

"Love you, too, Momma."

"I can't hear it enough."

I turned back around, put the car in reverse, and headed out.

Pulling into the football field, I looked around to see if Bear was here. Thankfully, he wasn't. I could handle making up excuses as to why he's not here. Making up reasons as to why he's showing up to his kid's football practice drunk is a bit more difficult.

I waited for Harlee to jump out of the truck as I pulled the pans over onto my lap. Handing her a tray of peanut butter brownies, I took the other trays and headed for the field. Seeing the boys scrimmage, I walked over to the middle set of bleachers and set the pans of goodies down. I waved at the other moms, most of them I had known since elementary school.

It was difficult for me to face them. They knew I didn't want to grow old in this town, but here I was. I could read their minds every time I approached one of them. They always were trying to figure out what happened, why I changed my plans, why Bear and I were together, and especially what happened between TJ and me. Even to this day, I could see their minds begin to work as they spoke to me.

I looked out to find coach and decided now was the time. I took a deep breath and headed for the middle of the field.

Hustling out onto the field, I saw Lucas grabbing a water bottle. I waved at him as I approached the coach. I stepped up beside Coach Kenny, but he didn't even turn toward me.

"Elle…"

"Coach Kenny."

"He ain't comin', is he?"

"No, sir. I'm sorry."

"Hmm."

"Coach…"

"No excuses, Elle. Don't really want to hear the bullshit anymore. I sure as hell don't want to hear you ever apologize for him again."

Steve Kenny, just like the rest of us, grew up in this town. He was two years ahead of us and played football with TJ, but his sister, Kelly, was in our class. So, Steve knew Bear and Bubba along with their reputations. Truth be told, Bear's behavior probably didn't surprise him.

"Yes, sir."

Truthfully, I couldn't blame him. This was becoming routine. "All I ask, Coach, is that you don't let this affect Luc. Please? He doesn't know what I had to come home to this evening."

Slowly, Coach turned his head toward me and looked me over as if he is looking for bruises.

Responding to his observation, I whispered so softly I wasn't sure if he heard me, "Just because you don't see anything, doesn't mean there ain't marks."

No more words were spoken. He nodded his head in acknowledgement and I turned to walk off. I heard the whistle blow then Luc's voice calling for me. Turning around, I saw him running toward me, pulling his helmet off. Meeting me on the side of the field, he looked at me quizzically. "Everything okay, Momma?"

Looking at his face, the same face I looked into in the car, I took a moment to quickly tell myself that his father sure would be proud of him.

I reached up to touch his face and smooth his raised eyebrow. I smiled and asked, "Is it too embarrassing to give your 'ole momma a hug? I've had a shit day and need a hug from my big man."

Not even hesitating, he dropped his helmet onto the ground, grabbed me, and wrapped his arms around my neck.

"It's gonna be okay, Momma".

Caught off guard by his reassurance, I giggled. "Hey, isn't that my line?"

"Yeah, but I just want you to know that."

"I know it is, sweetheart. Look, you better get back out there before Coach has you running laps. Don't worry, Luc. Be a kid, you only have one more year."

He laughed as he ran back toward the other players and I heard the best phrase a momma could ever hear.

"Love you, Momma!"

Finishing up with football practice, I gathered up my things and my kids. Saying goodbye to the other parents quickly, I headed toward the truck. I felt the buzzing of my phone before I actually heard the personalized ringer. I grabbed it out of my purse and looked at the screen. Seeing it was Bear, I pushed the ignore button. I really didn't have time for his bullshit. I also had the kids and they didn't need to hear any of his bullshit either.

We all got in the car and headed home. I decided to stop on the way and grab a bucket of chicken and the fixings. I wanted to get them situated and have a nice long hot bath. Easy ending to a long day.

Turning the corner to our street, I saw Bear's truck in the driveway. Quickly, I turned the radio off and slowed the car down.

"Okay, kids, listen up. Daddy's home. This is what's gonna happen. When we get in the house, Luc, you grab the food. JoJo, grab the plates and a couple cans of soda. Harlee, you grab silverware. Take the food upstairs to Luc's room."

When Bear had been out drinking, you never knew what kind of mood he was going to be in. So, I liked them going over to Luc's room because it was the furthest from mine.

"Ya'll sleep in his room tonight. Luc, as soon as the girls get in there, lock the door, turn the TV on, and turn up the volume. Harlee, take your PSP and headphones in there. Watch movies or play games with your headphones on. Luc and JoJo, tomorrow morning if I'm not up before you are, get Harlee up and get her dressed. Take my truck and go to school. Call Auntie Rachel and tell her to come over. Do *not* come in my room. I will call you during your lunch."

Looking at each other, this was not a new routine. I've never not been up before them, even if I was bad. I usually would put on long pants and long-sleeved shirts so they wouldn't see the bruises, but I always wanted them to know exactly what to do. All three of them acknowledged me and I knew that my long, hot bath was out of the question.

I pulled up to the house, took a deep breath, and pushed the garage opener. I waited a minute. No Bear, so I pulled in. We all got out and headed into the house. Walking slowly into the kitchen, we all looked around as if we were looking for a burglar. Still, no Bear. I helped the kids get into Luc's room and all situated. Kissing them goodnight, I closed my eyes and set the kiss to memory, just in case. I never took any of these moments for granted, I never knew if or when would be the last time I felt their lips on mine. I wanted to show them that it was just going to be like any other normal night and everything was going to be okay. I hoped. I told them I loved them and headed out of the door, reminding them to lock the door behind me.

I slowly walked down the hall to my bedroom. I never knew what to expect when I walked in there. Bear's mood changed so quickly, it was a daily guessing game. I heard the slight squeak as I turned the doorknob and attempted to open the door as quietly as I could. I said a silent prayer that he had just passed out and I was safe tonight. I stuck my head in and saw all the lights turned out. I was in the clear.

I walked in, shut the door, and locked it.

"Where you been?"

I closed my eyes. Hearing him slur those three words, I knew he was trashed. I couldn't see him, my eyes still hadn't adjusted to the darkness, but his voice sounded like he was sitting over in the corner where my makeup counter was.

"Luc had football practice, remember? You were supposed to meet me there. Coach Kenny wondered where you were so I told him you had to work late."

"Tried to call ya. Why the fuck do I pay for you to have a phone if you don't answer the motherfucker?"

"I'm sorry, Bear. I didn't hear it. I was helping Trisha Shepard stock the snack bar for the game on Friday night."

91

He doesn't pay for the phone, I pay the bill. As a matter of fact, I pay all the bills, but I wasn't going to argue this point with him right now.

"Well, aren't you queen of all the right fucking answers tonight? Doesn't take much for you to think of a lie to tell Kenny, who's to say you ain't lying to me right now?"

Walking closer to his voice, I was able to make out a silhouette crouched in the corner of the bedroom. "Bear, you're drunk, honey. I'm tired, I had a shit day. I just wanted to take a shower and go to bed. I have to be at the office early tomorrow."

I heard that menacing laugh coming closer to me. I stopped walking and began to back away in the opposite direction. My mind was going a hundred miles a minute.

"You've had a shit day? Well, well, queen bitch didn't get everything handed to her on a silver platter, huh?"

Mentally telling myself that I was not going to argue with him, I started walking over to the lamp beside my bed.

"Don't you dare touch that fuckin' lamp."

"Bear, I have to see where my nightgown is."

"Turn around." I knew that tone and it terrified me. Whenever he used that voice, I knew I'd better do what he said.

Quickly, I turned around so that my back was to him. I felt him come up behind me. Slowly he ran his hands down the front of my blouse. Closing my eyes, I couldn't stand the feel of his hands on my body. I could smell the booze and nasty perfume on him. I had to tell myself not to think about it. I pictured TJ's hands rubbing all over me. With my hair still up from work today, he started sniffing and breathing hard against the back of my neck. All of a sudden, he pushed the back of my head forward with vigor.

Bear moved away from me and yelled, "Fuck! You smell nothing like her! Why can't you love me the way she loves me!"

Feeling disgusted, I didn't say a word. I felt around for the bottom of the bed. Working myself around to my side of the bed, my fingertips touched the soft thin silky material of my nightgown. Blindly, I walked to the bathroom. Reaching my hand out, I felt the wall and then the switch. Flipping the light on, I saw Bear and knew I had made a huge mistake.

He looked like he had messed with the wrong person. Both eyes were blood shot and red-rimmed. A purple, blue, and yellow halo surrounded the complete area of his eye socket as red splotches marked his cheekbones. His shirt was all the way unbuttoned and blood stained. Thin lines of crusted blood creased the side of his mouth and streaks of tears ran down his cheeks.

Oh shit, I was in trouble.

All of a sudden, he was on top of me.

"Bitch, I told you to leave the light off!"

He quickly grabbed the top of my head and buried his fingers in my hair. Still pulled back tight in the bun, he had his hand fisted between the pins that secured my hair and the hair itself, making it into a lock around his knuckles.

I reached back, attempting to undo the bun so that it didn't pull as bad, but every time I did, his fist grew tighter. I tried my damnedest not to scream, but a yelp left my mouth. Finally, I got my hair out of the bun just as he went in to grab more. Dragging me toward the bed by my hair, I tried to apologize to him and explain I just wanted to get changed, but it did me no good.

As he stalked to the bed, he started talking.

"Oh, so you wanted to get undressed, huh? Queen cunt wanted to be a tease and walk 'round here in front of me without clothes on!"

As his words hit my brain, I was confused. None of what was happening made sense. Before I could truly comprehend what was happening, he threw me face first down on the bed and leaned his knee into my back, holding me down. I was gasping for air as he leaned his entire weight onto my back. I turned my head to the side in an attempt to take in a big breath of air. Out of the corner of my eye, I saw that he was reaching into his drawer.

Oh shit, oh shit, oh shit!

I couldn't help the panic that took hold of me. He moved his legs to straddle me as he stretched my right arm out to touch the headboard. I felt the leather strap being wrapped around my wrist right where I had the other scars tattooed over. I learned quickly to never pull against him. If I did, the strap would dig deeper into my skin and leave awful bruises. So, I relaxed as much as I could and allowed my arm to move with him. He did the same with the other arm and I began to beg with everything that was in me. Now that he had me backwards with my arms tied, he had total control over me. I couldn't protect myself at all.

"Queen Bitch thinks she's gonna walk 'round here naked like her pussy's made of pure gold. Well, let me tell you that pussy ain't worth the shit I done put up with for seventeen years! I missed out on so much because of your slut ass. The parties, the women…"

Quietly, he whispered, "Angie."

Angie…Angie? Who was Angie?

"You gettin' pregnant by that motherfucker and letting him go off to school while I raised them bastard kids was bullshit! I should've never offered you that arrangement. I think you owe me for seventeen worthless years and I will be collectin' on that debt right now!"

Before I could figure out his next move, I heard the tearing of clothes and then a tugging feeling. He was pulling what was left of my clothes off. I closed my eyes and went to my place.

It was strange. Subconsciously I was with TJ, yet I could hear Bear mumbling something about how he always knew I liked it rough. What I saw clear as day was TJ and I wrapped up in black sheets. His bedroom, his bed. Lying naked, facing each other, not a word had to be said, explanations were not needed. Contentment and indescribable peace washed over me. Once in a while, I sensed the feeling of his hand pushing back the piece of hair that continually fell in my face. I closed my eyes as I laid there, taking in the peace that surrounded me.

"Baby, look at me."

I opened my eyes and stared into those eyes that saw straight to my soul.

"Stay with me, darlin'. Don't leave me. Not yet."

"Never, TJ. I wanna stay here with you forever."

"Baby, you can't stay forever, just a little while longer. Hold on, honey, it's almost over."

I couldn't feel anything. I wasn't feeling myself being pushed and tugged. My head didn't hurt anymore, my stomach wasn't aching from the blows to the ribs, and my face didn't feel like it was on fire from the jabs Bear was landing. It was like I wasn't even in my body. I loved where I was because I was with TJ. I was wrapped up in his arms, safe and secure. No one could hurt me here. No one could take my babies from me. They were safe and I didn't have to worry about anything anymore. It was serenity being wrapped in his arms.

"Time for you to go, darlin'."

All of a sudden, I heard a high-pitched scream. I peeked through eyes that didn't want to open to see Rachel and Lilly standing over my bed, pure fear and pain all over their faces. Feeling my hands were still tied to the bed, I wasn't sure what to do. I was naked, my body was cold. Rachel's hands were attempting to touch me, but she acted like she couldn't find a safe spot to make contact. Lilly was searching for a clean blanket to throw over me, bawling. Both of their mouths were wide open and the only words I heard were out of Rachel's mouth

"Jesus Christ, Elle! What the fuck did he do to you, baby? There's so much blood!"

Tracy Lee

Chapter 5

August 1992

Being stuck in the hospital had been horrible. I was able to get out of bed and walk down the halls anytime I wanted as long as I had someone to walk with me, so I found myself walking several times a day. It was looking like I would be able to leave the very next day and I couldn't wait; I was ready to get home. Everything was staying down and my vitals were looking up.

Walking back down the corridor to my suite, I started thinking of how I was ready to go home so that I could start working on my new life. Now that school was out of the question, I knew for a fact that I wasn't going to stay in Richland. I just didn't know where I was going to go. New York, maybe? California?

Speaking of school, I had to tell Rachel that I wasn't going to be attending college. I couldn't tell her why, but she wasn't going to just accept the "I changed my mind" excuse. I had to come up with something good. I could hear voices approaching my open doorway. As they got closer, I started to recognize the tones. I lifted my head to look for my nurse call button just as Rachel and Bear walked through the door.

"Hey, sweetie." Rachel smiled as she greeted me.

"Hey, Rach...Bear."

"Hey."

I grabbed my call button and pushed it. My plan was that the nurse would come in and I would suddenly come down with some type of quick healing sickness. I still wanted to go home tomorrow, I just didn't want visitors right now. I had a lot to think about and chatting about local gossip was not going to help me make plans.

"How are you feeling?

"Better, they're pumping me full of all kinds of shit."

The nurse silently walked in and went straight to my IV bag. The three of us just sat there. Waiting for the right time, I began mentally cuing her in on my plan. Suddenly, she took out a syringe and injected something into my IV.

Wrong answer.

"What's that?" Rachel asked the air.

"Oh, this is Ms. Barker's prenatal vitamin. Since she can't handle the tablet, we give it to her through her IV. Gotta make sure that baby gets its nutrients."

My eyes got big as I slowly dropped my head into my hands. I was in deep shit now. Where did I start in this mess? I picked my head up and looked at Rachel and Bear. Their eyes were as big as saucers and their mouths were hanging open. Too bad there weren't any flies around, that would've made my day.

No one said a word until we saw the nurse leave the room.

"What the—" Rachel started.

"You can't say a word to anyone. Not even Lilly. TJ doesn't know and he's not gonna find out. Swear it, Rachel. Swear it on our friendship right this very minute. This doesn't leave the three of us. I've come to the decision that I'm keeping it. I'm not going to school and I'm not staying in Richland."

Not a word was said for a minute or two. Finally, I broke the silence.

"Well, you gonna say anything?"

Rachel and I had been friends since we were two years old. We knew each other better than we knew ourselves and she understood how I felt about TJ. She realized the reasoning behind my decision. She knew I only wanted what was best for him.

"I understand and I swear it to you. On our friendship, this information won't leave this room."

I nodded as I smiled a weak smile at her. Rachel rolled her eyes at me.

"Bear, swear it. TJ cannot find out about this."

Bear sat there for a few minutes, his eyes staring off into the space behind me.

"What if I could do one better than promising not to tell him? What if we made a deal, just the two of us? I don't say anything to him about this, he goes to school, gets his degree, and then gets picked up by the NFL to live happily ever after, if—"

He stopped talking for a second, looked at Rachel and then back at me. I sat up, looked at Rachel and then back at him."

"If what, Bear?"

"You marry me and let me raise that baby as my own with my last name. Other than the three of us, no one else knows any different."

I looked at Rachel and burst out laughing. Rachel looked at me and smiled a small demure smile, but that was it. There was no giggling.

I looked back at Bear who wasn't even smiling.

"You're serious?"

"Dead."

"Rachel, what do you have to say about this?"

Rachel, being the lady that she is, uncrossed her legs and crossed them the other way. She looked at her rings to make sure that all the diamonds were lined up directly under her knuckles before she replied, "Well, we have been discussing this for a while. I didn't want to go away to school with us as a couple, so we agreed that we wouldn't be a couple anymore."

Tracy Lee

Caught off guard with this information, I had to ask, "When did ya'll decide this?"

Like it was just casual conversation, Rachel replied, "We've been talking about it for the last month."

"Bear, do you have anything to add to this?"

"Nope."

Well, okay then.

"So, you wouldn't have a problem with this, Rach?"

"Fuck no, I'm going to college!" she said with a smile that went from ear to ear.

She knew that Bear would never leave this town because, truthfully, he didn't have the ambition to go anywhere else. He didn't have a college degree and didn't have any plans to get a college degree or technical training. Bear had experience welding and working on cars, but he wasn't going to get through life doing much more than that.

Rachel...well, Rachel was Rachel. She was the only daughter of a millionaire and an eighth generation Richland Locke which said more than me being a sixth generation Barker. She was not going to be tied down to a podunk town like Richland with a husband that worked on cars. Truth be told, I think they both knew that.

"If we do this, you both are going to have to work with me when it comes to TJ. I can't see him at least until after the wedding and enough time has passed that he won't become suspicious."

"Well, there is one condition that you need to know before you say yes. You'll have to know exactly what you're getting' into."

Stipulations, seriously? Oh, this I've gotta hear.

"Okay, Bear. Go on."

"If we decide to do this, get married, that is, you can't ever have anything, and I mean anything, to do with Trevor McHale again. No phone calls, no visitation. Nothing. I don't want him to have a chance to see the kid and try and figure out what we did. That's my kid and it always will be."

I could see his point on this. I really didn't want to have any contact with TJ, either. I knew he would give up everything if he knew and that wasn't an option.

Thinking about how much I loved TJ, there wasn't any other option. Not just for him, for me as well. If I didn't do it, TJ would find out that I was going to leave and would eventually talk me out of my decision and into raising the baby together. The vision I had before came back. I knew that wherever I ended up, TJ would end up finding me and talking me back into his arms. Then we would be right back to that image. This had to happen and it had to be with Bear. TJ would feel so betrayed, so angry, he'd write us both off. At least, that's what I was hoping for.

"Okay, Bear, you've got a deal."

"Holy shit! Is this really gonna happen, Elle?" Rachel replied like she thought this was an April fool's joke.

"Sure as shit, Rach!" Bear exclaimed as he jumped up and froze.

"When we gonna do this? I think it better be soon seein' as how you're gonna be showin'."

"Well, one thing at a time. We have to get Rachel and TJ off to school and then we can take care of everything. I guess we kind of need a story, too, don't we?"

"I guess we should think of one. People might get suspicious."

Rachel rolled her eyes and uncrossed her leg. As she stood straight out of her chair, she reached in her purse for her cigarette case. Grasping it, she opened it up and pulled out a long, white, nicotine filled tube. I hoped she wasn't going to light up here in my hospital room.

"Good God, ya'll. Me and TJ left for school, you two were lonely. Ya'll got together. Simple as that."

"See, there's a reason you're my best friend."

I heard a soft knock on the door and tender eyes that I had grown to care about more than myself peeked around the corner.

101

"Is it okay to come in?"

"Of course, darlin'. Please, come in," I told TJ as I saw Rachel and Bear whispering in the corner.

"We're gonna take off, babe. I'm glad that you're finally getting over this food poisoning, I'll see you at home," Rachel said, winking as she bent down to hug me. I caught on quickly and told them both thank you for the visit as they left.

"So, food poisoning, huh?"

"Uh, yeah. They should be letting me out today, I'm ready to go home."

"Me, too. Well, I'm ready for you to be home, that is."

"Yeah." I wanted to drop this subject and quickly. I was never a good liar and TJ always could tell when I was.

"How's the packing going?"

"All done, except for the bag of dirty clothes I have. Momma says she's going to wash them and then UPS them to me." He chuckled softly. "I think I will be just fine without one bag of clothes."

You could sense the tension in the room. I was scared to talk as to not give anything away and he was scared to talk because he knew something just wasn't right with me.

I felt like someone was stabbing me in the heart and wouldn't pull the blade out, just kept pushing further and further into my chest. It was taking everything in me not to burst out into tears.

There was nothing more in this life that I wanted than to have a little bit of Trevor mixed with a little bit of me growing, feeling it move deep inside of me. Having this pure bundle of love nestled right under my beating heart as the sound and rhythm calmed it. This being was something made from two people so in love, they would die for one another.

I would want this baby to know a love like that; a love that its parents would share for the rest of their lives. If we lived in another time and another place, I would want nothing more than to see that love grow not only for this baby, but for us as a family. But, that wouldn't happen in this whole fucked up scenario. Not now, not ever.

I didn't think I could go through with this. I didn't think that I would be able to keep this from him. Just as I was about to let tell him everything, I heard a rasp on the door.

"It's only me," my dad said before he came in with a large grin on his face.

"Well, Dr. Robbins is letting you go. He's filling out your discharge papers as we speak."

He caught eyes with TJ and nodded as he walked over to me to plant a small kiss on my forehead.

"Wonderful," I replied through an artificial smile and as little feeling as possible.

TJ clapped his hands together. "That's great. Is there anything you want me to take? I can grab some things and bring them over. You know I leave in three days, so I'd like to spend as much time as I can with you."

"Nah, I think I'm good. If you'd like, you can go on over to the house. We should be there shortly. You can find out what Clara made for dinner and call to give me a head's up. I'm ready for some home cooking."

Dad gave a little chuckle. "Yep, I can see you're feelin' better. Already thinkin' about food."

TJ closed in on me and laid a soft kiss on my lips. I couldn't hold back anymore. Luckily, he turned his back to me and headed out the door.

"Baby—"

"Daddy, it's for his own good."

"Is it?"

"You know he'll end up resenting me for holding him back."

"He'll end up resenting you for not telling him he has a child."

"Either way, I lose. How can I choose? In my heart, I feel like I'm doing what is right. How can I go against that?"

"I know you are and I have to say that I admire you for that."

"Well, there's something you don't know. Rachel and Bear came and saw me this afternoon. Bear and I have come to an arrangement.

Daddy grabbed a chair and pushed it closer to the bed.
"Oh?"

"We're getting married, Daddy, and he's going to raise the baby as his own. That way, TJ will never find out about this."

"Elleny, I don't think—"

"It doesn't matter what you think, Daddy. I'm marrying Bear Jackson."

I tried to get up but whether it was the dizziness from being dehydrated or from being broken inside, I sat back on the bed and sobbed silently.

"Elleny—"

"Daddy, can I just be alone for a minute? I just need some time to myself."

He exhaled because he knew I had made up my mind. "Sure, baby, I'll just take your things down to the car." Grabbing the bag of clothes and the two flower arrangements that were there when I woke up, my dad headed to the door. "Elleny, I just have one more thing to say. I'm just going to say it and then I won't bring it up again. What you're doing takes an immense amount of courage. Courage people your age don't necessarily have. Honey, I know you're scared of a future that you have no control over for yourself, but now for that innocent grandchild of mine that you're carryin'. What you are doin' is so beyond selfless that it amazes me. The people who don't know what you're about to do, don't get to appreciate it for what it really is. They don't even realize the gifts they are missing out on seeing, but I know. So do you. Don't ever forget that. Do not let anyone try and put you down over it and most importantly, don't ever forget why you're doing it. I am so honored that you are my daughter. Your momma is looking down on you, beaming with pride. I love you and I am so pleased that you have become the woman you are."

With that, he walked out of the room and I sat there alone. Getting ready to lose my best friends to college, my life as I knew it was over. And, in three days, I would be walking away from the greatest love of my life. How was I going to survive this?

Standing out in front of Rachel's house, I didn't know how to feel. I was a jumbled mess of emotions. Saying goodbye was hard enough for the average person, but I was pregnant and alone. I wrapped my arms around her and it took Lilly and TJ to rip me away from her.

Rachel reassured me that she would call and be home on holidays, but it didn't make me feel any better. I wanted out of this town more than anyone I knew and now I was stuck here for good with a man I would never be able to love as a husband. The future I had been planning since I started kindergarten wasn't even an option now.

Since I left the hospital two days ago, TJ had been with me almost twenty-four seven. He would come to the house early in the morning, crawl up in my bed, hold me, and talk about what he was looking forward to when he went away to school. He tried to pacify me by telling me how many days there were until Thanksgiving and that he'd be counting down. Then, there was Christmas. I just laid there, head tucked nice and tight underneath his chin, becoming lost in his smell. I took it all in, everything that became reminiscient of Trevor.

Every breath, every smell, every touch, the sound of his accent—I memorized it all. To him, it was all about the comfort of knowing there would be a tomorrow. For me, I held tight to what I could for today, knowing there would never be one.

We'd get out and head to breakfast either grabbing something quick and light from Clara or he'd take me to a restaurant. Then, we'd either walk the streets of town or just go out to a field, jam the radio, and make love in the back of his truck. I thrived for every touch and every kiss. I had to get my fill, but it never felt like it was enough.

Finally, the day had arrived.

Though I was throwing up all night, I drove to his house early in the morning. I knew I couldn't miss this. I pulled up to his drive and saw that his truck was already warming up and packed to the brim. I opened up the driver's side door and stuck two gifts that I had beautifully wrapped in my favorite color in the back seat. On top of the larger gift, I laid a card that I would give specific instructions on when he could open it. I didn't want him opening that letter until after the wedding. It was my goodbye letter. I couldn't take the chance of doing it face to face because I'd give in. I needed him to be far away and busy enough to where he wouldn't have a chance to come back. With that done, I crawled back out, went to the front door, and rang the doorbell.

"Morning, Mrs. McHale," I said to TJ's momma who looked like she hadn't slept all night.

Wiping at her eyes, she whispered, "Sweetie, what am I to do? My baby boy is…is…" her tears fell in full force as she sobbed. I hugged her tightly as tears came to my eyes as well.

"It's okay, Mrs. McHale. He'll be back in just a few weeks."

"I know, this is just really hard. I bet your daddy's happy as a lark that you've decided to stay and help him with his practice for a year."

"Yes, ma'am, he is. But, he feels he's holding me back as well," I replied as I came up with that little ditty on the fly.

As we hugged, I heard TJ coming down the stairs laughing loudly.

"Now, now, I can't have my two best girls cryin' like this as I pull away. I will be a nervous wreck driving, worryin' about ya'll".

"Hey, honey," I said as I wrapped him in a hug, pleading with my emotions to leave me the hell alone for the next thirty minutes. They listened for about three. He began walking out to the car with his momma under his arm. I followed them out and let him say goodbye to her. Then, she left and let us have our time.

Pushing my hair back from my face, he stared into my eyes. "I'm gonna call you tonight, okay?"

"I know you'll be busy, just text me to let me know you arrived safely. Get settled, meet your roomie, and get back with me when you get a chance. I'm not your first priority anymore."

I had to pull my eyes down to my fingers that were busy pulling at the bottom of his t-shirt. "Have fun. Remember, I will see you in a couple weeks and we will have fun making up for the time apart," I said in a flirtatious way as I winked. This was the hardest thing I ever had to say and I couldn't believe I made it through without crying.

"Okay, sounds good." He kissed me deeply, passionately, and I ate it up. Wanting this kiss to continue, I lingered slowly and teasingly on his lips. He fell for it until he had to go.

"Baby, I put two gifts in your truck. One, you can open any time after tonight. The second one, you can open any time after you get to missing home, I mean really missing home. It will help with the nostalgia. The envelope, please don't open it until after your first day of school. Promise me you will follow these instructions."

The look on his face was humor mixed with curiosity. "I promise, but the one I can open tonight better be a picture of you wearing nothing at all."

"Ha ha, Mr. McHale, you'll have to see. Drive safe, baby, and remember…" I got up close and I ran my palm over his cheek as I looked directly into his eyes, "I am anchored to you forever, Trevor McHale."

The smile left his face and his eyes became serious. He placed his hand over mine as he replied, "Love you, babe."

As he hopped up into his truck, he turned around quickly. "Oh hey, Elle, you'll always be my first priority." I smiled and lifted my hand in acknowledgement. Quietly, I whispered to myself, "Not anymore," as watched him pull out.

He had no idea that he would never see me again. I would never hear his voice again. I got in my car and drove faster than I had ever driven before. I ran red lights and I didn't care. My life was over. I had no idea how I made it to my driveway, but I did. Once I got there, I put the car in park and screamed as loud as I could until I had no voice left, then cried until I didn't have any tears left to cry.

Chapter 6

Present Day

"Holy shit, Rachel, I don't know where to touch her. She's black and blue everywhere. Look at the inside of her thighs, what the fuck did he do to her?"

The only thing I could get out of my mouth was, "Where is he?"

"Baby, don't talk. We have to call the police and get you to the hospital."

At that, I began throwing and tossing my body around. They both immediately tried to hold me down.

"No hospital, no cops, he'll take my babies. Is he here?"

I knew what my main priorities were and I needed to get those settled first.

"Where are the kids?"

"Look, Elleny, the kids are fine. They're at school. Luc called me this morning when you didn't come down for breakfast. He said that Bear was gone before they even got up. We had a bitch of a time getting into the house. The locks were apparently changed and I didn't have a key. We had to break in through one of the back windows."

That son of a bitch!

He went and changed the locks on my house. Since the kids and I always used the garage door, I never would've known. Did he think he was going to kick me out of my own home? This was my house. His name was nowhere on the deed.

"Shower. I have to get to the shower."

I looked up at them as I shook my hands, silently asking them to untie me. Their eyes met for a moment until Lilly yelled, "Shit! Seriously? You cannot really think that I'm okay with this. I mean, come on! Look at you, Elle! You are bruised everywhere and have blood in between your legs. That shitbag hurt you and you want me to help you up, put you in the shower, and help you get dressed like any other normal day?"

"Yes."

That was all that I could get out. I hadn't had a chance to look down at my body and I couldn't really feel any of what she was describing.

Through my own tears and a scratchy throat with lungs that seemed to only fill when I made them, I explained to her how it was. The threats that he had made to take my kids down to the swamps of Louisiana where I would never see them again. Lilly had a baby, she understood the bond between a mother and her child. She knew there was no other option for me.

This wasn't the first time that he had done this to me and it probably wouldn't be the last, but I had one more year to deal with it for the twin's sake and four more years for Harlee. Then, they would be on their own and I could divorce this madman. This was not the same person that I had known all my life. The man that I had spent the last seventeen years with was not the man that I use to respect and trust. This man had the mind of a psychopath. The question that I always asked myself after times like this was why. Why was he was staying? I couldn't figure it out. I knew my reason for staying. I gave up on love seventeen years ago outside of my children.

Slowly, they untied my wrists. The cuts were still raw and open, you could see pieces of meat where skin used to be. Walking slowly, they helped me to the bathroom where I sat down in a warm bath. Rachel washed my hair as Lilly sat over in the corner and cried.

"Lils, I didn't feel a thing, baby doll."

Lilly picked her head up to look at me as she lowered the finger that she had been nibbling on.

"What did you say?"

"It was strange. It was like I wasn't even there. I was with TJ. He kept telling me to look in his eyes and that it would be over soon. He told me to stay with him."

As I was telling her this, she began to cry more. Not like she was afraid of what she was seeing, but because she knew there wasn't any other place that would bring me the ultimate peace. The place that would bring me the stillness I would need to get through something so horrifying.

Rachel stopped massaging my head and came to sit beside me. She touched her palm to the side of my face and looked into my eyes. I stared back. I saw a sheen of moisture build up over her pupils. We didn't say a word, I knew what she was saying and I didn't blame her at all. She felt guilt from knowing that if she hadn't brought him to my hospital room that day, he would've never made me that deal and I wouldn't be in this situation.

I grabbed her hand as she continued to look into my eyes and just shook my head. A single tear left her eye and she nodded her head. She understood. She stood back up and continued washing my hair.

Feeling a bit rejuvenated after my bath, I went into my closet and remembered my job.

"Shit!"

Both women came running as though someone shouted, "Fire!"

"What!" they both screamed at the same time.

"I didn't call into work. I bet Loren is freaking the fuck out."

Rachel exhaled in relief.

"Shit, Elle, don't scare me like that. I called this morning and told him you weren't feeling good. He told me to stay in touch with him if you couldn't make it in tomorrow."

I knew he wanted to keep in contact due to the McHale merger; the meeting that I had yet to tell the girls about. They were going to shit golden bricks when I told them I was having lunch with Trevor McHale.

"Oh, thank God! Thank you. Let me get dressed and I will meet ya'll downstairs. There's so much I wanted to tell you tonight but I guess right now is as good a time as any."

"Are you sure? Do you need any help?"

"Honey, this isn't the first time I've been through this. This is just the first time it's been bad enough you've had to find out."

With this information, Rachel jumped as if a bolt of lightning hit her.

"You mean to tell me that this…" she pointed her finger up and down my body, "This has happened before and…and you didn't even call anyone to come and help you? You had to deal with this…" again with the finger, "all alone?"

"Rachel."

"No, no Rachel bullshit! You mean to tell me that I live not more than ten minutes from you, I have no children, a husband who works from home, and you can't call me? You're telling me that Lilly lives not more than fifteen minutes from you and Curt is home every night to watch Austin and you can't even call her? You can't ask us to come and help you get situated from your piece of shit husband hurting you? Am I hearing you right?"

"Rachel, this is my problem, my responsibility. Like my piece of shit husband tells me, I've made my bed, now I have to lie in it. I'm a big girl, I can handle myself. Just like you pointed out, you have families. Besides, I really didn't want you to see me like that, it's kind of humiliating."

"If it happens again and you don't call me and I find out about it, I'm going to the police. That's a promise. You get me?"

With that, she left my closet, walked hard to my bedroom door, opened it, and slammed it shut.

Yeah, I'd say she was a little upset.

"She's just worried about ya, babe. That's all."

"I know that, Lils, but I can't be calling ya'll to save me every time he comes home and feels like being an asshole. I've dealt with it this long, I can deal with it a while longer."

Lilly walked up to me and grabbed my hand. "Honey, no one should have to deal with any of this."

She kissed my cheek, walked out of the closet, and walked downstairs.

Though, she did it a lot quieter.

"Holy shit on a stick!" Lilly shouted after I just told her about the merger meeting I would be attending tomorrow afternoon.

"Well, fuckin' A!" Rachel exclaimed.

"Yeah, that's what I said, too. I was still shell-shocked from seeing him and now all of a sudden I'm supposed to sit down and have a drink with him? The nerve of him! Leaving a sit down meeting, refusing to sign the contracts, and demanding a meeting over drinks with the contention of signing the papers and delivering them to me."

I have found that the older Rachel gets, the more she likes to cook when she's pissed. So, I came down to an amazing lunch of grilled shrimp over cheese grits with fresh roasted tomatoes straight from the garden. She also made a fresh mango chutney that was to die for. Needless to say, I wouldn't be eating dinner tonight.

"Are you going to tell him?"

The infamous question. One that had been beating around in my brain for forty-eight hours now. Do I tell him about his twins or not? Not only do I have to think about something that would change his life forever, I have to think about something that would change the life of the twins forever. A lie that had been unspoken for seventeen years.

"I don't think so."

"Elle, he has a right to know. You did what you did so that he could fulfill his life's dreams. The way it sounds, he's achieved just about everything he's going to achieve."

"Yeah, but it's not just about him anymore. I have two others that this could be devastating to. Growing up thinking one man is your daddy and then one day, *bam!* Nope, sorry, I've been lying to you all your life, this man is your real daddy. Talk about a Maury moment."

I looked at Lilly sitting across from me, fork halfway to her mouth, staring at the wall behind me with the biggest shit-eating-grin on her face."

"Lilly, what is wrong with you?"

"Could you imagine his surprise of finding out that he had a kid? He'd probably mess his shorts. Now, imagine him finding out he has twins. I'd love to be a fly on the wall when that conversation took place."

All three of us burst out laughing at once. I was holding my side because of the pain, but I didn't care. She was right. That would be a sight to behold. I could picture his mouth falling open when I'd tell him he had a son. Then I could picture his knees wobbling when I continued on with, "Oh, by the way, you have a daughter, too."

I wasn't sure what to expect from this meeting. Was it going to be a bitch out session for the way I left him, or a reunion? Maybe he still had feelings for me, maybe he wanted to introduce me to his wife and rub it in my face the way Bear rubbed it in his. Shit, now I was getting nervous. I didn't know what to expect. Maybe I was just getting myself into a tizzy and it was going to be exactly what he said it was going to be: picking up signed contracts and possibly a drink.

I stood up and asked the girls if they wanted dessert. I had an apple pie in the freezer. I always made my desserts from scratch but I kept a pie in the freezer for emergencies. In Georgia, you never knew when someone was going to stop by to lollygag.

They both agreed to pie so I got up, set the oven to preheat, and brewed some coffee. Since it wouldn't be long before the kids got home, I pulled out a package of cookie dough as well and threw the dough on a cookie sheet.

See? Always prepared.

"You know, darlin', as soon as you walk through that door tomorrow night you have to call me and let me know what happened," Lilly demanded.

"I was waiting on which one of ya'll was gonna be first," I responded with a little laugh as I got down the coffee cups and dessert dishes and set them on the table.

Not wanting to bring up any more of that, Rachel quickly changed the subject.

"Remember that time when we were in the eighth grade and we all spent the night at Lilly's just to sneak out of her house so we could each visit our boys?"

Throwing the pie and cookies in the oven, I replied, "Rachel Locke-Harrington, you know that's not what happened. We went to Bear's first. He decided that he wanted to join up so the four of us headed over to Curt's. We ended up picking him up and heading over to TJ's. Remember how we all climbed in his window and played a game of Truth or Dare?"

"Holy shit, how do you remember all that?"

Pointing to my head with my index finger, I informed her, "I remember all."

Laughing, she reminded me of the time that we all went out for milkshakes after a movie one Friday night. "Dana Cisco was staring at TJ like she was undressing him with her eyes. Remember how the boys started talking about it? So, you decided you were gonna ask her, very politely, if she liked what she saw?" Lilly leaned her head back as she visualized the exact memory of that night. "Then, Dana got brave when she told you that it would be better if she could see what was going on under those clothes? I swear, Elle, you were as fluent as water. Sweetie, when you grabbed her up by the hair and tossed her to the ground, I couldn't stop laughing. Before anyone could get to you, she already had a split lip and you got some good punches in. The bitch deserved it. Seven stitches to her cheek and two to her lip. Bet she didn't wonder anymore what TJ was wearing underneath his clothes."

I started laughing and realized that I heard laughing behind me. Turning around, I noticed Lucas, JoJo, and Harlee standing there listening.

"Momma!" Harlee shouted and ran over to hug my waist. I grimaced a little, but I didn't let a sound out aside from my normal greeting.

"Hey there, my sweet angel! How was school?" It made it all worth it to feel those arms wrapped around me, to be able to rub circles on her back. That was my reassurance that she was real and standing in front of me.

Harlee let go of my waist and babbled on about her day. I told her to go upstairs, work on her homework, and I would call her down when the cookies were ready. After, of course, giving her aunties some love.

Rachel and Lilly loved on her for a few, then she flew upstairs, I'm sure to play on her PSP or PlayStation.

Both Lucas and JoJo came up and hugged me together. Again, I winced, but not as bad. They were gentler with me then Harlee was.

"Momma, we've been so worried. You said you'd call, but we never heard from you."

"I'm fine. I'm sorry I didn't call, it took me a little more time than I thought to get situated. Your daddy and I were up late discussing some issues."

"mmhmm, sure."

"Luc, baby, look at me. It's fine, I'm fine. Don't you worry about me, it's all good. Now, go on upstairs and get to your homework. I'll call you down when the cookies are ready, okay?"

"I'm gonna bash his skull in."

I stopped dead in my tracks and looked at my seventeen year old son and thought to myself, *My God, what have I done?*

"Darlin', I'm fine. See?" I turned in a circle with my arms up, reassuring him that I was okay. I looked over at Rachel and Lilly. They were looking at Luc like they knew he wasn't fucking around anymore with this bullshit.

"Momma, I am not a fucking idiot! I may not know what exactly he's doing to you, but I know he's doing something. I find out that he's doing what I think he's doing, I swear to God, I'll kill 'em."

"Dylan Lucas, look at your momma," I demanded as I grabbed his face with both hands to look him straight in the eyes. "For one, I love you more than my life itself. Anything and everything I do is for you and those two girls up there. I know that you're seventeen and you think that you're big and bad and can take on the world, but if something were to ever happen to you, I couldn't go on. Do you understand that?"

He was quiet for a moment.

"Answer me, son."

"Yes, ma'am"

"Good. Now, second, no one is ever worth losin' your life over, whether it be by death or by prison. They ain't worth it. So, let it go so that you can see another sunrise and another sunset. You got me?"

"Yes, ma'am."

"Okay. I love you, my protector."

"Love you, too, Momma."

"Mm-kay, now say hello to your aunties, tell them you love them, then get on up there and do your homework. Call you in a bit."

Luc teasingly rolled his eyes at me as he headed off for the stairs.

"Yes, ma'am. Hey, Aunt Rachel, Aunt Lilly. Love ya'll." He planted a swift kiss on both their cheeks.

"Oh, and Luc? I didn't miss that "F" word comin' out of your mouth."

Luc chuckled like he thought he got away with saying it and quickly ran upstairs.

The girls and I continued talking as we sat around the table. After a few minutes, we became silent, allowing everything we had just talked about and the events that happened with Luc to soak in. I heard the timer for the cookies, so I got up and took them out of the oven. Setting them on the cooling rack, the smell of baked goods took over my kitchen.

"I totally believe Luc would kick Bear's ass."

Yep, that came out of Rachel's mouth.

We all laughed for a second and it wasn't like a laugh that just broke the silence, it was like we all had lost our minds. The kind where you want to stop laughing, but every time you think to stop, you just laugh more.

They both continued to laugh while I went to the fridge to pull out more creamer. I opened the door and stopped, feeling sick to my stomach.

Their curious eyes came to me.

"Oh my god! TJ is going to own Bear's company."

Both smiles were wiped off their faces in an instant. They hadn't thought about that either. But, what had hit me thirty seconds ago was just now hitting them straight between the eyes. Bear was going to know that he was back in town, which meant shit was about to hit the fan for me.

As the timer went off for the pie, I slowly went back over to the stove, removed it from the oven, and set that on the cooling rack as well. Not waiting, I went to the freezer and removed a tub of vanilla ice cream. I sliced a hot piece of apple pie and placed it on a dessert plate with a large scoop of vanilla ice cream that immediately began melting. Then, I made two more plates.

Lilly asked, "What can we do? Can you specify that the new owner's not be named? Or that their offices not be located there?"

"People around town are going to be talkin', Lils. I can't put a stop to that. This is a small town and you know how the people are. TJ is gonna want to see his family. I can't stop him from comin' back."

Rachel concurred and added the Richland Gazette was going to have a field day with this. "Not only had the prodigal son returned home after seventeen years, but he came back with power and money and bought the one enterprise that keeps Richland functioning. He is either going to be the one who liberates this town or he's going to be its demolisher in the eyes of those who share the same mentality as Bear."

"Maybe he hasn't fulfilled everything he had set out to do. I think I would want retribution for the way that Bear treated me, don't you think, Elle?" Lilly said as she lifted her coffee cup to her mouth and looked me straight in my eyes.

Tracy Lee

Chapter 7

September 1992

It had been two weeks since TJ left. He had called several times within those two weeks but I stuck to my guns and didn't answer. I didn't think I had the self-control, but as it turned out, I did. Bear and I were leaving for Tennessee the next day. We didn't plan a big wedding, deciding that we would just stop at the first town we thought looked decent. Bear didn't think it would be a good idea for us to wed in town since people liked to talk and I didn't need rumors flying. I needed TJ to find out when he read that letter. I wanted to be the one to tell him and by the amount of times he *hadn't* called, I suspected he hadn't read it yet.

Bear and I had started to take our relationship to the next level. He was sweet and he didn't push me. He knew I wasn't experienced so he was giving me the time I needed. We had our first kiss a couple of days ago. Trevor was the only man I had ever kissed and we were used to each other, so with Bear, it was awkward. Don't get me wrong, Bear definitely knew what he was doing, I just kept waiting to feel that amazing spark I felt with Trevor, but it never came. I can say that I was definitely thankful for one thing, he was gentleman enough to take the dip out of his mouth before he came in for the kiss. I could still taste it a little, but it was sweet that he was thinking of me. I desperately wanted to find something that had a bit of Trevor in Bear. Since they were best friends, I thought I'd find it, but they were completely different.

We hadn't talked about the intimacy issue as of yet, we were trying not to rush this but we didn't have a lot of time. I guess we'd get to that bridge after the wedding.

It was decided that we would stay with my father and Mona just until I could find a job. When my momma died, life insurance money was given to my father. He never used it, instead he stuck it in a savings account for me. I hadn't touched it, nor would I ever think of touching it. That was all I had left of my mother. To me, spending it frivolously was like throwing my mom away for just anything. Besides, I liked to work. It kept me busy and I felt useful; that was important to me.

My visits to the doctor became more frequent due to morning sickness. The sickness was so bad they would have to hook me up to an IV for intravenous pre-natal vitamins and something for the nausea. This was another reason I wanted to stay with Daddy. If anything went wrong with the baby, he'd be there and could do something right away. Even if his office was a ten minute drive from the house, it made me relax a little knowing he wasn't far. I wasn't taking any chances with this baby, he or she was all I had left of TJ and I wasn't ready to lose all of him.

As I was packing a bag, my daddy came in and sat down on my bed.

"How ya feelin'?"

"Good, I ate some toast and broth for dinner and so far—"

"Excellent. You know, I was looking over your chart, you've lost another ten pounds."

"Yeah, that's what Norma said when she weighed me yesterday. I'm not gonna worry about it," I paused for a second and looked at my daddy, "Are you?"

"Well, you're just in your first trimester and some women do lose some weight, I just want you to be watchful over it. Stay light and high in fat or protein, if you can. Jell-O, I know has become somewhat of a passion of yours, but it's not nutritious."

"I know, I'll watch it. I'm only going to be gone for two days. We will be back in no time. Have Clara make some of her chicken soup and put it in the fridge. That way when I get back, it will be good and blended together."

Laughing, my dad assured me there would be chicken soup in there for me to feast on when I returned. Yawning, he took the hint that I was ready for bed. He stood, walked across the room, and wrapped up what he came in to say.

"You're gonna make an absolutely wonderful wife. You know this, don't you?"

Softly, I whispered, "Thank you, Daddy."

I saw him wipe his eye. "I wish your momma was here to see…"

I quickly got up and hugged him.

"She is, Daddy. She's watching over us in everything we do."

He reached into his back pocket for his cloth handkerchief and wiped his eyes and then his nose.

"I hope he ends up loving you more than I loved your momma."

"Daddy, I don't think anyone could love someone more than that."

"Well, he damn well better try because I know how to make it look like he died of natural causes."

Laughing, yet kind of freaked out, I scolded him, "Daddy, you're not supposed to say things like that out loud."

"I know, I just wanted you to know what I just spent an hour talking to him about."

"You didn't."

"I did, and he understands perfectly."

Well, even though we weren't having a traditional wedding, I guess it didn't mean the traditional father, son-in-law talk wasn't required. I could feel the blood as it raced to my cheeks in embarrassment.

"Tell me again, Daddy."

My dad walked back over to my bed and sat down beside me.

"Tell you what, Elleny?"

"What you said to me in the hospital. Right now, I need some encouragement. I feel like such a coward."

"Why? Because you're thinking with your head instead of your heart? Because you know that Trevor was never meant to grow old in this town? Trust me, baby, no matter what he decides to do or where he decides to go, he will never find better than you."

Standing, he walked to the window and looked out into the starry night. The moon shedding just enough light into the window, I could see as it shined on his face. It showed the reality of this whole situation. My father's age and his concern was all over his face. The crow's feet around his eyes were noticeable, his laugh lines that had once been there from the joy he shared with my mom had diminished to just short wrinkles around the top of his lip. He looked truly exhausted.

"No matter how much you think that you are holding back from him, things would be so much worse if you held him back."

As tears welled in my eyes, I knew that was true. TJ was too special and had too many wonderful abilities for him to grow old in this town. He needed to go out into the world and let them see all the beauty and potential that I saw in him. The problem was, I didn't want to let him go. Call it selfish, call it jealousy, I didn't give a shit, I loved him. I wanted him here to experience all that I was going to undergo with this baby, a baby we made out of love. All it would take was a phone call, one small little phone call and everything would be perfect…for me.

"Honey, I know that your heart belongs to Trevor, but I really respect Bear stepping up to the plate. He didn't have to do what he's doing; take on the responsibility he will be taking on. I think he'll truly be someone you will grow to love in the long run."

Looking down at my lap so my dad didn't see the tears, I needed him to understand. "I will never love another, Daddy."

Daddy turned and looked at me and I saw that he understood my pain. My dad had lost the one who held his heart and he would never get her back. He would go the rest of his days and never know that kind of love again. It destroyed his life. I mean, don't get me wrong, he lived, but he wasn't living colorful. His day used to begin and end in pure happiness. Now, it was monotonous and uninteresting.

"Don't say that," he whispered. I saw a tear run down his cheek by way of moonlight and it took everything for me not to break down. I walked to over to where he was standing at the window and hugged him. We cried for what seemed like hours for the loss of what was so essential for our life force: love.

The next morning was uneventful. I packed my overnight bag and threw it in the trunk. I hung my garment bag in the back seat of my car, kissed my dad goodbye, and waved at Mona who didn't wave back. This didn't surprise me, she wasn't thrilled we would be living with her, but I didn't really care. As we got going, I asked if we could stop for some breakfast. We ended up going through a drive through, which was fine with me. As long as they had coffee and something to put in my stomach, I didn't care where we ate. I nibbled on a biscuit with jelly, drank my small coffee, then laid back, watching the landscape through my passenger window.

Driving through the mountainous terrain of North Georgia, the view never got old to me. The colors of the leaves were just starting to change so I got a variegated backdrop of gold, rusty red, brown, burnt orange, and yellow. Some trees were already losing their leaves but that didn't change the spectacle surrounding them.

Bear and I chatted a bit and I was learning more about his childhood. I didn't realize that he and Bubba had lived with his uncle and aunt before he came to live with his granny. He revealed that their parents would forget to come home and they would eventually run out of food. I thought they were shitty parents by what was rumored, now I thought they were even shittier parents.

Bear continued telling me about his granny. Being from Louisiana, she taught him creole and he and Bubba would only speak to her in her native tongue before she passed away. His granny had meant the world to him, you could hear it in his voice when he spoke of her. She wasn't the perfect parent, but she met their needs as best she could and both boys respected her for that.

It grew quiet again in the car with the hum of a radio station barely coming through as the background noise.

"Tell me what's on your mind?" he asked at he stared at the road.

"To be honest, nothing really." This realization kind of freaked me out because my mind hadn't stopped since I found out I was pregnant.

He chuckled and grabbed my hand. "It's gonna be okay, Ellie. Things are gonna work out for us. We're gonna get married and then we'll be a family."

I started to laugh at the thought of future family pictures. The images that once stood in my mind with Trevor now had Bear replacing him. I couldn't get over how ironic this was. When Bear heard me laugh, he asked me what was funny. I started to reply when I heard the chirp of my cell phone.

I pulled my phone out of my purse and looked at the caller ID. It was TJ.

"Holy shit!"

Bear's eyes looked concerned. "Who is it?"

126

"It's TJ."

I saw Bear stiffen, but he didn't reply.

"I'm just gonna ignore it."

Still, no word from Bear.

I hit the ignore button and shut my phone off. If he had read that letter then he was going to be calling off the hook and I really wasn't in the mood to deal with that. I put my phone back in my purse and stared out the window at nothing. I reached in the back seat and grabbed a pillow and a blanket and laid my head back and closed my eyes.

"Look, I'm gonna rest for a minute. Can you wake me up when we get there?"

Bear rubbed my hand in acknowledgement so I shut my eyes.

I stood on the edge of the mountain overlooking a valley. Nothing grew there because water couldn't reach it. As I stood there, wrapped in an Indian style trade blanket, I realized I was naked. Feeling the cool air hit my face, my hair blew back off of my shoulders. I felt warm arms wrap around me as a face nuzzled in between my neck and shoulder.

I pushed my head to the side to give him better access. His lips were warm against my chilly skin, so much that I felt goose bumps develop all down my body. Bear began moving a little faster. I could feel him as he pushed his hips into my backside a bit harder each time his kiss lingered on my skin a moment longer.

Hands wandered until they found their way inside the blanket. His fist opened up as it molded around my breast. I began to feel nervous, yet it didn't bother me.

I leaned my head back onto his shoulder and waited for the prickling of his beard against my cheek to stimulate my senses. I never felt it.

"You shaved. Your beard didn't bother me, Bear," I said as I turned around and reached up to cup his face.

It wasn't Bear. It was TJ.

"Bear? Why would Bear come up behind you like this?"

My mouth dropped as I felt my eyes widen.
"Answer me, Elle. Elleny?"

I jerked awake and looked around needing to remember where I was and who I was with. I looked at Bear and found him staring back at me.

"Jesus Ellie, you okay? You're soaking with sweat."

Damn hormones! I mentally screamed.

"Honey, we're here."

Looking up, I saw the hotel we would be staying at for the next two days. Shit, this was really happening. My emotions seemed to be all over the place, processing all of this was nearly impossible. If I had a say, I would just throw myself down on the ground and curl up into a little ball until this whole clusterfuck was over. But, it wasn't going to pass. This was my life now. I had to decide on whether to embrace it or fight it and all that was going to do was make it worse.

I decided to not fight it. With that settled, I got out of the car, reached my arms way over my head, and stood on my tip toes. Being cooped up for hours did not do wonders on a body. I stretched and looked to the man that was going to become my husband as he started approaching me from the hotel office. *This wasn't going to be a bad thing*, I kept repeating in my head. Bear was a decent man. I had known him all my life, grown up with him. I would just be spending the other half of my life with him as well. I grabbed my garment bag and waited for Bear to pop the trunk. He grabbed my other bag, along with his, and carried them up to our room.

As soon as he unlocked the door, I dropped my purse and garment bag and ran for the bathroom. This baby was doing a number to my bladder.

When I came out of the bathroom, Bear was sitting on the bed. His arms were stretched out behind him, hands flat on the bed, holding himself up.

"Sorry, I had to go really bad."

"It's okay, I should've stopped. I forget sometimes, this is all new to me"

"Yeah, me too. But, from what I've been reading, my body is going to start looking gross and disgusting. Shit is gonna happen, so be prepared."

Bear's face turned white and he swallowed hard.

"We don't have to do this, ya know. There's still time to back out."

Bear quickly answered back, "I ain't backin' out."

"Okay then. Let's go get married," I said before I chickened out.

Thirty minutes later, after we both showered and changed, we went to go get married.

"Yep, we did it!" I announced to Rachel once we got back to the hotel room. I had already called Daddy and now that the two of them knew, I could go to bed. I was exhausted.

After we left the courthouse, we went and grabbed a bite to eat. Nothing fancy, just some barbeque. But, it had to be the best BBQ in Tennessee. After we stayed at the restaurant for close to an hour and a half, we walked around the small town just window shopping. Several of the stores were mom and pop boutiques but the items they were selling were unbelievably beautiful. One shop sold homemade quilts. They were so simple, yet so elegant.

Another store carried beautiful silver jewelry. The owner handmade all of the items and the work was flawless. Bracelets made of thick silver bands that had been stamped with vines outlined in black. Some were etched with simple curved lines. They even carried rings that were wide strips of silver and engraved with hearts and charms.

"You like these, don't ya?"

"They're exquisite. Look at what the creator has envisioned and put himself into. Each piece is unique."

Bear didn't say a word, he just smiled and grabbed my hand. It surprised me when he brought it up to his mouth where he kissed the back of it. I smiled a thoughtful smile as we began walking again.

We found a small café at the end of the block that had little desserts and coffee. After ordering coffees and a small piece of cheesecake, we both agreed it was time to head back to the hotel. With the day we had, we both were spent.

As we were walking back to the hotel, Bear asked quietly, "How you feelin'?" Surprisingly, I felt good. I hadn't been sick for a couple of hours and, if only for a moment, I felt normal again.

"I feel good. It's nice to have a couple of hours of not throwing up," I said as I giggled.

"That's not what I meant. How are you feeling about what we did?"

That was a good question. I hadn't really thought about it. I didn't think the reality of it all had hit me yet. I was trying so hard not to think of TJ, but he was continually on my mind.

"I feel good about what we did, Bear. I don't regret it at all," was the only reply that I could honestly come up with. At my response, Bear took my hand and we walked hand in hand back to the hotel room.

Walking into our room, I hadn't noticed that there was only one king size bed. Bear must have seen the apprehension on my face.

"I'll sleep on the couch."

I looked over at Bear, I knew this was coming. Sleeping with my husband scared the hell out of me. What if I wasn't enough for him? Here I was, pregnant with another man's baby. What if he didn't want to touch me? I was going to drive myself insane with all of the *what if's*. What I needed to do was get in there and figure it out.

I let out a breath in an attempt to calm myself down. Quickly, I told him that it was going to be fine, we could share the bed. After all, we had better get used to it; we'd be sharing one for a long time.

I rambled through my bag until I found my night gown. Grabbing my cosmetic bag that also carried my toiletries, I headed for the bathroom to get ready for bed. I could feel the panic overwhelm me. I braced myself on the sink and glared into the mirror.

"What the hell did you expect, Elleny?"

I tried with the, "It was going to happen at some point in time" speech, but that wasn't helping. So, I took my dress off, hung it up on the back of the bathroom door, and stood there looking at my belly. I wasn't showing yet but as I rubbed my hands over it, I knew there was something growing in there.

"I hope you understand what I'm doing and that I'm doing it because I love your daddy so much. Please, don't end up hating me." I took another deep breath, pulled my night gown over my head, and finished with my normal night time ritual.

Entering the room, I noticed all the lights were off. Bear was already in bed lying on his side with his hand holding his head up. His shirt was off and the top part of his chest was above the covers as he was watched TV. From the reflection of light coming from the television, I could see that his eyes were focused on me. I knew I was shaking and had to tell my legs to walk to the bed.

Pulling back the covers, I could see the top of his sweatpants and every ripple of muscle that protruded from his stomach. *Breathe, Elleny. Breathe.* I laid flat on my back with my hands over the covers and my arms laid at my sides as I looked straight up at the ceiling.

"Fuck, Elleny. If I pull you over here by me, you'll break in two. You're so tense, relax. Girl, I ain't no stranger."

He was right. Shit, we used to skinny dip down there in old man Jones' pond. I had seen this man naked before. Problem was, I was looking at him differently now. This was

131

my husband. We weren't kids anymore and his body damn sure didn't look like that when we were kids. I slowly moved my body toward him. Finally, I felt his arm go around me and drag me over to him. When he did this, his body ended up partially lying on top of me. His eyes met mine as he moved my hair out of my face.

"I never thought you needed makeup. You sure are pretty without it."

"Bear...I think that you deserve to know that...that I've never been with anyone other than TJ."

"Well, no shit. I know that," he spoke through a smile.

I knew I was blushing, but I thought I owed this explanation to him. I whispered, "I'm not experienced."

His eyes never leaving mine, he slowly brought his face closer to mine as he whispered quietly, "Well then, I guess we have a lot of practicing to do."

And with that, his lips gently touched mine for a chaste kiss on the side of my mouth. Then, he moved to the other side of my mouth, his eyes never closing. He laid another kiss on my chin before moving to my lips; a delicate, innocent, slow, closed-mouth kiss. It was nothing like I had envisioned. His tongue touched my lips ever so softly before he pulled back.

"You taste so good, Ellie."

He swiped his tongue over my lips again and I puckered my lips this time. My eyes blinked lazily of their own accord.

"Just like honey on my tongue."

"Bear," I breathed. This time when he came back for another taste, I parted my lips just a tad. The tip of my tongue touched the tip of his and he moaned. His thumb brushed my cheek as his hand held my head, bringing me closer to him. I could feel him laying on my leg, hard and long.

Holy shit...holy shit...holy shit.

"Baby, you gotta relax."

"I'm trying."

He came back in to kiss me again. Grabbing my bottom lip, he sucked it into his mouth. I pulled back, but his hand resisted my getaway, bringing me back up to him. I wrapped my top lip around his bottom lip and touched my tongue to his. That was all it took. He kissed me again. His tongue touched between my lips and I parted, allowing him in. I closed my eyes and all I could picture was TJ. He was the one I wanted here with me in this bed, on our wedding night. I just kept kissing Bear as though it was TJ. The kiss got hotter and the moans coming from him were getting louder. His movements came directly from his hips, grinding against my pelvis. I could tell he was wanting more than I was offering at this point in time. I wrapped my arms around him and ran my hands up and down his back. He seemed to be thicker than TJ, he was much broader. As our kiss deepened, my hands became braver, exploring as I went further down his back. Slowly, they began creeping into the top of his sweatpants.

"Yeah, baby. Grab my ass."

Oh shit, did he just tell me to grab his ass? I wasn't used to being directed on what my actions should be. With TJ, it was all natural. I had to keep telling myself that my time with TJ was over.

I squeezed his ass in my hands and dug my nails into his cheeks. I heard Bear mutter, "Fuck," and took that as a good sign. Gradually, he moved himself so that he was between my legs. I opened and allowed him entrance. Pulling my nightgown up over my head, I was naked. Other than my panties, nothing covered me up. I knew that he wasn't looking at me like I was back when we were kids, I could see that lust had consumed him. I suddenly felt very self-conscious. My hands went immediately over my breasts.

"Baby, don't cover yourself. Do you know how long I have fantasized about this moment…with you?"

Was he serious? I had to tell myself to breathe in, breathe out. I couldn't even answer him.

"I…I…didn't…um…know…that, Bear."

133

He stopped for a moment and we both sat up against the headboard. He looked down at his lap.

"Don't get me wrong, I loved Rachel. But you..." He shook his head. "You were like...a fantasy. It always seemed you and Trevor would be together forever, inseparable. I never thought I was good enough for you, Ellie. I wasn't rich. Hell, my parents were fuckin' fruitcakes. I didn't have the best and you grew up with the best of the best. Plus, you were too far up TJ's ass to ever even look at me as anything other than his friend," he chuckled.

Shocked by this confession, I didn't know what to say. Did I even say anything at all? The only thing that came to mind was, "I guess you're right, I was pretty high up there. In his ass, that is." I was not about to bring TJ into the middle of us right now, especially like this. Bear's erection was knocking on my vagina's front door and these fucking hormones were sprinting to let him in. I was also having a hard enough time trying to stop Bear from becoming totally invisible and TJ popping up in his place. *Shit! I had to stop this.*

"But, now I'm not. I'm here with you, so let's not think of him okay, sweetie?" I wasn't sure if I was trying to convince him or myself. I rubbed his cheek with my hand as I blocked TJ from my mind. "Now, where were we?"

Consumed with desire, Bear didn't smile as he removed my hand away from my breast. For a moment, he just stared at me. I was naked...open for him. His gaze was taking all of me in as he eyed my body up and down. His eyes went from my chest to my face, back to my chest again.

"I can't believe this is happenin'," he murmured as he went down to run his tongue over my left nipple. I closed my eyes as I arched my back to urge him to keep going. He took the hint and shifted over to my right one. His warm breath and the soft tissue of his tongue sweeping over me was an amazing feeling. I bowed further into him.

"Goddamn, girl. You want it bad, don't ya?"

I could feel the blood rush to my cheeks as I blushed at his words. I could also feel my temper rising from embarrassment and I didn't know how much more I could blame on these stupid ass hormones.

"I'm sorry. If you want to stop, I will understand."

"There ain't no way in hell I'm stopping. I love having you like this."

Shut the hell up and keep going, was what my hormones were telling my brain to say. I had to close my eyes and wipe those thoughts away from my mind.

While still showing my breasts ample attention, Bear began to move his hands down lower. I felt his soft touch tickle as he moved over my stomach. His hand sauntered down over my panties and that was when I realized I had no control over my body anymore. Not one single cell was mine to command. Bear ran his fingers between my legs, pushing the material up against my skin. I felt the moisture that had built on the material and I tensed. I knew he noticed, but he didn't say a word.

My mind was going in all four directions at one time. I didn't know whether to cry or scream. Should I jump up and leave, or did I lay here and let him finish? I closed my eyes and cleared my mind. I wasn't going to live like this. By now, I was positive that TJ had moved on, why couldn't I? This was my husband, I didn't want our honeymoon night to be like this. I opened my eyes and decided that old Elleny was dead…this was new Elleny.

I reached up and kissed Bear's mouth gently but fervently. He ran his finger up the side of my panties and then back down. I pushed the sides of my panties down so that he would take them off and he did. I pushed the back of his pants down, hinting for him to remove those as well, and he leaned up and followed through.

I suddenly felt him entering me, slowly. His head lowered so that his face was in my neck, his moan was low in his throat. His face moved to face me and his eyes locked with mine. I felt him move slowly. Inch by inch, he penetrated me completely. I was no longer known as a woman who only had one lover. I started to move, but Bear stopped. I looked up as our eyes locked.

"Are you going to move, babe?"

"Give me a minute, Ellie. You're pretty tight. I really would like to enjoy this for more than a minute."

"Oh…."

Slowly he pulled out, before slowly entering me again. As he pulled almost completely out of me, he let out a breath of air. Eventually, his movements became faster as we found a rhythm that was amazing, but something was off. The sex was good, physically, but emotionally, we didn't fit together like TJ and I. I shook my head, I had to stop thinking about this. That was never going to be again. I couldn't keep comparing Bear to TJ.

Just as I cleared my mind, I felt my stomach tightening. My legs automatically wrapped around Bear's back so I could bring him closer to me. My breathing became erratic. Oh god, this felt good. I could feel my orgasm building and slowly closed my eyes. By the moans coming from Bear, I could tell he was almost there, too.

My orgasm hit me like a tidal wave. I opened my mouth to scream, but nothing came out. I didn't think it would ever end. One moment I thought it was over, then it would start over again. Smiling, I knew what it was—it was the hormones.

"You okay?" I heard Bear's voice somewhere in the background.

"Yeah, how 'bout you?" I asked, staring back at the ceiling.

"I'm fan-fucking-tastic."

I looked over at Bear. He was lying next to me on his back, staring up at the ceiling with the same smile I was sporting on his face. I couldn't help but burst out laughing.

Chapter 8

Present Day

Waking up that next morning was worse than waking up the day before. My whole body ached and I knew that the bruising would look worse today. It was going to be a skirt and jacket kind of day. I could tell Bear was in the bed with me. He was sprawled out all over with the covers wrapped all around him. Christ, just looking at him made me want to vomit. I eased out of the bed and headed for the shower. I knew I needed to get to work early today, not only to catch up on what I had missed yesterday but I also had to have time to mentally prepare myself for today's meeting. I was looking forward to this meeting as much as I wanted Bear touching me.

I picked out my clothes, but all I could find with a jacket was a suede suit. *Shit, I was going to have a heat stroke wearing that in this weather. Well, considering that fuck-nut didn't think about that before he beat the shit out of me, I guess I would have to tough it out. Why would he give a shit that I had meetings to attend and people to meet?* Shaking my head to clear my thoughts, I jumped in the shower.

Finishing up, I turned on the radio in the bathroom to the news channel, making sure I kept it quiet. I'd prefer he didn't wake up at all, but hey, fairy godmothers weren't real and murder was illegal. I applied my makeup and kept my hair up in a towel. Deciding I was going to wear my hair up, I put a ponytail around my wrist and headed downstairs.

When I went by the kid's rooms, I opened the doors and went in. I loved to watch my children sleep. They were so innocent and beautiful. I prayed that none of this would affect them. I reached down laying a soft kiss on their cheeks in an attempt to wake them up.

"Good Morning, my sweet baby. Time to get up for school."

"Mornin', Momma," Luc groaned.

Going into the girl's room, I turned on the light and headed to JoJo first since she was the hardest to get up.

"Morning, my angel," I said quietly in her ear. "Time to get up."

"Mornin', Momma," I heard come from Harlee in a sheepish morning croak.

A moan was all I got from JoJo.

I went downstairs and brewed myself a cup of coffee. I pulled down four different boxes of cereal and set them out on the counter for the kids to choose from along with three bowls, a pitcher of milk, and a quart of orange juice. I went to the fridge, grabbed a yogurt, and leaned against the counter to eat breakfast and read the paper. I heard the TV in the kitchen come on so I knew one of my kids had joined me.

"Gotta hurry today. I've got lots to do since I missed yesterday," I reminded them as I set my coffee cup down for a refill. I looked into the breakfast nook and noticed it was Luc. He was such a good boy. Other than wanting to kill the man he knew to be his daddy, I never had to worry about him.

"Luc, can Evan give you a ride home today? I have to work late, then I'm meeting Rachel and Lilly. I'm not sure what time I will be home. I'll leave money on the counter for you to get pizza."

"Pizza? Did I hear pizza?" Harlee said as she came zipping down the stairs so fast, it's a wonder she didn't fall.

"Yes, I have something to take care of this evening," I replied while handing her a bowl of the only kind of cereal she would eat. Both kids planted themselves in front of the TV and tuned me out as they ate their breakfast.

"Momma, can I have a yogurt?" JoJo asked, her voice still sleepy as she came into the kitchen.

"Sure thing, babe."

I walked to the fridge and bent down to grab her yogurt.

"Damn, look at that ass! It looks like two pigs fuckin', baby. You better lay off the sweets!"

The kitchen became instantly quiet. I just closed my eyes, stood up straight, and acted like it was a normal day.

"Coffee?"

"Yeah."

I went to the single serve coffee maker, plugged in a container of his favorite coffee, and set his mug underneath. Not wanting to look at him, I went into the breakfast nook to grab any dirty dishes that were on the table. Just as I collected the last empty bowl, I felt an arm wrap around my neck.

Luc dropped his spoon into his bowl and stopped chewing. Harlee yelled for me and JoJo just stood up. She wasn't sure what to do first, get Harlee out of the room or run for the phone. I opened my eyes. Surprisingly, I didn't even realize they were closed. I could see the anger building up in Luc's eyes. Needing for him to see that I was alright, I smiled a fake smile back at him as if this was just a friendly game. I felt Bear begin to scoot back, so I didn't fight as he dragged me out of the room.

"Bear, let go of me. You're scaring the shit out of the kids," I muttered through my teeth.

I could feel and smell his breath on my skin near my ear. Even after brushing his teeth this morning, the smell of alcohol permeating the air was putrid.

"Bitch, shut the fuck up," he whispered while dragging me into the foyer by the stairs. "We need to talk. Some things need to be said 'bout the other night."

139

"I'm not gonna say anything, Bear. Nothing happened, remember?"

"Yeah, you better think twice about runnin' your mouth to someone."

It took everything in me to not vomit on this man. I didn't even want him touching me—ever. Now because of what he did to me the other night, I was going to have to go visit my doctor to be tested for any STD's that he might have picked up from whatever stripper he was sticking it to.

I put my mask back on and choked up the words.

"Honey, it's okay. You just drank a little too much. We worked everything out, remember? Look, baby, I've got to go. I have to get to work and I still have to take the kids to school. You gonna be home for dinner?"

"Fuck no, I ain't gonna be here for dinner. Am I ever?"

"Okay, I just wanted to check. I might get us some pizza or something."

Good, I didn't have to worry about him being home before me. I didn't want my kids left here with him when I wasn't home.

"Well, your coffee is ready. I'm gonna finish cleaning up breakfast and take the kids to school. I'll see you later."

I quickly walked back into the kitchen and Harlee was on me like butter on bread. I rubbed her back.

"See, everything is okay. Daddy just needed to talk to me." I looked up at JoJo and Luc and they were staring at me.

"Okay, put your dishes in the sink and get your stuff together. I've just got to dry my hair and we will be on our way." As they passed, I told the twins to make sure they kept themselves and Harlee up in their rooms until I was done.

I drove the kids to school and gave Luc the money to order pizza. I told him to rent Harlee a movie and that they could both have one friend stay until I got home. I kissed each one of them and told them I loved them before heading into work.

Just as I was about to enter the highway, my phone rang. Not being able to look at the caller ID, I answered it like it was a business call.

"Elle Barker-Jackson."

"Hey, honey. Just checking on ya."

"Lils, oh sweetie. It's so good to hear your voice."

Not wanting to bring Lilly or Rachel into this anymore than I already had, I didn't say a thing about what had happened this morning.

"You okay, Elle?"

"Yeah, I'm fine. Just a little nervous about this afternoon."

"Well, just remember we are with you in spirit and then tonight, we are meeting at Rachel's to drink the spirits away."

"Oh god, Lils. That was bad."

"I know, I was just trying to cheer you up."

Laughing, I told her that I would talk with her tonight and I wouldn't dare leave out one single detail.

I made it to the office and walked up to my desk. I had beat Loren there which was good. I didn't want to be bothered. I turned on my computer and waited for it to boot up. Going into the break room, I made a pot of coffee which I knew I would probably drink before anyone else made it in. Coming back to my desk, I noticed my welcome screen was up. I removed my jacket and put it on the back of my chair. Sitting down made me wince a bit. I knew I would be sore but every time this happened it seemed that I took longer to heal. I pulled up my email. Three-hundred and fifty emails.

"Fuck me. What did I miss?" I whispered to myself.

Not opening up the main email page yet, I dug in my purse and grabbed my iPod. I knew I was going to be here for a while. I put my iPod next to me, place the earplugs in my ears, and turned it on. The first song that hit my ears was George

Strait "I Cross my Heart". Hearing the lyrics took me back to my place.

We were dancing in a country bar. Sawdust covered the floor. I was wearing jeans and a cute tan leather vest that fit me perfectly. My boobs were perky enough to make an appearance but not be the guest of honor. Best of all, I was wearing the one thing that made my whole outfit, my tie up ropers that matched my cowgirl hat. Oh yeah, my outfit was rocking.

TJ was wearing a black and white quartered Cody's western shirt, just like the one Garth Brooks wore in his video. Black boots and black cowboy hat. He so wanted to get laid that night. He knew how I felt about that outfit. I loved being out on the dance floor with him. Looking into his eyes, I ran my fingers through his soft blonde curls that hung out of the back of his hat.

"Ah, now that's more like it," TJ said as he pulled me further into him.

I giggled my flirty laugh. "We're out in public, Mr. McHale. Let's keep it clean."

We began swaying back and forth. I laid my head against his chest as TJ began singing along with the song. I looked up into his eyes and heard every word. They weren't just lyrics, they were a vow; a promise that he belonged to me; body and soul. As he sang the chorus, he crossed his heart and held up his fingers like he was doing the scout's honor, which he never was. I giggled a little and shook my head. Brushing my fingers across his cheek, he closed his eyes and turned into my hand. TJ continued singing along with the song. I loved his voice.

I leaned up and kissed him fervently. His mouth covered mine in a long, loving kiss. TJ's tongue softly touched the inside of my mouth, dancing the slowest dance with my tongue. He wasn't just saying his promise, he was showing me he meant every word he had just sung to me.

We broke apart as soon as the song was over, but the two of us had just begun.

"Let's get out of here," TJ lustfully commanded.

I was waiting for him to say the word. I was just as needy and wanton as him. If I knew we could get away with it, I'd have let him prop me up against the wall over in the corner. I could never say no to him.

"I'm ready when you are," I informed TJ.

We couldn't leave fast enough. We made it out to the parking lot where he started kissing me again. Jumping up, I wrapped my legs around his waist. This time, the gentleness was gone, only need left in its place. He ripped my vest open as we walked to the truck. I was kissing wherever I could taste him. His lips, hips neck…his skin was a free for all. We made it to his truck where I jumped in the back seat as he locked the doors.

Immediately undoing his belt, we were insatiable. I had to have him in my mouth. I wanted his taste, craved it. No words were spoken, speech wasn't needed for what we had to say. I got his pants undone and gripped his length in my hand as I directed my mouth down to him. Closing my eyes, I enjoyed everything my senses were offering me.

His scent, the smell of his body wash and cologne mixed together, made my head spin. The flavor of him, the earthy taste of his masculinity and the hint of saltiness from his pre-cum quenched my thirst. The sounds of him moaning and whimpering because of the pleasure I was bringing him, filled my heart with an overflowing amount of joy. This whole experience was so overwhelming, I wanted to cry, laugh, and scream all at once. But, my main priority was to fulfill my man's needs, so I licked up and down, running my tongue around the tip of him.

"That's it, baby. Tease me." TJ barely got the words out of his mouth as he tilted his hips toward my mouth. I took everything he offered to me.

"Suck every drop of me into you. I want to mark every inch of you."

Instead of answering him, I hummed my enjoyment to him but that just made him thrust deeper down my throat.

"Fuck, baby. I love you so much." Those words were what I lived for. Trevor grabbed my hair back so he could watch me suck him into my mouth.

I could feel him tightening up in my hand. My motions became harder, faster. I raised my hand up to touch his stomach, running my fingers over his rippled muscles.

"That's it, baby. Take all of me. Don't ever stop loving me, I won't make it without you." My intensity told him that I wasn't going anywhere.

I felt the first gush of saltiness enter my mouth before he could say a word. I continued to suck long and slow until I squeezed every last drop out of him. I gently kissed the tip of him one last time and tenderly slid his pants up to cover him.

I got up off my knees, straddled his lap, and kissed him deeply. The blending of our taste together was my way of reassuring him I wasn't going anywhere. We would always be one.

Hearing Hinder's "You Deserve Much Better Then Me", I decided that I had had enough of going down memory lane for the moment. I turned the iPod off, took out the earplugs, and picked up my coffee cup to take a sip. Opening up my email page, I dropped my cup of coffee. They all had the same sender—Trevor McHale.

What. The. Fuck!

Flying to a standing position, I winced at the tenderness I felt from raising up too quickly. I swiped at my skirt a few times, hoping to get the excessive liquid off of me before the spot became larger. Luckily, there wasn't much left in my cup.

Grabbing the first piece of material I could find to clean up the mess, I trudged back to my desk and wiped up the rest of the coffee as I huffed and puffed. I wasn't in the mood for this bullshit this morning and damned if Trevor McHale didn't make me crazy. I cleaned up the mess and sat back down, wondering why I had so many emails from a man I hadn't heard from in seventeen years. I opened up the first one. The subject line: **The first of many firsts**. Looking down slowly, a picture was being downloaded.

"Shut the fuck up!" I screamed. It was the picture from our first official date. We went to our sixth grade dance together.

Was he kidding me? I had a feeling Trevor McHale was literally trying to drive me insane. He had to be, why on God's green earth would he be sending me pictures of us together…on a date? Maybe he was trying to get me fired, or even better—he was trying to get me killed.

I closed that picture quickly. I couldn't look at it anymore, it brought back way too many memories. I went to the next: **Second, but still first in my book**. Oh shit, I knew what this was. He was sending me pictures of all of our dates. He was sending me pictures of us together. The picture popped up on my screen and my mouth dropped. It was the picture from our second date. He had received an award for football that night.

I exited out of that picture and went to the next email, then the next, until the pictures became harder and harder to look at. I began skipping emails, each one had a subject line that had something to do with him loving it as much as our first. I picked a random one: **Just as good as the first.** I downloaded it and it was a picture at one of Lilly's parties. We were at her dining room table, probably playing a game of quarters. I was leaning in, kissing his cheek as he wore a smile from ear to ear.

This was complete torture, but I was drawn to the images. They brought me peace. I looked at myself in the picture, I recognized something I didn't think existed anymore—true happiness on my face. I knew that I had loved someone so much that the ripples of that love still continued to affect me and I never wanted to lose that feeling. Every time I thought of him, I got goose bumps. I could remember how it felt to have his arms encompass me. I felt safe, something I hadn't felt in years. It seemed like a lifetime since a smile like that had ever touched my face and Trevor McHale was the reasoning behind it. Even though he wasn't standing there in front of me or even in the same city as me, just the thought of him brought me that feeling of warmth. I didn't worry whether he was thinking about me, I didn't really care. He was my security when I needed him most and that's all that mattered. The emotion that I felt for this delusion was the only concept that made me feel whole and unharmed.

I scrolled through picture after picture, reliving my childhood and teenage years. I could recall every single picture; where it was taken, by whom, and what time of the day it was. I memorized every single minute of my time with TJ and those minutes gave me the strength to go on each and every day.

I finally made it to the last picture he sent to me. I opened it. The subject line read: **The day I died.** I downloaded the picture and I lost it. Tears began streaming down my face.

It was a picture that his mom had taken. Without us knowing, she clicked a picture of us on the day he left for college. I was looking up in his eyes, his hand was on my cheek, my left hand covered his, and the silver ring he had given me glimmered on my ring finger. The ring I never took off until the day I married Bear. The promise that he made to me and I to him. *"Forever and always, babe."* In the picture it was me telling him that I was anchored to him.

That was it! I couldn't take anymore. I ran to the bathroom and collapsed onto the stall floor. I tore off huge pieces of toilet paper and buried my face as I silently cried. I cried for all the years I lost with TJ. I cried for all I had been putting my kids through with that fucking piece of shit I was married to. I cried about not being able to kill him without going to jail. I cried about having to go in a few hours to see the man I still loved with every fiber of my being. The real father to my children, yet I couldn't do shit about it. And then, I just cried. For everything, for everyone, my emotions pounding for a release. All the tears I had held back for years decided to make their escape. Finally,I heard people scrounging around the kitchen next door and I knew I had to pull myself together.

I went out of the stall and looked at myself in the mirror. Talk about a mess! I splashed some cold water on my face to refresh myself a bit before I went out among the living. I quickly made it to my desk, grabbed my purse, and headed back to the restroom. Loren was in, so I told him I would be with him in a bit. I knew he was worried about me missing yesterday, so I really didn't need to walk into his office looking like hell. He'd send me home and I couldn't be there. I needed to be right here. So, I went back into the bathroom, fixed my makeup, put a smile on my face, and got ready for the day…again.

Walking up to Loren's office, I wrapped my knuckles against the wood softly just in case he was on the phone. I heard his cheery morning voice welcoming me in.

"You busy?" I asked softly as I looked around, not wanting to disturb him.

"Ah, Elle, everything okay? I saw your stuff at your desk, but I didn't see you. How are you feeling?"

Picking my head up, I answered with fake enthusiasm, "Better than I did yesterday. Yikes, that flu almost wiped me out."

"Yeah… I bet." He hesitated for a minute. "Listen, I don't want to get up in your personal life…"

"Then don't, Loren. I'm serious. This is my job, I love it just about as much as I love my kids. I'd make it my home if I could. Don't take that away from me."

Looking at me like he had pain in his eyes, he smiled a small smile and quietly agreed. He knew that I wouldn't survive without this job or the friendship I had with him. I needed this to keep my sanity. It made me feel somewhat in control of my life.

I couldn't deal with anymore drama. He knew that my marriage was rocky, but I would never allow someone to know just how bad it really was. I didn't need their money and I sure as hell didn't need their pity.

I went back to my desk and started working on the presentation that was scheduled for tomorrow morning when my phone began ringing.

"Loren Stevens' office, this is Elleny..."

There was silence.

"Um, hello? This is Elleny."

"Mrs. Barker-Jackson."

Oh shit.

I knew that voice, I'd know it anywhere. It was deep and gravely rough like he smoked cigarettes but I knew he never smoked a day in his life. No matter how hard he tried, I could still hear the southern accent coming through on some of his words. It could be seventeen years or a hundred and seventeen years, I would know that voice without even second guessing myself.

"Mr. McHale. So nice of you to call. Is there something I can help you with?"

"Should I answer that question truthfully, Ellie-bean?"

Shit, I set myself up for that one. Damn, Elleny get on the ball here. No wait, not ball...Ah!

Ignoring the metaphoric punch I just felt in my stomach, I straightened my back and asserted myself.

"Mr. McHale, I don't mean to be rude, but I am a very busy woman. Can I ask what this phone call is regarding?"

YES! Good one, Elle. Way to stay on point.

Hearing his cunning laughter, I could tell that he knew he made me nervous. I tried my hardest not to let it be heard in my voice, but that laughter meant only one thing. He could still read me like a book.

"Yes, Mrs. Barker-Jackson, I thought maybe you would like to know where you will be accompanying me for lunch here in about…oh, an hour or so?"

Looking at the clock, I noticed it was 11:24. Taking a calming breath, I closed my eyes and imagined a peaceful beach somewhere far away.

"I would appreciate that very much, Mr. McHale."

Hearing the laugh in his words, I knew I had done it again.

"Maybe I could find a way for you to show me how appreciative you are, Mrs. Barker-Jackson."

Every time I heard that name come out of his mouth, I wanted to scream. I couldn't stand an everyday Joe Smith saying it to me, so it bothered me even more hearing it come out of his mouth. And, as luck would have it, he felt compelled to address me by it every time he spoke to me.

"Mr. McHale, you can call me Elle. As a matter of fact, I insist you call me Elle."

"Ah, but we are professionals here, Mrs. Barker-Jackson. I insist we keep it that way."

"Very well," I grunted through a clenched smile.

"Waldorf Astoria, Atlanta. Do you need directions, Mrs. Barker-Jackson?"

"No, Mr. McHale. I think I can find my way. I look forward to our meeting."

"Oh, not much as I do."

I heard the click as he hung up. No goodbye, no see ya, just a click in my ear. "Holy shit," I muttered to myself. Maybe this is my payback and he's ready to collect.

I began to imagine what I looked like sitting here, carrying on a conversation with myself. I had to stop this shit.

I sat there for just a second with my eyes closed trying to reign in my composure. I rearranged my desk so that it looked mildly decent as I turned off my computer. I walked to Loren's office and informed him that I was leaving. I was nervous, I didn't know what to expect when it came to Trevor

McHale. The last time we had seen each other, it did not go well. I nervously walked down to the elevators feeling like I was walking down death row. I wasn't ready for this meeting. It was either going to break me or make me stronger. I was hoping for stronger because I was going to have to be the strongest I had ever been in my entire life.

I reached the hotel a little after noon. No one could predict traffic in downtown Atlanta, so you always left a little early hoping to arrive right on time. Fortunately, I was a bit early.

Since I had time, I called Dr. Peterson's office to make an appointment to come in and have that STD test done. I knew the front office manager, April, so I called and spoke with her. I knew if I spoke with her, it would be confidential and not leaking down to Dixie's Café by tomorrow morning's breakfast rush.

I pulled the mirror down and looked at my face. The last time I was face to face with this man, I hovered over his body lying in the street, sobbing, my arms wrapped around his neck, holding on for dear life, pleading with him to just leave me alone, yet having to be wrenched away from him by two other people. *Oh Jesus, I couldn't do this. I couldn't sit down with this man.* "Pull yourself together, Elle. You can do this. Now, get it together and get the hell in there."

I finished my pep talk, grabbed my gloss and swiped once over my lips. I checked my hair and got out of the car. Clicking the button to lock the doors, I reached in my purse, dropped my keys, and grabbed a small bottle of perfume. I sprayed a mist of it in the air and walked through it. Stepping up to the hotel, I kept my head high and my thoughts blank.

I walked into the restaurant bustling with activity. Waiters were dashing around in black pants, tuxedo shirts, and bow ties with large trays up above their heads, delivering food and taking food away. Waitresses were wearing the same uniforms as the waiters but with black skirts. They were rushing around delivering drinks, taking customer's orders, and getting the orders back to the kitchen. It was complete chaos, but the place was still extravagant. All around me sat prominent executives and extremely wealthy people.

"Excuse me, Madam. May I help you?" Hearing a very strong Spanish burr brought me out of my thoughts.

Clearing my throat, I politely informed him of my information, "Yes, I am meeting my party here."

"Last name?"

"McHale."

"Ah, yes. You must be Barker-Jackson?"

That fuckwad.

"Umm, yes. That's me."

"Please, I am Ricardo. Follow me if you will, your party has reserved the private room upstairs."

Really, the private room? Could he be any more shallow?

I followed Ricardo through the dining room, back almost to the kitchen. Out of nowhere popped a small hallway where a tiny stairwell sat nuzzled far in the back.

"Umm, are we supposed to be going up there?" I asked, feeling like this man was taking me up to the slaughter house to make homemade chili ala Elleny.

"Yes, ma'am. We are just taking the back way up. If we were to go in the front way, we would have to go to the other entrance on the other side of the hotel."

"Gotcha. Yeah, this way is fine. Thanks," I said to Ricardo as I led the way up the stairs. We walked up the cramped set of stairs until I reached the door. Opening it, I came to the conclusion that this was no little private party room. This looked like a bed and breakfast dining room straight out of a Norman Rockwell magazine.

Small wooden tables were set up to seat two. In the middle of the tables sat small crystal vases that were filled with beautiful pink and white tulips. Formal silverware arrangements adorned each place setting as did the most superb china collection I'd ever seen. Waterford crystal water goblets sat perfectly at one o'clock while champagne flutes sat directly to the right of the wine glass. There was a roaring fire crackling in the fire place directly located in the center of the room.

I took a breath and exhaled.

"Please, sit," I heard from over in the corner. I turned my head to see where it was coming from.

There he was. *Oh god.* I knew he could see the emotion that washed over me. My legs grew weak and my heart started thumping like it wanted out of my chest. I didn't need oxygen because he was what kept me alive. I sluggishly walked over to him as he stood, the butterflies in my stomach flying aimlessly around.

"Mr. McHale."

He held out his hand toward my chair and I sat down. I lifted my napkin and placed it softly in my lap while Ricardo poured water into our glasses.

Ricardo turned to leave as TJ thanked him with a nod and I thanked him softly.

Before he could get too far, TJ caught him. "Ricardo, please wait ten minutes before sending someone up to take our order."

I looked at TJ quizzically, wondering what he was up to.

His face was so much more beautiful than I ever could have remembered. I never noticed how strong featured he was. He was tan still, as though he still spends a lot of time outdoors. His eyes always stood out like emeralds gleaming in the sunlight. His hair had just a sprinkle of gray in it which I thought made him look so handsome and sophisticated. He kept it short now which made his neck look more prominent. I was reminded of all the times I had run my tongue up and down that neck. I writhed apprehensively in my seat at the thought. It literally pained every part of my body to look at him.

A smile brought me out of my mental striptease of Trevor McHale.

Shit, busted!

"So, Mr. McHale. The contracts?"

"Ah, yes, we will get to those momentarily. First, we have some catching up to do."

I straightened my back and rolled my eyes. "Look, I didn't come here for a high school reunion, Trevor."

"So, now we're back to first names, huh? Well, as I recall, in second grade I asked you not to call me Trevor."

"Trevor, TJ, Mr. McHale…look, what does it matter what I call you? This little get together you thought you'd force me into is strictly business. I'm here to pick up contracts and that's it. I'm not really in the mood to reminisce."

"That's hurts, Mrs. Barker-Jackson. Here I go out of my way to make you feel comfortable, have a nice meal, nice conversation, and you blow me off like I'm some stranger off the street."

"That's another thing, Mr. McHale," I said, enunciating mister cynically. I knew what he was trying to do. He was trying to get under my skin.

"Why do you feel it necessary to continually call me that? It's very annoying"

"Well, Mrs. Barker-Jackson, like I said, I want you to feel comfortable. I know that you're a married woman and I don't want to do something…inappropriate."

Oh, he was good, but I was better. This was going to come to an end right here and now.

"Mr. McHale, my personal life is not your concern, nor does it have anything to do with this lunch meeting. Now, are we going to discuss the contracts or not?"

He grabbed his water and took a sip. As he sat back in his chair, he placed his fingertips together, touched them to his mouth, and stared at me. I stared back for a moment before giving in first to look away. I wanted to explode. Both anger and desire filled me from the tips of my toes to the tiniest hair on my head and I had no clue which one would end up rearing its ugly head first. This was one battle that I was losing fast and there was no other way but down from here.

"Very well, if that's the way you want to play this game, then let's play. I have a proposal for you and I want you to hear me out before you answer. I have a feeling that this is one proposal you won't turn me down on." I clenched my teeth together, I knew he was inferring to our past history but I wasn't going to give him my emotions. "I have spoken with Loren and let's just say, he's given me his full support." His words peaked my curiosity, what could he possibly need my help with? Obviously, he had plenty of money, why wouldn't he just hire someone that would want to be near him?

I allowed him to continue. "I am moving the main headquarters of Mac-Gentry here to Richland." At this confession, I stopped breathing. It was true, he was moving back to town and I would have to see him and his beautiful family every day. I definitely needed to find a way out of this town now. I put one hand in my lap and started to play with the corner of my napkin. I set my eyes back on Trevor and realized he hadn't stopped speaking. "…legal work that needs to be dealt with before I can make this transition. Since the newest partner of Richards, Klein, and Daugherty, Mr. Loren Stevens, has been put on retainer by my company, I need you to accompany me back to Burlington to help me conclude my business. We have eight days to get all contracts drawn up, presented, signed, and filed. Then, we have to make sure that they are sorted away and packed, ready to ship down to the new headquarters here in Richland."

I had to sit there for a minute and replay this whole conversation back in my head. Did he just admit that he bribed my boss? And, that I had to go to Vermont…with him?

Just for shits and giggles, I had to know.

"How many contracts are we talking about here?"

"Two hundred and fifty," he replied immediately.

Laughing, I had to ask him to repeat himself.

"I'm sorry, I thought you said two hundred and fifty."

Smiling that oh so sexy smile, he replied, "I did."

My laughed turned into a smile as I politely grabbed the napkin out of my lap, set it on the table, and inched my chair back.

"Mr. McHale this, well we won't call it a lunch because I never got the chance to order, has been…enlightening. Now, since you feel that you have enough money to sit here and waste your time, that certainly does not give you the right to waste mine. Please, hand me the contracts."

As he stood, I watched him fidgeted with his tie. "Ms. Barker-Jack—"

Leaning over the table and getting as close to his face as I could, I rasped through clenched teeth, "Don't fucking call me that name again." I didn't smile. I didn't move my eyes from his. He knew I was completely serious.

He moved his eyes away from mine first. "Fine, Elle. Can we please sit down and discuss this rationally?"

I didn't hold back, there was nothing more to say. I tried to stay professional, but he was making this personal. "There's nothing rational to discuss. There's no way in hell that you are going to pull that off. Besides, I can't be away for eight days. That's ridiculous!"

We were both standing strategically, as if we were in a standoff. We were both waiting for the other to make a move. Our breathing was just about the same, rapid and shallow. The only difference was that the contemptuous smile had left his face.

Softly, the way he used to speak to me after we made love, he said, "Elleny, can we please sit down and discuss this? I have a plan and it will work, but I need your help."

At that voice, he could have told me to blow him and I would've consented. I slowly took my seat again. Resuming my position, I removed the napkin off the plate and placed it back in my lap.

"Let me finish my proposal."

155

Sitting back in my seat, I heard my phone chirp in my purse. I had a text message.

"Excuse me one minute, I need to check this."

Turning to the side to check for my purse, I reached down inside to pick it up. As I came back up, I saw TJ shudder. I didn't think anything of it as I looked down at my phone and noticed it was from Luc.

Evan no drive 2 day catch'n ride w Charlie.
B home 4 Har have fun luv u

I quickly replied

TY 4 txt, call me win nside w her
Wont b late luv u 2

I set the phone down beside me and smiled. "So sorry about that. Kids."

TJ stretched his eyebrows up and smiled while he took a sip of his water.

I sat back and allowed him to continue on. "I leave tomorrow evening to head back, so you'd be flying back on my company jet. I would set you up in a five star hotel which happens to be in walking distance of downtown Burlington, so you would be able to do your own thing in the evenings. A car will be sent for you every morning to drop you off at Mac-Gentry. You would not have to worry about anything. Financially, that is. Plus, I'm willing to pay you an ungodly amount of money that will be deposited into your personal account upon completion of the project."

"Leave tomorrow?" I stated like he needed it repeated back.

"Yes."

"How much are we talking about here?" I took a sip of water. I had to do something to bring me back to reality. I couldn't figure out if I was stuck in a dream or a nightmare. How was I going to leave for eight days? How would I explain this trip to Bear?

Where the hell was this waiter? I needed something stronger than water.

"I will triple your yearly salary."

I almost spit out my water. *Triple my salary? Holy shit!* Not only would that be enough for me to put away for the kid's college fund, but I could stash some of it away to maybe disappear. My foot began to bounce underneath the table.

I needed to play this smooth. "Mr. McHale…" I got raised eyebrows at that. "Trevor, do you know how much I make a year? You couldn't afford to triple my salary." Okay, maybe he could.

Looking down at his water glass, Trevor wouldn't make eye contact with me as he uttered, "I think if you turned this opportunity down, it would be the second biggest mistake of your life."

I had to get away from this man or my head was going to explode. I closed my eyes to calm myself.

"Look, go home, talk with Bear about it. I will be at Richland Manufacturing at six tomorrow evening. If you want to take advantage of what I am offering, meet me there. If you decide not to, well I don't know what else to offer to make you say yes."

It was quiet for several minutes. I looked at him, but his eyes never met mine. He twisted his water glass as though he was uncomfortable with this whole situation. I eventually broke the silence.

"Can we order? Not only am I starving, but I need a drink. Something really strong."

He laughed a bit and looked up at me. Trevor's eyes beamed and something that had been missing this entire time made an appearance. That spark I loved returned to his eyes.

"Sure."

Beside him, next to his menu, was a small box that looked like a garage door opener. He pushed the button. A moment later, a waitress came and took our order.

I ordered my drink, two of them. A wonderful full bodied white wine and a shot of tequila. I also got my food. An amazing vinegar braised chicken with leeks and peas. I ate as if I hadn't eaten in months.

"So, tell me about your children."

Oh shit, what did I say? Stay calm, Elle.

"Well, I have a set of twins, a boy and a girl. Their names are JoJo and Luc, and I have a fourteen year old, Harlee."

"That's wonderful, Elle. I'm so happy for you and Bear. Speaking of Bear, how is he?"

I really didn't want to talk about that shithead. But, if I didn't say something, he'd become suspicious. However, if I lied and told him that he was the perfect husband, he would know something was wrong and I didn't want him knowing shit. So, I chose to ignore the question.

"Enough about me. Tell me about you."

The waitress set a dessert coffee down in front of me and I thanked her before returning my focus back on TJ. I couldn't hear a word he was saying, something about a farm and some horses, I couldn't stop staring at his mouth.

That mouth had touched places on me that no other mouth had ever touched. I knew what that tongue could do when it wasn't being used for speaking. How it felt like satin against my inner thigh, how he could relax the muscles in it and use it to lap against me. How he could contract it to use as he tickled my inner core.

He continued talking, something about the pool in his backyard. I was still locked on his delicious body parts. His lips were tender yet wild. They could suck on any part of my body and I would orgasm. His lower lip was plump and was a perfect fit between mine. I envisioned reaching over and taking his top lip between my front two teeth—

"So, what do you think?"

Busted again.

"Sounds wonderful."

"Yeah it is, but it's time to move on," he said with a smile. Trevor could've been talking about selling my soul to the devil and I would have agreed because I had no idea what he was talking about.

"Speaking of moving on, I really have to go. Trevor, it's been a pleasure. Thank you for lunch and I will make sure to think about your little proposition. Now, if you wouldn't mind, I need those contracts."

"Wait, let's have another coffee, I could call—"

"I can't, but thank you." I cut him off. I couldn't sit here anymore. First off, I was sitting in a wet spot. I had to clear my mind because neither my brain nor my vagina could take any more visuals of this man naked, sprawled out, ready to fill my every need. "I have another appointment to attend, so I really must go."

"Cancel it."

I laughed inside. The nerve of him, who did he think he was telling me to cancel my appointment?

"I'm sorry, but that's not an option for me."

"Fine, I will call Loren and have him cancel it."

"Are you serious? Do you really think that you can just show up here and start ordering people around? Because I've got news for you, it's not happening."

I watched him pick up his phone and press a number.

"Hang up the phone, Trevor."

"No, this meeting is not finished and you're going to sit here until it's done since I'm paying. By the hour, I might add."

Glaring at him, I muttered, "Shit, fine. Whatever. Just hang up the fuckin' phone."

Watching the smile reappear on his lips, I knew I was in for it.

"Tsk, tsk, Ellie-bean. No need for language."

Feeling trapped and not in control of this situation, I leaned in close to enlighten him of a very important detail. "You're not making a very good case for yourself when it comes to me deciding on whether or not to go with you tomorrow evening. Now, I don't know who the hell you think

159

you are, because you sure don't look like my daddy or my husband, but if you want me to even pass a second glance at your proposition, I think that you need to tone down the alpha because it doesn't make my panties wet, it just pisses me off."

I leaned back in my chair and pushed my bangs out of my face. When I did this, the arm of my jacket rose up. I nonchalantly pulled it back down.

Looking at TJ, I noticed his brows were low like he was disturbed by something.

Rolling my eyes, I asked, "Oh Jesus, did I hurt your feelings?"

Acting like he couldn't think or talk, he stuttered, "Ah… no, it's fine."

"So, with that being said, let's continue."

"Let's talk about your husband."

Quickly, I responded, "Let's not."

I didn't want anything about that man to leave my mouth. I was doing what my daddy had taught me to do. If I didn't have anything nice to say, I wasn't going to say anything.

"Why? I'm curious to know how he's doing."

"Well, you can stay curious. I thought we had discussed this already, I don't talk about my personal life. Telling you that I had children was as far as that was going."

"Okay then, how's your daddy?"

"Dead. Next question."

An uncomfortable silence fell between us. I was afraid to lift my head, knowing what I would see in his eyes. I didn't need that from him.

"Christ, Elleny. I'm sorry. I didn't know"

"Me too, next question."

"What happened to you?"

Shocked, that question threw me off. I wasn't expecting that to be asked. I had two options. Option one: break down and tell him that my husband beats me and sleeps with every piece of trash around town. He works when he feels like it and what he does make, he puts in the string of some herpes infested whore down at the local strip club. And, oh yeah, the only reason I married him was so that I didn't have to tell you I was pregnant with your children. Which, by the way, he has threatened to kidnap if I ever left him. Or, option two—lie.

"Life happened to me, Trevor. Just like it happened to you, except it seemed to like you a whole hell of a lot better than it liked me. Now, if you'll excuse me, I'm going to go use the powder room." Standing up, I pushed in my chair and grabbed my purse. I went to turn around when I noticed that he was watching me.

I asked, "Do you need to call my boss and make sure it's okay for me to go to the powder room?"

He just continued staring at me with a smirk on his face and dammit if that wasn't cute, too. I turned back around and headed to the ladies room.

I made it to the ladies' room without falling into a million pieces. Leaning against the sink, I couldn't do anything other than stare at myself. I made a mental note to find out the maximum amount of money I could withdraw from my account would be. Then, I would pack up the kids and fly to some deserted island. Just Gilligan's Island it until we were old and gray.

I had to regroup and find my composure because I felt like I was one bird away from flying over the coo-coo's nest. I took some deep breaths. Inhale, exhale. Inhale, exhale. I went to grab my phone to call Rachel to cancel our shopping trip.

My phone...my phone. Where's my..."Fuck, shit, goddammit! Can't anything go my way?"

I left my phone on the table. I took three more calming breaths, washed my hands, and headed out of the powder room. As I was coming back to the table, TJ stood again. Like a gentleman, he waited to sit until I was comfortable where I was seated. There was my phone, sitting in the same spot I left it.

161

"Would you mind giving me one more moment? I need to postpone my next appointment."

He smiled an "I won that battle" smile as he granted me permission.

"Postpone away."

I sent a text to Rachel.

Rach still w dicklord

Won't let me leave, rain ck on shop'n?"

I immediately received a text back.

Ur gona fuk him, r'nt u?

Sure, scream my name bitch <3 u

She was so dead tonight, payback was a bitch. I couldn't deal with two members of the McHale family right now, so I pushed her off until later.

"Could I get another coffee please? Since it seems I'm going to be here a little longer."

"Of course."

He hit the button again and, swiftly, the waitress appeared like she materialized out of thin air.

"Can we get two more dessert coffees? Please, hold the ice cream. Thanks."

As she left, I regretted not asking for a double shot of Kahlua in mine.

"So…" he started as she left the room.

"So…" I repeated. This was going to be a fun conversation.

"Look, I'm sorry, Elle, if I seemed demanding. I just want to spend some time with you, I haven't seen you in eighteen years and I just want to catch up."

Hearing the sincerity in his voice, I relaxed a little. I didn't want to talk about my life and when he told me about his, all I had was personal mini orgasms, so I felt it was good to talk about Lilly and Rachel.

"You weren't being demanding," I assured him with a smile on my face. "It was more like bullying," I revealed as I laughed.

He laughed a bold, hearty laugh and it made my heart leap with joy. With hearing the emphatic gruff that originated from the bottom of his belly and escalated to a happiness that I haven't heard or seen in seventeen years, I felt intact and complete again. My laugh died down to a smile but my eyes didn't leave his face. He looked like he became alive when he laughed like that.

The waitress returned with our coffees and we thanked her. As I took a sip of my coffee, Trevor began speaking.

"So, tell me about the ink?"

I looked at the floor and grabbed my purse. I pulled out my pen and laid it in front of him. He looked at the pen and then looked back at me. I looked at him and looked back at the pen.

"What the hell is that?"

"A pen." He asked for a pen, maybe he had had one too many dessert coffees.

"You asked for a pen."

"No, I didn't."

"Yes, you did. You said, 'where's an ink pen?' I handed you an ink pen."

He chuckled loud. "No I didn't. I asked you to tell me about the ink."

Still not understanding, I looked at him like he had lost his mind.

"What the hell are you…?"

It hit me like I had run into a sliding glass door. As if this day couldn't have gotten any worse.

I immediately ripped the ponytail out of my hair and threw it in my purse. I'd had enough of this reunion.

"I have to go."

I instantly stood up and threw my phone in my purse as I ran for the door. I didn't give a shit about papers, tips, nothing. I just had to get out of there.

TJ was running after me, attempting to stop me. But, I didn't, wouldn't. I needed to keep running. I couldn't believe I had been so stupid as to put my hair up for him to see it.

It being a tattoo, an anchor. A tattoo that was my penance to look at every day and remind myself that I had that one regret that I'd never get over until the day I died. No one knew about it. Not my best friends, not my kids, not even my husband. This was mine and mine alone.

I got to my car and beeped the locks. My mind was nothing but a jumbled mess, and my heart…I couldn't even explain what I felt. I don't know how, but I started the car and buckled my seatbelt before I drove away from the hotel.

Crying my eyes out.

Chapter 9

September 1992

Coming back from Tennessee was enjoyable, we ended up taking our time. We actually woke up early and stopped by an all you can eat buffet. I thought I was in heaven until I actually ate and could only finish half my plate. I didn't take a chance of going back for seconds. I could still remember the after effects of morning sickness, no thank you. After breakfast, we took the scenic route. We saw a beautiful waterfall and decided to stop.

The sight was breathtaking. A beautiful massive waterway rushed by us so fast it was difficult to focus in on the rocky bottom. As the stream got closer to the mountainous drop-off, the watercourse turned to the sound of thrashing waves that were so loud we could barely hear each other talking. We both watched as it overflowed down the side of the mountain in a roaring thunder. At the bottom, peace silenced the stream as it made its way to a crystal blue lagoon that just begged to be jumped into. The surroundings were so beautiful, I didn't pay attention when Bear grabbed my hand.

"I'm not good at the sweet shit, Ellie, but since I didn't get you a weddin' ring, I thought this would do." He had a ring. He had gone back to that little shop that we stopped in front of and bought me that ring. It was so beautiful, I was speechless. "Bear, it's absolutely gorgeous. Thank you. You did really good at the sweet shit, hon." I gave him a little laugh and leaned in for a chaste kiss.

We got back in the car and continued toward home. We talked and laughed the whole way there. Bear had a great personality. He could make me laugh at the drop of a hat, always could. Both Bubba and Bear were not easy to get to know, they weren't the type to give a stranger the shirts off their backs. But, if you knew them and they thought you were good people, they would be the first ones there if you ever needed something. Plus, his accent always made everything he said sound so funny even when he didn't mean it to be.

We ended up stopping at an outlet mall so I could stretch while looking around. I even stopped in a baby store and looked at all the outfits and pictured specific outfits on what my mind detailed as my baby.

Then my mind wandered to TJ. I began to feel like my heart was being held down by tons of bricks. I suddenly felt guilty that I was keeping this big of a secret from him, especially because it wasn't mine to keep. I knew he deserved to know about the baby, but I also knew he wouldn't make the best decision for himself. This baby had a momma and a daddy now and I was fine with that. TJ had his life to live in his way. At least, that's what I kept telling myself. I made the decision and he never had to live with the guilt of turning his back on us.

We both got back into the car without a word being spoken. We weren't more than two hours away from home so I decided to take a nap. I felt Bear gently shake me. When I raised my head, I noticed that we had entered my dad's subdivision.

"Ellie, we're here." I slowly stretched as best as I could still being cramped in the front seat of my car. It was dusk out. The day had flown by. When we turned into the long driveway of my childhood home, my heart froze. TJ's truck was in the driveway.

"Oh, shit," I muttered.

Immediately, Bear instructed for me to wait in the car. As he put the car in park, he demanded that I not open the door.

I snickered and rolled my eyes. He was being ridiculous. "Bear, he's not gonna hurt me, I think I owe him a chat, at the very least. I'll tell him to go home and not to come back."

This time when he spoke, his voice was low and scary. I stepped back, surprised by his tone. "Didn't ask you that. I asked if you understood what I said."

"Sweetie, you're making a big deal outta nothing."

He repeated the words again.

I agreed and looked anxiously around as we pulled up next to TJ's truck. I was kind of hoping that he was just about to leave. No such luck. I didn't see him anywhere. Bear quickly came around to my door, glancing at the surroundings before opening my door. We both began to relax just as both front doors flew open.

"What the fuck, Elle!" TJ yelled as he stalked out of the door. Daddy and Mona rushed after him.

"What the fuck is this...?" He was waving a piece of paper around in the air. It was the letter I wrote him. "I have been calling you for days. Your phone has been going straight to voicemail and I've left you hundreds of messages."

TJ's appearance was shocking, he looked like shit. He was thinner and looked really pale. His eyes were red rimmed like he had been crying for days.

Oh, this was not good.

"TJ...I ah, I turned my...p...phone...off." It seemed like it had taken me twenty minutes to get that statement out, but I was in shock. I wanted to go up to him and touch his face, comfort him. I wanted to make him better.

Bear grabbed my hand and squeezed tightly, tearing me from my thoughts. I didn't care, I couldn't take my eyes off TJ. He was in so much pain and it killed me to see him this way. I was just about to tell Bear never mind, that I couldn't go through with this, when I heard his stern voice.

"Elleny, go in the house. Don't say a word to him, just walk right past him."

Attempting to calm this situation down before it got totally out of hand, I turned and smiled nervously at Bear.

"I truly don't think that's necessary."

Bear squeezed my hand again and I winced. "Go!" he yelled, and I jumped back in fright.

As I began walking toward TJ, he stopped. My eyes were glued to his huge eyes, his eyebrows touching his hairline. He was so confused. I walked past TJ and didn't say a word, but he did.

"Babe?"

"Don't talk to my wife!" Bear shouted.

TJ froze where he was. As did I.

I closed my eyes and bowed my head at the announcement Bear decided to make public. My plan to diffuse this whole clusterfuck was to get Bear in the house so I could speak with TJ. I wanted to tell him to go back to school, to go on with his life, in my own words, on my own terms.

"Bear…"

I heard TJ cackle. "You're fucking joking, right?"

This was not the way I had this planned out. He wasn't supposed to ask questions, I was supposed to be doing all the talking and he was supposed to do exactly as I said and that was the end. We both would go on our merry way. I couldn't take hearing the sorrow and dejection in his voice anymore. It was killing me. I gently breathed, "Go home, Trevor."

"You married him?"

Turning his head back and forth between me and Bear, his hand matching the rhythm of his head, he said, "What the fuck am I missing here? I'm so lost I don't know which way to turn."

Louder, Bear demanded, "You heard her TJ, go home!"

TJ started walking toward Bear. He drew his eyebrows in and silently reminded Bear of something I'm sure he didn't forget. "You…you were my best friend, my brother, and you'd do this to me?"

"Dude, you ain't the big bad football star anymore, are you?" Holding his hands out, Bear began a dialogue that had my mouth dropped to the ground. A speech he must've had planned for a very, very long time. Either that, or he had some hostile emotions bottled up towards TJ and he was letting them all out at once. "You lost this one, my brother!" He repeated TJ's words in a cynical snarl that brought goose bumps to my skin. "How does it feel to be the fucking loser? Mr. My Shit Don't Stink! You just thought you had it all, but in the long run, I ended up having everything. *Your* everything! In high school, you always acted like heartbreak and misery couldn't touch you. Well, how's that workin' out for ya there, buddy? I hope you fucking choke on it!"

I turned to Bear and looked at him. I couldn't say anything, nothing would come out. He rolled his eyes at me as he yelled once more, "Ellie, I told you to get the fuck in the house!"

I couldn't take anymore, I broke down. This man that was being broken down and humiliated right in front of me was the man that I fell in love with in second grade. I was pregnant with his child, everything I was doing was because I loved him whole heartily. So why did this feel like someone was literally taking a knife and stabbing me in the heart? The pain that I was feeling would haunt me for the rest of my days. I would never forget the way his face looked right now. The look of pure suffering and agony. He was a fish out of water, gasping for air that he would never breathe in because Bear and I had sucked every last drop from him.

I told myself that I was doing this because I loved him, but all I had done was break his heart. Jesus, this was torture. Not only for me, but for him. His body language was begging

169

me with every part of him, but I couldn't say yes because he would screw his life up.

Why couldn't he understand? I was beginning to get pissed off. I was furious that he didn't understand that this was for his own good. But, I was really infuriated at myself. He didn't know why this was happening, didn't know that I was pregnant.

He saw the tears streaming down my face for the pain I had caused him, yet he came toward me to wrap me in his arms. And, I wanted him to. I wanted to be engulfed in all that was Trevor. His smell, the feel of his skin, the taste of his sweat and tears. I had resigned myself. I was done with this, we would find a way to work it out. The baby, his schooling, my schedule, we could work it out. I began walking toward him, holding my arms out to him when Bear's shouting got louder by the second as he charged at TJ.

"Don't you fucking touch her, cocksucker!"

Bear tackled TJ. It all happened so fast. When I saw one of Bear's fist hit him square in the jaw, I expected TJ to fight back. He did nothing. He didn't even protect himself.

I started screaming at the top of my lungs. Daddy and Mona came dashing toward me.

"Get her in the house!" Bear yelled as he sat on top of TJ's chest, striking TJ in the face, over and over.

Wriggling and straining to get out of their grasps, I was screaming, "No! Get your hands off of me! Let me go! I have to help him!"

Daddy demanded that I hurry inside so that he could go and get Bear off of TJ, but all I could hear was Bear yelling at TJ. And TJ laid there, taking every punch to the face. He was bleeding from his mouth, nose, and the corner of his right eye.

"Go ahead, finish me off," I heard TJ mutter. "Fucking kill me, Bear! I ain't got nothing to live for now. Come on, do it, you asshole! Finish this! You've taken the only thing in life that matters to me, I'm fucking nothing!"

I was screaming, pleading to Bear for him to stop. I finally broke away from Mona and Daddy and ran over to where Bear was straddling TJ on the ground. I found strength that I didn't know I had and used it to push Bear off of him.

I fell to the gravel driveway, scraping my knees all to hell as I cradled TJ in my arms as tight as I could. His face was against my shoulder and I cried hysterically. He was breathing, but unconscious. I brought his head up from my shirt to look at him as I wiped his face, attempting to get the blood off. But, more gushed out in its place. I was covered in his blood.

I heard Bear mumbling something about the stupid motherfucker deserving everything he got, but I really wasn't paying attention to him.

Daddy and Mona made their way over to me and pleaded for me to let go so that they could get him some help, but my grip on him wouldn't falter. I couldn't let go of him. I wiped his face with my hands. Blood was dripping from me. I repeated, over and over, "I can't do this, don't make me do this. I've changed my mind. I can't do this, don't make me do this."

They attempted to pull me away, but my arms were locked around his neck. Still unconscious, I had made the decision that I was never letting him go. As they were pulling, I was screaming at the top of my lungs.

"I'm sorry, Trevor. I'm so sorry, baby. I don't deserve you, you're too good for me. You deserve so much more than me. Don't come back here, just go home!" I couldn't take my eyes off of him. If I let him go, I wouldn't have a heart anymore. I wouldn't be able to live. I would only be a hollow shell.

Finally, they unlocked my hands. Mona dragged me into the house while my dad took TJ to his car and drove him to his office. This was the first time since I had known Mona that I've seen her look like she actually cared about something or someone. She helped me walk to the couch as she sat down with my head in her lap.

171

She began brushing the hair out of my face, a continuous motion that was supposed to be soothing, but I felt nothing. I was in shock. I wasn't talking, screaming, my tears had dried up, and I was just staring. Staring at nothing. I was barely breathing. If I could have stopped, I would have. I was not a person anymore. I didn't have feelings anymore, my heart had totally shattered into millions of miniscule pieces that just blew away like dust particles in the wind. There was nothing left. I didn't care about me, I didn't care about Bear, my parents, this baby...nothing.

"There, there, baby. That's it, calm down. Momma's got you." That was all I heard for hours, like a bad song track set to repeat. Then, it stopped. I thought maybe Mona had fallen asleep. I wasn't sure of the time but I knew it had to be late. I was still looking straight ahead at the television that was showing some infomercial.

I was blank. I had no thoughts roaming through my head. I didn't feel like I needed to use the bathroom or eat or drink. I could see a bright light coming from the opposite side of the room where the lamp was turned on, so that must've meant that it was getting ready to be daytime.

Days began to run into each other and everything just kept repeating over and over. During the nights, Daddy would come. I would see him carrying in full IV bags and leaving with empty ones. He would do his little snapping and hand movement tests in front of my face. Yet, nothing.

Then, it happened. I could hear my daddy speaking to Mona. The worry and anxiety in his voice was terrifying to me. He sounded weak and his voice sounded shaky. Knowing him, he probably hadn't been sleeping or eating. "I don't give a shit, I'm calling Trevor and putting the phone up to her ear. Maybe his voice will bring her out of this. I have tried everything else I can think of."

I didn't know where I was and why I felt so stiff. My body didn't want to move. I heard mumbling again and I saw my dad sit down beside me.

I wanted to tell him that I was okay, but all that would come out was a grunt.

I could see my dad's reaction to my noise as he stood up and came to the edge of my bed. "Shit, she's awake. Mona!" He acted as if he didn't know what to do first, check my vitals or hug me.

"Elle…Elleny. It's Daddy. Can you hear me?"

I desperately wanted to say yes, I wanted to put him at ease, but all that would come out was another grunt.

I was officially getting scared and starting to panic. Why couldn't I say what I wanted to say?

"Elleny, can you move your head to look at me?" I winced as I slowly moved my stiff neck to look at my dad. It took all the energy I had to turn to the side. I had a feeling I was in deep shit. "Honey, you've had some emotional trauma. You haven't moved in almost a week and a half. You're speech will come back, baby. Just give it time. I know you're scared, but you're fine. The baby is fine." I saw him smile and it was a gorgeous smile. I knew he was relaxing. "You've had fluids and I've checked the heartbeat of the baby and it's strong, which is really good. You need to just take it easy and everything will be okay."

I slowly and stiffly nodded before closing my eyes.

I fell asleep.

I was standing in a beautiful meadow. The grass came up to my knees and there were daises growing as far as the eye could see. In the far off distance, I could see hills, picturesque rises that had grown almost as tall as mountains.

At the bottom of the slope, I could see someone walking…no, running.

I didn't know what to do. I loved where I was, it was so delightful. I just wanted to sit down and let the daisies cover my body. I wanted to feel them embrace me. I picked one up and put it to my nose. The odor surrounded me. When I looked down, another one had already grown in its place.

I looked back at the person coming toward me. They weren't close enough for me to recognize, but they were waving their hand at me. I was hesitant.

The flowers began to grow thicker and the feeling of serenity became stronger. I now yearned for it. Suddenly, I heard a voice. "I'm here with you. Come. Come now. Run to me as fast as you can. Don't lay down, baby!" At hearing that voice, I instantly ran. It was TJ.

I couldn't get to him fast enough. I didn't want to waste another second.

I was speeding toward him. The feeling of peace and serenity were now fleeing. Deep down, I was frantic. I kept hearing his voice tell me that I was almost to him. The promise of forever and always were the words that he spoke to me, which made me refuse to stop. I felt breathless, but I didn't care. I was running to TJ.

"That's it, my love. Come to me." I was running as fast as I could, but he kept getting further and further away.

"Trevor!" I yelled.

"Yes, babe, come to me. I'm right here."

Running and running, I couldn't reach him. I was sweating and crying. My breathing was so rapid I felt like my lungs were going to burst.

That's when I woke up.

I was in the back of an ambulance, soaked in sweat. I heard a voice I didn't recognize. I looked up to see a smiling face looking down at me. He was breathing like he had just run a marathon. He was holding a set of electrical paddles in his hands. Letting out a refreshing breath, he finally spoke, "Good of you to join the living again, Mrs. Jackson."

Chapter 10

Present Day

During my drive to Rachel's, all I could think about was this offer. I really wasn't sure how I felt about it. I didn't want to put myself in a precarious situation because I didn't trust myself and Rachel knew that. She proved that with her text. Yes, I would totally be with him. This was why the situation at hand had to be handled with extreme caution. Just because I wanted to, didn't mean I would allow it to happen.

As I drove, I heard soft bells playing. I looked out my window to see if I was near a church, maybe even a train track. There was nothing.

"Where the hell is that noise coming from?" I asked myself.

The sound became a whisper, so I continued driving.

Think, Elle. Triple your salary. That's a good thing. The kids could stay with Rachel, she wouldn't mind. Bear wouldn't have an issue with the kids gone, he'd be able to stay out with his weekly whore. Shit, speaking of whores.

I called my doctor and made the appointment to come in. Then, I called Rachel to tell her I was coming.

"Well, did you scream my name?" she asked upon greeting. I snickered.

"Girl, you are not going to believe what I yelled and how many times I yelled it. I will tell you all about it when I get there. I'm on my way but I have to stop by the doctor's for some blood to be taken. I'm not taking any chances of getting

175

something from that douche. Give me ten. What time will Lilly be there?"

"You're a bitch! I can't believe you'd make me wait! She said she'd be here in about thirty."

"Sounds good. By the way, I will explain everything when I get there, but it looks like I'm going to have to go out of town for about two weeks. Do you think you can keep the kids? You'd have to take them to school and do the momma thing. You think you can handle that?"

I knew Rachel didn't do the mommy thing naturally. I knew that my kids would be on their own, but I also knew she had Kevin and a state of the art alarm system. It would be a cold day in hell before Bear got his hands on my kids in Rachel's care. I didn't doubt Lilly at all, but Curtis was now a detective with the sheriff's office and they had Austin. My three kids would just be in the way and I really didn't want Curt in on what was going on.

"Fuck that! I'll give Lucas my Mustang and he can do the big brother thing. I'll make sure they eat."

Laughing, I admitted that she spoiled her nieces and nephew.

I hung up with her as I pulled up at the doctor's office. Grabbing my purse, I began to head on in. Suddenly, I heard the bells again. The noise was coming from my purse. I stopped in front of my truck and dug for my phone.

It was playing, "Alone" by Heart?
How in the hell...Trevor!

I didn't recognize the number but when I saw the caller ID, my blood started to boil.

Your Destiny. *Really, Trevor?*

Not wanting to give him any ammunition, I answered politely.

"This is Elleny."

I heard silence for a second then my ears picked up on that deep throaty voice that sent my body in a whirl of emotions. I had a feeling this wasn't a courtesy call. That voice sounded like it meant business.

"What the fuck is wrong with you?"

Not in the mood to deal with him, I needed to nip this in the bud thirty seconds ago.

"Mr. McHale, I'm sorry, but this is not a good time."

"I have been calling and calling you." TJ's voice was dark and deep. "Do you know how fucking worried I've been?"

Whoa! Hold the phone. Did he just say that he had been worried? I pictured him pacing the marble floor in front of his huge king size bed made of pure gold.

I rolled my eyes, this was ending right now.

"I'm sorry, Mr. McHale, but I believe I told you I had another appointment on my schedule for this afternoon."

"Cut the bullshit, Elle!"

Well, that caught me a little off guard. I was expecting something more along the lines of smartass. Dickhead; no, didn't see that one coming.

"I'm sorry, Mr. McHale, but I don't know what you're talking about."

He was losing his temper. I could tell by the puffs of air blowing into the receiver. The whispering voice that he replied to in almost brought me to my knees. Fear engulfed me.

"You know exactly what I'm talking about. How dare you run out on me like that! It was totally uncalled for. You were distraught when you left, that concerned me. Then, you screw with me by not answering your phone? I'm not a happy person here, Mrs. Barker-Jackson."

What was he not understanding about this alpha-male bullshit? Throwing my purse on the hood of my truck, I leaned up against the side of the driver's side door, I figured this conversation wasn't going to be as short as I wanted.

"I apologize, Mr. McHale...Trevor, I meant no disrespect by leaving so suddenly. As you can see, I am perfectly fine since I answered my phone. And, as for you not

177

being happy, that really sounds like more of a personal problem. Now, if you will excuse my rudeness, I have to go have some blood drawn. I will speak with you later. Oh, by the way, since you decided to be a dick concerning the contracts, I will expect them couriered over by late morning tomorrow. Please make sure they are signed, and you're picking up the bill for the courier service."

I didn't know if he heard the ending because, again, I was expecting some smartass remark but that didn't leave his mouth. What left his mouth made me roll my eyes. He couldn't get it through his thick skull that I was not his business anymore.

"Blood work…you're having blood taken? What for? Are you sick?"

"Ah, Mr. McHale, I believe that would be a personal question. Have a wonderful evening."

Click

High-five, Elle! Talk about leaving him hanging. That makes up for the cell phone ringtone bullshit.

I grabbed my purse, looked at my phone, shut the ringer off, then dropped it back into my purse. I sauntered into the doctor's office feeling pretty good, since I put Trevor McHale right in his place.

"Shut the front door!" Lilly yelled when I told her the part of the story where he offered me triple my salary. Since she had Austin, she's tried not to swear around him. So, she'd picked up little sayings that her three year old could repeat.

We kind of learned the hard way to not let Rachel watch Austin for long periods of time. Since Rachel's favorite word had always been "fuck", he would come home with a colorful vocabulary. My favorite instance was when he was running through Richland public library, slashing his toy sword at everyone shouting, "Twat," at the top of his lungs. Or the time we were in the grocery store when he waved and greeted everyone we passed with, "Hello, pwick!"

That was when Curt made Lilly promise that Austin wouldn't be left with Rachel unattended for more than thirty minutes.

"Are you going to do it?" Lilly asked

I smiled. "I think I am. But I'm doing it for the money."

Both Rachel and Lilly looked at each other and burst out laughing. "Yeah, sure, you're doing it for the money. You're gonna fuck him," Rachel said with an exhale of her cigarette.

"Really, Rach? I am not going to fuck TJ. Besides, I thought you didn't like talking about your cousin's sex life."

I continued recanting this afternoon's events from my unforgettable lunch with TJ. I had to break down and tell them about the tattoo and what it meant. Lilly cried as Rachel rolled her eyes.

I told them how I acted a fool and ran out on the luncheon. I was embarrassed now that I looked back on it. It was stupid of me to act like a child over a tattoo that only meant something to me. I saw how he smiled when I got up quickly. He must've thought I was stupid for permanently etching a symbol onto my body that meant something seventeen years ago to two children. I didn't know how I was going to show my face around him again.

I brought Rachel up to speed on the kids, their favorite foods, and schedules. I told her that she needed to stick to the schedule because it was hard for them to get back into the normal routine once they returned home. She told me, "Fuck you". Apparently, they were her kids while at her house and she planned on feeding them junk food, and letting them do what they wanted. She bragged about how there would be football and lots of shopping. Lilly and I giggled. They weren't going to want to come home.

179

After finishing two bottles of wine, we wrapped up the evening. I needed to get home before Bear did, I didn't want him showing up drunk and running his mouth to the twins again. I was so burnt out on trying to maintain control, the stress was horrendous. Make sure Bear doesn't beat the shit out of me, make sure he doesn't start doing it to the kids. I knew he hated my children, even his own. When he talked to me about the kids, he wouldn't call them by name. They were those "bastard children". Even Harlee who was his biological child.

Bear's jealousy over TJ consumed him. I never knew why. Maybe it was over something in high school, maybe it was because TJ was better looking, or maybe it was Bear knew he would never hold my heart. I didn't see that as a reason though, Bear never gave a shit about me. But, something about Trevor ate Bear up with jealousy. It was a cancer that had consumed every part of him.

Bear always did pay better attention to the soles of his shoes than me. I think it was the money. Maybe he thought he would eventually be able to touch what was left of my inheritance. Before my dad died, he went to the bank and talked to Mr. Young. He made sure that his new life insurance policy would be added to what was left of my mother's, but he also added stipulations to the trust account. Bear would never see a dime of that money. He ended up putting it in my and the twin's names. Since he didn't live long enough to see Harlee grow and since Bear was her father, Daddy didn't want to take a chance. I didn't blame him.

I was walking out the door when I told Rachel that I would drop the kids off at her house around four-thirty before heading to the airport. I gave her a hug and a kiss and thanked her for her doing this.

I got in my car and texted Luc that I was on my way home and he responded immediately with a "K". I started my drive, making a mental note on everything that needed to be done by tomorrow evening. I figured it wasn't late, so I called my boss and he answered on the second ring.

"Hi, Elle." Loren sounded like he was either dozing off or he was getting ready to.

"I'm sorry. Did I wake you?" I kind of wished I hadn't called now.

"No, did the meeting go well?"

I wanted to hesitate, but I answered honestly. "Yes and no."

"Oh...."

"The contracts will be couriered over by noon tomorrow, I know you know what's going on and I have decided to go."

"Really?"

"Well, did I really have a choice, Loren? I was told that you were required to follow along. Besides, he told me that if I didn't go, your partnership would be in jeopardy and I'm not taking that chance. You've worked too hard for someone like Trevor McHale to walk in and take it from you. It's no big deal, it's just eight days."

Now, I was wondering if I was trying to comfort him or myself.

"Elle…"

"Loren, it's fine. Really. Rachel's gonna watch the kids and I'm gonna get a room to myself."

It got quiet for a moment.

"Call me if you have any questions. You are the best at what you do, Elle. I have no doubt that you will get everything he needs done and do it better than any of his employees."

I agreed to call him if I needed him before I hung up. Pulling into my neighborhood, I prayed Bear wasn't home. My prayers came true. I turned the corner and didn't see his truck, so I pushed the garage door opener and drove in.

I went into the house, it was so quiet and all of the lights were out. I liked seeing my house like this, it looked like a normal family lived here. I went to the fridge and saw that the kids left a note on top of the pizza box telling me that they loved me. I grabbed a piece and took a bite as I grabbed a piece of paper to write Bear a note.

Bear-

I have to go out of town on business tomorrow evening. I leave at six. The kids won't be here so you will have the house to yourself. If you don't want to stay here, then stay wherever. I will be gone for eight days.

-Ellie

I left it on the kitchen counter so he'd see it when he walked in. If he wasn't too drunk, that is. I went ahead and headed to bed. As I went upstairs, I stopped by Luc's room and told the kids that I was going out of town and they would be staying with Rachel. The girls squealed and jumped up and down on Luc's bed for a minute while I smiled. Luc didn't smile at all. I asked the girls to get to their rooms as I kissed them all goodnight and headed for my room to jump in the shower.

The shower felt great. I was exhausted and ready to hit the hay. It didn't take long for me to fall asleep.

Bear's fist was full of my hair. My fists started flying around immediately. I thought someone had broken in and was attempting to hurt me. It didn't take me long to realize it was just my husband. All I could do was pray the bruises weren't going to be too bad.

"So, queen bitch is going out of town on business, huh?" I didn't answer. He had his face right up beside mine and I could feel the spray of spit as he spoke. I had to close my eyes. I tried to turn my head to the side, away from him, but he wouldn't let me.

"On business, huh? What, some dick gonna pound that pussy? Is that what kinda business you're gonna be taking care of?"

I didn't say a word, it didn't matter either way. He wasn't going to believe me. So, I just shook my head.

He let go of my hair and pushed me back down to the pillow, his hand covering my face as he straddled my chest.

He leaned back for a minute, his hand reaching for his pants. I heard his zipper being ripped open.

"Open your mouth."

I shook my head again frantically. He was going to have to cut a whole in my cheek if he wanted to stick that nasty dick in my mouth.

"I told you to open your mouth," he slurred at me. I folded my lips into my mouth, showing him that my mouth was sealed tight. He balled his hand up into a fist and punched me as hard as he could in my ribcage. His hand grabbed the back of my head again and pushed my head up toward the ceiling so that my mouth would automatically open. I fought him. I was yelling through my nose, refusing to open my mouth for him.

"I'm gonna put my cock in your mouth, bitch. If you even think about biting me…" He reached next to the bed for a bottle of whiskey I didn't even know was there. He tilted it up and the liquid poured into his mouth. I could see his throat gulping it down in large amounts. He lowered the bottle and didn't even bother wiping the access off of his mouth before he leaned back down to my face. "I'll kill ya. Then, I'll take you out to the hog farm and let the hogs finish you off. You know they'll eat anything. Now, open your fucking mouth!"

He punched me again and pulled on my hair, making my mouth fall open. As soon as he saw his chance, he crammed his length down my throat. He reared up, pushing keeping, his scrotum falling against my chin. I was gagging and crying at the same time. My feet were kicking, trying to get him off of me, but I wasn't doing anything but wearing myself out. He was too high up on my chest.

Tracy Lee

"You taste that, cunt? That there's the taste of real love!"

He pulled back for a moment, but never left my mouth. The odor hit my senses before the taste did, the smell was almost unbearable. Just as I was about to gag, he thrust forward, going in again. I watched his hand wrap around my neck as if that was going to help. I could taste some nasty whore's remnants on his unwashed penis. I began to vomit as he crammed himself back down my throat, over and over again. The foul, musty fluid that covered his shaft was thick and encrusted in his pubic hair along with the stench of urine and feces.

"That's it, whore, clean that shit off my dick. How does it taste licking a real woman's pussy juice off my cock? You like it?"

He began to thrust faster, harder, hitting the back of my throat. "That's it, you aren't half the woman she is. You deserve to be eating her shit. You can't even suck my cock worth a shit!"

I just laid there. I stopped kicking, my hands fell to my side, and the only sound I could hear was myself gagging. The tears from my eyes slid down my cheeks until they combined with the vomit that dribbled out from the sides of my mouth onto my nightgown and the front of my chest.

He finally pulled out, his cum spurting all over my face. He traced my forehead and nose, making sure that it covered every inch of skin. He climbed off of me as I turned to fall to the floor. I was coughing and vomiting beside my bed, needing to get that taste out of my mouth. He staggered to the bathroom and turned on the light. I was pissed and defeated. I could barely talk from the beating my throat had just taken, but I croaked out, "Why the fuck do you stay if you don't want to be here?"

I could hear him laughing. "Bitch, you think I'm gonna leave someone whose got money in the bank? For the shit I've put up with, I'm gonna get what's owed to me."

184

I got up on my knees.

"How much?"

He turned from the doorway and stood where I could still see his face. "This arrangement was your idea, not mine. I didn't ask for you to stay, you could've left to be with whoever the fuck you wanted. So, how much would it take for you to get the fuck out and leave me and my children alone?"

"All of it."

I couldn't believe what hit my ears. He couldn't be serious. He had to have lost his mind. He was not going to take all the money my momma and daddy left me. I had never even touched it. That was for my children. Who the fuck did he think he was? I didn't say a word, I just turned back toward the bed and slowly got up. We both knew this conversation was over.

I heard him get in the shower so I went to the sink and brushed my teeth and used mouth wash—twice. I washed my face and chest, took my nightgown off, and put on a t-shirt. I looked at the clock. It was four twenty-two in the morning. I couldn't go back to sleep, so I started a load of laundry. I kept thinking back to that conversation. I was stuck with him. I had a decision to make. A life changing decision—another one. I came to the conclusion that I wasn't very good at deciphering between the right and wrong answers, so I went to the couch and cried. I didn't know what to do, I had nowhere to even look for the right answer.

That's when I saw my purse sitting on the coffee table in front of me. Laying on top was my cell phone that always seemed to be resting at the very bottom of the junk. I grabbed my phone and pushed the button to reveal my contacts. Using my finger, I scrolled down through all my friends who had no idea what was really going on between me and my husband. They knew he was a drunk mess, but they didn't know the nightmares that became a part of my life. I looked down through my contacts and found what I was looking for, what I had been looking for all along.

Your destiny was staring me right in the face. It didn't take much for me to tap out that message. I needed someone to take me away. I wanted a hero so bad I could taste it and I would be spending two weeks with him.

Meet u @ RL mfg 6pm

Placing my phone down, I continued to cry, thinking about what had happened to my life. I didn't deserve this, I sure as hell didn't ask for this. I couldn't think anymore, I didn't want to think anymore. I just wanted to cry until it was time to get the kids up. Then, the crying would stop, breakfast would be cooked, and kids would be taken to school. That was exactly what happened.

I got the kids off to school then came home to pack everyone up. I packed a little bit of everything for Harlee. She was so picky, I never knew what she would be in the mood for. Lucas and JoJo were so much easier, they basically laid everything out for me. All I had to do was put it in their suitcases with the extras I thought they would need.

Last was mine, I made sure that I packed professional, yet cool and added some lounging items for around the hotel room. I also packed something elegant, just in case I wanted to grab a drink in the hotel lounge or go have a bite to eat in a nice restaurant. TJ said it was a five star hotel so it wasn't like I could walk in wearing jeans and a tank top. I packed my toiletry items and what seemed like five hundred pairs of shoes. Women could never pack enough shoes.

I put everything downstairs by the door leading out to the garage. I checked the clock. Unbelievably it was almost twelve-thirty. I called the office and sure enough, the contracts were delivered at nine that morning. I smiled a small smile knowing that I was woman and he heard me roar.

While I had my phone, I just checked to see if anyone had texted me. No texts, but I had a voicemail. I pushed the code and put the phone up to my ear.

I heard the voice; rough, domineering, extremely deep with a hint of a southern accent that he tried so desperately to hide. His voice incessantly drove me senseless with hunger—for him. I couldn't help but smile and the grin went from ear to ear. The sound of his voice was ironic to me—it provided me strength, yet left me powerless. He was my paradise but I felt like I was in hell because I couldn't physically have him.

"Mrs. Barker-Jackson, Trevor McHale here, I received your message this morning, don't you ever sleep?" I could hear the laughter in his voice. *"I am pleased that you have changed your mind about this arrangement. I look forward to working with you. I will see you at six sharp. Please, Mrs. Barker-Jackson, do not be late. I'm a stickler for punctuality. Have a good day and if you have any questions, please feel free to give me a call back."*

It took everything in me not to call him back. I wanted to speak with him so badly. I wanted to tell him about all that had happened. I needed to give all of this to someone and just get the pressure off my chest. I wanted someone to tell me it was going to be alright, that I wouldn't have to deal with bullshit like that again. Instead, I pushed the number seven and saved his message. If I wanted to hear his voice, I could listen to this message over again.

I made some cookies for the kids and put them in a plastic container and began to pack the back of my truck. I was going to pick up the kids and go straight to Rachel's. I hadn't spoken a word today, in hopes that the back of my throat would heal quickly. I didn't want to answer any questions that I knew were bound to fly once they heard my voice.

I put the cookies in the passenger seat and headed out. I went over my mental list three times while on the way to the kid's schools. I didn't want to forget anything. So far, nothing came to mind. I got the kids and headed for Rachel's.

Reaching Rachel's house, the kids were overjoyed. As soon as we came to a stop, all three doors opened and the kids went running to the front door screaming that the first stop was to the pool. I had no worries they would be a problem.

Kevin opened the door and greeted us warmly. He smiled at me and winked as he informed the kids that the back door was unlocked and the Jacuzzi was turned on and ready. Auntie Rachel was already out waiting on them and Greta had some snacks and drinks laid out for them. The kids ran past him as though they were in Pamplona and the gates were opened for the bulls to run free. We both watched and laughed.

Walking into the foyer and then into the enormous kitchen, I smiled at him.

"Thanks, Kevin, I truly appreciate this. I know they'll be safe here with you," I croaked out.

Stopping next to the center island where the large eight-eyed gas stove was mounted, Kevin looked at me with his right eyebrow raised. "Darlin', you getting sick?"

I leaned up opposite him on the bar and stiffened. I opened my mouth to speak and hesitated for a moment because I hadn't really thought of what I would say if someone asked me. If I said yes, they'd go into this long spiel of how I shouldn't be traveling sick, but I sure as hell couldn't tell him that my husband came home from fucking some whore and then face fucked me against my will. I'd have a rebellion on my hands. So what would I say?

"I'm fine, I…uh, just woke up like this. I feel fine. I…uh, think it might be just a case of laryngitis."

"What did I hear?" I heard Rachel's voice and pictured her sashaying in like she was on the runway in New York during Fashion Week. Coming in from behind me, she said, "You've got a touch of something?" She started walking toward the kitchen. As she entered, I could hear the clip-clop of her petite slide-on evening slippers that had white faux ostrich feathers across the bridge of her foot, her coordinating French manicured toes popping out the top of them.

"Come here, I have a flashlight. Let me check out the back of your throat. I don't want you flying if you're getting ill, I don't care who's in the cabin with you."

I began this conversation whirling leisurely through a web of lies. I was handling it quite well, so I thought, but it all went to hell in a hand basket.

I began faltering and stuttering. "Ah, Ra…Rachel, that's just…not necessary. I'm fine, really, I'm okay."

Scrutinizing me, a peculiar look peaked on her face as if she was trying to figure out what I was hiding. "Get over here now, Elleny. Let me look at your throat."

I walked closer as panic began to fill the inside of my body. I knew it showed on the outside as well. There was no way in hell she was looking in my mouth. I didn't know what she'd see, but she would no doubt see something.

I got up face to face with her and did the only thing I could think of that quick. I threw my arms around her and squeezed her as tight as I could.

"Hug me, Rach. I need your support right now. Don't fight me on this. Everything is fine. Don't ask me to do what you're thinking of doing, please? I love you, baby doll, with everything I am. Without you and Lilly, I would have nothing and I wouldn't be able to go on. What you would find when you looked at my throat would make you vulnerable because you wouldn't be thinkin' with your head, you'd be thinkin' with your heart. This is not the time for you to become soft, I need you to be strong. Strong for you and Kevin and strong for my kids. You understand me?" I whispered.

I felt her arms come around me as she let out the breath she had been holding.

I craved for someone to throw their arms around me and just take this load off of me, and she gave that to me. She always did. I closed my eyes so tight, I fought back the urge to lose it. I wrapped her into my body and absorbed every sense of power and strength she allowed me to take. I eventually let go of her and looked her in the eyes. She was weepy, I couldn't take leaving and her being in this state. I looked at her and smiled. "I'll be okay, sweetie. You enjoy your nieces and nephew. When I get back, I wanna hear all the stories of how you let them play fashion show and watch UFC." She giggled a small giggle and I kissed her cheek. I left before I lost it for sure.

I asked Kevin if he wouldn't mind driving me to Richland Manufacturing. I really didn't want to leave my car where Bear worked, he'd know something was up. As we drove to the factory, I saw a long limo sitting out in front of the main office building. We pulled up beside it. As the driver got out of the front, the back door opened. TJ stepped out of the back and glowered at Kevin.

Without saying a word, Kevin handed my bags to the driver. I grabbed Kevin's hand and took him to the side of the car.

"Kevin, I'd like you to meet Trevor McHale, Rachel's cousin. Trevor, this is Kevin Harrington, Rachel's husband."

The scowl left TJ's face and his hand went straight out to shake.

"I guess that makes us kin now. Nice to meet you," Kevin greeted as he took TJ's hand.

"Same to you. Thank you for helping Elleny here."

"No problem, she's also a part of our family. Ellie-bean, you stay safe. Don't worry about the kids and take care of the um…throat."

I hugged Kevin and told him thank you again in my raspy voice as I jumped in the limo.

I sat there for a second before TJ jumped in the back. I noticed his face was beat red and he was grimacing again. I went to the seat across from where he was sitting and looked out the window next to me.

"You okay?"

I didn't want to speak because I didn't want the same shit I got from Kevin and Rachel so I looked back at TJ and nodded. He was holding a glass out to me.

"It's water."

I smiled and nodded in thanks. I took a sip and placed it in the holder as I resumed my position of looking out the window. I saw the same scenery I had looked at every day for the entirety of my life. Suddenly, I was hit with a burst of envy. He got to do everything he set out to do. I was the one who wanted to leave and see new places, but that was the difference between him and I, he didn't have to answer to anyone.

The thoughts in my head were as loud as a freight train going full speed on a journey that never ended. I needed to quiet the noise. Out of nowhere, I heard myself say one word.

"Why?"

His head shot around from looking out the same window and his mouth opened but nothing came out. He had to think for a moment.

I repeated, but elaborated a bit more, "Why did you come back here?"

He went back to looking out the window as though I hadn't said anything at all.

"Elle, this is my home. I have been away for almost eighteen years. Years that I felt like I was adrift, everything was always temporary and indefinite. I never made plans long term because I knew I would never follow through with them. I've felt like I didn't truly have anything. I had money in my pocket, I had money in the bank, but it was all meaningless."

I had turned around in my seat and sat facing him. Somehow, I felt betrayed by his words. I would've liked to have heard that he lived it up. Went to the best parties, had celebrities as friends, and had models for girlfriends. At least that way, I wouldn't have given up everything in vain. "You would've never gotten what you have now if you had stayed in this town, and you know it."

He glared at me for long minutes and I was beginning to feel uncomfortable. I didn't know whether he was going pounce on me or throw me out of the car. Finally, he spoke and his voice sounded harsh and bitter. "You're wrong, Elleny. I would have had all I ever wanted if I had stayed."

I was astonished he would even make that inference. How dare he bring that up? We hadn't even been on this trip for twenty minutes and he was already stirring the shitpot.

Now I was incensed and offended. He had no right to bring up what happened eighteen years ago. We were children that had no clue what life was about outside of stupid movies with happy endings. We didn't know shit about reality, the reality that I knew.

I closed my eyes, took another sip of my water, and tried to calm myself down.

"What, you have nothing to say to that?"

I didn't even turn my head away from the window to give him my attention, I just shook my head. If I opened my mouth, he would definitely throw me out of the back of this car and my shoes were not made for walking.

We sat in silence the rest of the way to the airport.

The limo stopped and I reached for the door, Trevor grabbed my hand. My eyes went straight to his. I couldn't help but get lost in his eyes. I loved thinking of having a future where those eyes are continuously searching what was deep within me. I felt a cold shiver come across my skin.

"…the door, Elle."

I shook my head to break me out of my thoughts. I didn't say anything, instead I kept getting drawn back into his eyes.

"Are you sure you're okay? Let the driver get the door, Elle."

I heard him that time. I wanted to die of embarrassment. Once the driver opened the door, I stepped out of the limo and to the side while I waited on our bags to be handed over to the flight crew. I decided this was a good time to text Luc and tell him that we were getting ready to take off. I gave him text kisses and hugs and told him to pass them around.

I boarded the jet and was met by a delightful and charming young flight attendant by the name of Jasmyn. She offered me a champagne and I resisted since I was going to be in a cabin for two and a half hours at twenty-nine thousand feet with a man I didn't want to walk past at an Atlanta Braves game. I went to the back of the jet, found the last seat in the corner, and readied myself for takeoff. I grabbed a magazine and started flipping through the pages when I saw two legs that were fitted in a pair of oh-so-delectable jeans.

"Change much?" I asked, still flipping the pages of the magazine. I had decided that I didn't want to wear something too professional, but I didn't want to be too casual either, so I settled on a skirt. A black pencil skirt that hit right at the knee and a black and white-striped scooped-neck, short-sleeve shirt that fit just tight enough to show that I do take care of myself. I also had a light sweater on to hide my wrists where the bruising was still apparent.

I could hear him blushing when he replied, "Why yes, there are some things that have changed and yet, there are so many things that are still the same." At this confession, I slowly raised my head and looked at him, page still half-turned. I knew what he was inferring to, but I wasn't playing this game with him.

Closing my magazine, I knew I had to put a stop to this once and for all. This was not going to happen. My heart couldn't take it and it wasn't fair for him to even imagine that this was a possibility. He deserved someone so much better than me. He deserved someone who wasn't so broken.

I closed my magazine and returned it to where it belonged in the pocket on the back of the seat. I crossed my legs, placed my hands in my lap, and dressed my face with a smile. "Look, Mr. McHale, whatever you have going on in that brain of yours," I raised my hand and began swiping air, "let me assure you, it's not going to happen. This trip is strictly business, nothing more. I have never given you any indication that I am interested in your flirtatious manner, nor will I. So, if you know what's best for you, I suggest you go up to the front of the cabin and secure yourself for take-off."

TJ knelt down in the middle of the aisle, grabbed my hand off of my lap, and brought my attention back to him by saying, "Are you done? That was an excellent lecture, Ms...." he hissed the end, as if in his mind I was single, "...Barker-Jackson. Now, let me tell you the way it's going to be."

He began to rub circles over my hand. I attempted to pull away but his grip became stronger and his eyes became fueled with desire. "By the time this trip is over, I will have not only fucked you in ways you've never been fucked before, but you will be pleading for me to stop." His eyes never left mine. No blush came to his cheeks. He meant every word he was saying. Still circling his thumb on my hand, he continued. "I will have tasted every part of your delicious body. I will take my time and lick you in places no other man has even thought of licking you. I will drink every bit of you into me because...fuck, how I have missed your taste. My fingers will do things to you that will have you sobbing with pleasure."

He came in close, his nose was practically touching mine. I could smell his cologne mixed with the freshness of his breath and it was driving me wild. "What you don't know, and I am gonna let you in on my little secret here, is I won't ask you for any of this. It will be you, Ms. Barker-Jackson who will be begging me."

I just sat there. My eyes were glued to his, my mouth was dropped open, I was speechless. He raised my hand to his mouth and kissed it very gently. Before he pulled it away, he ran his tongue over where he had just kissed. "Oh yes, that's the taste I have dreamt about for the last eighteen years." I pulled my hand away swiftly as he silently laughed and stood up. Walking, away I heard him say, "I will leave you with your thoughts. Enjoy the flight."

Shit! I was in trouble.

Chapter 11

November 1992

Thanksgiving was coming around way too fast. The smell of autumn was strong in the cool air and the people around town seemed to be in happier. Maybe it had something to do with the fading of the hot summer. I seemed better, but bigger than I expected to be. I was getting ready to have a sonogram the following day to find out if I was having a boy or a girl. I didn't care as long as he or she was healthy.

I recovered from my emotional breakdown quickly with the help of my dad and Mona. They were so encouraging. My relationship with Mona had flourished since my breakdown and we had become friends. We weren't best friends, but she had changed that night. She opened herself up to me and I was thankful for it. I understood where she was coming from now.

We would talk about baby things and she was excited about becoming a grandma. She never had a chance to have any babies of her own. When she married into my family, I was almost a teenager. We talked about going shopping for the nursery and baby clothes. I felt like she respected the love I felt for TJ, like she knew exactly what I was feeling. That no matter what happened in the future, I would never love another man. It was the same way she felt for my daddy. Unfortunately, my daddy didn't feel the same way and it made her hopeless. We were in two separate worlds but burdened with the same issue.

195

Bear, on the other hand, took a step back. He seemed very distant. I would ask him what was bothering him and his answer was always the same. "Nothing, just things at work." I could tell work was far from the problem seeing as he practically lived there. He even crashed on the couch in the break room overnight. He seemed like he was happy about the baby, but something just felt off. The night of the fight, I had lost all respect for Bear. I didn't even want to be around him. I felt betrayed and angry by his actions and words.

But, I wasn't in this pact for love. There was nothing that said I had to hand my heart over to him. Truthfully, I didn't even have to make love to him. I was just throwing that in for convenience. We agreed to marry and raise this baby together, no one had to know the reality of the situation. I just knew I had to stay with him and see this thing out.

We decided that after the baby was born, we were going to start looking for a house of our own. I was beginning to get excited. I could picture it all, a federal styled home filled with antique furniture. Looking out the front window, I could see the white-washed rocking chairs lining the beautiful wrap around porch that overlooked the small garden out front. Stepping inside the foyer, it felt as though you were taken back in time, to where things were simpler and life was lived as a blessing, not a curse. To the right would be the quaint, artless dining room that seated the enormous carving board table where my family would sit down to eat the nightly meal I cooked especially for them.

Ivory colored walls connected to dark wooden flooring, cross-stitched samplers adorning the stairway as you walked up to the second floor. Four out of the five bedrooms upstairs held a four poster bed painted a rustic brown wash. On top of each pillar was a beautiful, yet simple finale. The baby's room was almost over-the-top with the amount of pink that ornamented it. The walls were a soft, pale pink that represented the softness of a little girl's skin and was enhanced by sunshine yellow throws. The white of the floorboards brought it all together and made the room blissful. Subconsciously, I think I was set on having a baby girl.

I wanted to play the role of housewife in my own home so bad I could taste it. I could picture the smell of peach pies baking in the oven as I would roll dough to cut out for homemade biscuits while the batch of fresh apple butter was simmering on the stove. The scent of cinnamon and spices wafted through my nostrils just daydreaming about it.

I had a lot to occupy my mind as of late, but there was one person I would never stop thinking about. With Thanksgiving next week, I knew he would be coming home and it was going to be impossible to not run into him. I was going to have to explain to him what had happened and why. I felt that he was owed a large apology. It had only been two months, but he didn't know I was pregnant. He would be getting an eyeful now.

Standing at the kitchen sink peeling potatoes, I felt Bear come around me and plant a kiss on my cheek. I smiled. I had to keep telling myself that Bear was a good guy and I would learn to love him. That's what everyone kept trying to cram down my throat and I was trying as hard as I could. Just coming home from work, I knew he would be hungry so I told him to grab a beer and dinner would be ready shortly. Daddy and Mona had decided to take a cruise for the holidays, so it would only be me, Bear, and whoever stopped by after spending time with their families. I knew Rachel, Lilly, Curtis, and Rachel's new boyfriend, Kevin, were going to drop in. I couldn't wait to see them.

I finished with dinner and got everything set up on the table. I had made fried chicken, mashed potatoes and gravy, candied carrots, homemade biscuits and apple butter, and homemade peach cobbler for dessert. I was starving. I couldn't wait to tear into some chicken. The morning sickness, more like all day sickness, had slowed down and I was finally keeping food down. I sat down and Bear handed me his plate. I made his, handed it back to him, and then started on mine. I

197

took a couple bites, then decided that I needed to state my upcoming plans to him.

"I wanted to let you know, I'm planning to see TJ when he comes into town for Thanksgiving. I owe him an explanation."

Bear stopped chewing for just a second, set his chicken back down on the plate, and dug into the mashed potatoes. "That's not gonna happen."

I knew he was being serious but I wasn't asking him for his permission, this wasn't that type of relationship. Yes, he was my husband, but only on paper. I had to stand my ground here. "I'm sorry, but I wasn't asking you. I was telling you that I am going to see our friend that we have known since we were kids, and I'm going to talk with him."

"You want to go talk with him? Yeah, right. You want his cock to talk to your pussy."

How dare he talk to me that way! That was not the reason I was going and he knew it! Completely losing my appetite, I pushed my plate away from me. As I went to stand from the table, I whispered, "The hell I'm not." He must've heard me because he came back madder than I've ever seen him. Standing, he growled, "No. The. Fuck. You're. Not!"

"Yes. The. Fuck I. Am!"

That did it. He exploded in anger and lunged toward me. Roaring, he hurled Mona's elegant, marble topped dining room table over onto its side with one hand. Everything that I had been cooking since ten this morning was nothing more than a stain on her non-blemished white carpet. Out of nowhere, I felt a flash of red heat on my cheek. My head swirled around. Out of the corner of my eye, I could see Bear's arm as it followed through on the slap.

He had struck me.

Slowly, he lowered himself down to my level and gritted, "I told you when we made this fucking deal, you weren't going to have contact with that fucking dicklicker again. What the fuck aren't you understanding about that?"

Kneeling on the floor with my hand against my cheek, tears were flowing down my face. "You hit me…" was all I could get out of my mouth. I was in total shock. Here I was pregnant, and he had whacked the shit out of my face.

Whispering in my ear, he sounded like pure evil. "And if you bring that motherfucker's name up again in my presence, it will be a lot worse next time. You understand me, bitch? Shit, now look what you've done. You fucked up my dinner. I'm going to the fuckin' bar. Don't wait up."

I just sat there, still in shock over what had just happened. I began to pick up plates. Slowly, I stood. Staying still for a second to get my equilibrium centered, shock and guilt fought for possession as I cleaned up the mess that was made because I opened my stupid mouth. I touched my face again and could feel it beginning to swell. Damn, did it sting. I continued to scrub the floor to get the peach cobbler out until I curled up into myself right there and fell asleep at eleven thirty. Bear still hadn't made it home.

I woke up the next morning, confused as to why I was on the floor. I was stiff and felt exhausted. Looking at the clock, it was eight thirteen. I had to be at Doctor Leonard's office by nine. I hurried to get dressed. Using a ton of make up on my face, I tried to cover up my family drama. But, the more I dabbed the powder puff against my bruised cheekbone, the more it stood out. I hoped that Dr. Leonard wouldn't notice.

I checked my watch one final time as I walked to the car. I had a feeling I would be finding out what I was having by myself. Calling Bear's pager number and leaving a message with the operator didn't do any good. However, I wasn't so sure I wanted him around me. I replayed everything that happened last night. I had a really bad feeling that if I wasn't pregnant, he would've kept hitting me.

Sitting anxiously in the waiting room, I grabbed an out of date magazine and acted like I was reading it. I was lost in my thoughts, mainly about last night's events as well as Bear's absence. Suddenly, I pictured TJ. What would he say if he had the chance to experience this with me today? Would he be the kind of father that would pace anxiously around this waiting room as he waited to find out what would be calling him daddy? Or, would he sit here silently, lost in his thoughts as he held my hand, being the supportive man he was? I heard my name being called, bringing me back to the present. I slowly got my things together, trying to give Bear a few more seconds just in case he was frantically running up the stairs.

Finally, I couldn't wait any longer. I followed the nurse back to the triage room where she did what she needed to do with my weight and blood pressure. I didn't really pay attention to the nurse. This whole check-up routine was becoming monotonous.

"How many weeks did you say you were, Mrs. Barker-Jackson?"

Nervously, I told her that I had recently hit the twenty week mark. If she looked in my chart, she probably could've found that out herself.

I thought back to when TJ and I were at the lake and started counting. Whether or not it was that weekend, I had never been with anyone else. I guess I could've been off a week or two.

"Well, you're measuring a little bigger than that. Let's just see what the sonogram says, you might be further along than you think," she said with a smile.

Now I was growing anxious, was there something wrong with my baby? What if it was deformed? I had drank alcohol while I was pregnant without knowing, what if I hurt our baby? I wanted to break down right there in the office.

Dr. Leonard came in and her bubbly attitude hit me like a lightning bolt. I wasn't in the mood for cheery. I just wanted to see what was wrong with my baby.

"Shall we go ahead or are we gonna wait for Daddy?" she asked, her smile taking up most of her face now.

"No, let's just start," I quickly responded.

"Very well. This might be cold." She squeezed the gel on my belly and began rubbing the instrument across my skin.

"Well, here's the—" She stopped talking and the smile left her face. She pushed several buttons on the machine and then went to the phone to call for the nurse to come in the room, "Stat".

Seeing her reaction to whatever was on that screen caused me to panic. What if Bear did something to the baby when he hit me? I couldn't breathe. I remembered the nurse telling me I was measuring big and now the doctor ran around the office like she was ordering major surgery.

"Dr. Leonard, what the hell is going on? I'm freaking here."

The nurse who measured me earlier came running in.

"I want an HCG count done and I want results by the end of business today!" she demanded to the nurse. The nurse turned to leave and closed the door behind her. Dr. Leonard sat back down and stated, "Elleny, I want to show you something."

I was beginning to think that my kid had two heads.

"Do you see this right here? This is your baby. I'm going to do some measurements on it here in a minute, so far everything looks good. Do you want to know the sex?"

I looked at the monitor where her finger was pointing and could see what looked like a small curled up body. I saw its head, its small hands and feet jerking around. I smiled, everything looked normal.

"Yes, yes I do."

"It's a girl," she said with a smile. I felt a rush of warmth fill my body at the thought of having a daughter. I was going to be the momma of a girl, TJ was going to have a daughter. I wiped the tear from the corner of my eye.

She continued, "Now, do you see this over here?"

I didn't like the tone in her voice. I followed her finger to a bump on the screen. All I could see was a large bubbled blob, I was trying not to hyperventilate.

"Oh shit, what is that?"

"It's a butt, Elleny. Do you see this right here?" Again, she pointed to something on the screen. "That is the penis. It's another baby, Elleny…and it's a boy."

I let out a small laugh. *She was kidding, right?*

"What the hell did you just say?"

"You're having twins." There was that smile again, taking over her entire face.

She did her measurements and played their heartbeats out loud. No wonder I was having a dance party in my belly, they were excited to throw me into another emotional breakdown.

I couldn't handle this. I thought finding out I was pregnant was emotional, that was a walk in the park compared to finding out that I was having twins. I was back to feeling like I couldn't breathe.

"I can't breathe."

Raising off the stool, Dr. Leonard grabbed my hand and helped me sit up on the table. She told me to breathe in and out of my nose, this would pass in a minute. But, that was a lie. I still had another four months with two babies growing inside of me. I had to push two babies out. Not only was I going to be responsible for one of TJ's babies, I would be responsible for two. I had enough problems remembering to feed myself.

Dr. Leonard informed me that the nurse would be coming in to take some blood and then sat there for a minute until my breathing regulated. She excused herself, giving me a minute to come to grips with the news I had just received.

I didn't know what to do first, so I cried. I cried hard. Then, I thought about what to do next. Should I call my daddy who was out in the Caribbean enjoying himself? Should I call Bear? He didn't give a shit about me and one baby, why would he care about another? Decided, I called the one person I always called when I needed to talk.

"Hey, babe. Whatch'a doin'?"

Rachel's voice immediately calmed me. I never needed to question her loyalty.

"Rach...there's two."

"What, Elle? I can't hear you, speak up."

I was quiet for a second so I could pull myself back together. I felt the sob rise in my throat and I needed a minute to push it back down. I heard whispering on the other side of the line, then I heard a door shut. "Elleny, is something wrong? Talk to me, babe."

I gathered myself, and on a large inhale of breath. I repeated, "There are two."

"Oh, honey, you scared the shit outta me. I thought something was wrong with the baby. There are two what?"

I couldn't hold it back any longer. I had never felt so helpless in all my life. This was supposed to be a happy time, I had just found out I was having twins. I looked at every aspect of the situation and I couldn't find one shred of happiness in the circumstances I found myself in.

"Babies, Rachel, babies," I blubbered.

"Jesus, Elleny."

Yeah, that was an understatement. I was lost and alone.

"I'm sorry, Rach. I shouldn't have called you. Go back to whatever you were doin'."

"I'm coming over, where are you?" This was what I loved about my friends. They were my family and I could depend on them as such.

"I'm at Dr. Leonard's office."

"Can you drive?"

"Rach, I'm fine. You just spend time with your—"

"Shut up! I'm coming over. Now, do I need to come and get you or are you going to meet me at your house?"

Yep, that's Rachel.

"I'll drive home. See you there."

"Lilly's coming with."

On my way home, I kept picturing two babies swimming around in my belly. Our babies that we made out of love, the babies I would get to look at every day for the rest of my life. I started to look at my glass being half full instead of half empty. I was going to experience part of him inside me for the next four months, growing stronger day by day. Maybe I wasn't so unlucky after all. Maybe I had been doubly blessed.

I made it home and saw Rachel's car sitting in the drive. I walked inside and both Lilly and Rachel were sitting in the living room. As soon as they saw me, they ran to me. We hugged a strong, deep hug as we cried together. They both recharged me mentally and emotionally.

Rachel dropped to her knees and started rubbing my belly. I grabbed her hand and lifted her up until she was standing. Then, we went into the living room and all three of us sat hip to hip.

"Did you find out the sexes?" Lilly asked hesitantly, scrutinizing my face to determine her reaction. I smiled and the smile grew bigger and bigger, as did theirs.

"Ya'll will be happy to know that you are the proud aunties of a little girl and a little boy."

All three of us hugged and cried together. I needed this comfort, I felt so deserted. This was better than anything I could've dreamed. Finally, we all stopped crying and separated just a bit. Rachel and Lilly's heads turned from side to side when Lilly decided to speak.

"Where's Bear and what the hell is wrong with your face?"

First I grabbed my face and scoffed. When it came to Bear, I just shrugged. I hadn't heard from him all morning. For all I knew, he could've been lying in a ditch somewhere.

Lilly stood up quickly and started for the back of the house. "You mean to tell me, he didn't go with you to find out the sex of his baby and he wasn't with you when you found out you were having twins?"

I shook my head. Really, what could I have said?

I decided to tell them what happened. "Last night he got upset with me. I told him I was going to go see TJ and talk to him about what happened that night." They both got quiet for a moment. "We've been friends since we were able to form sentences, I can't leave things the way they ended that night."

Still nothing, so I continued. "Ya'll think it's a bad idea, don't you?"

I looked at both of them and saw they were agreeing with Bear. Not for the same reasons. They knew deep down I wouldn't be able to handle it emotionally.

"So, how do I give him his stuff back? He deserves his shit back, right?"

Not one word.

"I am not a fucking mind reader! You have to talk here!"

It was Lilly who finally responded to me.

"Don't do it, Elle. Don't put yourself in that place. I mean, do you know what it's like to hear that something is wrong with your sister and there isn't shit you can do about it? It almost killed me, Elle. I can't go through that again. Neither can your babies. You have to think of them now."

She was right and I knew it. TJ was like my drug. I needed just a look, a small peek to get my fix. I had yearbooks, pictures, anything with him on it stashed away in my room where Bear would never even think to look just so I could get my fill. I had to see him. I just knew that it would make this unbearable ache go away. I was obsessed. But, if I saw him and we interacted, I had a feeling it would make the aching even worse.

"Is he here, Rach?" I whispered. I wasn't really sure that I wanted to know. She didn't answer. I didn't ask again, for fear that I would hear the answer I didn't want. Rachel knew the deal, but Lilly didn't. I wanted to keep it that way. I had to walk away and catch my breath.

I walked into the kitchen and grabbed an apple juice. Rachel followed me. "Don't do it, babe. You did the right thing by letting him go, so let him go."

It took everything within me not to throw something, anything. I wanted to destroy the whole kitchen, I was so frustrated. I knew I had to let go, but I just couldn't.

"I can't. It eats at me every day. I lay next to a man that doesn't mean shit to me and I dream about another man who I love so much I can't see straight. I can't do this, Rach, I'm not going to survive."

"Honey, you've done it this long, it will just take time. No one said it was going to be easy, but it will work out."

Just as we were finishing up, Bear and Lilly walked into the kitchen. I just stood there and glared at Bear. I really didn't want to get into anything while the girls were here so I just ignored him.

Taking Lilly and Rachel by the hands, I led them out to the back porch. I had Clara make some of her chicken salad before she left yesterday to go spend Thanksgiving with her family. We sat out on the back porch enjoying the beautiful scenery as we ate chicken salad and drank sweet tea, laughing and catching up.

They told me about their time at school and even Rachel told me more about her new man, Kevin. Lilly had been spending time with Curtis and he was loving every minute of it. He missed her so much. You could tell when you looked at him he was having a difficult time with the separation.

After several hours of catching up, they left and I was left alone with Bear. He was in the living room watching TV, so I went in the kitchen to clean up what was left of the dishes. I felt Bear's hands moving my hair to the side. My hands in the water stilled. His nose came up against the back of my neck, I could hear his loud inhales and exhales as though he was sniffing me, his breath warm against my cool neck. Suddenly, I felt his wet tongue up against where his nose had just been. He was tasting me.

"I'm sorry, Ellie," he said quietly. I clutched my eyes closed.

"You missed an important appointment today, Bear. I needed you with me and you weren't there, where the hell were you?"

"I stayed in the back room at work again and then they asked if some of us wanted to work some overtime. I had to get away, Ellie. You promised me that you wouldn't have any contact with him after we got married and now here we are, married, and you're insistent on seeing him. I told you that was my baby, not his."

"Babies, Bear."

He looked back at me quickly. "The fuck you say?"

"I said babies, Bear. There's two."

"Two babies...twins?"

Now that he was repeating everything I was saying, I was starting to get nervous. Was he going to change his mind and back out of this agreement? With the way he acted last night, I don't think I'd be too upset.

"Yeah, Bear, twins. Why are you repeating everything I say?"

His eyes were huge and he wasn't moving.

"Ellie, baby, I'm so sorry. I fucked up. Big time," he pleaded as he hugged my back. "I missed out on seeing my babies, something I can't get back." He sounded like he was sniffling. "Did you find out what they were?"

I felt guilty. Maybe I was overreacting. He seemed like he was sincere and sorry. I smiled and he knew the answer to that question.

"Do you want to know?"

He shrugged. "I don't know, do I?"

Every time he called these babies his, I cringed. They weren't his and I died a little inside each time knowing that their real daddy would never experience any of this with me.

"One's a boy and one's a girl," I said as I smiled a fake smile.

"Oh, Ellie, I'm so fucking excited! I've got a son and a daughter, we've got our little family!" Bear said as he hugged me again. I closed my eyes and just listened to him chatter about how he had planned on spoiling his daughter to death and how he was going to teach all of his football secrets to his son.

Rachel's words popped into my head. Maybe she was right. Maybe I needed to give it a chance. He sounded really enthused about having the babies and he didn't have to do what he had done. I started reconsidering what I was feeling.

I hugged him back. He pulled his head off my shoulder and looked me in the eyes as he laid his forehead against mine. He apologized again as he kissed me softly.

"I'm so sorry, baby. I'm sorry for everything. I didn't mean it…any of it."

He continued to give me small chaste kisses all over my face. "I'm sorry I hit you, baby. I swear to god, I will never raise a hand to you again. I love you so much. It's just…thinkin' of you spending time with him, it makes me crazy." He worked his way back around to my lips and began kissing me harder. "You're carrying two babies, my babies. I love you so much."

Love? What the hell was this I love you crap? He had never said that to me before, that was not what we had talked about.

His hands slowly crept under my shirt as he went for my breasts. Through my bra, his thumbs rubbed coarsely against my nipples. My head fell back against his shoulder, it felt amazing. His hands were hot against my skin, his breath against my face was warm, and my body was demanding contact.

"Bear, don't stop." I wrapped my hands around his upper arms for balance while he raised my bra up over my breasts so he had full contact. He began to roll my nipples between his thumbs and forefingers, pinching slightly. My nipples were so sensitive, it felt incredible. He lowered himself, kissing me as he went down, whispering endearments. He unbuttoned my pants then ran his hands over my bulging belly.

"My babies, I'm your daddy. I've got two of ya in there," he said as he kissed my belly. I could feel the babies tumbling around at the sound of his voice.

"Bear, I need you."

To be honest, I didn't need *him*. I needed to be full of someone's cock and he just happened to be there. Call me selfish, but I blamed it on the hormones.

He stood up and kissed me, walking us backwards to the bedroom. As soon as I felt the side of the bed on the back of my legs, I laid down and let him pull my pants off. He laid down beside me and pulled me on top of him.

"I wanna see your belly while you ride me, baby. You're givin' me more than I could've ever asked for…two babies."

Every time he said babies, my mind automatically went to TJ. I couldn't take thinking about him anymore. It was wearing me down.

I lowered myself down on him and heard him hiss. I closed my eyes and went to the place I always went to inside my head whenever I wanted to be with Trevor. This time, I was in my room and TJ was lying underneath me while I rode him. My hands were running all over his muscled chest and stomach. I couldn't get enough of how he felt underneath me. Feeling myself getting wetter, I began moving up and down, releasing and contracting.

"Yeah, that's it, baby. Ride that cock."

I ignored his coaching and kept my eyes closed.

In my head, I was smiling. I loved how TJ would hold his breath when he was coming and a moment later, let it out in the sexiest of moans. The way his stomach muscles tightened as I fluttered my fingers across his skin. I would lick, tasting every bead of sweat off of his ripped stomach and neck as he'd thrust deep inside of me. I could feel every inch of him, but my body wanted more; wanted all of him. His lips, his touch, his skin—I wanted to own him, body and soul. It was so erotic. I sped up, needing just a little more to push me over into my own orgasm.

"Oh yeah, baby. Make me come. Goddamn, I'm gonna fill you up."

Bear moaned as his orgasm took him over. I dropped my fingers down between my legs and began to rub hard and fast. Finally, I climaxed. It wasn't mind blowing, but I felt relief.

"Well, I sure as shit needed that," Bear said as he immediately pulled me off of him,got up and headed for the bathroom.

"Darlin', you cookin' dinner tonight? I'm starvin'."

I looked at the clock, it was only three-eighteen. After cooking my ass off yesterday and him throwing it all over the floor, that was a big hell no.

"You wanna go out?"

"Sure, we can go out."

I jumped in the shower, threw my hair up in a messy bun, and got ready in record time. We decided on a little restaurant in town. The ride was quiet and short, lucky for me. As we got out of the car and turned to head to the restaurant, I heard a voice I thought I would never hear again.

"Bear, Elle, wait up! I wanna talk to ya'll!"

Shit, shit, shit!

Turning around, I saw TJ jogging over to us. I turned back around to Bear. His breathing had turned erratic and his face was as red as a beet. This was not good. I quickly told Bear not to open his mouth and took control of the situation the only way I knew how.

"TJ, turn around and go back to where you came from. I guess you didn't learn when Bear kicked your ass the first time that I never wanted to see you again. Get outta here! Why can't you just leave us the hell alone!"

He halted in his tracks. The look he gave as his eyes traveled down to my stomach killed me inside. I wanted to scream that these were his babies. The smile left his face and I could see his jaw clenching. He looked at me a moment, nodded once, turned, and walked away. On the inside, I was screaming.

Another piece of me died that day.

Tracy Lee

Chapter 12

Present Day

The flight from Atlanta to Burlington was only two and a half hours. To me, it felt like seven hours. With nothing to do, I continued to replay the conversation that TJ and I had over in my head. I couldn't help it, I was captivated.

This was a dream that I had been having since I was eighteen. Now, it was being offered to me on a silver platter. All I had to do was just ask him. No, scratch that—I had to beg him.

He had obviously put plenty of thought into this plan. I must've been scowling and blushing at the same time because he laughed as he passed me on his way to the bar to grab himself a bottle of water. *But, really, beg?*

"Something funny?" I inquired.

"Just you," he replied, smirking.

"Would you like to elaborate on that, Mr. McHale?"

"You're giving great thought to my offer, aren't you?" he responded, bluntly.

My cheeks must've blossomed into a deeper shade of red because he smirked again.

Busted!

However, I was not going to let him think he could talk to me that way. I was a married woman. So what if I fantasized about this man while I use my battery operated boyfriend. So what if I dreamt about him and used him as my savior when my husband abused me. He wouldn't be finding any of that out.

I rolled my sleeves up, preparing for a fight.

"I will have you know, Mr. McHale, that I—"

"What the fuck is that?" he barked, slamming his bottle of water down on the bar. Looking around the cabin, I had no clue what he was talking about. I sat there for a moment listening, thinking maybe he heard an odd sound.

"I don't hear or see anything, what did you see?"

"What I see better not be what I think it is. If it is, someone is going to die and it won't be a fast death." His voice was dark and menacing. It sent a chill up my spine and I actually felt sorry for whoever he was speaking about.

Making his way around the bar, he picked up my hands so fast, I didn't have time to pull my sleeves back down. TJ's eyes began to examine the bruises that had become a faint purple and green. My tattoos seemed to cover up most of what was left.

"Mr. McHale, please…" I pleaded, pulling my sweater back down and silently cursing myself. *How could I have been so stupid?*

"Don't you fucking Mr. McHale me, Elle. Where did these bruises come from?"

Snatching my hands away, I found myself defending that fucktard, Bear. Not because he deserved it, because I needed to save face.

I stood straight up and croaked, "You've been away a long time and things have changed. People have changed. Don't you come up to me threatening me with your alpha-male bullshit."

He looked at me. His eyes had softened, but his smile had disappeared. I tried to get my breathing back down to a normal rate, but I was pissed and he knew it. I was not that little girl anymore.

"Look," I rubbed my forehead, trying to get my thoughts in order, "I apologize for losing my temper. To be quite frank, I've had a shit night and I'm extremely tired. I just want to get to my hotel, take a long, hot bath, and fall asleep. If there is anything you would like me to work on for the rest of the flight, please feel free to bring it to my attention."

He just kept staring at me, not saying a word. I looked away and then looked back at him just as he mumbled something under his breath.

"Glass," was the only thing I could understand. I looked over toward the bar.

"I'm sorry, are you in need of a glass? Here, let me," I offered, since I was already standing.

As I went to step out into the aisle, he stopped me.

"That's not what I said." I turned to look down at him. His face was blank. "What I said is, your husband should touch you as though you were made out of the most delicate piece of glass; regarded as if you could disintegrate into the finest of dust."

I stepped back to my seat and sat down. I cleared my throat and breathed, "Mr. McHale—"

He pounded his fist on the arm rest that divided us, cutting me off. "Don't call me that again. Do you understand me? You call me TJ…that's my fuckin' name!"

I blinked quickly, trying to stop the tears that were threatening. Softly, I murmured, "I'm not made of glass, TJ."

He closed his eyes and whispered, "God, I've missed hearing you same my name."

I was still barely able to catch my breath. With what breath I had, I informed him, "I've changed, TJ. I'm not that naive little girl anymore."

"I know you, Elle. I know you better than anyone. I know that you still think of me, because your all that's on my mind."

"Shut up!"

I knew what this was: some stupid mind-fuck joke because of the way I ended things. He wanted to get back at me for hurting him. Well, it was working. He destroyed me. For eighteen years, I died more and more inside. Now, to have to face it? I couldn't handle it. He was my life force whether he knew it or not.

"I know that you still feel something for me, because you consume me, Elle. All of me. This won't stop. This pain that I feel down to my very essence, won't stop. We are anchored. Together, you and I, forever, and you know it."

"TJ, shut up!"

"I've seen it permanently inked on you. And, I know it because you're always next to my heart." He opened his shirt and there upon a silver chain was my anchor ring. The same ring I had slipped in his pocket the night of the fight.

"It never leaves my neck. You are with me constantly."

I couldn't take anymore. I was trapped. The tears were building up and closing my eyes was the only way to stop them. This was what I wanted my entire life; what I basically would've sold my soul to the devil for. Why, all of a sudden, after seventeen years, would he just pop up and offer me eight days of pure TJ time? There was a catch; had to be.

"TJ, this is never going to happen. You can't even begin—"

Just then, the captain's voice came over the intercom, informing us that we were starting our descent into Burlington. I fastened my seatbelt and TJ got up to move back to his seat. Before he turned to leave, he bent down and kissed my forehead.

"That's it, darlin', you think about all I've said to you. You have an hour to get in your room, shower, and dress. You're joining me for dinner, nothing fancy. Jeans will be fine." He laid another small kiss on my forehead before finally heading to his seat.

Oh shit, I was in so much trouble.

Looking up at the hotel as the driver turned into the unloading area, I felt like I was in Vegas. The hotel was lit up with lights you could most likely see from miles away. I followed TJ into the lobby and stood there in amazement at how posh the inside lobby was. I couldn't even imagine what the rooms would look like.

"Ah, Mr. McHale. Nice to see you again, how may we assist you this evening?" I heard coming from the front desk. Looking in that direction, I saw a handsome man who appeared to be in his mid-thirties, dressed charmingly, conversing with TJ.

"Why, hello, Simon. I need a suite, perhaps the penthouse is available. I apologize for the last minute scheduling but this trip wasn't expected."

"Of course, sir, the penthouse suite is available. Two rooms, both with king size beds. Would there be anything else this evening, Mr. McHale?"

"No, that would be all. Please, bill it to Mac-Gentry."

I walked up as I heard him say, "…your stay with us," and walked with Trevor toward the elevators.

"What did he mean by your?" I whispered curiously, so that the very influential people walking by us didn't hear.

Smirking, he mumbled, "What do you think he meant, Elle?"

I smiled so it looked like we were having a wonderful, loving conversation. On the inside, I was livid. "I'm thinking that statement was meant for me, not you."

Entering the elevator, it filled up quickly, pushing us against the back wall. He laughed at my response, concluding, "I'm thinking you misunderstood something."

My face blanked as realization set in. He could tell by the alarmed expression on my face that I was clued in on his plan. He laughed louder this time.

"You're not… no! That's not possible. Why would you stay here? Wait, you're not staying here, right?" I was mumbling even I couldn't figure out what I was trying to say.

Hitting the first floor we passed, some of the riders got off. The doors shut again and we continued our journey to the top floor. We stood in silence, hip to hip, squished like a can of sardines. Slowly, I felt his hand gently stroke my hand and goose bumps shot straight up my arm. I closed my eyes and savored the feeling. Quickly, I tugged my hand up and folded both of my arms over my chest. I was not going to give into him, especially if he thought I would be begging him for anything.

Looking over, that sly smile was still adorning his beautiful face.

We went up four more floors and more people stepped off. The elevator was becoming increasingly less crowded, yet we stayed right where we were. Hitting the ninth floor, all but one stepped off and there we stood. I looked over at him through the reflection on the wall and noticed that he was staring straight at me.

Looking straight ahead again, I dropped my arms straight down in front of me and asked TJ if there was a problem.

Slowly, he leaned over and I felt a warm rush of air hit my ear as he blew. I was covered in goose bumps again. *Damn him!*

"Oh, no problem, Elle. I was just imagining what you would look like with your legs wrapped around me while you rode my cock up against this elevator wall."

Oh shit, oh shit, oh shit!

My head snapped toward him, mouth agape. I really should have been slapped for that question, considering what was said on the plane. I left myself wide open. I told my brain to close my mouth as I turned my head straight ahead and prayed that this ride was almost over. With the way today was turning out, I was going to have to burn this pair of panties.

I heard him laugh under his breath as the doors opened and the last man stepped out of the elevator. Sliding the keycard into the slot to get to the penthouse, I stood there with my eyes closed. I didn't want to look at him. Or hear him speak. At this rate, I would be begging for him to take me before dinner.

Finally, we reached the door to the penthouse.

I informed him he was going to have to give me a little more time considering it was almost nine and I needed to call Rachel and check on my kids. He agreed and unlocked the door. When I stepped into the foyer of the immaculate hotel room, I thought I had died and gone to heaven.

"Like it?"

"Amazing," was my only reply.

TJ walked around me and headed to the left, so I figured my room was on the right. As I walked into the living area, I couldn't believe my eyes. I was looking out over a night sky that dazzled like the stars on a cloudless night. All around us were skyscrapers with almost every floor illuminated. Looking out further, you could see the residential neighborhoods.

The houses glowed with the warmth of the families that lived in them. You could see small flames in the backyard from where they were grilling or having a bonfire. These were happy, loving families that probably watched movies together, or played board games. It crushed me inside that my children didn't have that kind of home. I tried as hard as I could to give them a decent, normal childhood. They had holidays, routines, chores and most importantly, a momma's love. But, Bear didn't make it easy. The kids and I would sit down to watch a movie and Bear would come in, drunk off his ass and screaming at me, scaring the shit out of the kids. That would always be the end of our loving, warm family night.

"Beautiful, isn't it?" I turned my head to the side and saw TJ standing right behind me, offering me a glass of champagne.

"It's breathtaking." I plastered a fake smile on my face. Though the view was phenomenal, I couldn't help but feel nauseated by it. I took the glass of champagne and sipped it slowly. I was exhausted from last night's festivities and if I drank too much, I would be in a coma before dinner.

Feeling him move in closer, I could feel the heat coming off of him, and I liked it—maybe a little too much. I heard him speak softly. "It so peaceful, it's like no one has a care in the world." I closed my eyes and moved away to head for my room. "I better call the kids so I can get ready for dinner, thank you for the champagne." Looking back, I saw him looking up at the ceiling, his eyes were closed.

I ignored him and headed for my room. The bellhop had already brought my bags up, so I began to unpack a little, hanging up the pieces of clothing that wrinkled easily. Moving to the bathroom, I plugged in my iPod and turned the shower on. I could barely hear Knight Ranger's "When I Close My Eyes" as I rubbed the shampoo into my hair. I knew the lyrics though, and they hit close to home with me. I would always turn this song on while washing the dishes, ear buds stuck deep in my ears and the volume all the way up, as I settled into my fondest memories of TJ and me. Like the time we were supposed to go out to dinner with Lilly and Curt.

I knew staying at TJ's house after school and getting dressed there was going to be a mistake. Before the evening even began, we had already made love twice. I was in the shower in the guest room while he was getting dressed in his room. It took me two hours to get ready as I used the curling iron to create curl after curl. Pleased with my appearance and snuggled into my little black dress, I headed down the stairs. As soon as I hit the foyer, TJ came out of the kitchen and froze. I could see the hunger back in his eyes.

"You look delicious," he mumbled as he slowly moved toward me.

"TJ, we are going out to dinner. I am not the first course," I laughed as he planted his lips on my neck. "And I will have you know that I worked long and hard on this hair. Please try not to mess it up." I tilted my head back to allow him better access.

I couldn't say no to him. In fact, I needed him. I felt like my brain never turned off, never relaxed. It was absolute chaos in my head until I was bound to TJ in some way physically. Then the pandemonium would disappear, leaving tranquility in its wake.

His lips left my neck and he brought his face up, eyebrows raised. "Oh, baby, while you were working long and hard on your hair, I was working on something long and hard. Wanna see it?"

I threw my head back in laughter. I laughed so long, tears were pooling in the corners of my eyes.

Pulling myself together, I kissed him softly, pulling his lower lip in between my teeth. At the sound of his deep, throaty moan, I knew we were going to be late for dinner. I wrapped my legs around his waist as his hands settled on my ass. He walked us back upstairs toward his bedroom and I began gyrating my hips, reveling in the feel of him straining against his pants. His thick erection rubbed me deliciously through the barricading fabric and I moaned, trying to get closer.

Finally making it to his room, he laid me on his bed, teasing me further.

"I knew you were gonna mess up my hair, TJ McHale," I teased. I moved myself up to the pillows, trying to create leverage. When he didn't immediately climb over me, I sat up on my elbows and looked at him. I raised my brows in a "what?" look. He unbuttoned the top button of his jeans.

"What do you want, babe?" he asked, his eyes blazing.

"You," I shyly replied.

Stepping back a little, TJ began to unbutton his shirt. "No, darlin'. I want to hear you tell me what you want."

I looked at him like he had lost his mind. I wasn't talking dirty to him. I was a shy, southern lady, after all.

Like the room was full of party guests, I whispered, "TJ, I can't say the words. You know what I want."

"I wanna hear it come out of your mouth, Ellie-bean."

"Okay...fine. I want your dick, babe. There you happy?" I quickly got the words out of my mouth as I rolled my eyes and felt the blood rush up to my cheeks.

"No, I'm not happy. You love me?"

Now I was getting angry.

"Why would you even ask me that?"

Now that he saw I was getting apprehensive, he came over to sit next to me on the bed and laid his hand on my chest. I went to sit up and he stopped me quickly,

"No, baby, just lay back. Close your eyes."

I trusted him with everything that I was, so I did what he told me to do. I laid back and closed my eyes. Slowly and very gently, he ran his fingers up the inside of my leg.

"Feel that?"

"Yeah, babe, I feel that."

"Now explain what you're feeling."

I had never really concentrated on the description of the feeling. I laid there and just...felt. He slowly ran his finger up the other side of my leg but stopped mid-thigh. I became frustrated. I slowly opened my legs wider thinking he would take the hint. He didn't. Again, he stopped mid-thigh.

"I feel frustrated and disappointed."

"Good girl, why?"

"Because I want you touch me."

"Mm, beautiful, babe. Where do you want me to touch you?"

I pointed to my core and I heard him huff.

"You want me to touch your pussy?"

"Yes, please. This is killing me TJ, you're teasing me."

He laughed and replied coquettishly, "Then play along, darlin'."

At this point, I knew he wouldn't give me what I wanted until I played along. I started moving my hips in a circular motion and licked my lips. "Baby, I need your cock inside my pussy. Please, I'm so wet. I need your cock buried so deep that all I feel is you."

That's all it took. TJ ripped his shirt off, his buttons flying all through the air. His pants weren't even all the way unzipped as he tugged them off of his legs. His motions were erratic, his kisses fevered, as he worked his way up my legs. Reaching my core, he stopped. He laid his cheek against my upper thigh and just breathed me in. My hands went straight to his hair and began to softly push it back from his face.

Quietly, he whispered, "You know my life is yours, don't you? I am nothing but skin and bones without you."

Tears filled my eyes. He was everything to me. He made my day begin and my night end. He was my happiness to the point where I felt physical pain.

"I know, and you're mine, my love." I couldn't even fathom the depths of despair I would feel without him.

"Come here," I breathed, needing him more in this moment than ever before.

He slowly crawled up my body, his eyes never leaving mine. I ran my hand over his cheek. "Make me whole, babe."

As he entered me, tears of emotions that I couldn't describe were running down the side of my cheeks. He pulled out of me slowly before thrusting back in forcefully, his eyes still connected to mine. I moaned, needing this. I needed him. I wasn't whole without him.

My hips moved of their own accord, matching him thrust for thrust. I needed more, needed him deeper. I readjusted, lifting slightly so my clit rubbed against his pelvis with every forward movement. I was lost, caught in a haze. I didn't know where he ended and I began.

"That's it, babe, make me yours. God, you feel so good. So deep, so perfect. Shit, TJ. Show me who's pussy this is."

I lowered my hand to his back, raking my nails against his flesh. His muscles tensed under my fingertips, his hips pounding faster. As I felt my own orgasm approaching, I whispered in his ear, "Baby, give me all of you. You have all of me."

That was all it took. TJ groaned and my orgasm shattered through me at the sound. As I came down from my climax, I could still feel him slowly moving in and out of me.

He raised his head from my neck with a smile on his face. The color in his cheeks hit me straight in my chest. He was happy and satisfied. TJ started laughing as he pushed the hair out of my face. "We will be doing that again soon."

I laughed again. Hard.

Coming back to reality, I felt the water prickling my skin, and it was cold. It was past the time to get out. TJ told me that this was casual so I dressed casual. I threw a smidge of makeup on and lip gloss before I threw my damp hair up in a messy bun. That was as good as it was getting, I thought as I walked out of my room and into the living area.

A mishmash of several different entrees ranging from hamburgers with fries to fish and grits was laid out.

"It's been eighteen years since I've had a meal with you, I wasn't quite sure what you would be in the mood for," he said as he pulled the cork out of a bottle of wine.

If I were wearing boots, I would've been knocked right out of them. He had taken a shower and was dressed in a pair of faded blue jeans that were worn in all the right places. The t-shirt he was wearing was navy blue and fitted — quite nicely, I might add. His feet were bare and even they were gorgeous. I could smell the fresh scent of his body wash heavily in the air. I brought my attention back to the food, I was starving but I wanted something light and soft, my throat was still a bit sore.

Clearing my throat, I told him that I wasn't picky and went to sit down at the rather large dining room table. He had hooked his iPod up to the stereo and had some soft music playing in the background. I wasn't really paying attention to the music.

"Please, have a seat."

"I thought we were going out."

Smiling at me, he poured me a glass of wine "Never said we were going out. As I recall, I think my words were, you have an hour to get dressed because you would be joining me for dinner. We're doing that. Plus, I kind of wanted to keep you to myself tonight, maybe finish what we started the other day at lunch."

Looking at him, I knew he had to recognize the questioning smirk on my face. "I think where we left off was treading dangerous waters, Mr. McHale. I said nothing personal."

He poured himself a glass of wine, pulled his chair up beside me, and sat down. "I don't want to sit that far away, I don't want you to strain your voice any more than you already have." I smiled as I brought the glass of wine up to my lips. "Back to the question at hand. I don't think you can ever get too personal, Ms. Barker."

Now he was using my maiden name. I didn't understand him.

"What would you like to eat?" TJ asked as he glanced over at the buffet. I followed his eyes over to the counter full of delectable goodies. My mouth began to water as I fixed my sight on that gorgeous bowl of mixed greens they had arranged in a beautiful serving dish. I started to push my chair back when he put his hand over mine.

"I asked you what you would like to eat. Nothing in that question said to stand up and leave the table." His voice was deep and stern.

I sat back down and put my hands in my lap. "I'm sorry. I thought I would just help myself, I didn't know."

He rubbed his hand over mine, his facial expression growing softer. Quietly, he asked, "Now, what would you like to eat?"

Not sure of everything that was up there, I told him to put a little of everything on my plate just so I could say that I had tasted it. I was more interested in that salad, a cup of soup, maybe a sandwich, and Jell-O. He nodded once as he squeezed my hand gently, then he stood up. "So, are you going to tell me what the tattoos say?" He blurted as he dished out some soup

225

into a small porcelain bowl. I knew that he had noticed the tattoos on both my wrists when he saw the bruises and the one on my hairline behind my ear.

"I wasn't planning on talking about them, no. All of my ink is very personal and they mean something very sacred to me."

"I could tell that the ones on your wrists were in different languages. Why would you have tattoos on your wrists if no one can read them?" He said as he chuckled.

He placed the bowl of soup down in front of me as he continued speaking. I smiled in gratitude. "Well the reason that I have them in different languages is that again, they're for me. No one else."

"Miss Barker, you are making this reunion a little difficult if you're not willing to talk." He said as he winked, setting a plate of food down in front of me.

"Thank you, sir." I graciously said as I picked up my fork to take a bite of my salad. He winked again as he left to go back up to make his plate. If he wanted to play this get to know each other game then I could play.

"So, are you married...girlfriend?" I said between bites of the delectable sandwich.

"Now she wants to get personal, as long as it's her asking the questions, huh?" He playfully retorted as he sat down with his plate.

"I'm not married, had a girlfriend but nothing serious. No kids, just me."

"Oh, sorry to hear that."

He took a bite of his hamburger and began to talk again. "Sorry for what? I'm not sorry. I told you, Elle nothing was permanent for me and as I recall, I made a promise a long time ago that I planned on keeping."

I almost choked on my food. I quickly chewed and swallowed then took a gulp from my wine, a huge gulp.

"You're kidding, right?" I chortled.

Shaking his head. "Did you think I was kidding when I made that promise?"

"TJ, you were in second grade".

Now I was laughing because no one made promises about their future in second grade. "Why of course I thought you were kidding. Besides, that's not even possible."

Taking another bite he answered. "And why's that impossible?"

I took another sip of my wine and shook my head. "I'm not talking about this."

"Oh yes you are. You brought it up."

I laid my fork down and looked up at him.

"Okay, fine I brought it up. I'm ending it now. Next subject." I picked my fork back up and began stabbing at spinach leaves.

"Ok then, I can work with that. Subject change, why won't you just admit that you're still in love with me?"

I changed my mind, back to the other subject.

"That promise can never be acted on since I am already married. Remember? And from what I know about multiple marriages is that polygamy is illegal."

"Oh, so you want to go back to that subject? This is getting interesting."

He smirked again.

It was my turn to ask another question and I decided that I was getting this conversation back on track. I was growing sick of always discussing myself.

"So, since we are going to get started tomorrow, can you give me a rundown on my day?"

"Here we go, back to professionalism 101."

"Yes, sir. That is what this trip is about, isn't it?"

"It's about a lot of things, Elle."

"I'm sure it is. For you, maybe, but I think it would be best for both of us if we keep this strictly professional."

Still sitting beside me, he threw his napkin over his plate. Obviously, he was finished eating. Maybe he was just about as fed up with this conversation as I was.

"What does the ink represent, Elle?"

Maybe not. I didn't answer him. Grabbing my hand, TJ turned it over seeing the ink mixed with the bruises that wrapped around my wrist. I knew he saw them, but he didn't say anything about them. I laid my fork down. He leaned into me, rubbed his nose against mine, and began to spell the letters of my tattoo against my lips.

"C-U-I-M-H-N-I-G-H."

"What's it say, Elle." I wasn't a question, more like a demand. He mumbled it as he rubbed his lips against mine. His sweet breath was warm against my skin and made my blood boil. My heart was beating two hundred miles per minute. I could only imagine that he tasted the same. I yearned for this moment for so long. I had dreamed of having his lips against mine again—if only just once. I closed my eyes and reveled in the sensory overload. This felt like a dream to me.

I sighed the translation. "Remember."

I felt his tongue poke out just for a second, sweeping across my bottom lip quickly, and then it was gone.

"Remember," he said as he smiled. He then stood up and headed to get another plate of food. I opened my eyes and felt anger rush up from the bottom of my feet to the top of my head.

I'd had enough of him. If I stayed in his presence any longer, I was going to punch him in the face. I grabbed my soup and spoon and excused myself from the table. I thanked him for a nice evening and begin walking to my room.

"Where are you going?" he asked as he wrapped his hand around the top of my arm, halting my movement. I looked at him then looked at my arm, showing him that he needed to remove his hand. He didn't, which just pissed me off more.

"I'm going to bed. I think I've had enough bullshit for one night," I uttered. I was going to my room, video conferencing my kids, and then I was going to bed.

"No, you're not."

He started to drag me back to the living area. I ripped my arm out of his hold and began walking to my room.

The nerve of him! Who the fuck did he think he is! "How dare he think he can order me around," I mumbled to myself.

I heard him laughing as I walked into my room. I set my soup on the nightstand next to the bed and went to my luggage. I grabbed my laptop, t-shirt, and sweats. I went to get on my bed and opened my computer when I heard a light knock at the door. I wasn't going to answer it, but he continued to knock. I reluctantly walked over and opened the door.

TJ was standing there with a cup of Jell-O.

"I would like to apologize for my behavior. I wanted to make sure that you got this before you went to bed. I will be up tomorrow at eight, if you'd like to join me for breakfast. They have a wonderful omelet bar during the week and then we can head over to the office and I can show you around."

Relaxing a little, I let my guard down and accepted his peace offering.

As I went to shut the door, he held out his hand as if to shake on it. I indulged him by sticking my hand in his. As I went to shake, I felt him tug my arm—hard. I went to pull back, but his lips were already on mine and he was kissing me, hard and slow. His tongue tempted my lips to open with little swipes. On its own accord, my mouth opened, allowing him access. And that was all it took. I was lost.

His taste, his smell, the way he moaned when he succeeded at accomplishing his task, broke down my defenses. I needed more, but this was leading us somewhere I couldn't go. I had already had one breakdown over ending this, I couldn't take another one. In a rush, I pushed him away. His breaths were rapid and short, and his eyes looked like the fire in them had been extinguished. I couldn't look at him much longer, I wouldn't be able to fight him off.

"Good night, Mr. McHale," I said as I began to shut the door before he had a chance to respond.

"Good night, Ellie-bean. Sweet dreams." I could hear the smile in his voice. I knew there was no going back to where we were before. Professionalism just took a nose dive right out the fucking window.

Chapter 13

December 1992

Richland was beautiful this time of year. Other than a disturbance here and there from a momma deer and her baby, the snow laid crisp and clean across the front yard. It was Christmas Eve and I was excited, my two favorite girls were coming home from school and I wanted to hear all about college life.

Things were going well for us. I was healthy; huge, but healthy. The babies were growing and everything looked good, according to my last sonogram two weeks ago. Daddy and Mona returned from their trip after Thanksgiving and I surprised them with two bibs that said, "I love my grandpa and grandma". One in pink and one in blue. It took them a minute to wrap their minds around what I was trying to say so I just came out and told them about the twins. They jumped up as I took my time getting up and we hugged and cried, but they were as excited as I was.

Bear, on the other hand, began to grow even more distant. He wouldn't come home for two or three nights a week and he barely even talked to me when he was. I was hoping with Christmas here, we would spend more time together; at least get prepared on what to expect when the twins arrived.

I was now in the homestretch of this pregnancy. I was due in March but from what I had been told, multiple births didn't usually make it to forty weeks. I was exhausted, my tummy felt sore from all the kicking, and I didn't think I would ever forget the feeling of a head or foot stuck up under my ribs.

I hadn't heard anything from TJ nor had I seen him. I wondered about him daily—how football was going, if his classes were going well, if he had someone in his life.

I was heading into the study so I could begin the daunting task of wrapping when I heard the doorbell ring. I went to the door and opened it, not even thinking to look through the peephole. A lady I had never seen before stood before me. As I stood there longer, I began to question myself on whether it was a lady or not. She looked like she was a vagabond.

Her hair was greasy and the color was dull. She had about three inches of root regrowth that was jet black while the rest of her head was bleach blonde. Her face had concealer caked onto what looked like a week's worth of already caked on concealer. Her fake eyelashes were barely hanging onto what thin lashes she had attached to her eyelids. Her eye shadow was powder blue and coated the entire skin above her eye, her rubbed on crème blusher was rusty red and her lipstick was just as red. It didn't even follow the lines of her lips, it just went all over the area under her nose and above her chin.

Grabbing the cigarette out of her mouth, she said, "The fucks Bear?" She must've smoked three packs a day. She proceeded to stick her head in around me and look into my childhood home, screaming Bear's name. She smelled like she had been raised in a brothel. The odor of nasty sex mixed with body odor, cigarettes and booze wafted into my noise. I held my breath as she continued to try and move around me. At this moment, I was thankful for my girth, otherwise she would've been able to get by me.

"Bitch, get out of my way!" she growled at me. I had to keep my wits about me. I was a southern lady with class unlike this scum that was leaving her trail of filth on my doorstep.

"Um, ma'am, I don't know who you are or why you're looking for my husband, but Bear is not home at the moment."

She looked at me eye level then dropped her sight to my feet as she inspected every inch of my beautifully washed body.

"So, you're the cunt who tries to hold him down, huh?"

I jumped back, shocked at this question. I put the fake, "get the hell outta here before I grab the bat that is sitting pretty behind this door" smile back on my face and explained again. This time much slower so she would understand.

"I'm sorry, I didn't catch your name but since trash seems too graceful of a title, I won't call you anything. However, I did call someone and that is the cops. So, I suggest you leave this property. Let's see, what's a small word that you would understand…" I held my index finger up to my lip and I stared into the sky, acting like I was contemplating a word. "Quickly, yes, that's a small word." She took one more drag off her cigarette, threw it down on the cement of the entryway, and bowed. "I'll be seeing you again," she threatened before she turned to walk away. I heard her mutter, "Cunt," as she walked away.

"Lovely," I retorted as I shut the door and locked it. I stood there for a moment to make sure she definitely had left the property. I then reminded myself to start using the peephole.

I ended up in the study with Christmas music streaming through the speakers when I saw Mona come in. I playfully yelled at her to get out before she saw something. She laughed, stuck her tongue out at me, and plopped down on the couch next to Daddy's desk.

I looked at her. "Everything wrapped?"

She smiled at me.

233

"I take that as a yes."

I threw another wrapped gift over in the pile. I had gone a little overboard this Christmas because of the babies. They weren't even here and I basically had everything I would need. I wasn't sure if I was going to have a baby shower so I took it upon myself to purchase what I thought we'd need and what I wanted. It was so much fun, seeing little outfits and picturing my babies in them. I also bought a two seated stroller where both the seats laid down. I was eager to put that thing to good use. I had no idea what Bear had bought or if he had bothered to buy anything at all. This was going on twenty-four hours since the last time I had seen him.

"Any word?"

It was as though Mona was reading my mind. I shook my head. I did not want to lose my good mood just because he was being stupid. I knew what he was doing, he was out at the bar. It was Christmas Eve and he should've been home with his family and pregnant wife, but he chose to shoot his paycheck down his throat.

I finished up the gifts I had left to wrap and noticed I had some little stocking stuffers for the girls I needed to still get, so I asked Mona if she wanted to go out with me. She agreed and we headed to the living room to grab our purses. As I went to put mine on my shoulder, I was flipped around quickly. I grabbed onto Bear's shirt to gain my footing.

"What the hell, Bear?" I squeaked out, attempting to get my eyes to catch up with my brain. Lowly, he whispered for me to get in our room. He was pulling me by my shirt as he stomped to the bedroom.

He stopped right inside the doorway, slammed the door, and locked it.

"I heard you had a meeting with a friend of mine this morning."

Did he really consider that skank a friend of his? The thought of that nasty woman spending time with him made me sick to my stomach. How could he stand to be near her? The smell was revolting enough. I wasn't about to let him yell at me for telling her to leave.

"Oh yeah, trash? I didn't catch her name before she called me a cunt, so I just named her trash since that's what she smelled like," I said, trying to hide my laughter.

His mammoth hand came across my face so hard that it slammed me into the dresser. Losing my stability, I fell to the ground.

"Don't you ever call her trash, Elleny. You got me? Ever! She is important to me."

I thought what I heard him say was that some repugnant woman who smelled like every man in Atlanta blew his load on her meant something to him. And what was I...chopped liver?

Standing up, holding onto the dresser with one hand and the other on the side of my face, I turned my attention to the door Mona was about to break down. I heard her screaming if everything was all right and to let her in immediately. My voice sounded as shaky as my legs.

"I'm fine, Mona. Just give me a sec, hon, and then we'll go."

I turned back to Bear and looked at him. "She that important to you that you'd give this up?" I grabbed my belly with both hands. "I've had enough of you and your flexible-matrimonial schedule. And, you promised never to raise a hand to me again, Bear. I am four months from giving birth and you're smacking me around like I'm a man in the boxing ring. Pack your shit and get out, I don't need this. I'm going out with Mona, you had better be gone by the time I get back."

He strode two large steps and was right in front of me, the veins on the side of his head throbbing. I could see he was beyond mad, he was fucking livid. He grabbed the back of my neck and pushed me down until I was on all fours. Stepping closer, he put his boot down in front me and proceeded to push my head down until my face was crushed up against the top of his boot.

235

"Lick my boot, bitch, because that's where you deserve to be. You think you're better than her? You ain't shit. Don't you fucking think you can order me in and out of this house. All you should be concentrating on is cooking my fucking meals and spreading those fat-ass legs when I can't seem to get pussy from a real woman. You ever threaten me again, you won't be able to walk for a month. You got me? Oh, and next time my lady comes by to see me and you don't treat her like the queen she is? It won't be a good time for you. Do you understand me, cunt?"

I felt like I had entered the Twilight Zone. I couldn't believe what I just heard. He called me a cunt. I was his wife and he called me a cunt. And, he thought I was fat? I didn't know whether to cry or get up and hit him. I went to stand up when he continued on.

"I asked you if you understood me, whore?"

I saw his boot go back but it all happened so fast. He brought his foot back up as hard as he could, kicking me in the top of my stomach. He kicked me so hard, I left the ground for a few seconds. I couldn't breathe, I thought this was it. I thought I was dead. All I felt was pain throughout my torso.

As he went to walk out the door, I heard him say, "I can see that we're on the same page now. Don't worry, I won't be home for a while."

He opened the door and walked out as I laid there on the floor. I saw Mona run down to my side, screaming for someone to call 911. I closed my eyes and passed out.

I woke up with my dad in front of me, stethoscope attached to his ears, listening to my stomach.

"Everything sounds good but I want a scan done."

I'd had enough of hospitals, I wasn't going to go back until I had these babies. "I'm not going to the hospital, Daddy," I said softly.

"Ellie, we need to make sure the babies are fine," he pleaded. I could feel them rolling around, one on each side. I knew he could feel it too, his hand was still resting on my abdomen.

"And no cops. Promise me, no cops. I refuse to become the talk of the town."

"Absolutely not, Elleny! He beat the hell out of you. I'm calling the cops." His voice grew stern and I knew he was as serious as a heart attack.

I sat up straight, a terrible pain shooting through my ribs. The pain was almost unbearable but I pushed through it.

"I said no cops!" I yelled right before I collapsed. Maybe refusing a hospital visit was a bad idea.

I heard my dad mumble under his breath, "Goddammit," as he walked out of the room.

I sat up from the couch and lowered my feet to the floor. Gently, I had to work myself up to standing. I walked slowly, taking measured steps as I made my way to the kitchen.

After an early dinner, Mona and I decided to tend to the errands we needed to do earlier in the day. I was sore so we took it extra slow walking through the mall. I got what I needed and picked up a few things I didn't need, but they were for the babies. That was always my justification.

As I was walking, I continued to feel like I was being watched. I turned my head from side to side to see if I recognized anyone. A cold seat broke out across my skin but I didn't see anyone. I shook off the feeling and finished what we came to do. In the back of my mind, I couldn't help but wonder if it was Bear's trash that was following me. Maybe I would see her again sooner rather than later.

We made it home by seven and I decided that I wanted to take a long bath. I began walking out of the kitchen when I heard the phone ring. It rang twice and then it stopped. I had started back down the hallway when the phone started to ring again. As it was going into its third ring, I caught it.

"Hello," I snarled into the handset.

Silence.

237

"Hello?"

Still nothing, so I hung up.

I continued my way out of the kitchen when the phone started ringing again. I stormed back to the phone.

"Hello!" I yelled into the receiver.

More silence. I had a feeling I knew who it was, so just to make sure she didn't call back, I informed her, "If this is you, skank, Bear's not here. I don't know where he went and he said he'd be gone for a while which a week or two, so don't call back."

I slammed the phone down and left the kitchen, finally heading to the bathroom. I ran my water hotter than normal, added bubbles, and sunk down.

The phone didn't ring again.

"Wakey, wakey!" I heard a quiet voice say next to my ear. I opened my eyes and there, nose to nose with me, was TJ. "It's Christmas mornin', darlin' and have I got some presents for you." He kissed my forehead. I reached up, wrapped my arms around his neck, placed my face into his neck, and just cried. I sobbed for so many reasons.

I wept for the way Bear had treated me and my babies the day before. I was so scared. I thought the only piece of TJ I had left was going to be ripped away from me permanently. I cried because he was here in my arms, how I left things the last time I saw him, and how I had been lost without him.

My ribs were throbbing, the babies were going a mile a minute, pushing against my skin that had grown tight with every month they had become more developed, but I didn't want to leave the position I was in. I was completely content with him here in my arms. My heart had found its normal rhythm again.

"Ellie-bean, don't cry. I'm here with you, always." He pointed to my chest. "I'm right here, anchored to you, babe." I put my head back in his neck and just kept telling him that I loved him so much.

I opened my eyes and realized I was still in my bed, the room was dark, and there was no one standing beside me. I was dreaming. I turned over onto my side and continued to cry. I couldn't go back to sleep so I went into the front room and turned on the Christmas tree. Sitting down on the floor in front of it, I was lost in my thoughts. At first, I blamed it on self-pity, but every way I looked led me back to my thoughts of Trevor. I cried so much, I eventually stopped producing tears. I wasn't weeping anymore, my heart was.

Christmas morning came and went. Daddy, Mona, and I opened all of our presents, leaving the babies and Bear's gifts under the tree. It was difficult not to think about Bear. Where he was, who he was with, what he was doing. This was our first holiday together as a family and he wasn't here to be with his family, it was a lot to take in.

Lilly, Curtis, Rachel, and Kevin had stopped by around four when we were just getting ready to sit down and eat. Smelling all the wonderful fragrances throughout the house had my mouth watering. I was eating for three and I was always starving. They got a little of everything and just picked while I ate a mound of food. We sat around the table talking about college and everything they were experiencing.

Kevin had moved into Rachel's apartment and they seemed blissfully happy. This was the first man that I had seen with Rachel who didn't put up with her shit. He stood his ground and she needed that. We laughed at how big I had become as I would lift up my shirt for them to see my stomach move around like on some Sci-Fi horror flick. They placed their hands where they could see the fluttering, feeling the babies turn over in circles. My sisters loved and kissed on them and then Mona served the pie.

This, to me, was what family had always been about. I didn't bring up Bear because this was about us, sisters. I missed them just about as badly as I did TJ.

At around eleven, everyone got ready to leave. Mona and Daddy said their goodbyes in the house and I walked them out to their cars. Curt and Kevin gave me a swift hugs goodbye and got in to warm the engines up.

Being all bundled up, the three of us girls attempted a hug that seemed to be all coats. I told them I loved them as I kissed them goodbye, once again. I hated when they left to head back to school. I watched them drive off until they were out of sight. As I was walking back up to the house, that eerie feeling washed over me again. I stopped where I was and turned around. I didn't see anyone. I waited there for a moment, but nothing happened. I walked back inside, shut the door and secured the lock.

"Wakey, wakey!" There was that soft voice again. I prayed to hear it. I opened my eyes and there he stood in the same place hovering over me. I felt his hands on my stomach. I pulled my arms up so that I could cover his hands with mine.

"TJ," I whispered.

"I am so proud of you, Ellie-bean. I love you so much, babe. Do you realize that there will be nothing greater under heaven than what we have made together? Our babies were conceived out of a love no other two people on this earth will ever understand. The devotion that we provide to each other is life-sustaining, my love. Even though I won't be there with you physically, I'm with you always. You hold the most vital piece of me right here within you."

When I heard him say those words, I knew that I would make it through this. I had to. This was crucial to the both of us. We were keeping each other alive, even though we weren't together. With that, I pulled his hand up to my lips and kissed it ever so softly. He was hot but that heat was what drew me to him.

"TJ, baby, you're burning up." I could feel it burning my lips as though I had kissed a stove.

"You feel it then, don't ya?"

"Honey, I don't know what you're talking about. Feel what?"

Then it hit me, like a bolt of lightning straight out of the sky.

Life-sustaining.

TJ was to me what I was to him. I was his heart and soul as he was my mine. To me, he was burning hot, providing me with the energy I needed to keep living. To him, I was burning hot, providing him with what he was in need of. That was why I was carrying the most vital piece of himself inside of me.

I was what was keeping him alive.

I woke up, drenched from head to toe in sweat. I was screaming bloody murder, not because I had a nightmare… because I was in labor.

Tracy Lee

Chapter 14

Present Day

I video conferenced the kids. I told them that the flight was good and I was in my hotel, getting ready to go sleep but I wanted to blow them a kiss goodnight. So, I put my fingers over my mouth, leaned back as far as I could go, and threw my hand out to them with a *muah!* They did it back to me, even Luc which surprised me.

I explained to them that I was going to be really busy, so I wasn't sure if I'd be able to conference them like this again every night. I reminded them to be good in school and keep the safety rules fresh in their minds. If Bear was to show up at the school, they were to call Uncle Kevin right away and to stay in the school office no matter what Bear said. If I was to send someone else to pick them up, Luc met that person at the car and asked the code word. Only then could the girls get in with them. And, finally, they were to go to bed at a decent hour so that they didn't give their Auntie Rachel any problems.

I told them I loved them and then told them to give me and Auntie Rach some space, we needed to chat.

"Put the laptop to the side, I wanna see him lying next to you," Rachel joked as she laughed.

"Rach, he's not in my bed, nor will he be in my bed."

"Don't tell me that shit. You're going to prove your own self a liar, I know you're gonna fuck him."

"He kissed me, Rach."

There went the hand with the cigarette in it. It was as if someone had screamed *Hallelujah!* Rachel's arm went straight up in the air and then pointed right back into my face.

"I knew it!" she screamed.

"Shh! It just happened and it wasn't because I wanted it, he kinda snuck up on me."

"Okay…well, how was it?"

"Seriously, Rach? This isn't high school truth or dare."

"Fuck you! I've been waiting eighteen years for this shit. You better start talking!"

"It was okay. He saw the bruises, though. I thought he was going to come unglued. He started with all that "Me Tarzan, You Jane, let me pull you by your hair back into my cave" bullshit, so I had to bring him back to reality and let him know that shit didn't fly with me."

"Maybe you need some of that, Elle. I mean you haven't had someone to depend on in a long time."

"And I don't plan on starting to now. He deserves something wholesome, someone that isn't tainted."

"How the fuck do you know what he needs? I swear, girl, you aren't as tainted as you think you are. You know that, right?"

I fought with deciding on how much Rachel needed to know. She wasn't really one you could tell one instance to and her be satisfied. I thought to myself if this was a good idea, but to prove my point she was going to have to know.

"Rachel, did you know that I had to go and get tested for STD's? Yeah, you remember, you had to help clean up the mess? I had to go and humiliate myself because he decided to lay with some piece of crap and then come home to me, remember that? I still have the bruises so it's pretty fresh in my mind. Well, last night he was with, I guess the same whore, who knows, then came home drunk and sat on top of my chest using me to clean himself off. Tell me how I'm not tainted, girl, because right now, I'm feeling pretty fucking contaminated."

I looked up at Rachel, she had her hands over her face, crying silently. I didn't mean to make her cry. She just needed to realize I was no good for Trevor.

"Rachel, baby, look at me."

She brought her hands down and her mascara had run all over her cheeks and down her chin.

"Honey, I'm broken. Irreparable. He doesn't deserve that."

"Why!" she screamed at me as she slammed her fist down on her desk.

"Why can't he fix you, goddammit! He's the only one on this earth that can fix you and I want you fixed! I am not giving up on you, Elle. You mean too much to me!"

Still sniffling, she turned her head to the side as though she was looking deep down inside of me. "I need you, Elle. Don't give up on me, let him fix you. You deserve this." Rachel whispered.

Wiping the tears from my eyes, I blew her a kiss, told her I loved her, and disconnected the call. I sat there a moment and cursed my luck for running into TJ McHale again.

I needed a drink, something strong. I got off the bed and went to the door. I put my ear up to it to see if I could hear anything. It sounded quiet, so I opened the door just a hair to peek out into the open area. Nothing. Lights were out, except for two small lamps over in the corners. I opened the door all the way and headed for the kitchen. I walked briskly, hoping if I hurried my chances of running into him were slim. I entered the small kitchen and opened up the cabinets. I saw regular size glasses but I didn't see any shot glasses. *Fuck it.* I grabbed a juice glass. The mood I was in, I probably could've just sucked it out of the bottle.

I went over to the mini-bar that was located in the living room and looked at my choices. Since having kids, I hadn't been a big hard liquor drinker, so I decided on the first bottle I saw. Grabbing the bottle of Jack, I unscrewed the lid, and poured half a glass. That looked like a shot to me. I tipped my head back and filled my mouth.

"Holy shit!" I whispered as I looked at the glass, there was about half of that shot left. I took a couple of short breaths to try extinguish the fire that was now ablaze in my mouth and tipped my head back again.

"Whoa," came out of my mouth a tad louder. I glanced around the corner just to make sure that his door was still shut. I watched it for a moment to reassure myself that he wasn't coming out. All was clear. I tip-toed back over to the bar and poured the same amount in my glass. Now that I'd had two shots, I was feeling pretty relaxed. My muscles weren't as tense and I didn't seem to be as uptight. I had forgotten how much I liked liquor. I was feeling pretty damn good.

"This one's for you, fucker. May you live short and die long."

"And who would we be toasting to? I am really hoping I'm not the fucker."

I looked back and saw TJ standing there in a pair of sweats and no shirt. His stomach muscles were rippling down into a luscious V where his sweats hung off his hips. His arms were still as large and very defined as they were in high school, just a bit bigger now.

"Christ Almighty, shouldn't you go put a shirt on before harems of women break down the door to lick every muscle on your body?" I murmured to myself as I turned back around and shot what I could of the liquor in my glass.

I heard him laughing—hard. Looking back again, his head had fallen back and his stomach was even tighter, which just made this harder. I turned to the bar again and downed what was left in the glass.

"Well, I wasn't expecting harems, just you," he said, still laughing.

I went to fill up my glass again. Considering I was pretty shit-faced, I may have filled up the whole glass.

Reaching for the bottle, TJ said, "I think we've had enough, don't you?"

My hand fell down to my side, because I couldn't feel it anymore. "Nope, I'm still standing, right?"

He chuckled again and started walking me over to my room.

"I thought you were asleep. I was just coming out to get a glass of water and here I find you attached to the bottle of whisky. Can I ask what brought this on?"

"You sure can," I slurred. "You know what brought this on, Mr. McHale? I'm gonna tell you," I continued, stumbling back into my room.

"Drama, that's what brought this on. D-R-A-M-A."

He walked me to my bed, pulled down the bedspread and sheet, and helped me sit on the side. As he stood there, I continued on.

"I hate drama, but it seems to continue to hunt me down."

As I was talking, I began pulling my blouse off. Fortunately, I still had my bra on. I reached for my t-shirt like I was in the room all by myself. I wasn't freaking out that TJ was standing right here in front of me watching me undress.

"Never can I go a day with some sort of shit happening to me."

I balled up my blouse and threw it on my suitcase over in the corner and pulled on my t-shirt.

"I thought if I got away, it would calm down. But, nope, here it is."

I reached up behind me, unhooked my bra, and pulled the straps out of my shirt on both sides. I flipped it into my suitcase, pulled my feet into bed, and covered up.

"Are you comfortable, Elle?"

"No," I said as I put my hands down to my side.

"But, I'm okay. Thank you. Good night, again, TJ."

"Good night, Elle. Sleep well."

I watched as he headed for the door, thoughts and memories bombarding my mind as I saw Rachel crying and slamming her hand down on her desk.

"TJ?"

I stopped him right as he was closing my bedroom door.

"Yes?"

"Would you mind laying with me for a bit?"

I heard the smile come back in his voice as he answered, "Not at all."

He shut the door and panic washed over my body.

I mentally fought with myself. *Oh god, what had I just done? TJ was going to be lying beside me in bed. Oh Jesus, what if Rach was right, what if we did end up sleeping together? What if I ended up begging like a dog? Oh shit, did I get waxed? Did I shave my legs? Oh god!*

Everything was running through my head as he walked around the other side of the bed and pulled the covers back. I watched him stand there for a moment.

"Do you mind if I lay in my boxers? I don't want to offend you or anything. I know you're a married woman and I told you I wasn't going to make a move on you, so you don't have to worry."

TJ in boxers? Oh yeah, I'm so going to get fucked this trip. No you're not, shut up, Elleny!

"That's fine, I have my sweats on. I think we're adults here."

Yeah, sure we are. The guy just kissed you and earlier told you that he wanted you to move up and down his cock in the elevator. Girl, you are so screwed.

I quieted the arguing in my head as I turned on my side toward him with my hands up under my face. I watched as he undressed and climbed into bed facing me. I could see him faintly from the bathroom light I had left on, I smiled at him and he smiled back. We just stared at each other for long moments.

"Wanna tell me what happened?" he said in his low rough voice.

"I made Rachel cry," I blurted out.

"Oh, I see," he responded, surprisingly.

We stared at each other again for another couple of moments before he spoke again.

"Do you wanna tell me why you made Rachel cry?"

"Because I told her I wasn't going to sleep with you."

He definitely wasn't expecting that.

"I see."

I brought my finger up to his nose, put the pad of my finger up to the tip, and held it there for a moment while I whispered, "I've missed you." I saw his eyes close. My eyes were becoming heavy, I felt sleep coming fast. I began to bring my hand down and back underneath my head.

His hand came up and wrapped around the back of my neck, his thumb running across my cheek, just like he used to do. I felt his warmth shoot throughout my body, his touch was burning against my skin and I wanted more. He moved his thumb down to brush against my lips. Back and forth he went, his eyes dropping to watch his finger.

He didn't say a word, just continued brushing back and forth across my lips. I didn't say anything either. I raised my hand and held on to his lower arm just to have some type of contact with him. Finally, he spoke.

"I'm sorry about your dad."

I closed my eyes at the thought of my daddy. I reopened them.

"I know."

We sat there in silence a little bit longer, my eyes taking in every square inch of his beautiful face.

"Should of been me, Elle."

Still looking at him, I lowered my eyebrows in confusion. I didn't know if it was the alcohol or the exhaustion but I became really confused as to what he was referring to. Was he talking about my dad still? I watched him pull me

249

closer to him, his hand still around the back of my neck. Closer, closer, until there was no space between us. He pulled my forehead down until it settled touching his. He closed his eyes.

"Goodnight, babe."

"Night."

I was just about to drift off into a deep sound sleep when I felt him put his arm over me and heard him say three little words I never thought I'd hear him say again.

"She's with me."

I closed my eyes and did something I hadn't done in seventeen years, I slept soundly; no worries of being woken up by Bear and the fear of him tormenting the kids was gone. I felt the safest I had felt in a long time. I was protected, and I loved it.

"Good Morning, Ellie-Bean." I heard inside my head. I felt soft, tickling touches down the side of my body. "I've missed waking up to you like this."

I'm having that fucking dream again.

"Goddammit, I forgot to drink the tea last night. I hate this dream. I've got to get up. Wake up, Elle, it's another day in hell," I murmured to myself with my eyes still closed.

I heard the quiet laughing coming from beside me, but it didn't sound like Bear's. In fact, I couldn't remember the last time I heard Bear laugh. I popped my eyes open and got a full view of the ceiling. "Oh shit, that's not my ceiling."

Memories from last night came flooding back to me. The hotel, the penthouse suite. Bottle of whisky, TJ in the same hotel suite. I sat up quickly, which was a huge mistake. "Oh god, my head," I moaned as I grabbed a hold of both sides to make the spinning stop. It didn't help. "What are you doing in my bed?" I asked through one squinted eye. "I said good morning, Elle. There is usually a response to that comment." Trevor grinned a very handsome one-sided morning smile.

"Morning, TJ. Now what are you doing in my bed?"

"You asked me to lay with you last night and truthfully, I enjoyed it…immensely. I forgot how much you talk in your sleep. I must say, I don't know whether to blush or feel honored that I make you, hmm…" he set his chin in the nook between his index finger and thumb as though he was engrossed in deep thought, "How would I describe those noises you were making after you said my name? Moans? Groans? Nah, not descriptive enough."

Oh shit, oh fuck, please let this still be the dream! I promise, I will drink my tea like a good girl every night, please let this be a dream.

"You're lying," I huffed as I threw the blankets back onto him so I could leave the bed. I plodded straight to my bedroom door and opened it. "Thank you for your comforting last night, but seeing as I have to meet you in…" I looked at the clock, "an hour and a half, I have a lot to get done before then." I opened the door and threw my arm out, showing him the way to his own room.

TJ slowly pulled the covers away and stood next to the bed. I saw him grab his sweats off the chair, but he failed to put them on. Walking toward me in just his boxers, I had to tell myself to keep my lower jaw up so that my mouth would stay closed as I wiped the greedy look off my face. I kept thinking back to when I'd had him. I had touched and kissed every part of that body, that man had been buried inside of me. I felt every thrust hitting against my internal wall, letting us both know he couldn't go any further. I could feel my eyes sluggishly blinking with all the dirty thoughts that were going through my mind. He went to walk by me and stopped. Staring into my eyes as though he could read every thought I was having, he smiled and touched his finger to my nose. Softly, he whispered, "I've missed you too, Ellie-bean." Then, he walked straight into his room.

251

I grabbed my iPod and immediately went straight for the shower. Turning it on, my all-time favorite song played. "Pain" by Three Days Grace. It described my life so well. I lifted my head up under the shower so that the hot water could revive me. I felt like shit, I hadn't drank like that since I was a teenager. I found out quickly that I was just too old for that shit. I washed my body and brushed my teeth accomplishing two things at once, so I might have time to do something with my hair.

I seized the towel from off of the warmer and wrapped it around my body. I grabbed another one and wrapped it around my head. Listening to the lyrics of Seether now blasting at full volume, I begin to wake up. I wouldn't officially be awake until I grabbed a cup of coffee. I went to snatch my makeup bag out of my suitcase when I heard a knock at the door.

I dragged in a breath and blew it out quickly. I walked to the door and stood there a moment to clear my head. Peeking through the door just slightly, TJ was standing there in his sweats again.

Oh, he was good at this game.

"I thought maybe you'd like a cup of coffee."

I look down to his hand and saw a porcelain cup full of slightly creamed coffee in his hand.

"One sugar, dash of milk…just like you like it. Go ahead, take it." He smiled that grin again.

I opened the door a little further and grabbed the cup out of his hand.

"Thanks," I replied truthfully, because God knows I needed it.

"Welcome," he said as he headed back into his room.

I closed the door and went back into the bathroom. I began with my make-up, I didn't want anything that was too dramatic, but I needed something to cover up this hangover.

Minutes later, I finished and was quite happy with the results. I needed to work on finding an outfit.

I grabbed my thin beige pencil skirt and my short sleeved V-neck top with the lace overlay out of the closet and neatly laid them on the bed. The shirt bunched at the sides to define my curvy hips. I grabbed my beige heels and set them beside the bed and *Voila*! my outfit was ready.

Back into the bathroom I went with my hair dryer to begin working on my hair.

I heard Damn Yankees' "High Enough" come on and I flipped the hairdryer off for a moment. I couldn't help but think back to when we were at the lake that weekend where we made our babies. How I thought that things would end up so differently. I threw that thought into the recycle bin and dumped it, I couldn't think of that now. This was about business and getting home. I turned the hair dryer back on and continued styling my hair.

I ran the straightener through my hair one last time and set it down. It wasn't bad but it wasn't "club hair". I spritzed some perfume all over my body—a nice floral scent—as I unplugged the straightener and left it on the counter to cool down. Walking back into the bedroom, I looked at the clock; perfect timing. I was feeling awake now. Still running a little slow from the drinking, but I could function. I threw my clothes on and then added a lime green and cream scarf around my neck that hung low. I was ready to start the day and I was doing it looking good.

I opened my door and walked out, shutting it behind me. TJ was sitting at the table with a cup of coffee in front of him and newspaper in hand. He was wearing a dark gray suit with a black tie. His hair was styled in a sexy messy look. He looked delicious. I glanced up at him with a fresh smile on my face and informed him that I was ready to go. He just stood there, frozen. I saw his eyes begin to move, scrutinizing.

I looked down at my outfit and turned my head to the side to look at the back of me.

"What? Is there something on me? I knew I shouldn't have laid this on the bed. Shit, give me a minute I'll go…"

"You look…you look beautiful, Elle."

I turned back around and had to swallow two or three times to get the lump in my throat to go down. I put my mask back in place and walked toward him.

"Oh please, you were already in my bed last night, McHale. It won't be happening again, by the way, and that sweet talk isn't going to work." I walked passed him straight toward the door and heard him humph as he followed me. He opened the door and held it as I went through and made my way to the elevator to push the down button. "I hope you're ready to work, because I'm not here to play."

I looked at him straight-faced and saw his lip had turned up into that handsome half smile as he replied, "Yes, ma'am."

The elevator dinged, the doors opened, and I walked in ready to kick some Mac-Gentry ass.

"So, I have two assistants. Mary and Sara who are now your assistants. Use them. Don't be afraid to tell them what to do and how to do it. Your methods are the best I've come across. You and Stevens have a nice system going, uncomplicated and very thorough," TJ stated as he picked through his eggs and hash browns.

Cutting my enormous egg white and mushroom omelet, I blushed. "Thank you, I've tried to work with functionality, what would take the smallest amount of time but would cover all that needs to be covered. I know how you business men are workaholics."

He chuckled while putting a bite into his mouth. "That we are."

"Sara will show you to your office. She knows you're coming in today and she can help you find the names of the clients and all their information. Mary, on the other hand, is fairly new so you can use her to make the copies and she can help with putting the presentations together."

"Great, I will need to have a memory stick for each client that has outstanding mergers with you. That way I can put each client's information onto one and everything we need is right there at our fingertips. I could, with Sara's help, probably have those done by tomorrow afternoon so that we can begin putting presentations together."

He'd laid his fork down and was looking at me with a look that I hadn't seen in seventeen years. His hazel eyes looked like they were on fire. The lust that had taken over his stare was burning a hole right between my eyes.

"You're staring again, TJ," I informed him as I went in for another bite of my breakfast.

"You're spellbinding."

I pulled my face up out of my plate as I looked at him for a moment, mouthing, "Stop."

"Stop what…why?" he said with the sexiest smile I'd ever seen on a man.

I laid my fork down and I asked him quietly, "Why are you doing this? Is this some game to get back at me for what happened between us?"

The smile that was on his face immediately left and I could see his jaw clenching. He got up in a rush but the path he was on didn't register until he had my wrist in his grip, pulling me behind him. I was wearing heels and his stride was longer, so it took me a minute to step into his rapid rhythm. He quickly turned the corner into a hallway and rushed down to the men's restroom. Throwing the door open, TJ looked inside to see if it was occupied. Finding it empty, he pulled me inside and locked the door behind us. Just as quickly, he pushed me up against the wall. His face was so close to mine, I could feel his hot breath on my eyelashes. He pushed closer.

"Do you feel that, Elle? Does this feel like a fucking game to you?" he demanded. I could feel it and I didn't want my voice to give me away, so I remained quiet. His cock was as hard as stone and his thrusts caused him to rest against my stomach. "Nothing about me and you is a game! Don't ever let me hear you say that again!" I felt his fist hit the wall right beside my head and I closed my eyes. I knew he wasn't Bear and that he would never hurt me, but I was still scared and I didn't want him to see that. He bent down further so his length massaged me right between my legs. His movements were so smooth and addicting that I didn't realize my legs were spread, allowing him passage to my now soaking wet center. I had to mentally restrain myself, I was on the verge of ripping my clothes off and mounting this man in front of me.

Feeling his breath blow up against the side of my face brought me out of my attempt at restraint. "Open your eyes and look at me, sweetness," he whispered in my ear. Sluggishly, I opened my eyes and noticed he had his face turned toward me with his lips right next to my cheek.

"Do you feel how hard you make me, Elle? My cock is pulsing, my body is vibrating. This has been going on since I saw you walk into that conference room. Do you know how excruciating it is to jack off, just to immediately get hard again? Do you, Elle? I don't think you do. You're destroying me." He grabbed my hand and brought it to his pants. I could feel him throbbing beneath my fingers as he closed his eyes in relief. Automatically, I wrapped my fingers around his hard shaft. Still looking straight ahead, I could see him out of the corner of my eye. His eyes were heavy and his breaths began to come faster.

"That's it, Elle. Do you feel that? That's what you do to me, it's all for you."

I moved my fingers over his pants, slowly up his length. I felt his breath break through his teeth as he hissed in my ear. I brought my fingers up and molded them around the tip before easing my fingers back down.

"Yeah, Elle. Fuck...you do this to me. This is how much power you have over me." I felt his lips coming around the corner of my cheek, but found that I was the one moving my face toward his.

"Elle, you don't know how bad I've missed your touch."

My hand was still working him, touching him slowly through the material of his suit pants. My fingers traveled down to the bottom of his shaft then worked their way back up to the tip, producing drops of heaven that soaked through to my fingers. His hips were moving in slow circles that mimicked the pace that I was working him at. His moans were deep and harsh, driving me wild. Touching his forehead to mine, I closed my eyes. I could feel his breath dance down the slant of my nose and touch the skin above my lip. I took in his scent and allowed it to absorb into me. I felt the sensation of his tongue touching the middle of my lips and that was my breaking point.

I opened my lips to give him full access to explore my mouth and ended up wrapping my lips around his tongue, sucking delightfully on the taste that was TJ. My fingers that were gripping him were spread wide and building up friction as his hips followed. I heard the sensuous moans echoing throughout the restroom and realized they were coming from me. I pushed my hips toward him while my other hand covered the button on his pants to get them undone.

Still kissing me deeply, he breathed, "Tell me, Elle. All you have to do is say the words."

I needed this so badly, I was ready to say whatever it was he wanted me to say. Then, it hit me.

It will be you, Ms. Barker who begs me for everything I have just said to you.

He wanted me to beg him. He wanted me to play his game. It was then I realized he hadn't touched any part of my body aside from my lips. My hands were the ones jacking him off.

What the fuck, Elleny!

I pushed him away with all my strength. That shove barely knocked him off of me. I needed oxygen, I needed to come back to my senses. Reality was beginning to crash down—hard. I was standing in the men's room, getting ready to raise my skirt for a man who wanted me to ask him to fuck

257

me. No… scratch that, he wanted me to beg him. I didn't beg for food, I sure as shit wasn't begging for dick!

I strolled very slowly over to the mirror to check my hair and lips that were now red and swollen from our harsh kissing. I turned around, straightened my shoulders and my skirt, and told him how it was going to be.

"I'm going back up to my room to freshen up, Mr. McHale. I will be ready to leave for the office in fifteen minutes. If you ever try something like that again, you won't be fucking anything again for a while, are we clear?"

He put that shit-eating grin back on his face, nodded once, and unlocked the door. I walked toward it and looked at him with the glare that told him to open the fucking door for me. He read my face and held it open as I walked through. I then proceeded to head upstairs to burn this pair of fucking panties.

I entered the bathroom in my suite, put my hands on the sink, and stared at myself in the mirror.

"What the hell are you thinking, Elleny? Don't be stupid. You're being fucking stupid! Think of how this will turn out. The kids, your own sanity. Stop falling for his shit! Nothing about this is for you, this is about work!"

I closed my eyes and took some deep, relaxing breaths. I pulled my hair up and jumped in the shower. My body betrayed me by flooding my panties like a dam that had burst forth. If this was what blue balls felt like, I promised never to cause them to any man again.

I jumped back in my clothes and headed out to the living area. I saw TJ had changed as well. Grabbing my gloss out of my pocket and swiping it across my lips, I headed for the door.

"By the way, love the gloss. Tastes like cotton candy."

I rolled my eyes as he closed the door and headed to the elevator without saying a word. The ride to the lobby was quiet and so was the walk to the car. The day was beautiful. I looked up into the clear blue sky and reveled in the cool breeze. I didn't even notice the black, sleek, convertible Audi R8 Spyder that pulled up right in front of us . That car was sex on wheels. I saw TJ walk around it. I opened my mouth to yell at him just as the valet handed him the keys. I smiled as the man opened my door and I got in.

"What the hell is this and how did it get here?" I asked in a high pitched voice I didn't even know I could produce.

TJ laid his head back on the head rest and proceeded to laugh for what seemed like minutes. I didn't see the hilarity of the situation, so I just sat there. Finally, he put the car in gear and took off.

"I had it brought over. I thought maybe after work I could take you out, show you the town." The idea sounded good, but I wasn't planning on it. I needed to work on those memory sticks so that I could stay on schedule.

"Maybe," was all I could say to him.

The drive from the hotel to his office was short but the city was beautiful. I didn't have a chance to leave Richland often so this was pure beauty. Big city, cars passing us at fast speeds honking their horns, sidewalks full of people walking shoulder to shoulder, cell phones plastered to their ears. This was living. I had always dreamed of being smack dab in the middle of the bustle of big city living. Small town life was so laid back, I was sick to death of it. I'd always wanted more than that.

Pulling up to the high-rise of Mac-Gentry was overwhelming. To think that small town Trevor McHale owned this twenty-four story building. I felt that everything I gave up was worth it. He would've never gotten this if he had stayed in Richland. The thought made me smile.

The valet opened my door. As I hopped out, a thought crossed my mind. "When I was putting together your contracts for Richland Manufacturing I would've never put you and Mac-Gentry together. Where did you come up with that name?"

TJ walked around beside me and grabbed my hand as we walked into the front lobby of his company.

"My last name is McHale, obviously, but I didn't really want to use that. So, I shortened it and dropped off the Hale, turning Mc into Mac.

"I went into a partnership with a guy I met in college, Greg Gentry. He was a madman when it came to buying out companies. We were partners until we became widespread. Greg got bored, he wanted out. He was in it for the chase and when you get to a certain point, that chase decelerates until you're ultimately sitting on the sidelines, catching your breath. We were making millions by this time so I bought him out. Now it's all mine," he explained with his hands out in front of him.

"Nice." I smiled.

Stepping into the elevator, I stared at the gold mirrored doors that were in front of me. I listened to the bell chime as we passed each floor. I saw TJ's reflection and his head was turned toward me again. I knew what he's thinking.

"Don't even think it, McHale. Not going to happen."

I heard him chuckle, but saw him step in front of me. He put his hands around my head to box me in. "But what you seem to forget, Ms. Barker is that this is *my* company. I make the decisions on what will and what won't happen here." He winked at me in his teasing manner.

I heard the last bell chime and watched the doors open to the top floor of the Mac-Gentry Firm. I walked out into a waiting area that was immaculate. Modern furniture surrounded the enormous space. On the left of me, was a waterfall wall with Mac-Gentry Firm etched into it. The water ran over the logo and the base of the wall projected out, as if it was meant to hold flowers. Instead of flowers, it was filled with stones and flood lights that illuminated the Mac-Gentry logo. To the right, were two very modern couches that faced each other. Between the couches sat a stainless steel coffee table with a glass tabletop. The table was home to one simple black vase that contained three, large-pedaled bronze flowers. The chairs were the same design of the couches and none of the furniture had arm rests or backs. The company probably paid thousands of dollars for this furniture and it looked like it was made all for under a hundred bucks. All the chairs faced a wall-mounted television, the sound was turned down low, but CNBC wasn't known for its soap operas or talk shows.

We walked deeper into the waiting area to see the receptionist desk right in front of a clear wall of glass with two doors right in the middle. One of the doors had a card reader on it so that employees could slide their badges quickly and go right through.

"Charlene, I'd like you to meet Elleny Barker-Jackson." TJ spit my name out as if it was poison on his tongue. "Elle, this is our receptionist, Charlene."

I smiled at Charlene. TJ continued. "Elleny is going to be working here with us for the next couple of weeks. I need you to make sure that she is given a badge so that she can come and go as needed." Charlene smiled at me. "Elleny, it's a pleasure to meet you. I can have your ID to you by the end of the day, will that do?" I smiled back. "Please, call me Elle. It's a pleasure to meet you as well and the end of the day is fine. I don't plan on going anywhere." Charlene seemed pleasant. She was attractive. Tall with long blonde hair, she looked that she might be in her early thirties. She was thin, actually a little too thin, but some men liked that.

"Elle it is, then. If you need anything, my extension is in the employee directory, just give me a buzz." At this point she looked down at our joined hands and her smile increased. I quickly pulled my hand out of TJ's and returned to my conversation with Charlene. "Thanks again, Charlene. I'll probably be taking advantage of your offer," I chuckled softly.

She hit a button under her desk and the door automatically opened. TJ grabbed my hand again, this time in a death grip. We walked into another room. This room was a large open area divided into small work areas. All of them

261

contained a large L-shaped table, a computer, a phone, and a chair. They provided their own decorations. Some workstations were all decked out where some only had the bare essentials. On the right side of the area, high up on the wall, was another television with the same channel on.

Around the perimeter were their manager's offices. These spaces were actual offices. The names of each manager were posted beside the door along with what department he or she administered. All of their offices overlooked the middle.

I followed behind him since I didn't know where I was going and he seemed to be pulling me along by my hand. He stopped by an office where an older gentleman was sitting on the phone looking at his computer. We stood there for a moment until I heard him tell whoever he had on the phone that he would get back to him later. We walked in and went straight to his desk.

"Trevor, I heard you were on your way back, I didn't expect you until tomorrow. Did everything go well?" The man's eyes glanced over my way as his smile grew wider. "Hello, who do we have here?"

"Sam, I'd like you to meet Elleny. Elleny, this is Sam Fordham. Sam is in charge when I'm not here."

Sam was maybe early forties and in shape. Not as good as TJ, but he looked like he could hold his own. Sam had some weight on him but you could tell that he was mostly muscle. His hair was black with grey streaks running through it; the gray made him striking. He was wearing a blue pin-striped suit and a light pink long sleeved dress shirt with a thick silver tie. His jacket was hanging over the back of his chair.

Sam's eyes looked me up and down as he held out his hand. I took his hand and he turned it over, kissing the top of it. "Elleny, such a beautiful name." His eyes never left mine. "Elle. Please, call me Elle and thank you. It's a pleasure to meet you, Sam."

I smiled at him and his eyes went back to TJ, as did mine, and he was not smiling. I quickly let go of Sam's hand

and attempted to break the tension in the room. "So, Sam, I am going to be working with Mr. McHale for the next couple of weeks." I looked back and forth between Sam and TJ, hoping that someone would give me their eyes in acknowledgement. Finally, Sam broke the eye contact and smiled back at me. "Wonderful, Elle, I look forward to getting to know you better. Maybe we can have lunch before you leave?" I looked back at TJ and saw his jaw clenching rapidly. I needed to shut this down—fast. "Well, I have a feeling I'm going to be pretty busy, but thank you for the offer. It was a pleasure meeting you. Mr. McHale, would you mind showing me around further?" I squeezed his hand and mentally demanded that he look at me. He must've heard me because he turned to me and responded. "Of course, please forgive me. Shall we?" I nodded to Sam and excused myself. He nodded back without saying a word and went back to sitting at his desk.

As we walked back out into the hall, I whispered through gritted teeth, "Your office, now!" I picked up the pace, even though I had no idea where we were going. I just had to calm down. *What the hell was he doing? He was not my husband, did he think this was high school?* We turned the corner and there sat another open space. Another reception area, not as big as the front but it was a good size. Big enough to fit a couch, two chairs, a desk, and another TV. He nodded to the lady sitting at the desk and pulled me into an office. I happened to catch his name plate beside the door so I knew it was his. As soon as we walked in, he shut the door and told me to not say a word. He went over to his desk and pushed a button that made the whole wall of glass that faced the reception area become opaque. He touched another button and the room filled with symphonic music. It was obvious he didn't want anyone to hear or see our little discussion.

"What the fuck is wrong with you? First, you parade around here holding my hand like we're boyfriend and girlfriend, then you introduce me to your second in charge, who ends up pulling some stupid "look at me, I'm a male!"

263

bullshit. Then, there's you. You're acting like you're ready to take him out in the parking lot and beat the shit out of him. This isn't high school. The pissing matches went out of style back in the eighties, buddy! Cut the shit out! Number one, I am not your girlfriend, and number two, you're making me look like I'm not be taken seriously."

He walked out from behind his desk and started pacing in front of it. "And how am I making you look like that?"

"By making it look like we're fucking each other, TJ!" I yelled. "What were you thinking about when you were staring at Sam?"

He didn't answer me, so I moved closer to him. "What, you don't want to say? Because you know I know. You were thinking like we were still seniors in high school and no one could put their eyes on me. Am I right? Well, I'm here to tell you, Trevor, we are not in high school anymore. I am not your girlfriend and we are not fucking each other anymore!" I finished.

As fast as I could draw in a breath, TJ was in my face. His teeth gritting, his breath coming out as though he was hyperventilating. "And why is that, Elleny? Why aren't we together anymore? Why are we not fucking anymore? Oh, that's right, because of Bear! What is it with him, Elle? Bear's cock bigger than mine? He give it to you better than I ever could?"

Before I could even think about what I was doing, the palm of my hand came up and made contact with his cheek. I brought my hand back down and covered my mouth, blocking the screams from coming out.

How dare him! He didn't know the shit I had to put up with! "Fuck this, I'm going home. This job is done." I went to turn my back on him and head for the door when I heard him whisper, "Wait."

I turned back around and found his eyes. "Wait for what, TJ?" He stepped forward that one step, our eyes never losing contact. "For this." He picked me up, carried me across the room, and pushed me up against the wall with his mouth on mine. My arms flew around his neck and my legs automatically wrapped around his waist. Everything was happening so fast, my mind was in a whirl. One minute, we were fighting like cats and dogs, the next, he was sucking my face off. This whole situation was so deranged, but I couldn't stop myself. He was a drug to me. I never had been able to tell him no. I opened my mouth wider as I grabbed the back of his head to pull him deeper into me. I couldn't get enough of him. He broke the kiss, our breathing fast and labored. I could feel he was hard again and my skirt had drifted up to my hips, giving him the perfect access.

His eyes were roaming over my face. I must've looked a mess, but he looked beautiful. I've missed this look on him. His cheeks were flushed, his lips swollen, his pupils dilated; absolute beauty was staring at me.

"Tell me your mine," TJ whispered, so softly. "Say it, Elle. Tell me your mine." It was like in a dream. One of those dreams I had when I was pregnant. I could hear a voice that sounded like me, but my mouth didn't move. "I'm yours, TJ," I heard my voice say.

"Tell me you belong to me."

I didn't even hesitate, I couldn't. I had always belonged to TJ, body and soul.

"I belong to you."

He kissed me softer this time as he rolled his hips under me.

"You with me?"

I heard those words and tears came to my eyes. I was gone, completely and recklessly. And damned if he didn't know it. Through tears and a voice that didn't want to cooperate with me, I finally got out what he had been waiting seventeen years to hear, "Anchored to ya, babe."

He touched his forehead to mine. Then, his lips came to mine and we kissed as though we were giving each other life—again.

265

Tracy Lee

Chapter 15

February 1993

Winter had seemed to diminish early this year. It was cold, but not as cold as it had been in February years ago. I was as big as a barn and really the only times I left the house anymore were for my doctor's appointments. Bear had come home after being away for three weeks. He begged and pleaded for my forgiveness. I gave in and allowed him to come back, but he wasn't back for long. It was only a week, and then he was gone again for another two. I was used to it now. This was how it was going to be and I really didn't care anymore. If he was here, he was here. If not, no big deal.

The babies were good. Back in December, I had a small scare. I thought I was in labor but they were small contractions called Braxton Hicks. The doctor said it was my uterus practicing for the big day. She monitored the babies for a bit and then let me leave the hospital. The babies weren't moving around very much anymore because, bless their hearts, they just didn't have any room.

I had a doctor's appointment today and Mona was taking me. Daddy didn't want me behind the wheel. I didn't have an issue with that, so I sat in the back seat and propped my feet up.

"Have you thought of anymore names, Ellie?" Mona asked as her eyes fluttered between the rearview mirror and the road.

"For a girl, I'm thinking Tatum. For a boy, Dylan."

"I like those names, sweetheart, they sound like good, strong names."

"I think so," I said as I rubbed the top of my belly.

"I think you're a strong woman, Elleny," Mona said out of nowhere. I looked into the rearview mirror and I could see her eyes looking at me. "Don't you ever let him break you, you understand me? You can give him your blood and your sweat but don't you ever give him your tears. You are stronger than him."

Her eyes were going from the mirror to the road, from the road to the mirror. I looked at her and through tears, I shook my head. It killed me that she and Daddy had to see what he was doing. I didn't care about him leaving or having another woman, Bear didn't hold my heart. What I cared about was that they had to clean up his mess when he was done beating me. That was something you just didn't want anyone to see.

Reaching the doctor's office, I stepped out of the car and felt fluid run down my legs.

"Well shit, Mona. I think I just pee'd."

"You what?" she laughed as though I was joking.

"I just pee'd down my legs."

"Honey, that's not pee. I think your water broke."

"Oh shit, it's not time. My babies, they ain't done cookin'." I was panicking so my southern accent was really coming through.

She told me to stay where I was, she was going to run in to find out what we should do. She was gone about eight minutes before I saw her running back toward me, taking in oxygen as though she had just run a marathon.

"Jesus, Mona, are you okay?"

"Girl, I am not a runner. I'm a lover and a shopper."

"What did she say?" I asked, trying to get Mona to focus.

"Oh yeah, I'm taking you to the hospital. She's right behind us." I nodded once and got back in the car. "Make sure when we get there, you call Daddy and have him bring all the stuff." I already had a bag packed and the two car seats were by the front door. I hadn't planned on having the babies yet, but it was good to be prepared just in case.

Although women told me child birth hurt, this wasn't hurting. Maybe it only hurt with one baby. Maybe with two, God felt so bad that you had to suffer double while being pregnant that he said that there would be no pain during the delivery.

"You want me to try and reach Bear?"

I didn't have to answer, my face said it all.

I got to the hospital and was admitted right away. Now, my feet were up and I could lay back and watch TV, this delivery would be a breeze. I rested for a bit until my dad came in with everything. He brought my bag, the babies' bags, and the car seats. That was when it hit me. When I left that hospital, it would be with my babies in my arms. I wanted to cry. I took a little bit of time to call Rachel and Lilly and let them know that I was in the hospital. They both wished me well and told me they loved me. Then, I just laid there and waited for the doctor.

Lying there in that bed, my stomach protruded out so far I couldn't even see my feet. I wondered what TJ would do if he was here. Would he stand beside me, holding my hand? Would he kiss my head and encourage me to keep going? Would he tell me he loved me and that this was the happiest day of his life?

I threw my hands up against my face and took a minute to revel in the meaning of what that meant to me. Two babies created from our love, a love that was so big it wouldn't be contained within just the two of us. I was happy but I was overcome with deep sadness for the perfect little life that was never going to happen.

At that very moment, I felt a twinge move from one side of my stomach to the other side as my whole abdominal section became as hard as a rock. The monitor I was attached

269

to began beeping uncontrollably. Before I could call for someone, the room was full of doctors and nurses.

"I want a sonogram STAT!" I heard the voice of one doctor as Mona and Daddy flew to my side.

I was looking around, shocked. I couldn't even get my mouth to move to find out what was happening.

I heard another doctor demand, "There's no time, we need to section her immediately." I didn't know where to look anymore, so I just grabbed my dad's hand and held on tight.

Finally, one of them addressed me.

"Mrs. Jackson, I'm doctor Duvall. I'm on staff here at the hospital, Dr. Leonard is on her way. Your babies seem to be in distress. Every time you have a contraction their heart rates decelerate. The way that they're dropping, I don't think we are going to have a chance for a natural birth. My recommendation is to do a caesarian section so we can get them out as soon as possible for you to enjoy both of them." My dad immediately told the doctor to do it. I just sat there staring, numb from what he just said to me.

"So…there's a chance…my babies will…" I couldn't even get the word out. I had made it almost thirty-five weeks with these babies fighting each other for who would get to jump on my bladder and now there was a chance that my pregnancy would be all I would get. That my babies could—

"That's why I would like to get you prepped for surgery. Doctor Leonard would be here in time to deliver your babies, but time is of the essence. We need to move now if we're going to do this."

There was no choice to be made.

"Let's go."

I laid there on that cold table, a paper sheet at my breast line covering my lower half. On one side of me was the anesthesiologist, on the other side was Mona all decked out in paper scrubs with a mask on her face.

"Look at me, sweetheart. You're doing so well."

I felt like I was in a dream, I couldn't feel my body from my chest down but I could feel tugging and pressure. "I can't feel myself breathe, am I alright? How 'bout the babies…how are they?"

The doctor beside me comforted me. "You're breathing fine, that can sometimes be a side effect. Everything is stable. You're doing awesome, Elle."

I heard Doctor Leonard's voice, "You're going to feel a lot of pressure. That's just me going in to grab a hold of baby number one, okay?"

I answered back a soft but anxious, "Okay."

I could feel exactly what she was talking about. It felt like someone was pulling my insides out. Then, I heard the best sound I could ever hear—a baby screaming.

"It's a boy!"

I felt so much emotion, I couldn't help but bawl and blubber. Once again, I felt the pressure and then the screaming. This time, not as loud, but still a shrieking cry.

"It's a little girl!"

I began blubbering again. My babies were here. They were both crying and breathing. I was overjoyed. They took both of them over to warmers and began doing what needed to be done. Weights were taken, hands and feet were stamped with black ink. Mona had met the nurses over at the warmers and was taking shitloads of pictures.

A minute later, she came up beside me and kissed my forehead. Tears were running down her face. Mona came down next to me and said quietly, "They're beautiful, sugar, they look just like their daddy." That's when I closed my eyes and lost it completely. My prayers had come true. I could look in my children's faces and see the twinkle of their daddy in them. Finally, when everything was done, they wrapped them up and brought them to me. I was still strapped down to the table and I could feel the doctor still doing things behind the paper wall, but I didn't care. Nothing else mattered. The three of us were alive and well.

I must've fallen asleep after being rolled into the recovery room because when I woke up, I was back in my room and I was in tremendous pain.

"Ow…"

"Hey, baby, you're awake. You hurtin' that bad?" I saw my dad come up beside me and lay his hand against my forehead.

"Oh shit, Daddy, this hurts."

"Well yeah, honey, you had major surgery. It's not like you went for a weekend to the spa."

I tried to laugh but that made it hurt even worse. He reached around me for the button to call the nurse and I heard her voice as she walked in the room.

"Hey, Lydia, can we get some pain meds for the new momma?"

"Sure, Doc. Can she sit up and drink some fluids?"

I heard my dad chuckle and I knew that chuckle. I was going to be sitting up and drinking fluids.

"She'll be cooperating here momentarily."

"My babies, can I see my babies?"

My daddy looked at me. "Let's talk when Lydia leaves."

I saw her walk out the door and I began to panic.

"What's the matter, Dad? What's wrong with the babies?"

"Nothing's wrong, honey. They're good."

I let out the breath I had been holding.

"They just have to watch them for a couple of hours to make sure they're breathing regulates. They seemed to be having a little difficulty with that, the pediatrician says that's completely normal with premature babies."

I took another breath and let it out again. I didn't think I could take much more of this.

"I wanna see my babies, Daddy."

He looked at me again. "You sit up and drink some fluids and I'll see what I can do."

It took me a minute to get my feet on the floor but I was set on seeing my babies.

I grabbed a hold of my dad's arm and put my weight on him. I smiled big when I realized I was standing. Mission accomplished! Now, to take a step. I had to tell my foot to pick up, move out, and step down. *Bam!* I took a step. Then, I did it again with the other foot. I was on a roll. We slowly made it down to the NICU and rang the bell beside the door. The nurse saw my dad and smiled. I saw the door open and a nice older woman greeted us with a warm smile.

"Are you here to take your pick?" she joked.

"Yep, we're only here for the cutest ones," my dad replied as he winked at her.

We followed her through rows and rows of isolates and baby warmers, some opened with stuffed animals and blankets in them and some were closed. Some incubators had holes in the sides of them where you could stick your hands through and have minimal contact with the baby, others were completely closed and the only opening was a tiny hole to allow tubing and lines for monitors.

We continued walking until we came to a larger open warmer where two babies were lying beside each other. One was wearing a tiny blue knit beany cap, the other was wearing a pink one. They both were naked, other than their diapers, and lying so still. They were sleeping. I could see the sticky pads that were affixed to their tiny protruding bellies. Attached were the lines of wires that connected them to their individual monitors. Once every couple of seconds, I'd see an arm or a leg jump involuntarily. They were so beautiful, they were angels sent to me straight from God's cradled arms. They dissipated into nothing more than a water spattered vision from my eyes clouding over with tears.

I couldn't even fathom the emotions I was feeling. I had just laid eyes upon both of these babies, yet I was so deeply in love with them. My life had died the moment they were pulled out of me, now it was theirs. There wasn't anything in this world I wouldn't do for them. It was almost terrifying that I could feel this deep for anyone other than TJ, but I did and that was not going to change.

I continued to just stand there, staring at them in disbelief, when the nurse's request made my head flash up at her.

"Would you like to hold them?"

"Oh god, I can hold them? They look like they'll break," I nervously replied.

"Why of course you can hold them, you're their momma. You've been their home for nearly a year, wouldn't you feel comfortable being close to that?"

She kinda had a point.

She led me to a large rocking chair where I sank very slowly into the thin padding that covered the wood seat. I saw her lift the little girl out of the warmer while she said, "It's always ladies first." I smiled at her and cradled my arm where she placed my daughter. I wanted to cry but I didn't think I could anymore. I just stared at her. I brought her head up to my lips and smelled her skin while I place a soft tender kiss upon her brow. She squirmed for a moment and then settled back in my arm.

"Hello, my sweet angel. I'm your momma. I've been waiting for you for such a long time. You are already cherished by so many, you have no idea what you have walked into."

My dad silently laughed as the nurse went to go bring me my son. She reached in and he bowed his back in his first stretch.

"That's it, young man, stretch those legs," the nurse said as she laughed.

She laid my little man in the other crook of my arm and I gently held him close to my breast. I pulled him up to my mouth as well and laid a kiss upon his brow as I smelled the baby smell exuding from his newly developed pores.

"My sweet little man, how I have prayed that you will thrive to become the man that your father is. Aside from your daddy, you are the only other man who holds my heart."

I totally understood where my daddy was coming from when he told me my mom had half his heart and I owned the other half. I didn't want to let my babies go---ever.

I sat there for hours, just holding them. The nurse asked me if I wanted to try feeding them and I, of course, said yes. I wanted to attempt breast feeding but I wasn't sure how I would do. Now that they were born, it all seemed so visceral. The nurse took my son back to the warmer while I pulled the side of my gown down to lay in my lap. I gathered my daughter in my arm and pulled her to my breast. She attached herself instinctively. I warmed her body with my heat and just sat in awe at the intimate moment I was sharing with my daughter. I sat and soothed her. Even though she couldn't understand, I knew I was communicating with her.

I did the same with my son and relished every second I had him in my arms. He was his father's son. He laid still against my breast as I stroked his skin and lulled him.

I noticed that the change of nurses was happening and I was exhausted, so I asked my dad to help me back to my room. I thanked the nurses and hugged the nurse who had given me the opportunity to have this once in a lifetime experience with my children.

I slowly walked back to my room, sat back down on the corner of my bed, pulled my legs up, and closed my eyes.

I woke to the sound of crying babies. I opened my eyes and saw a woman standing in front of me. "I've got two hungry babies here, Mrs. Jackson. Would you like to feed them?" My eyes opened wide and I made myself wake up. "Yes, please." I yawned. I slowly raised my body up to a sitting position while I waited for the bed to catch up with my movements.

275

She handed me my little girl as I opened my gown and put her up to me. This time, she began sucking harder. She was starving. "When do you think they will be able to come stay with me in my room?" I asked in a hopeful tone. "The pediatrician will be in in the morning to check them out and then come in to talk to you." As she was talking, I noticed my belly was cramping. I winced. "Are you still in a lot of pain?" I shook my head. "No, it's more like a harsh cramp." She reassured me that it was normal and I was welcomed to something to help with the pain. Since I was nursing, I decided to just tough it out.

I finished with my little girl and handed her back to the nurse. She instantly fell asleep. The nurse handed me my son and he proceeded to follow in line with his sister.

"Do you have names for your babies? The information for their birth certificates will be sent out tomorrow, it would be good if they had names," she said, smiling.

Holy shit, I hadn't even thought about that. I had an idea of what I was looking for but I didn't have anything definite.

"I have…ideas, but I guess I'll need to come up with something then. For the little girl, I was thinking Tatum and for the little boy, Dylan."

"Those are beautiful names, Mrs. Jackson. I think they both fit."

"Please, call me Elle."

She shook her head in acknowledgement and took the baby out of my arms, placing him back in the walking crib. I laid my bed back down and turned gently to my side. My eyes soon became heavy and I was on my way back to sleep.

"Wakey, wakey, babe." I opened my eyes and TJ was sitting in the chair next to my bed holding my hand. "They look exactly like their momma, they take my breath away." I smiled. "What are their names?" I looked at him and told him the names I had picked for our children. "I wanted to name our son the name you picked out, Dylan Lucas. For our daughter, I was thinking Tatum Jordan." He looked at me with a grim look on his face. "Honey, she doesn't look like a Tatum, but she does resemble a Jordan." I smiled at him and raised my eyebrows. "I've got it!" I announced her name to him and he smiled that beautiful smile at me and kissed me goodnight.

I awoke to a knock on the door. A very petite older woman stuck her head in. "Good Morning, Mrs. Jackson?" I sat up straight. The babies were brought to me early this morning and I was still holding my little girl while my son slept in his walking crib with a full tummy.

"Elle. Please, call me Elle."

"Very well, Elle. My name is Betty. I'm from the vital statistics department here in the hospital. I'm here to fill out the forms for your babies' birth certificates."

I smiled at her. "Great, I'm ready."

We started with my son. She asked me several questions: my name, my physical address, my mom's maiden name, my maiden name, the baby's father's name. I hesitated for a moment before telling her I didn't want it listed. She nodded once and continued on. She finally got down to the baby's name and I replied, "Dylan Lucas Jackson." She smiled and complimented me on such a handsome name. I didn't tell her that his daddy came to me last night in a dream and helped me decide permanently on their names. They'd never let me leave this hospital.

We finished with Luc's information and went on to my daughter's info. She repeated the same questions, I answered the same answers. She got down to her name and I announced her name for the first time out loud, "Jordan Taylor Jackson."

We finished up the interview and then the pediatrician came in. We discussed the health of the babies. He was pleased as pie that they were eating so well and that they had taken to nursing so quickly. He wanted to keep the babies in the NICU one more night just to be sure everything was perfect. He asked me if I had any questions for him, I shook my head and thanked him for coming in to speak with me. He was gone for about ten minutes when Doctor Leonard came in to check on me. She pushed on my belly, looked at my chart, and we talked about the babies. She asked me if I had any questions for her. I shook my head, thanked her, and she left.

I was ready for a nap. I laid down and closed my eyes.

I heard my dad's voice silently prohibiting whoever was on the other end of the line access to me and my babies.

"You will not come up here. If you do, I will have you removed." There was silence from my dad for long moments then a breath before starting up again. "She had to have emergency surgery. All three of them could've died and where were you? Mona was the one standing next to her holding her hand while the surgeon cut into her to bring those babies into this world."

Bear.

I heard his voice change as he cupped his hand around the phone's receiver and stated, "If you come up here, Willie Jackson, with God as my witness, you won't ever see my daughter or her babies again." He put the phone back down on the desk to hang it up and sat back down beside me. I turned over to look at him and tucked my hands up under my head.

"Sorry, honey, didn't mean to wake you."

I partially winced and asked, "Bear?"

He shook his head and closed his eyes. I knew that Bear's abusive manner was a slap in my dad's face. He didn't raise his daughter to be treated that way, but Bear had something over my head that I didn't want TJ to find out about. I really didn't have a choice. I either put up with it or else TJ's life was ruined. Daddy knew this was my reasoning. He knew I'd stay and continue to put up with it until one of us was buried in the ground. There was nothing Bear could do to me that would make me disturb the life that TJ was leading.

I made it through the two days I had left in the hospital. I was bored, hungry, and tired of either being woken up for my breasts or vitals. I knew once I got home, Mona would be there to help me whenever I needed it. She didn't have any babies, but that didn't mean her instinct was absent. She would do whatever she needed to do.

Daddy met me under the canopy with the car. They wheeled me out with JoJo strapped into her car seat on my lap while another nurse carried Luc beside me in his. I handed JoJo to Daddy and then got out of the chair. He strapped her into the car so I went around to the other side and got beside her. He appeared beside me with Luc and strapped him in on the other side of me.

Reaching the house, I felt like I hadn't seen it in months. I was elated to finally be home. I waited for Daddy to come around and grab one of the babies' seats then I jumped out and grabbed the other baby. I went in the house and heard, "SURPRISE!"

"Holy shit!" I screamed. I looked around the living and dining area. There were people everywhere. In front of everyone were my three girls: Lilly, Rachel, and Mona. I set the car seat down on the floor and ran to them with my arms straight out to give all three of them a huge hug. People began crowding around wanting to get to the babies. Mona pulled JoJo out and immediately began smothering her in kisses. Lucas went to Lilly who instantly began to cry. I needed to sit down. I was still so sore and exhausted.

The baby shower went on for hours. I opened presents, ate a few bites of cake, and drank some punch. I talked with people I hadn't seen in a while and spent time with my girls. They weren't going to be in town long, Lilly was flying out first thing the next morning and Rachel was driving back the next evening.

I left the babies with Daddy and Mona and walked with the girls into my room.

"Anything, Rachel?" She knew what I was talking about. I always hated to start out our conversations that way, but I just needed to know he was well.

She didn't have to say anything, I could see it in her eyes. He hadn't contacted any of his family.

I asked them how school was going and they filled me in on everything. We continued talking up to the point where Lilly announced she had to get up early for her flight. We hugged and kissed and I cried, but I said my goodbyes and walked them to their cars.

Back inside, Clara was helping Mona wash up the last of the dishes and Daddy was holding both sleeping babies. I plopped down on the couch next to him and gently grabbed Luc. I held him up in front of my face and kissed him. I laid him up against my shoulder and just sat there giggling at Dad who was trying his hardest to get JoJo to smile.

"Daddy she's only days old, I don't really think she's going to smile at your command yet." He laughed.

When we heard the front door slam and saw Bear walk in, the smile left my dad's face quickly. He got up and took JoJo in the other room. Bear walked over to me but I wouldn't even turn my eyes to him.

"Hey, baby." He acted like nothing was wrong.

I glared at him. "Don't you dare."

"Is that my boy?" I knew he was deliberately changing the subject. He began trying to claw Luc out of my hands. I heard the baby moan a small moan and knew Bear wouldn't stop pulling, so I released him.

"What's his name?"

I looked dumbfounded at him.

"Did you seriously just say that to me? Did you actually hear the words that just came out of your mouth? Don't you think something is wrong with that picture, Bear?"

He just kept shaking the baby and cooing loudly in Luc's face until he began to cry.

"Where were you while your children were being born, Bear?"

He didn't answer me, so I asked again.

"Did you hear me?"

He answered this time.

"I heard ya, bitch. I was somewhere that ain't your business." He looked over at me and glared. I knew with his tone that he wasn't fucking around anymore with my questions.

"What did you name my boy?"

"Dylan Lucas. I've been calling him Luc."

He nodded.

He looked back at me. "Go get my daughter from that motherfucker."

I had to clench my teeth to not say a word. I stood up slowly and went into the kitchen where my dad was standing with JoJo in front of him, ready to deposit her in my hands.

"I'm gonna kill him, you know this right?" my dad whispered to me as he laid JoJo in my arms. I hushed him because, again, I didn't need my ass beat this soon. And, really, stitches or not, he'd have kicked my ass.

I took JoJo out into the living room and laid her in his other arm. Then, I reached over and took Luc from him.

"Oh, my beautiful girl. You look just like my granny."

I didn't vocalize anything, but he had totally fucking lost it.

"What did ya name my girl?"

I didn't hesitate this time.

"Jordan Taylor. I've been calling her JoJo."

"Nice."

"Where's her bottle? I wanna feed her."

"Bear, I'm breastfeeding, neither of them takes formula." I tried to sound pleasant but obviously it wasn't working.

"You better figure out a way for me to feed them. If I wanna give them a goddamn bottle, I'm gonna give them a bottle."

He began to get up with JoJo. I was terrified at what he was going to do and where he was going with her. He took her to the nursery and put her in the crib. I laid Luc down beside her and turned on the monitor that was on the dresser beside them. I took the other half of the monitoring system and attached it to me so that I could hear everything.

I went to bed before Bear. Last time I saw him, he was sitting out in the drive with some man drinking beer. I checked on the babies and saw they were sleeping so I grabbed a quick shower and headed to bed. The last week played back in my mind: the first time meeting my babies, the baby shower, seeing my girls again. My thoughts lulled me off to sleep.

Just to be woken up in the middle of the night with Bear's hand over my face and his other hand up my nightgown.

Chapter 16

Present Day

I pulled my hands out of TJ's hair, brought my legs from around his waist, and set them on the floor. I couldn't believe what I just admitted to, face to face. He let go of my ass and kissed me on the tip of my nose.

"Now that we have that outta the way," he said, flirtatiously. I looked over at him; he was wearing a smile from ear to ear. "There's a restroom through there," he informed me as he pointed down the hall beside his desk. "Although, I do enjoy that thoroughly fucked look." I smiled back at him and corrected his last phrase.

"Ah, but you are mistaken, Mr. McHale. I was not thoroughly fucked." I kicked my foot up behind me and headed toward the restroom.

Turning on the light and shutting the door, I heard my phone going off in my purse. I walked back out to where I dropped my purse on the floor by the desk. I reached in and checking the caller ID. It was my doctor's office.

I scrambled back into the bathroom and answered the phone in a low voice.

"April?"

"Elle, hi. I got your results back this morning and I thought you'd like to hear them as soon as possible. Everything came back fine."

I exhaled out loud. "Thank you for calling me. By the way, since I have you on the phone. I've had another situation and I need to have another test done, but I'm in Vermont. Can you see if doc can recommend someone or knows someone up here?"

"Well, Elle, we just tested you for all STD's. You shouldn't need another one this fast. It—"

"Well, I need another one, April. Can you just ask and let me know?"

"Ah, yeah sure, but any health department should offer it."

If April hadn't known me personally, she might have thought I'd worked out on the street.

"Great, thanks again. Have a good day."

I hung up with April and set my phone on the sink. I looked in the mirror. *Holy hell!* I did look like I've been thoroughly fucked. I straightened my hair back down and attempted to reduce the swelling of my lips by putting a cold cloth between them. That didn't work, so I swiped some gloss on them and fixed my clothes. I walked back out into TJ's office and continued toward his desk. "Do you have a physician up here? One that is…discreet?" He looked at me funny and chuckled. "Of course I have one. He's the best in the country. Why, are you ill?"

I walked toward the couch and noticed that the music and opaque windows were gone. The lady at the desk in front of us was staring and waving at me.

I waved at her and mumbled through a smile, "That lady is waving at me." TJ burst into laughter. "That's Mary." I relaxed my shoulders.

"Oh, great!" I stood up and walked out the door to go introduce myself. As I opened the door, TJ's hand flew over it.

"Wait a minute, we're not done here. What's with the doctor?"

"Oh, I just need to stop by to see him quickly. If you would, please text me the number."

"When you tell me why."

I couldn't believe what was already happening. We had just discussed that he had no say in what I did or where I went.

"Jesus Christ, TJ. Didn't we just have this conversation? Just shoot me the number or I will find a clinic, it doesn't matter to me."

"As I recall, you said you were mine and that you belonged to me. That gives me every right to question you. Now, are you going to tell me now or on the way there?"

"Neither," I said as I pulled against his hand. I found out quickly that the door wasn't budging.

"I don't think I gave you that as an option, Elle. Start talking or I will find another way to get it out of you."

I probably would've told him why I had to go, I would've made some bullshit up just to get him off my ass, but now I wasn't saying shit. This was about principle now. I refused to say a word.

"Not gonna talk?"

I closed my mouth, put my fingers up to it like I was turning a key, and then threw it behind my back.

"Not happening, bud."

Out of nowhere, he removed his hand off the door and I pulled it open. I looked at him, he looked at me, and headed back to his desk. I headed out into the reception area.

"Mary? Hi, I'm Elle Barker-Jackson. I think we are going to be working together for the next couple of weeks."

She stood and grabbed my hand a little stronger than I was expecting, then proceeded to shake it briskly.

"Mrs. Barker-Jackson, it's such a pleasure. I have been looking forward to working with you."

"Wonderful, from what I'm understanding there's one more assistant, Sara…correct?" The smile seemed to be ripped off her face in a flash. "Sara, yes. Let me give her a buzz and see if she can come and meet with us."

I smiled, but didn't say anymore. I stood with my back to Mary, looking in at TJ sitting at his desk on the phone and saw him wink at me. I smiled back. That's when I heard her voice.

"Mary, I am up to my neck in wo—"

She stopped talking but continued to walk toward the both of us. Her eyes were squinting harder and harder in my direction. I ignored her. This wasn't the first time I've had to deal with other office assistants that thought they were H.B.I.C. Usually, I ignored it and eventually they would see they were just as normal as the rest of us.

"Sara, is it?" I started toward her with my hand out, ready to start this little game she wanted to play. I was already ahead, killing her with kindness.

"I'm Elle Barker-Jackson, it's a pleasure to meet you. I'm so pleased to have the chance to work with you."

I walked right in front of her. She looked at my hand and curled the left side of her lip up as she rolled her eyes. She intentionally walked right beside me without saying a word, right into TJ's office.

I heard TJ tell whomever he had on the phone that he would call them back.

"Trev—"

Did she seriously call him Trev? It took several swallows to keep from throwing up in my mouth.

"Sara, I see you had a chance to meet Elleny."

She smiled this calculated smile that made me want to smack it right off of her mouth.

"Trev, I am up to my neck in paperwork. Mary called me up here and now there is no way I'm going to be done by lunchtime. Do you think that there is any way she can work with me here? I have asked her not to buzz me, but every time I turn around—"

She totally dodged his question. So I made it known right in front of "Trev".

"Yes, Mr. McHale, thank you for asking. I did have a chance to introduce myself to Sara here. I have a wonderful feeling that the time we spend together is going to be enjoyable. Don't you think, Sara?"

I had a beautiful smile on my face, just like the one I had on my face when I mentally mashed TJ's balls for trapping me into that luncheon.

"Perfect! Sara, I'm pulling you off of Brooks and Fairfield account. You'll now be working under Elle, helping her with anything she needs. Nate will be swinging by your office to pick up anything and everything you have on them."

"Trev, this is bullshit! I have been working with them for months now. They won't deal with anyone else. They'll pull out," she claimed as she folded her arms over her chest and stuck her left foot out in front of her.

"I'll deal with them, don't you worry. Elle, what was it that you said you needed this morning? Oh yes, have Mary order a box of five hundred memory sticks, also call Chris over in IT and have a laptop checked out and brought up to my office for Elle by one-thirty. We have an appointment."

Damn, I thought she was pissed when he pulled her off that account. She was fuming now. If she were a cartoon character, smoke would have been coming out of her ears.

I raised my eyebrow at TJ and he just winked. Sara didn't say another word. She turned around and marched out. I kept my eyes straight on him.

"Where are we going and why are we not working?" I asked. Now my hands were folded over my chest and I was looking at him with a quizzical brow.

"You said you needed a physician. I made you an appointment and I'm taking you."

I dropped my hands down to my sides. "Oh, screw that. You're not going. I don't need you to go. I simply asked you what his name was, I am totally capable of finding him."

He walked over to me and rubbed my shoulders. "Shh, don't work yourself up. I am taking you by the doctor's and then we will have an early dinner. We will take our work back to the hotel and do as much as we can together. Possibly with a bottle of wine...or a bottle of whisky. Your choice," he said with an extremely large smile.

"You're an ass, Trevor McHale," I teasingly retorted. "You're not getting me drunk tonight, we have too much work to do. And, I think we've played enough for one day. Now, can I get someone to show me to my office?"

He tilted his head back and laughed heartily. Walking up beside me, he grabbed my hand. "Allow me, Ms. Barker."

Before we left for the doctor, TJ showed me the office I would be working out of, which was located right next door to TJ's. Coincidence? I think not.

He also showed me more of the building, taking me to the different floors I would mostly be working on before heading back to his office. Just as we were arriving back, Chris showed up with my laptop. Top of the line Apple Mac Pro with Retina display, it was sweet. TJ and Chris went back to TJ's office to trade his laptop with the same one I had.

While they were busy in TJ's office, Sara paid me a visit with a box of memory sticks. She walked in three steps and pleasantly threw them at my desk. Thankfully, they landed upright. Then, just as pleasantly, she walked out.

We gathered up what files we could, along with the memory sticks, and piled them all into a huge storage box. Flipping the laptops over our arms, we headed out for the day. As we passed by Charlene at the front desk, she attempted to hand me my badge. Since my hands were full, I pushed my hip toward her and told her just to drop it in my purse. Our ride in the elevator started out quiet, which I didn't have a problem with. It was obvious that TJ did. He would glance at me then turn away, glance back then turn away.

Finally, I'd had enough.

"What's the story with Sara? She seems like she wants to be your BFF."

He snickered. "She's very dedicated to her job."

I kept my eyes straight ahead as I replied, "Uh-huh."

His snickering turned more into a laugh. "Why, Ms. Barker, do I detect a hint of jealousy?"

I looked at him, my face straight as a board. "I don't get jealous, Mr. McHale."

The bell chimed. Looking up, I noticed we were on the eleventh floor. The doors opened and several executives stepped in. As I stepped over into the corner, I noticed Sam. He did a double take as he walked closer to me.

"Elle, how are you doing so far?"

I looked over at TJ, who was standing in the other corner staring laser beams into Sam's skull. I was surprised his head didn't explode.

"Sam! It's going great so far. I'm just on my way with Mr. McHale to a meeting. Thank you so much for asking."

"Well, again, if you need anything, please feel free to give me a call." He smiled as he reached inside his jacket pocket, pulled out his card, and placed it in my fingers that were clinched around the bottom of a box.

I smiled pleasantly at him and nodded my head. The bell chimed as the doors opened and everyone began to exit the car. TJ and I stayed back and let them go out the front first.

"Where's that card, Elle?"

"It's in my other hand, why?"

His face was as hard as stone. "Hand it to me now."

By the tone in his voice, I knew he was not playing around.

"Hold on, the box is heavy."

He stopped right where he was, in the middle of the walkway of the beautiful atrium that was located in the lobby, and piled the boxes of files he was carrying, right in front of his feet. He grabbed the box out of my hand and dropped it to the ground as held out his hand.

"Here. Christ, it's only a business card."

"Don't fuck with me on this, Elleny."

289

"Why Mr. McHale, do I detect a hint of jealousy?"

He didn't even look at me. He ripped up the card and threw it on the ground. He picked up my box and handed it to me. Picking up his own box, we began walking when he replied, "Fuck, yes you do!"

We went by the hotel on our way to the doctor's to drop off the computers and files. While we were there, I decided to change, freshen up again, and change another pair of panties.

I walked out into the living area and saw TJ sitting on the couch, texting. He was still in his suit pants and dress shirt.

"You changed," he said as he put his phone down.

"Well yeah, I figured since it was such a nice day, maybe we could drive with the top down so I could see the sights along the way."

He smiled a huge smile and jumped up from the couch.

"Give me ten," he said as he placed a kiss on my forehead.

TJ ran into his room and shut the door behind him. I picked up a magazine and began thumbing through the pages when I heard my phone ring. I picked it up but didn't recognize the number. Putting it on speaker phone, I answered in my professional greeting. "Elleny Barker- Jackson."

No one said anything, so I was quiet for a moment before repeating, "This is Elleny, is anyone there?" Still flipping through the magazine, I heard his voice.

"Yeah, I'm here bitch, where the fuck are you?"

Fuck! I put the magazine down and looked toward TJ's bedroom door to make sure it was still closed.

"Bear, I thought we had discussed this the other night. I left you that note because you weren't home. I told you I had a business trip. Remember?"

He was quiet for a moment. My eyes stayed glued on TJ's door.

"Where the fuck are my kids?"

"They're safe, Bear."

"That's not what I asked, whore!" he yelled.

I winced and kept my eyes on that door.

"Bear, I'm not out whoring around. Can you please stop calling me that?"

"Listen here, you nasty whore…"

Just as Bear was going off, TJ's door opened. I quickly picked up the phone, took it off speaker phone, and put it to my ear. I replaced the mask on my face with a beautiful smile.

TJ however, did not.

"…y, you ever try to tell me what to do again, I'll kick your ass so far into next week, you'll be fired for not showing up. Now, where are my fucking kids?"

I looked at TJ and put my index finger to my mouth, asking him to be quiet

"Bear, you were out…wherever you were, and I wasn't sure if you would be home. They're staying with Lilly."

I wasn't about to tell him Rachel's, he would go over there. Since Curt was a cop, I figured that he could protect his wife better than Kevin could.

"Well, I'll go pick them up and bring them home, that way they're in their own beds and with their blood."

The mask dropped from my face. My face went from happy and beautiful to white and scared shitless.

I screamed, "NO! No, Bear, please don't do that. Lilly and Curt have been planning so much with the kids, and you know how much Austin looks up to Luc. He was planning on teaching him some of your best football plays. JoJo, Harlee, and Lilly were planning on going shopping. It's fine, they wanted to stay over there and they have plenty of room. You just enjoy your time alone. Go out, have a good time."

I didn't realize it, but I was pacing back and forth and I was pacing fast. I was biting all of my nails down as sweat beads formed on my hairline.

"Yeah, maybe your right. Some of the guys at work are going down to the titty bar for some beers, maybe I'll join 'em."

I stopped moving, put my head back, and closed my eyes. My mask went back in place. "That sounds like fun. Well, hon, I've got to get back to my meeting. I'll let you go, ya'll stay safe tonight."

"Uh huh, what the fuck ever."

Click.

I threw my phone down on the coffee table and headed for the couch.

"Just give me a moment, please?" I asked, my mind nowhere near where it needed to be.

I sat, put my head in my hands, and just closed my eyes. I took some breaths and opened my eyes again.

"Luc."

I reached for my phone and immediately called Luc's phone. I began to think of his schedule. "He's at lunch," I said to myself. The phone rang, and rang…

"Momma?"

I closed my eyes and forced the tears back. My baby boy's voice.

"Momma, what's wrong?"

I took a breath and put the smile back on my face so he didn't hear any different.

"Hey, my sweet angel baby."

"What is it, Momma?"

"Hey baby, do your momma a favor this afternoon. No practice, I'll call coach. Just get in Auntie Rachel's car, pick up JoJo and Harlee, and go back to Auntie's house, okay?"

"Momma?"

"Baby, I'm fine…everything is wonderful. Just do this for me. Send me some pics of ya'll swimming this evening okay? I will video conference you before I go to bed so that I can kiss you good night."

The tears were welling in my eyes. I looked up at TJ and he was staring at me. He looked absolutely helpless, but there was nothing he could do. I brought my eyes back to the magazine.

"Love you, my big protector."

That was when I saw TJ turn his back to me as he headed for the kitchen.

I heard Luc's voice.

"Love you too, Momma."

"I'm gonna call coach and JoJo and tell her to wait in the office. You remember safety rules, right? Stay alert today, baby. I'm calling you tonight."

"Okay, Momma. Bye."

I hung up with him and immediately called JoJo.

Her phone went straight to voice mail. I pushed the end button, put the phone to my lips, closed my eyes, and prayed that she answered this time.

"One more minute, okay?"

There was no answer from TJ.

I dialed her again.

"Momma, what's the matter. Luc's texting me."

"First off, hey, my sweet angel baby. Momma misses you."

I was screaming and destroying shit on the inside of me. I had never felt so helpless in all my life. I was hundreds of miles away from my babies and they were sitting ducks. I swore this would never happen again.

"Hey, Momma."

"Luc's not staying for practice, no cheerleading today. I'll call Sandy. Stay in the office 'til he comes inside to get you. I'm gonna call Leslie over at Har's school and tell her to keep her in the office until you or Luc come in and get her. Safety rules, okay? Pay attention, stay alert. Okay?"

"Okay, Momma. Love you."

Two tears strolled down my cheek but my voice didn't falter.

"Oh, baby, I love you, too. I wanna see pictures tonight of ya'll swimming your tails off in Auntie's pool, okay?"

"I'll send some."

293

"Good girl. I'm gonna go now. Talk to you tonight, my sweet angel."

"Bye, Momma."

I instantly called Harlee's school and told my friend from high school that Harlee needed to stay in the office until one of the twins came in and picked her up, hand in hand. I even lost my temper by telling her not to fuck this up, it was important. She hesitated but agreed.

I headed to the kitchen and found TJ facing the counter, holding himself up with his arms balanced on top. Out of nowhere, he raised his hand, slamming the cupboard above his head as hard as he could. It opened and shut three times. The sound of the slam made me jump.

"What the fuck is going on, Elle?" His voice was scary low. I'd never been scared of TJ, but right then, I was terrified.

"Let's go, TJ."

"We're not going anywhere!" he yelled at the top of his lungs.

"I heard that whole fucking conversation, Elle. He called you a whore."

I closed my eyes and started to walk away from him.

"No, no, no! You don't get to walk away from this, Elleny. Don't you dare fucking close me out! You don't get to decide what I get to know!"

I couldn't take it anymore. I lost it. Built up anger from years of being beaten and abused erupted inside of me and I lost it on the one person I had spent my life trying to hide it from.

I took a moment and then walked right up into his face. He wanted to hear it, he was going to hear every bit of it.

"I don't get to decide what you get to know? You don't want me to close you out? Are you shitting me? You don't know how many times I've been hurt by that man, how many times he's beaten me so bad that I haven't been able to stand up, sit down, lay down...nothing! He made me get rid of babies, Trevor! My throat? It's sore because he came home to me just the other night while I was sleeping and held me down by sitting on my chest as he face fucked me until I cleaned his skank's nasty shit off his cock! The reason I need to go to the doctor's is because I need to find out if I caught something, anything from him! You wanna know the truth, you're gonna know! These…" I held up my wrists in front of his face, "these are from Bear tying me up with leather straps. He's damaged me internally, TJ! He's hurt me so bad, Lilly couldn't even help clean me up. There was so much blood, she thought I was dead, and that wasn't even the worst time! You wanna know what my tattoos are? The remember isn't about us, it's a promise to myself. To remember that no one will ever love you the way you deserve to be loved. It means to remember to hide your heart away, lock it heavily away, and don't ever let someone touch it. Ever! This one is the most important advice anyone has ever given me in my life. It says you can have my blood, you can have my sweat, but you will never get my tears. I'm broken, Trevor. I'm tainted and I will never be repaired!"

I was breathing heavier than I had ever breathed before in my life. Tears had stained my face and I had no idea I was even crying. I had to get away from here. I looked over at TJ, his face was blank, expressionless.

I turned around to walk away when I felt him grab my arm, turn me around, and pick me up.

"What?" My voice was rough and cracked. He didn't say a word, just carried me toward his bedroom. He opened the door and shut it with his foot. Still nothing was said as he sat me down.

"What are we doing?" He just stared at me again. He unbuttoned my pants and unzipped them.

"TJ, you can't do this. I'm not begging."

Still, nothing. I felt him grab my pants. He slowly pulled them down to my ankles. He tapped the top of my foot, I pulled my foot out of my pant leg. He did the same on the other side, I obliged again. Standing back up, TJ gently removed the chain from my neck. Just as tenderly, he removed

295

my shirt. I was standing there in my panties and bra. He went over to the wall and hit the light switch.

As he was walking, I begged him, "Please, TJ! No, please don't turn on the—"

That was as much as I got out of my mouth as I looked down at my body. I saw TJ slowly walk up beside me. Leisurely, he ran his fingertips as gently as he could over the purple, pink, and green marks that covered my whole abdominal area. He circled around me, studying my body, using very little pressure as he touched my skin.

I closed my eyes. I couldn't even imagine what he thought of me now that he could actually see me for who I was.

"TJ—"

"Shh."

He circled around me one more time, coming to a stop behind me. He unhooked my bra and came around to the front of me. I had my arms folded across my chest. He gently pulled my arms down and I complied. He then went back to my shoulders and pulled my straps down until the bra was hanging from one of his fingers. I went to put my hands back up to hide my breasts.

"Don't you even fucking think about it," TJ said in that low, terrifying voice again.

I dropped my arms back down to my sides and turned my head to look away from him. He gently kneeled in front of me and slowly pulled my panties down my legs. I hesitated and began to say his name, but he beat me to the punch.

"Don't say a word."

He pulled them down to my ankles and, again, he tapped on my foot.

There I stood. Nude, bruised, and extremely humiliated in front of the one man I never wanted to see me like this. Still kneeling in front of me, he began to slowly run his hands up my calves, then my thighs, moving so slowly. I wanted him to say something so badly, I needed to know what was running through his mind. Maybe he was wondering when the last time I got my ass kicked was.

He reached my stomach and rubbed his fingers over my C-section scar from the twins. I squeezed my eyes shut. His actions were killing me. He touched my ribs again, making his way up to my breasts. Gently, he ran his fingertips over my nipples. They became hard and erect from just that little touch of his finger.

He brought his hands down around my waist and gently placed them on my hips as he pulled himself closer to me, placing tiny kisses on the bruising that covered my stomach. He moved over to my hips and ribs and placed kisses on that area as well. Pushing himself back, he moved to the other side and repeated the same actions. He eventually worked his way back to my middle and kissed my stomach as though he was kissing my uterus for the babies I had been made to get rid of.

He wouldn't look at me, but by the tone in his voice I knew he meant what he said.

He whispered to my stomach. "He's dead, Elle." Standing up, he didn't say another word. He turned and walked into the bathroom and closed the door. I stood there for a moment wondering if we were done. Should I get dressed again? That's when I heard all hell break loose. TJ was screaming, not saying any words, just screaming at the top of his lungs. Glass was breaking, things were being thrown, and punches were landing against the wall. Toiletry items were being pushed off the sink, landing and breaking all over the tile floor. Quickly, I pulled on my panties, shirt, and shoes. I grabbed his shoes that were resting by the bedroom door and flew to the bathroom. I threw the door open and saw him standing in the middle of an enormous mess. A mess that I essentially created. I couldn't keep my anger under wraps and had let everything except the most important secret out.

I looked at TJ, he was looking back at me, huffing and puffing from his exertion. His eyes were bloodshot and his face was so red. "Oh Jesus, TJ. This is entirely my fault," I said through my tears. I walked over to him and asked, "TJ, honey pick up your foot. There's so much glass, let me slip on your shoes. I don't want you to cut yourself." He didn't say anything but he did what I asked of him.

We walked back through the bedroom, grabbing jeans and a shirt for him. I snatched the rest of my clothing up and headed for the bedroom door. We went into my room and I walked him into the bathroom. I turned on the water so that it could warm up.

I began to do what he did to me. Taking off his shirt gently, I silently begged for forgiveness from this man whose heart was breaking right in front of me again. It seemed like all I brought him was hardship and pain. I owed him something, I owed him this. I undid his pants and pulled them down, leaving his boxers on. I didn't want him to feel uncomfortable, so I left that up to him

"Would you like me to leave while you get in the shower?"

"I'm sorry, Elle."

I stopped what I was doing and just stood there.

"I'm so sorry, baby," he said as he bent down, grabbed my cheeks in his hands, and pulled me up to him.

"Shh, TJ. None of this is your fault."

He was restraining himself, I could tell. His voice and hands were shaking uncontrollably and he acted as if he didn't know where to touch me. He needed to control himself by limiting his contact with me, I knew he was on the edge.

He still had my head in his hands as he pulled me up to his face. He touched his lips to mine, repeating over and over again, "I'm so sorry, baby."

"It's okay, everything is fine," I began repeating, needing to placate his frame of mind.

He sealed his lips over mine and swept his tongue into my mouth, swirling it with mine, as though he was wiping away all the damage Bear had done. His kiss became harder as we lost control. My hands flew up into his hair and I wrapped my fingers in it, bringing him closer to me. He broke the kiss and worked his way down my neck with the lightest of kisses. "TJ, I'm not glass." As he continued kissing me, he replied, "Yes, you are. You should never have had to hurt like that." He began walking me backward. As we passed by the shower, he reached in and turned it off. I didn't stop him. We continued walking straight back into my room. Our kisses were so desperate, we couldn't get close enough. There was no turning back now. I couldn't, I needed to feel him within me.

He curled his fingers around the bottom of my shirt. I lifted my arms, breaking our kiss long enough to get my shirt over my head. My hands went down to the top of his boxers and began to push them down. His lips sucked my tongue deeper into his mouth, gently nibbling against it. I felt his fingers dive into the corners of my panties as he let go of my tongue. "Say the words, Elle. I have to hear them from you. I have to know that you want this just as bad as I do. This can't be all me." I looked him in the eyes, put my nose to his, and gave him exactly what he was waiting for. "Please, TJ. I need you, baby."

He pulled my panties down and laid me gently on the bed. He continued kissing me as he reached down and pulled his boxers off. I gripped my hands around his neck, wrapped my legs around his waist, and allowed him to drag me up the bed where he had better access. "TJ, honey, please...I'm begging you."

He began to slowly nibble at my throat and worked his way down. He licked my right nipple and I bowed up into him. He brought it between his teeth and bit gently, teasingly. I writhed in pleasure as TJ worked his way over to the other side. He sucked and licked and bit, I closed my eyes and relished the emotions pouring out of him.

"I've missed this, baby. You're still so beautiful. You will never fully comprehend what you do to me." I was holding on by a thread. I couldn't take it all in, it was overwhelming—the kissing, the touches. Slowly, I watched him work his way down. I was lost in the moment, until I felt him blow gently against my clit. I retracted up the bed and pulled my knees up to my chest as I yelled, "No! Anything but that. You can't do that. You can't put your mouth on it!"

He sat back on his knees and looked up to the ceiling with his eyes closed.

"What is it, Elle?"

I continued to shake my head. "No, anything but that."

Frustrated, he ran his fingers through his hair. "Why, why can't I put my mouth on it?"

I put my head down on my knees and answered, "He says it's nasty, that it's not clean."

In one swift move, he grabbed my legs and pulled them down to him so that I was lying flat on my back. My legs were hanging over his shoulders and his face was buried between them. His tongue laid flat against my skin as he moaned, lapping up every drop of wetness. "I'm gonna make you come with my mouth and I'm going to drink you up. You understand me, Elle? This is beauty. This pussy right here…" Lick. "This is my heaven…" Lick. "This is my sanctuary…" Lick. "My refuge…" Lick. "That motherfucker doesn't even deserve to lay next to this treasure. He will never in his entire fucking piece of shit life be worthy enough to put his fingers against this pussy." He opened me wider to get to my clit and teased me with the tip of his tongue. "Do you feel how good that feels? My tongue licking up every bit of you? That's how you make me feel. My mouth is against the most perfect jewel and it's all mine. The wealthiest of wealthiest men will never find a gem as perfect as yours. It's so beautiful and pink, just for me, Elle… every bit of it is mine." He continued flicking his tongue against me. I'm not sure what I was feeling. Happiness, sadness, maybe a little of both.

I unwrapped my fingers from the sheets and ran them through his hair. I pushed his head against me. I was on the verge of an orgasm, so I began to lift my hips up and down quickly against his tongue. "That's it, Elle, work that beautiful pussy against my tongue. Come all over my face, baby. You look so gorgeous when you move like that." Just as I was about to come, he stuck two fingers slowly into me and that was what it took to push me over. I screamed at the top of my lungs. It has been so long since I climaxed like that, it was overwhelming. He continued to lap at my core, moaning that sexy moan. "Give it all to me, babe. I want it all. Everything he's taken from you. I'm giving it back."

I pulled him up to me and welcomed his rock hard shaft into me as he began to push deep. "Shit, Elle, I'm trying to take it slow. Tell me if I hurt you."

I nibbled on his ear as I whispered, "Do it, TJ, I need to feel you move inside of me."

Slowly, he entered me completely and didn't move. He pushed his arms up so he was hovering over me "Do you feel my cock deep within you? That is how deep you are within me. You are so deep, Elle, I can't find a way to get you out." He began to pull out and I bowed toward him, closing my eyes. "I want your eyes, Elle." I wrapped my arms around his neck and brought my mouth up to his. I locked eyes with him as my lips barely touched his. I asked the same questions he asked me that night, seventeen years ago.

"Tell me you need me, TJ." He kissed me as his thrusts became faster. "Elleny, I need you so much, baby. I can't function without you. For seventeen years, I've been sleeping. Then, you were brought back to me and I'm finally awake." His thrusts were harder, deeper, faster, as his breathing accelerated. He was getting close, I could feel it. "Tell me what you want, TJ. Describe it."

He didn't hesitate. "I want you beside me for the rest of my life. When I wake up, when I go to sleep. I want you to give me babies and I want to be able to share this love that is overflowing inside of me with you." I began to tense. I felt my orgasm building. I knew he felt it too because he began to moan. "Fuck baby, you're squeezing me so tight." He thrust twice, three times, and filled me up with every drop of him. He eventually stopped moving and just stayed inside of me.

"Can I tell you something without you getting mad or upset?" TJ pushed himself back up again as he rolled his eyes at me. "Yes, but hurry before I change my mind." I took a breath. "When Bear was…you know…doing what he was doing, he kept asking me if I liked the taste of what real love was, but it was rancid, horrible. Nothing about it tasted like love. Love shouldn't be disgusting and nasty, should it?" Looking me in the face, I could see he didn't set himself up for a question like that. He gently pulled himself out of me and bent back down so that his face was between my legs again. He began licking me again and moaned so sexily. I loved to hear him make those sounds. It was beautiful. He came back over me and looked in my eyes. "I want your mouth." I gave him my mouth. He stuck his tongue in and I could taste a part of him mixed with a part of me. It was sweet yet salty and had just a hint of bitterness. I swirled my tongue in his mouth to taste more of our combination. He broke the kiss. "Do you taste that, Elleny? That's what real love tastes like. Pure, uncorrupted, virtuous, untainted. That's what straight-from-your-fucking-soul-love tastes like. You got me?"

He wiped the tear from my face and licked it off his thumb as he whispered, "Let me put you back together. Babe, you're not broken, you're just damaged. Remember, bendable…not breakable." He kissed my nose. I turned my head away from him and whispered, "TJ, there's so much that you don't know. Things that are shattering."

"Then, when the time is right, we'll get through it. Let me heal you, Elle." I closed my eyes, laid my head against his, and just said, "Okay."

Chapter 17

August 1995

Please, oh please, let that stick be broken, I thought as my head was stuck in the toilet for the third time that morning. I had a feeling something wasn't right, so the moment I got a break from my one on one with the toilet, I packed up the kids, loaded them in the car and headed down to the drug store. I wasn't sure if I should get one or two, but who could go wrong with an additional pregnancy test? I hurried back home since I felt the urge coming back. I pulled into the drive and stuck my head out the door.

"Son of a bitch!"

The morning went by pretty slow, probably because I needed to get up there and take that test. I ended up feeding the twins lunch an hour early and then laid them down for their naps. I went into the bathroom, followed the directions, and waited. I set the timer for exactly five minutes. And waited.

Being pregnant was not going to be good at all. Bear didn't wait the allotted time he was supposed to wait after the last one. Having them, however, was getting easier now. After my first one, I felt like a murderer who didn't deserve the two kids I had. I attempted to stay in bed for days crying, but I had two babies and I was by myself, so I grieved when I could. Bear would drive me to the clinic, sit out in the car with the kids, and then drop me back off at home before leaving again. Bear deserved to burn in hell for what he had done. These were still my babies and that son of a bitch made me get rid of all five of them. He was using it as a birth control, since he wouldn't let me be on birth control. I tried sneaking it, but he found my pills and beat my ass. I finally gave up, it just wasn't worth it to me. Well, I was done now.

I was going to have this baby. The twins were older now, they were getting ready to turn three, were in daycare, and I had a job.

Hearing the ding from the timer brought me straight back to the matter at hand. I picked the stick up to look at it and began crying. There was no chance that there weren't two pink horizontal lines. I sat down, my back against the tub, and thought of what was going to happen.

I hadn't seen him in weeks, which was fine with me. When he did come home, he always smelled of cheap ass perfume and liquor, so I knew he had been taken care of. Which I was thankful for, it took a lot off of me and I really didn't want him touching me. Ever.

Rachel and Lilly were supposed to be spending their last weekend in town with us. We were taking the kid's to the zoo. They loved it there, so we were planning a whole day of it. They were getting ready to finish their last year in college and I was thrilled for them. Curt, I had a feeling, was getting anxious, too. He ended up going to college here and had joined the police academy. Now, he was a police officer here in town. I was so proud of him, plus it always made me feel a little bit safer. Daddy and Mona would come over several times a week to see the kids and to make sure I was alright. Usually, I would make dinner and we would sit down and eat, that was a great time for me. I missed my dad.

TJ had been on my mind a lot the last couple of weeks. The dreams had stopped coming years ago and I had never felt more lost. Every day I would wonder where he was and if I ever crossed his mind. Every year I would get a phone call. It started the Christmas I was pregnant with the kids. I'd answer the phone and no one would say anything. Now, every birthday and Christmas my phone rings at 7:43 p.m. and I answer. I wasn't sure who it was, but I always pretended it was him. I'd say hello and just talk to the air.

I was cooking dinner when I heard the doorbell ring.

"Who is it," I asked."

"I'm looking for Elleny Barker-Jackson, ma'am," a strange voice answered. I asked again.

"Who are you?"

"Ma'am, are you Elleny Barker-Jackson?"

Not knowing who this was, I was getting scared. Since that visit from the skank, I didn't know what other trash Bear hung around and he obviously didn't care who he gave our address out to.

"Umm, no I'm not. She's not available."

"Ma'am, I think you're lying to me."

What the fuck!

I opened the door to bite this person's head off and froze.

"Gotcha, biatch!!"

Rachel was standing at my door. I wrapped my arms around her neck and hugged her as tight as I could. She and Kevin went up north for a few weeks before school started. They wanted some time to themselves and needed to get away.

"Oh my god, you bitch! You scared the living shit outta me! What are you doing here? I'm so glad you're here! Come in, come in. I thought you weren't going to be back 'til Tuesday. Come see your kids."

I kept on and on, I was so excited she was standing there.

She started laughing as she walked through my door. I begin to shut it.

"Wait, Kevin's coming in. He's bringing the bags." She sauntered in, unlit cigarette in hand.

"Where are my kiddos!" she screeched. At the sound of her voice, JoJo and Luc came running into the foyer from the living room. She threw her arms out as she dropped her cigarette and ran toward them. I laughed and bent down to pick it up as Kevin walked in behind me.

"Hey, Kevin," I greeted while he was attempting to put down the bags. I hugged him. I loved Kevin. I always thought he was so perfect for Rach.

Kevin and I both stood there watching New York runway model Rachel, sitting on the floor in her designer jeans and stiletto heels smothering two kids that had messy faces with kisses, while they laughed and called her Auntie Way-Shell. I giggled.

"Ya'll come on in, I've got dinner in the crock pot. I'll make you a plate. I never know when Bear will be home, so I've got plenty," I said as I led them into the kitchen.

"What are ya'll doin' here?" I asked while scooping a large helping of mashed potatoes into a large bowl and ladling a big helping of chicken and dumplings over the top.

Rachel pulled a bracelet out of her pocket for JoJo and smiled at my daughter. JoJo took the jewelry as she yelled, "Pwetty!" all through the kitchen. "Well, we came home as kinda a surprise, right, Kev?" Rachel looked at Kevin and I looked between them as I ladled dumplings in a bowl for her. I walked toward them with their bowls as I told JoJo to get up in her highchair.

"Okay, what are ya'll not telling me?" I asked as I put Luc up in his highchair.

"Well, fuck, Elle. We took a small honeymoon."

I stopped. "You...ya'll got married? And you didn't even call me?"

"Elle..." Rachel looked back at Kevin. I felt like I'd been run over by a train. We had planned our weddings since we were five. She wasn't there for mine, but Christ almighty, she at least knew about it. I didn't even know about this one. I would've at least called her and told her my maid of honor speech.

I couldn't help it, I started crying. I wasn't mad at her. I was furious with myself. Nothing in my life was going the way I wanted it to, nothing. Everything was a total fuck up and no matter how much I tried for it not to be, the worst it seemed to get.

She came up and hugged me. "Honey, no one was there. We just went down to the court house while we were up there and did a twenty minute ceremony. It was spur of the moment, baby doll."

"I know," I whimpered. "I'm not mad or anything, I'm ju… ju…just sick of everything fu…fucking up."

Shit, the pregnancy hormones were already kicking in. Kevin probably thought I was a fucking fruit loop.

I raised my head and used my shirt to wipe my eyes and nose. "We had plans, Rach. I had plans and everything has totally been shit on. Everything we planned growing up together, it's all over and done with."

Rubbing my back, she attempted to comfort me. "I know, hon, but those were little girl dreams, look what you've got here…"

I looked behind her and saw my children shoving fists full of mashed potatoes in their mouths. I felt warmth settle over me. I looked at her and smiled. She nodded because she knew what I was thinking. *His children.*

"I love you, Rach."

"I know you do, Ellie-bean. How could you not, I'm irresistible!" She joked and the three of us laughed hysterically, with the two kids joining in when they heard us.

I got the kids in their beds around eight and shut the door. I didn't want to take the chance of anything waking them up. I wanted to spend as much time as I could with my girl and her new husband.

"Have you told Lils?" I asked as I raised a cup of coffee up to my lips to blow on it before I took a sip.

We were all sitting in my breakfast nook drinking coffee and eating some peach pie that I threw in the oven after my little breakdown. Rachel and I cleaned up dinner while Kevin took the bags to the room they would be staying in. We had a five bedroom house and only two rooms were being used, so they had their pick.

"I called but she didn't answer. I didn't want to leave that kind of message over a voicemail so I figured I try again tomorrow."

I took another sip of my coffee. We talked about how happy her parents were at the news of the marriage. I asked if she was going to be known as Rachel Locke-Harrington or just Rachel Harrington. I knew she would keep the Locke in there. She was eighth generation.

"Ya'll stayin' til the weekend? Are we going to be able to do the zoo?" I asked, hopeful it would be longer than two days.

"Fuck yeah we're doin' the zoo. But, I think we might go take a couple days to go up north, maybe show him the lake we used to go to."

Oh, that would be fun. Take your new husband up to where you used to go for week-long sexfests with another man. Sometimes I wondered if Rachel thought stuff through before she said it.

We finished talking and by 10:30 we were all exhausted, so we headed up to bed. I turned on the alarm and locked all the doors before I climbed into bed.

I woke up on my stomach to the feeling of being suffocated and squished at the same time. I opened my eyes and felt weight on my back with someone's hand over my mouth.

"Don't you fucking scream," his raspy voice said into my ear. I smelled liquor and something musty on his hands.

"Who the fuck's cars outside? You got someone here fucking you? I can't believe you'd do that shit with my kids in the house, I always knew you were a whore." I closed my eyes and just shook my head, trying to move his hand away from my mouth.

I tried to speak, but his hand just made it muffled. Finally, he let go but he didn't get up.

"It's Rachel and her husband Kevin, Bear. They just got married and came home to tell everyone. They're right in the other room. Why are you doing this?"

He sat up and stared at the wall behind my head. "Well then. Hot, tight pussied Rachel is here, huh? I wonder if her husband would let me pound that for old time's sake." I just closed my eyes and laid my head back down. I was still gasping for breath since he outweighed me by a hundred pounds.

"No?" he answered his own question. "Well, maybe I'll just pound you since I'm in the mood to tear me up some whore cunt tonight. I suggest you don't scream loud."

I knew what he was implying; if I screamed, I would get hit. If I took it like a "real woman", he'd only bruise my inner thighs from where he would viciously ram his hips against me. I saw him reach in the drawer.

"Oh no, Bear. I won't move, I prom—"

He reached back around and covered my mouth. "Did I tell you to beg, cunt? I don't wanna hear your stupid, fucking voice," he whispered through gritted teeth next to my ear, spit flying on the side of my face. I had no choice, he was gonna strap me to the bed. He grabbed my arm and pulled it out toward the head board, I resisted. *Slap!* Bear's open-hand came across my face. "Don't you resist me. Give me your arm." I closed my eyes. *Don't you cry, don't you cry, don't give him your tears, Elle. Don't you dare.*

"It's pretty sad when a husband can't stand looking at his wife," he uttered as he strapped my other arm up. I could already feel the leather digging into my skin. I didn't want to imagine what I looked like. My arms were completely stretched out. They felt like they were going to pop out of the socket at any moment. He raised my gown and ripped off my panties. He must've looked at them because he laughed wickedly and said, "You're not even woman enough to wear sexy panties for your husband. This cotton shit is not the way to get a man to want to dig into that snatch of yours, Ellie." I

309

wanted to beg him not to do this, but that would've just gotten me smacked again. So, I just laid there.

I heard the unzipping of his zipper and closed my eyes. The feeling that I was being spread open sent panic throughout my body. Mercilessly, Bear pushed himself into me as hard as he could. I drove my head down into the pillow and screamed in unbearable pain. He pulled out just as fast and did it again. Only, this time, he jammed two fingers right above where he was ramming without lube or stretching. I screamed again, barely able to catch my breath the pain was so bad. "That's it, bitch, scream. I want to hear you scream. You like that pussy tore the fuck up, don't ya?" he whispered in my ear. He pushed forward again. This time I just moaned. My eyes became heavy and by the next thrust, I had passed out from the pain.

I woke up the next morning to the kids crying on the monitor next to my bed. *Shit, what time was it?* I heard Bear's voice come over the monitor. "Well, mornin', my princess, that stupid bitch of a momma neglecting you? Well, we will have to keep up with that. I just might have to take ya where you'd be taken care of properly." I looked at the clock, it was 7:10 in the morning. I attempted to jump out of bed and almost fell straight to the floor. My legs were like jelly, my ass hurt, and my thighs were so raw they were probably bleeding. I made it back to the bed to sit there for a moment. I had to get up and get JoJo and Luc from him. I breathed through the pain all the way to my dresser. I reached in, got a pair of panties and sweat pants, and threw them on real quick. I stumbled to the door and threw it open. I walked awkwardly to the nursery which was next door to my room. I threw the door open and walked straight to my child who was being held by Bear. "There she is, I thought that would motivate her. Sometimes, JoJo, you have to tell those lazy ass people what will happen if they don't get up off their fat asses."

I officially loathed this man. If I didn't have these babies, I'd probably shoot him and enjoy the rest of my life in prison.

I grabbed JoJo out of his hands and kissed her cheek. I smelled her head and that brought me back down from my panic attack. I held her to me and just closed my eyes. I opened them and saw Bear smiling at me. I didn't ask him what he was smiling at, although he must've wanted me to because he said, "I thoroughly enjoyed last night, sweet cheeks." I still didn't respond to him, there was nothing to say. "I think we might have to do that again here in the near future."

As he said that, he walked by me. "Now, where's that sexy lil Rachel. I can't wait to smack her ass."

Fucking dick!

Before he left the room, I thought I ought to go ahead and get the news out. I knew this wasn't going to go pretty, but I didn't give a shit. I mentally prepared myself for the ass beating I was getting ready to take.

"Oh, hey, Bear, since you wanted to be a cocksucker when you decided to have sex with me two months ago, you got me pregnant again and it's too late to have it dealt with. So, guess what, you're gonna be a real fucking father now."

He hated TJ being brought up in his face. The twins were his biological kids in his eyes and no one was going to say differently. This motherfucker even said that they looked like him. He slowly entered the kid's room and shut the door.

"You think I'm afraid to have you walking around with a fucking bruise on you, whore? 'Cause I ain't. I will mark you all over your disgusting body and they won't know a fucking thing. Say the word, Ellie. Give me permission to fuck you up into next week." I smiled at him and walked past him. "That ain't my baby, whore." I kept walking, "Whatever, Bear."

I needed some time to myself. Since I looked like a punching bag, I didn't think I could walk around the mall, so I decided to go where I haven't been in a while—to see my momma. I didn't remember her, but my daddy always said I looked like her. I had seen pictures. She was beautiful. Long, dark hair that she wore up on top of her head in a high ponytail, her eyes matching the shade of her hair.

The only memory I had of her was when Daddy wouldn't let me have sweets. Only on special occasions was I allowed one, maybe two pieces of candy, and that was rare. One evening, my momma strapped me in the car and we rode into town. I remembered playing with the toy she had given me to keep me busy while she drove. We ended up going to the sewing shop to get some ribbon. I couldn't tell you what it looked like, but I could never go into that shop again. We got back in the car and drove to the ice cream shop where we ended up staying for a while. I got a cup of ice cream, she had a cone. I remembered licking more of hers than I ate of mine. I slept all the way home. Her smile lit up the night, it was so bright and beautiful. I don't ever think she yelled a day in her life. I missed my momma, though I was glad that she wasn't around to see how I turned out. She might end up blaming herself and this had nothing to do with my parents.

I asked Rachel if she'd sit with the twins a bit while I went to run an errand. I ended up just going in the shorts I had on, I wasn't going for a fashion show. I needed my momma. I drove all the way there in silence, thinking about where I had gone wrong. What did I do to make Bear hate me so much? He wasn't like this in school and I knew he never treated Rachel like this. There was no way she would've allowed it, she would've dropped his ass. I never felt so alone in all my life.

I pulled up the road that my mom's grave was near and parked. I didn't bring her any flowers and I felt guilty for that. I hadn't come to see her in years, I don't even think I had brought the twins up here, but in my time of need, here I sat. Maybe I was being selfish.

I walked down the middle line of headstones, so careful not to step on the area in front of them as I came up on my mom's. Beautiful daisies sat on both sides of her marker, pictures of my babies were placed in a picture frame that said, "I heart my grandma!" Daddy must still come up here. He used to make it an every Sunday ritual. I was comforted that he had this as therapy. I had nothing. There was nowhere for me to go to mourn the loss of what was the most valuable relationship I'd ever had. I knew my daddy's pain and there was no way that I could comfort him enough for that pain to go away. I felt a tear hit my cheek at the picture of my children. Every day they looked more and more like their daddy, it made me smile. I wiped my cheek as I sat down in front of my mom's headstone and laid my cheek against the smooth rock. "Momma, I need you," I whispered as I tried to hold back the tears. "I can't be strong much longer, I'm breaking. I'm so ashamed at who I've become. I gave up everything for him, Momma." I got louder as the tears came. I couldn't hold them back anymore. "Tell me what to do," I whispered as I began shaking from silently crying.

I sat there for hours, just chatting to myself.

"I wish you could tell me that I'm a good momma," I said, looking at her name written in pretty calligraphy. Nancy Elaine Phillips-Barker was etched into the marble and underneath was her date of birth and the date she passed. My dad made sure she knew exactly what he felt as he had "You are loved and cherished" inscribed on her marker as well.

"I feel so lost, like inside of me is disorder and confusion and I can't be like that. I have to stay in control. I have to be aware of every move Bear's making, Momma. If I'm not, he's going to take our children…and I'm tired, I'm so fuckin' weary. I have another one on the way… just found out yesterday. See my face?" I took my sunglasses off. "Got this because I'm stupid, lazy, fat, ugly, a bad mom, a bad fuck and…"

I kept going, naming off all the names that I heard every day of my life. Names that I've gotten so used to being called, I started to believe them. "Oh, don't worry, they don't bother me anymore. Nothing bothers me anymore. I found out that true love isn't real…never was. It's some bullshit story that we tell our little girls to get their hopes up that some man out there will treat them with respect. We teach them that one soul mate will keep them safe and never, ever harm them. That

313

they'll keep your secrets and show you how special you are. But, see, that's not how life truly is! In reality, the word love means hatred and malevolence, disrespect and cruelty. They don't keep your secrets and they *don't* treat you special. They don't keep you safe and they *do* harm you."

Chapter 18

Present Day

Sitting in the waiting room of TJ's doctor's office, I felt as though all eyes were on me. I saw people whispering and I automatically wondered if they were whispering about the lady that was having another STD test—two in a week.

TJ saw me fidget. He grabbed my hand and held it in his lap. Turning toward me for just a moment, he smiled a reassuring smile and went back to looking at his lap.

"Miss Barker?"

I glared at TJ. It was going to look real funny when I had to hand them my insurance card with my full name on it. The nurse walked us back to the triage room where she weighed me and took my blood pressure…again. Twice in two weeks, I think I was up to date on my vitals.

"So, Miss Barker, what are we seeing you for today?"

"I just need an S—"

"She's going to need a physical. I'd like Dr. Callahan to check her out thoroughly."

I looked at TJ with my eyebrows raised. "What on—"

"I'm sorry, Mr. McHale the appointment was scheduled hours ago and we still have three other patients to see. Maybe you can resch—"

Since my appointment was scheduled at two and we didn't arrive until four because of getting caught up in some "unexpected business", I was thankful they would still see me.

Now here he was, making waves. They'd probably end up kicking us out.

"Listen to me… Jackie, is it?"

"Yes, sir, my name is Jackie."

"Well, Jackie, I bet if you go and have a discussion with Dr. Callahan, he will not have a problem with us sitting in the exam room while he finishes with the other patients and then returns to our room. He will be compensated very well for his time."

She nodded her head and placed us in an exam room.

"That was totally unnecessary, I don't need an exam. I just want to have him take some blood and be done with this," I protested, flipping through a celebrity magazine.

"Elle, you are covered in bruises. I want to make sure that you don't have anything broken."

That was truly none of his business. I didn't want to discuss this with him anymore than I had and I sure as shit didn't want some doctor poking his head into this situation. If Bear got wind of this, he'd have my kids up and gone by the time my plane landed back in Atlanta.

Still flipping through pages, looking for something to read to take my mind off this, I shrugged and casually informed him. "It wouldn't have been the first time and it sure as hell won't be the last."

Suddenly, TJ ripped the magazine out of my hand and threw it across the exam room. "It sure as fuck was the last time!" He tightened his jaw and his eyes were lit with pure rage. "Don't you think for one fucking second that he won't get what's comin' to him for what he's done! You are not going back to that, and that is final!"

Quickly, the room seemed to cave in on me. The air seemed to dissipate, I couldn't catch my breath. I bent my head down between my knees and began taking longer breaths.

"What's the matter, Elle?"

"I can't breathe. I think I'm having a panic attack."

"What…why?"

I sat up swiftly, so quick my ponytail flew through the air.

"You have no clue, TJ. Don't tell me I'm not going back to that because I don't have a choice. I have to go back."

He walked back over toward where he was sitting. "What do you mean that you don't have a choice? You do, and I'm making it for you. When we leave Burlington, I'm going with you to your house. We're packing up what you and the kid's need for a couple of days and coming back to my house. Then, I will have professionals pack up the rest of your things and put them in storage."

I began to laugh a maniacal laugh.
"You think it's just that easy, huh? You think he's gonna let us go just like that?" I asked him as I snapped my fingers. "You don't think I've thought about that or even tried? Do you know what happens if I do that again?" I saw his jaw twitch. His face was so hard, I knew this wasn't going to be any easier for him to hear. "You see these?" I picked up my shirt and reminded him of what going to sleep brought me. "This will be a day at the fair for me. You see these?" I held up my wrists. "These won't look like this if I try that again. There won't be anything left for Rachel and Lilly to bury. My kids won't have a place to come visit their momma. Now, do you really want that for them?"

He sat there, his face stone.

I saw his mouth attempt to move. "Why?" he asked with a shaky chin. He was enraged and trying to keep it buried deep.

I looked down at my hands that were sitting in my lap, contemplating on whether to lie the same lie I've told myself for the last seventeen years or to make up a new one. I decided on the latter. I knew I could never take the chance on him seeing the twins. If he ever caught a glimpse, he'd know.

Quietly, I answered, "I've changed, TJ. Bear has turned me into a harsh woman, hon, and I can't be brought back. I've come to the conclusion that it's better to be unhappy and have my kids safe and with me, than to be happy where my children would always have to watch their backs."

He just shook his head. "I can protect you, Elle," he said, staring at me as if he could see down into my soul. He meant every word. He'd die protecting me and my children—our children. But, who would protect him?

He was still young enough to get married and have a family of his own. I couldn't let him make a mistake like wasting more years on me. He should be able to find the last element he needed to complete his life—his happiness.

At that moment, the doctor walked in. "Well, Ms. Barker, I hear we've had a change in plans. Let me—"

Out of nowhere, TJ spoke up. "We'll just take the test, Doc." His eyes shot to me. "We'll reschedule for the physical."

I breathed a sigh of relief.

We finished up at the doctor's and left. TJ fought me because I wanted to pay for the visit but he wouldn't hear of it. He paid cash and a little extra for the doctor's time, he also paid for a one day turn around on the results. We got in the car and headed for the city.

By this time, it was almost six in the evening. The sun was attempting to set so the sky was a beautiful orange color. The top was down on the car, I had my sunglasses on, and I just laid my head back against the headrest and felt the breeze on my face. I laid my hand on TJ's leg and he covered my hand with his own. I felt like I was in my place, sitting next to him in his old truck with the windows down.

I asked him if he would turn on the radio. He turned it on but played a CD instead. It was Whitesnake's "Slow and Easy". I opened my eyes, lifted my head from the headrest, and looked over at TJ, smiling. He smiled back.

He was trying to let the song tell me what he was thinking. I smiled bigger than I had in years. The top was down on the car, Bear was not anywhere around, TJ was sitting beside me and all of those feeling I felt when I went to my place came rushing to me in an instant. This was real.

Freedom. I turned the song up louder. I began bouncing my head to the beat. I heard the chorus come on and I sang just as loud as the lead singer did. I didn't care about what the people around me were thinking. I was unbound, released from the hold Bear had on me for the past seventeen years. At least, for now. I hadn't tasted this in so many years, I forgot what it felt like—the loss of control. The wind was blowing away all the feelings of dread and anguish I had lived with most of my life. I began laughing, loud and frenzied. I laughed so hard, I began to cry. I wanted to know this feeling for the rest of my life. I raised my arms up in the air and just opened up my palms, letting go of everything that had been a part of me for so long. I forgot who I was, letting it go. The secrets I'd been keeping trapped up inside of me, the stress of being found out, it went out in the wind. The consequences of TJ finding out those secrets, the thought of taking my kids and running off when this was done and over with, I let all of it go in that Audi going down the interstate. I'd deal with it all another day.

We made it back to the city and decided we were in the mood for Mexican food. We drove to a restaurant that TJ said had the best Mexican food around and a back patio where a live band played. The choice was obvious, we were going to eat outside and enjoy the music and amazing sunset.

Finishing up with my enchiladas and my second margarita, I talked TJ into one more drink. He added the stipulation that I give him one dance. I accepted, had one more margarita, and then attempted to do a little Spanish dance that looked more like a seizure. We decided we needed to leave so that I could get a head start on what I needed to do.

We made it back to the hotel. I took a quick shower and settled in to call Rachel and video conference my kids to tell them goodnight. I had received pictures from them this afternoon while they were swimming, so I knew they made it back to Rachel's with no problems.

I sat down on the couch and called Rach, it rang two times before she answered.

319

"Hey, babe."

I smiled, she sounded so laid back.

"Hey, sweetie, how are the hoodlums?"

She giggled. I could hear them in the background, something about Kevin and ice cream.

"They're wonderful. They said something was up this afternoon. I didn't know what to do with that, but I figured you would call me and let me know when you got a chance."

She knew me too well. I'm controlled and panicked at the drop of a hat. She's just as calm and collected and well, if trouble happens, she'll find a way out…in a bit.

I walked to my room and shut the door.

"Where are you?"

"I'm in my room, why?"

"Oh my god! You did it, didn't you?"

"Rachel!"

"Holy shit! Well…give me details…wait! No, I've changed my mind, fuck that. We'll leave it with you did it."

I laughed then I got serious.

"I told him all about Bear, Rach. Bear called when I was in the living room and he was in his room. I had it on speaker phone, but I didn't know he could hear and Bear called me every name in the book. TJ started yelling at me, asking why I wouldn't tell him what was going on…so, I did. He went ballistic, Rach. Throwing shit, it was nuts."

She was quiet for a minute and I heard her sniff.

"Did you tell him?"

I knew what she was talking about and there was no way I could tell him. If he threw that big of a fit when it came to Bear doing this to me, I couldn't imagine what he would do if he knew Bear was raising the children I withheld from him as his own. Not only that, Bear was beating the shit out of me with his children in the same house.

"You know that's not possible, Rach."

She knew. She also knew how much I wanted to, but time had passed. Like building a house brick by brick, it had taken me seventeen years to build this house from the foundation up. Telling him about them would tear the whole house down and hurt all that was in it.

I told her that I was going to call the kids to tell them goodnight and remind them to stay aware of their surroundings for the next couple of days. I did my call, grabbed a shower, and was sitting at the dining room table with my laptop with my first file and memory stick. As I began my eleventh file, TJ popped up behind me and moved my hair to the side as he kissed the back of my neck.

"Now, now, Mr. McHale, I am trying to work here." As I said this, I saw him drop down in the chair next to me with his computer. He was laughing. "I know, I just wanted to see if I could distract you."

I laughed, never taking my eyes off the screen as I replied, "I cannot be distracted. I am a lean, mean, working machine".

He started laughing again. "Oh, I think I can think of a way to distract you." I felt his hand touch my thigh and my head turned his way to jump his ass—

"Gotcha! Just call me the master of distraction."

I stuck my tongue out at him.

"Don't tease me. I might take you up on that offer."

I leaned over toward him and barely touched my lips to his as I whispered, "Oh, Mr. McHale, that was so not a tease. That was a taste of what will be available to you tonight, if you let me get this box finished."

I leisurely laid my tongue on my bottom lip so that it touched his lips. TJ drew it into his mouth for a moment as he kissed me and then immediately grabbed a folder and began to enter information.

"Fuck, Elle, take it deeper, baby." I leaned in further to take more of him in my mouth. I loved the way he smelled and

321

tasted, I would never get enough. "Shit, baby, I love your mouth. It's like stroking my cock against silk."

I hummed my pleasure at the thought. Not wanting to take him out of my mouth, I stroked down and sucked harder as I came back up his shaft. Running my tongue around the tip of him, I heard him hiss in enjoyment. "I wanna be inside you."

After we finished the whole box, it wasn't as late as I thought it was and I wanted to do something since he treated me to an amazing afternoon. So, as soon as he stood up, I went for the button on his pants. Catching him off guard, I got down on my knees and unzipped his pants slowly, never taking my eyes off of his. I reached into his pants, encircled him in my hand, and closed my eyes. I felt so at ease doing this to him. I didn't feel embarrassed or that he was going to make fun of me. It was as if he was made to be a part of me. Whether it be my hand, my mouth, inside me. He was made for me.

I lifted him out of his pants and touched the tip of my tongue to the head of his cock. I tasted a drop of him on my tongue and I closed my eyes in gratification.

"I taste you on my tongue, TJ. I like knowing all I have to do is touch you to see you glisten for me." I ran my fist down and back up him to find another drop of his sweetness drip down the side of his shaft. His eyes were closed and his head was back as I continued, "Or all I have to do is lick you." I ran my tongue down the side where that drop was running down his length and caught it as I swept back up to the tip. His eyes were back on me. "I can taste you anytime I want."

"Fuck baby, it's all for you," he answered in a heady voice while he pushed the hair off my face, continuing through to the back where he gripped, tugging it gently.

I put my lips around him and sucked hard. I heard him moan as he tensed his muscles. I teased him with my tongue, flicking over where I had just sucked. I felt his hand in the back of my hair, pushing gently down, encouraging me to take all of him in. I didn't hesitate. Starting out slowly, I drew him into me, working myself into a faster rhythm.

"That's it, honey. Take my cock. God damn, I've missed you." I moaned and dropped my fingers between my legs. I was on fire, I could feel the heat even before I touched myself.

"Yes, play with yourself. Touch that beautiful pussy while I watch you take my cock. Shit, you're gonna make me come."

Beginning to rub my fingers against myself faster, I moaned while taking him all the way down my throat. This made him go wild with desire. He began to push my head, faster and faster. I began to suck harder.

"Don't stop." I followed his direction. I felt the first jet hit the back of my tongue and heard his long groan.

"Fuck, Elle, I love you!"

I giggled and stood to my feet. "Yeah, I bet you do."

I heard the alarm clock start to go off. I hit the snooze button. This two in the morning shit and being up at six was not doing anything for my beauty sleep. I rolled to my side and saw TJ sleeping soundly beside me. He looked so gorgeous and peaceful, his face was relaxed and I couldn't help but smile.

I could see the grey in his hair right at his temples now. I gently ran my hands through it. He snuggled closer to my hand reflexively. Leaning into him, I kissed him softly on the lips. I pulled the covers off of me and headed to the bathroom. I turned on the shower and let the water heat up. I grabbed my toothbrush and toothpaste, slathered a bit on the brush and set it aside. I put my hand in to test the water. It was perfect.

I undressed, grabbed my toothbrush, and jumped in. I got under the stream of water, closed my eyes, and just enjoyed the hot water against my face. Without opening my eyes, I stuck my toothbrush in my mouth and brushed my teeth. As soon as I was done, I threw my toothbrush over the glass enclosure to hear it landed right where I wanted it to in the sink.

"Nice shot!"

I opened my eyes and screeched in shock.

TJ was standing right in front of me, totally naked in the shower.

"Goddammit, you scared the shit outta me."

He laughed and kissed me long, hard, and wonderfully wet.

"Mm, you taste like peppermint."

"Well, duh!" I said sarcastically, as I squeezed the shampoo in my hand.

"I had to repay you for the wonderful morning kiss you gave me just a minute ago."

"You shit! You were awake?"

Laughing, he shook his head. "You were having a moment, I wasn't going to spoil it."

I smiled and just stared at him. "Here, wash my back while I wash my hair. We're gonna be late."

I finished showering, leaving him to wash his hair. He ended up washing my entire body, and I his. We made out hot and heavy for a bit until I stopped it because we were here for work and I needed to remember that. I stepped out of the shower, grabbed a towel, and went to work on an outfit. Since I was going to be sitting in an office doing data entry all day, I decided on my black pant suit. I left my hair down but put in a nice pair of silver hoops along with several silver dangle bracelets. My black stilettos were thick platforms with a thin heel. With these shoe on, I reached TJ's shoulders. My makeup was flawless. I felt hot for a thirty-six year old mother of three.

I walked out of my room quickly. I smelled coffee and I was desperate. I heard TJ in the kitchen on the phone yelling something about not caring about someone, that we were on a time crunch, blah, blah, blah. I packed up most of our stuff last night after our little interlude, so all I really had to do was organize the box of memory sticks, and grab my purse.

I walked in the kitchen to grab my cup of coffee and stepped up behind TJ while he was talking, I leaned against the cabinets a minute just to admire the view. He was still on the phone blabbing about work, standing there in his pants and a dress shirt. He began backing up. His back hit my front and he stopped. He rested his phone up against his shoulder and reached his arm behind him. He grabbed my hands and put them around his waist. I heard him unzip his pants and he continued his conversation as he opened his boxers and inserted my hand.

I gripped my hand around him as he slowly moved my hand up and down his shaft. His voice never faltered. I leaned my head up against the back of his designer shirt while he jacked himself off using my hand. I couldn't get the thought of how erotic this was out of my mind. He wrapped up his phone call but continued thrusting into my hand. I was so turned on, I had to close my eyes and wish that the call would go dead. Finally, I heard those words. Two words that made my heart beat fast. "Good bye."

He threw his phone down, immediately turned around, and slammed his mouth down on mine. We were both fighting for control over the kiss until I finally gave in. I decided on going in another direction—south. I unbuttoned his pants while he unbuttoned mine. I flung my shoes then kicked my pants off as he walked me backwards to the living room. He broke the kiss just for a moment to tell me to lean over the couch. I hesitated. I didn't like to be backwards, Bear always made me turn backwards. He said he didn't want to look at my ugly face. I stood up and told TJ, "No. I'm not a dog, you're not going to fuck me like one." He jumped back like I had caught him off guard. I probably did. "Baby, I wasn't even thinking that, why would you even say that?" The mood was ruined. I began pulling up my panties and searching for my pants. As I was looking for everything, I explained, "Bear says the only way he can fuck me is from behind so he doesn't have to look at my ugly face." I didn't see what happened, but I heard it. TJ picked up a fifty thousand dollar vase and threw it across the room, where it hit the wall and shattered into a million pieces.

I turned around with my pants in my hands and my shoes on my feet when he spoke. "Don't you ever compare me to that fucking piece of shit! I would never think that of you. I have never treated you that way and don't you ever think that it would start now!"

I was scared. I didn't mean it that way. I didn't even know what I was thinking saying it so casually. I was used to being treated like a piece of trash, TJ wasn't used to me feeling that way.

I ran over to him and hugged him. "Honey, I'm so sorry. I didn't mean it to come out that way. I would never compare you to him. I just don't like being turned backwards. I feel self-conscious. The whole time, I would be wondering if you felt that way, too. You are nothing like him. Please, I'm so sorry." I began kissing his cheeks and lips, whispering my apologies against his skin, over and over. My lips trailed down to his mouth. "Please, I need to show you I'm sorry." I kissed him frantically, plunging my tongue into his mouth. I needed him to see how important it was for him to forgive me. He grabbed my head and held me against him as we twined our tongues together.

"Please, TJ." I reached down and grasped him within my hand again. He was immediately hard and I fell down to my knees. I was out of control, I needed him like I needed my next breath. He was my savior, he allowed me to be uninhibited. "Trevor..." That was all I needed to say. He reached under my shoulders and picked me straight up in the air. I felt the desperation in him, he needed me as badly as I needed him. "Tell me what you want, baby." I wanted him to know I felt the ache just as much as he did. He pushed me up against the wall.

"You are no longer his!" He rubbed the tip of his cock against me and I tensed in anticipation. "I never was his, Trevor," I admitted as I felt him slide gently into me. "You are mine now," he said as he filled me all the way up. I closed my eyes in the relief I felt of having him connected to me. "Open your fucking eyes!" he yelled, not out of anger, but out of desire. I opened my eyes. "I've always been yours, Trevor." He drew back out and I gripped my hands in his hair. I wanted him to go faster, I needed him to fuck me faster. "Say the words, Elleny." I pulled myself up and slammed myself back down on him, searching for what I was looking for and not finding it. "Goddammit, Trevor, I'm fucking begging you. I need you to fuck me now and hard. I'm not gonna break, please," I pleaded, desperately.

He pushed back in slowly again and I was ready to scream. "What the fuck do you want to hear? Tell me, I'll say it!" I bawled. I felt him touch the top of me internally, but it wasn't getting me anywhere. I was so turned on, I took my hand out of his hair and put it between us, needing the friction.

"You don't get to come! You say the words and I make you come! It belongs to me. You hear me, Elleny?" That was when it hit me. I knew what he wanted to hear and he could go screw himself, I was never saying those words again. I said them to him seventeen years ago and I had an emotional breakdown trying to forget them. "Get off of me," I whispered. He was using shit that he knew for a fact would break me, just so I would get him off. "No, say the words!" He became still, his cock still buried deep within me.

I began moving, but it wasn't enough. He pushed my blouse down, pulled my breast out of my bra, and began to suck on my hard peak. "Elleny, your pussy is so wet, it's dripping down my balls, baby. All you have to do is say the words and I will get you off." I closed my eyes and he began to suck harder. He moved to the left one and sucked my nipple almost painfully, but the feeling was so intense I could feel my orgasm rising.

Feeling my internal muscles clench, he let go of my nipple and lowered his hand between us. He pulled it back up, his fingers shiny and dripping wet. "This is all you." He stuck his fingers in his mouth and licked them clean. I was ready to scream in sexual frustration. "I could eat you for dinner, every night. My cock is ready to bust here, Elleny. Just say the words and I will move." I'd had enough. "Fuck you! I'm not saying it again! I won't be able to survive this time, goddammit!"

He stopped everything. No more talking, no more teasing, nothing. He began to move again slowly. "I can't say any more than what I've said to you, Elleny. I told you how I felt last night. I need something from you, baby." He was slowly working himself inside of me.

I began to rock my hips, again. "I want the words, Elle. I need the words." My heart was so full for him, but I didn't want to say the word love when it came to TJ. I didn't believe in love anymore. I couldn't risk it. He started to thrust harder, deeper. "Ride my cock, Elleny. You love it." He was beginning to build up friction. "I do love it." I rolled faster. "You love my cock don't you, Ellie-bean? I love that you only come for me."

"Yes, only for you."

He was banging into me now, going so deep and so fast my back was building up friction on the wall. "That's it, baby, come all over me. I want you marked by me. I want to smell you and know that that's my smell on you. I'm gonna come so fucking hard."

I opened my mouth to enjoy the high and quickly, he stopped.

TJ screamed, "Say the fucking words, Elleny!" "I love you!! Shit, Trevor! I love you so much, I've never stopped loving you. I can't see anyone else but you! But, I can't go back to that. I won't go back! Is that what you want to hear? Is it, you sadistic motherfucker?"

He thrust into me so hard, I felt like I got whiplash. I was over the top, almost to the point of passing out. My orgasm was so big, I sat there for ten minutes, just feeling the high pass over my body. With my head on his shoulder, I just started sobbing. I couldn't even bring my head up to look at him. "Elle, baby, don't…"

"No you don't, Trevor!" I pushed him away. I was standing there naked from the waist down, my breasts exposed, crying. My heart wasn't even a heart anymore, it was just a puddle of shit in my chest cavity. I didn't want to say the words because I knew it was inconceivable for us to be together.

I walked to the bathroom to clean up and TJ followed me. "Don't what, Elleny? Let's be honest here, what is it you're not telling me? Why can't we be together?"

"Honesty…" I laughed manically. "I don't even know what that word means anymore," I mumbled to myself, but obviously loud enough for him to hear me. "Look, if it's about Bear, I understand."

"You do? "I laughed again. "You understand…?"

"Yes, I understand that you have children with him and you don't want to pull the kids out from him. You're a good mom and you don't want your kids to suffer. But they won't suffer darlin', they'll grow to love me."

I'm a good mom. That phrase echoed through my brain. Suddenly, I thought of all the things that I had done to be a good mom. The lies I had told, the people I had hurt, the damage I had caused for allowing my children to grow up with a monster. I didn't say another word. I fixed my hair, cleaned up my face, and went to find my clothes. "Let's go, I have work to do."

The ride to work was extremely quiet, my eyes didn't roam. They looked straight ahead. As soon as the car came to a stop, I opened the car door and exited out onto the pathway that led up to the building. "Elle, wait up!" I heard him, but I paid him no mind. I had a job to do and I wanted it done so that I could get the hell out of here and get back to my shitty life of beatings and lies. I pushed the button to the elevator and stood. TJ finally caught up to me. He sounded a bit out of breath but maybe he needed that exercise. We stood there, waiting for the chime, and finally we heard it. We both stood back and waited to see if anyone would step off. No one did. We walked in and as soon as the doors closed, I beat him to the punch.

"I'm here to work, Trevor. I'm not here to fuck my boss. I'm finishing my job and I will leave as soon as the last contract is signed. I will be finishing up the memory sticks this morning. This afternoon, I will get the clients scheduled for the next several days' worth of signings and I will be out of here before you leave for lunch."

He laughed. "You done?" I looked at him. *Was he serious?* This was all a big fucking joke to him. Well, I was done being the punchline.

"You won't leave until I say you leave. If you remember correctly, your boss, Mr. Stevens, is depending on you."

That piece of shit! I moved quickly in his face and I was fucking furious. "Don't you fucking dare threaten me with that shit!" I gritted. "I was called here to do a job of collecting and storing two hundred and fifty signed contracts. I just told you that will be accomplished. Don't you fucking think you can toy with me, McHale."

I went back in my corner and looked up at the numbers, praying that this elevator had warp speed. Unfortunately, it didn't. Not another word was spoken. As soon as the elevator doors opened, I put my mask back into place. My face was adorned with a smile that could light up the dark. He allowed me to exit first, but as soon as he walked off into the lobby, he passed by me and mouthed with his finger circling his face, "Nice mask." I flipped him off. I greeted Charlene with a smile and a warm, "Good morning." I walked to my office, making the mental note to ask Mary if there was another one available. I really didn't want to see him today. I dropped my stuff off at my desk and then headed for the kitchen to get a much needed cup of coffee. I passed TJ's office without even looking in and continued down the hall. I passed several offices until I heard a distinguishable voice. "Well, hey there, good lookin'." I rolled my eyes to myself, put the smile on, and turned to step into the doorway of Sam's office. "Morning, Sam, how are you today?" He sat up and smiled his creepy ass smile. Sam reminded me of the men my daddy would tell me never to take candy from. "Well, I'm better now that you walked in," he responded with a wink. "Headed somewhere?" God, please don't follow me to the kitchen. "Just going to the kitchen to grab a cup of coffee, then I'm heading back to my desk to get the day a rollin'," I said with a little Georgia accent that I was trying my best to hide.

"What? You mean to tell me that you're away from your family working for Trevor and he hasn't even taken you to get a decent cup of coffee? Here, let me grab my jacket and we'll go grab one real quick. You have not tasted coffee like this. It's heaven in your mouth."

I thought about a smart ass comment along the lines of, 'no, I had that in my mouth late last night', but I thought it would be best to not announce that to practically a stranger. Before I had a chance to say anything, Sam grabbed my hand, pulled me out of his office, and walked us straight back down to TJ's.

No, no, no! Please don't say that we're going someplace together!

"McHale!" Sam teasingly shouted as he walked into TJ's office. I stayed out by Mary's desk. TJ was busy looking at some papers, I don't think he'd had a chance to even sit down yet. TJ looked at Sam and then looked at me before Sam had even said a word. I just looked at him, attempting to hide my surprised expression. I had a feeling it wasn't working.

I heard muffled talking from the glass, only catching a bit of the conversation from where the door was open.

"She's here in town and I'm gonna show her how northern gentlemen behave and take her down to the Coffee Cabana for a cup, we'll be right back." He was smiling, TJ was not. Sam walked back out to me and wrapped his arm around

331

my shoulders, pushing me gently toward the elevators. Still in a daze that this was really happening, I kept waiting for TJ to come up behind us and start in on a rant. Surprisingly, he didn't.

We walked to the elevators where Sam was telling me all about how great this coffee was and how many different ways you could order it. The doors to the elevator finally opened and we stepped in. He pushed the button for the first floor.

"So, how do you know Trevor McHale?"

I really didn't feel comfortable talking about my relationship—past or present—with this man so I just shrugged it off and told him a half-truth. "My boss is his attorney back in Richland."

"Ah," Sam countered. I faced forward, trying to figure out how all of this came about—me going from my office to the kitchen to now. I was on my way to a coffee shop in a strange city with a complete stranger.

"...have kids?" I heard kids and that brought me back to my current predicament.

"I'm sorry?"

He chuckled. "I asked if you had kids."

I smiled politely. I think I was overthinking this whole scenario. "Yes, I have three. I have a set of twins who are seventeen and a fourteen year old."

"Yikes, teenagers!" He laughed and held his hands up in front of him as though he was protecting his chest.

I laughed quietly. "They're really not that bad. My kids and I are...close. We only have each other to depend on."

All of a sudden, his eyes perked up, his body language changed, and he seemed curious. "So, no loving hubby?"

"No, not at all." Again, I wasn't lying.

"Hmm."

What is up with this man's vocabulary, could he respond like an adult?

The doors opened up and Sam flung his arm out as to say, "Ladies first". I nodded and walked out. I stopped by the doors since I had no clue in what direction we were going.

We walked again with very little conversation. He eventually broke the silence with his tactless way of making it known that he was divorced with no kids. He explained how his ex was a bitch and he didn't see any point in bringing kids up with a mother like that. Suddenly,I pictured my kids.

We came to stop in front of a rocket. That was no car, it was either something that should only have its tires on a closed, well supervised course or launching from Kennedy Space Center.

"You're shittin' me, right? You want me to get in…that?" I asked with a gurgle.

He laughed. "Honey, this is not a that. This is next year's model of the Porsche 911. She is a sleeping baby right now, but here in a minute, she will be raring to go and play." He beeped the locks and opened the door for me. I folded into the seat and tried hard not to throw up. I felt like I was in a soda can, the dashboard four inches from my face.

Sam came around the back and got in on the driver's side. Pushing the start button, he looked over at me, showing off. As he went to put the car in reverse, his hand gently caressed up against the outside of my thigh. I turned to look at him but he was looking behind us, attempting to get out of the parking garage as though nothing had happened. I let it go because we were in a very tight space. He put the car in drive and did it again. I looked back over at him. He looked at me this time and it took a moment for him to see that I was not going to allow that to happen again.

"I apologize, Elle. Small, cramped area." I didn't respond, just turned my head to look forward.

"How long are you going to be in town?" I smiled as though I was the only one in on a secret. I only had a couple more days and I would never have to interact with Trevor McHale again.

"I should be out of here by Wednesday."

Sam looked disappointed. "So soon? I thought maybe I could show you around my town a little."

I put my mask back in place. "Well, I appreciate it but I am going to be pretty busy this weekend with paperwork and computer programs," I uttered.

"Elleny, you still have to eat." He smiled crookedly at me since he was looking out the window driving.

I was becoming tired of this game. I felt uncomfortable and I had no way out or anywhere to go. This coffee shop could have been in Puerto Rico for all I knew.

"Ah, but see the good thing about living in the twenty-first century? Hotels have room service."

He looked over at me and broke out in hysterics. "Oh, girl, you are too much!"

He actually thought I was joking. I turned back around. "Hey, I didn't know there was a coffee shop around here, that's my hotel right there." Sam smiled as he passed my hotel and went to the next block. There was the sign for Coffee Cabana. He parked on the street another block away, and we walked right to the shop. The café was packed.

The people ordering were screaming orders in code words while the people behind the counter were repeating orders and yelling people's names. There were bodies coming in on one side of me and out on the other. I felt Sam at my ear, his nose in my hair. It almost seemed like he was smelling me. I backed away the second I noticed how close he was.

"I asked you what you like in your coffee," Sam attempted to say over the crowd's tone. It was really loud in here. "I'd like a large coffee, nothing fancy, one substitute...one creamer." He ran up to the counter beside the line where the people were waiting to order and shouted someone's name. The man came up to him and shook his hand. Both set of eyes came to me as Sam pointed me out. The older gentleman nodded his head as they continued talking. Sam said a few more words then shook his hand again. I watched Sam cut back through the crowd, ending up right by my side. "Okay, give him a minute. He'll have us hooked up in no time."

"Great." Really, that was great news, I was ready to get back. I watched groups of students grabbing coffees and walking out the door on their way to class. Other's walked in with hard hats under their arms as they were getting ready to start the day.

"I could sit here and just people watch all day," I said to Sam. This was so surreal to me. The longest line I'd ever seen was waiting for a turn on the tree swing over Ferguson Falls and that was maybe two or three people.

"I bet. They're a whole different bree—" Suddenly, someone hit me from the side, knocking me straight into Sam. I would've fallen but he quickly reached out and wrapped his arms around me. The back of my head felt like it was on fire. I didn't know what had caught me but it was hard, like an elbow. He stood me up and held me like that for a moment so I could get my balance back. Sam instantly bent down to look me in the face. "You okay?"

"Yeah, I think so," I replied as I felt to see if there was a lump or even blood. He let go of me and looked around. "Stay here, listen for our names. I think I saw the kid that ran by you."

I nodded my acknowledgement and stayed right where I was. I looked around a bit more, making sure I didn't feel dizzy and that my sight was fine. I heard Sam's name called so I went up to the counter to grab the coffees. I thanked the gentlemen and walked toward the entrance. Walking back out to the sidewalk, I looked both ways down the street. I didn't see Sam anywhere. I began walking back in the direction of where we had parked. "Need a lift, pretty lady?" I turned back quickly, my guard up, ready to tell some asshole off, but noticed it was Sam with the car. I walked toward the car without a smile on my face. This little escapade was done and over with. He opened the door as I handed him his coffee and I got in. "How much do I owe you for the coffee?" I asked. He shook his head. "Your company was payment enough." I just smiled, I would make sure he was reimbursed. I didn't want to give him any ideas. I sat back and planted my face straight ahead while I took a sip of my coffee.

We stepped off the elevator onto the top floor of the Mac-Gentry building. I was in a hurry to get back to my office and start working. I thanked Sam for showing me the coffee shop and for the coffee before I excused myself. He seemed to be following me. I almost turned around to see if he needed something, when he turned down a hallway that I had never been down before. I continued walking back by TJ's office and entered my own. I turned on my computer and waited for it to warm up. My mind began to wander to this morning. The vivacity I had been feeling the last couple of days, I knew once I stepped foot back in Richland it would be gone. My thoughts left me speechless, I couldn't imagine not feeling this again, but I knew it was because of my time with TJ and I was not going down that road.

My computer came on and I signed into the network's terminal and began to work. I was sort of stunned that TJ hadn't been in to bitch me out for going with Sam. But, when I had passed his office, I didn't see any movement from the corner of my eye.

I worked harder than I had ever worked. I knew I had a personal deadline to meet, so I continued through the final box of client information that had now been efficiently organized on memory sticks. I looked at the clock, it was 12:42. I mentally patted myself on the back for a job well done. As soon as the last file was entered and then placed in an orderly fashion back into the box, I buzzed Sara's extension. No answer. She was the assistant that had access to the confidential client records, so she would have to be the one who returned them back to where she got them. Because she was a bitch, I wouldn't have put it past her to do some stupid shit. So, to cover my ass, I wanted someone to know what I was doing. I got up from my desk and walked by TJ's office. The glass was opaque. I turned around to ask Mary if he was in a meeting and noticed she wasn't at her desk, so I went up to the door and knocked.

"Come in," a familiar, yet irritating voice called from inside. As I opened the door, I saw Sara sitting on the couch across the room from TJ's desk applying lip gloss to her incensing smile. TJ stepped out of the back hallway and came to a stop when he saw me. He was buttoning up a new pressed shirt after he just tucked it into his pants.

"Obviously, I have interrupted something. I'll come back later," I responded quickly and turned to leave just as fast. I was so fucking mad, I couldn't seem to get anything else out. Why I was mad, I had no idea. It wasn't like I owned him or we were married. He didn't owe me anything.

"Elle, wait!" TJ stated, but I didn't listen. I walked straight back into my office and picked up the box that was sitting on my desk. I could hear TJ following me but I turned right back around and headed out, meeting him right outside the entrance to my office.

"Elle, let me explain."

"I was just looking for Sara. These files are done and ready to be put up so that they don't get lost. I actually took some time and arranged them alphabetically so that she would have an easier time with filing them."

I tried to move past him but he wouldn't let me through. He grabbed the box and attempted to take it away from me. "Elle, let me have the box and let's go back in the office and talk for a minute."

I held onto the box tighter when I snickered. "Talk about what, TJ? There's nothing to talk about. Look, I'm really busy. I have phone calls to make and papers to file. I need to get this back to Sara and—"

I didn't have time to say anything more as the box was ripped out of my hands. He marched swiftly back to his office, box in tow, running into Sara as she was exiting. "Sara, go files these and keep them organized just as they are. Now!"

Her mouth dropped and her eyes came to me. She didn't have time to reply, he was marching back to me just as swiftly. Her large eyes turned into a glare when what had just happened finally dawned on her. I didn't know what had happened in that office and I sure as fuck did not want to know. I stood there at the door, arms folded over my chest, just watching him walk toward me. As he passed, he grabbed my hand, pulling me into my office. He then slammed the door behind him.

"Sit!" he demanded as he pointed to the couch.

"Fuck you!" I said furiously.

TJ closed his eyes and drew in breath to calm himself. "Elleny, don't start this shit again. We're both aggravated and I have something I need to say to you so please, don't fight me on this."

I was not going to sit down to hear him tell me shit. I didn't want to hear that he had been fucking Sara, too. As a matter of fact, he could sit, I was standing. I didn't feel he owed me an explanation for whatever he had going on with her, it just would've been nice to know that I wasn't the only one. Here I was, having an STD test done yesterday because my husband slept with anything that drew breath, and, there was TJ, sitting beside me, holding my hand, knowing that he was doing the same thing all along. *Fucking men sucked!*

"Really, TJ, to be honest, I really don't care what you have to say. And, I really don't think you owe me an explanation on who you do and who you don't do, just like I don't owe you an explanation on what goes on in my bed. It's not like we're married, I just would've liked to have known so that you could've used protection."

He came at me, his lips in a perfect straight line. He put his hands around my waist, lifted me up, and carried me to the couch. Once there, he tossed me on it.

"I said, sit!"

I gasped, "Trevor McHale!"

"You're gonna sit and we're gonna talk...and don't call me Trevor again!" he demanded as he came to sit next to me.

"I don't have time for this bullshit, TJ. I have calls to make." I looked at my watch so I didn't have to look at him.

I took a breath. From exhaustion or to calm myself down, I wasn't sure. TJ saw that I was still irritated. He picked up my hand and kissed my knuckles.

"Babe...where did you go this morning?" he asked in a softer tone. The tone I could never say no to. This was the TJ that I fell in love with twenty four years ago, sitting in a circle on the sidelines of a soccer field playing telephone. This was the man that told me that same day he was going to marry me and no matter how much I fought it, it was happening. His tone told me he still felt the same way. I looked over at him and my eyebrows must've been drawn up because as soon as I looked over at him, his went up as well. I still didn't say a word, just moved my eyes over him.

I noticed him—Trevor. I looked at his hair and brushed it off of his face just to bask at all that was him. "Elleny?" I didn't respond. I touched his brow that was raised up in confusion and curiosity. I ran my thumb over the little wrinkles that had taken up residence due to stress and time. His skin was delicate to me, so soft and warm. I wanted to take those lines of stress away, I wanted to take everything that made him not be this Trevor, I wanted to take it off of him.

I would've done anything to be eighteen years old again, back out at the lake where we hadn't a care in the world, just laying down on a mound full of sleeping bags discussing how Layla was a slutty name. I wanted to be his savior as he was mine. I looked deep in his eyes: long, beautiful, thick eyelashes that curled just enough to see the hazel eyes that reigned over me. Eyes that flared red when he was lustful or angry. Eyes that also glimmered when things mattered to him. I became mesmerized every time I looked into them. They possessed me. When he looked at me, his eyes didn't stay still, they flickered back in forth as they took in what I was thinking through mine.

They could look at me in an instant and interpret everything I felt. They knew me, *he* always knew me. Those eyes read my soul and I couldn't be away from him another day. I barely made it an hour. I slowly moved my fingers down his cheek to his lips. Lips that were always fleshy and plump and the perfect color of pink. With one touch, they could drop me to my knees and command me to do anything. They have tasted me, aroused me, they have even comforted me. I ran my finger over his bottom lip and felt him take it in his mouth and swirl his tongue around it. I closed my eyes, he knew every thought, every idea, every emotion I felt. Still, not having said a word, I threw my leg over his and straddled him, still just gazing at him. I touched my nose to his and slowly rubbed them together, taking in his scent, a fragrance that captivated me.

I would become wet just from having his scent in a room. It enthralled me, enchanted me. I touched his ear. Ears that have heard my moans of pleasure and pain. Ears that had taken in my pleading as I begged with hunger; heard me laugh and cry. I pulled his earlobe in my mouth and bit down gently. I heard a soft hum in his chest. Softly, I whispered against his ear, "Do you like it when I do that?" He didn't answer my question verbally. Instead, he gripped my thighs with his hands. I could feel how hard he was between my legs. "I'll take that as a yes."

I flicked my tongue on his ear again. I began moving back and forth in his lap. I held the power now, he was under my command. I pulled my head back and looked at him, his eyes were closed. I leaned my cheek up against his cheek and brushed him with my breath again. "Tell me what you're thinking, TJ." His eyes opened and they were flaring. I knew this man too well. "Do you really want to know what I'm thinking? I'm wondering what in the hell I have to do so that you will never leave me again."

Talk about coming to a complete stop! The moment was ruined.

"Fuck!" I yelled as I hopped off of him and headed back to my desk. I grabbed my purse and headed for the door. "Where the hell do you think you're going?" TJ asked. Grabbing for the knob, I turned it and realized it was locked. Spinning on my heel, I glared at him. "Nice, Trevor. Real nice." He hadn't wanted to talk at all. As I passed Mary's desk, I heard him yell, "We need to talk!" I didn't even look back. I just keep walking and replied, "Go talk to Sara! I'm sure she'll eat your bullshit up!"

I had no clue where I was going or what I was doing, I just had to get out of there. I went to the elevators and waited. Growing impatient, I decided it would be easier to take the stairs. I asked Charlene where the stairwell was and she directed me to it. I walked through and noticed the stairs only led up. I followed them until I saw a door that had to lead out to the roof. I opened it. Not sure if it locked automatically or not, I put my purse between the door and the jamb. Standing on the rooftop and looking over the city, I didn't want to go anywhere else. I walked out to the edge and looked down. I felt dizzy but I felt alive. The wind was cold and gusting, yet it didn't feel cold. I sat down and lifted my head up to the sky. The sun was beating down on my face. I closed my eyes. No one was around and all I heard, other than the wind, was silence.

I sat up there for an hour, alone with my thoughts and nothing else to bombard me. I came back down and went straight to my office and began working. I didn't go to see TJ and he didn't come to me. He had caused enough waves in the office this week, he didn't need anymore. I called and booked five signings for Monday. Since you never knew how long it was going to take to go over everything when it came to company buy-outs you had to give plenty of time, I learned two hours was a good time span.

Monday was booked up until six-thirty. Tuesday, I booked seven up until eight-thirty. Then, I was catching the red eye out of here. He was going to have to work Saturday and Sunday if he wanted all of these done and we were probably still going to have to come back to do more. If I had to work all weekend, every hour, we were getting this shit done. I was getting up to go talk to him about this weekend when Sara walked into my office.

Shit!

She came in without knocking and closed the door behind her.

Double shit!

"Is there something I can help you with, Sara? I was getting ready to have a meeting with Mr. McHale and to be quite honest, I really don't have the time to deal with shit drama."

She stood in front of my desk looking down at it, moving shit around like it was hers. "I just have one thing to say to you," she informed me. *Oh, really.* "Oh, I'm sorry. I forgot who I was speaking to, please forgive me. I'm used to dealing with professional executive assistants, ones that have college degrees. When I say I don't have time for drama," I leaned over the desk and spoke slow, "I mean I don't have time for drama. Now, if you'll excu—"

"He won't fuck you and if he does, he won't keep you."

Whoa. Where did that come from?

"I beg your pardon?"

"Oh, I know what you're trying to do, Elleny. Work right next door to the main man who is worth millions and flaunt your..." she looked me up and down one time and curled her lip, "flaunt your shit in front of him, which to me looks like he could do better. I'm onto you and let me let you in on a little secret, I've been here working my ass off for four years now. If anyone is in the seat for him next, that seat belongs to me."

I was speechless, I couldn't even think of what to say. I wanted to bring her back down to reality, but I'd blow my very intricate cover of professionalism. Then it hit me, she said if anyone was in the seat for him next…did that mean what I thought it meant? What was this, fantasy-fucking with TJ McHale? I was so going to have fun with this. It was time to piss this little bitch off.

"Oh, so you mean that you're next, huh? You weren't good enough to have him first? You get to have someone else's sloppy seconds?" Sara shrugged. "I'll take it." That's when I was slapped in the face. "She didn't work here long, he wouldn't let her. Her name was Natasha, she started here when they got together and it got serious quick. She'd come in to have lunch with him and we'd talk. Said she thought they'd be planning a wedding soon. She was practically living with him. Then, one day, about eight months ago, out of nowhere, *Bam!* Dropped her like a hot potato. Didn't call her again, moved all her shit out of his house. He got tired of her. So don't think you have a chance to make him into the perfect husband, he isn't husband material."

I couldn't see. I couldn't hear. I had to sit down. I felt like I was going to pass out. I had to finish this conversation and get the fuck out of here.

I was pissed, so I didn't have to act very much but I put on a good show for her. "Is that how this works…he gets passed around like a tray of hors d'oeuvres around here? Well, you can pass me by because I don't do any bitch's sloppy seconds. Oh, and if you ever come to me again with high school drama, I'll kick your ass. You got me?"

I didn't even wait for an answer, I just got my shit and walked out the door. I couldn't let on that I knew about Natasha. I was ready just to go and get a new hotel room, but then he'd know something was up. I just had to bite my tongue and move the fuck on. I walked by his office and noticed he was in there by himself. I walked up to his desk.

"I have booked you solid on Monday until six-thirty, Tuesday until eight-thirty, and you're going to have to do signings all weekend long to even start to get ahead of this. I talked to Mary, she's calling me a cab. I've had a shit day. I'm going to the hotel to work and then going to bed. Have a good evening."

Chapter 19

May 1996

It was spring again. I stared out at the raindrops streaking down the window of the nursery where I had just laid my new born daughter, Harlee, down in her crib. We had gotten back from my check up to make sure everything looked good and I found out that I could get a contraceptive shot, that way Bear wouldn't know and I wouldn't have to find myself in this predicament again. Don't get me wrong, I was thrilled now that she was here, she was beautiful. She looked like me. Dark strands of hair wisped on her small head, her soft skin was pale, not tan like Bear's. I felt like my prayers had been answered; I couldn't see anything of him in her.

He still had his JoJo. She was his favorite and he showed it. Luc was an identical image of TJ and that infuriated Bear. I was shocked no one in town ever said anything to me about it. Every time I looked at him, my heart would stop in my chest.

In the past months, the twins had turned three and were in daycare. They loved it. I was chomping at the bit to get back to work, seeing as Bear never brought home a paycheck. He told me that I had enough money, I didn't need to take his too. I began taking what I needed from my momma's money to support me and the kids.

Daddy and Mona had went on vacation in Europe and had just returned. They stopped by to see Harlee since they missed her birth. Daddy didn't want to go, but I told him I'd be just fine. He needed time away, for himself, and I was kind of hoping that maybe he'd begin to finally see what Mona was trying to tell him.

She had changed since I had the twins. I think she really just wanted to feel involved in a family and before, it was always the two of us, and she was the outsider. Now I needed her, just as much as I needed him and that made her happy. She needed to be needed.

Lilly had graduated early and had moved back to town last weekend. I was so thankful she was here. She moved all of her things into Curt's house and was in the process of looking for a job. We were spending so much time together, he'd have to pry us apart.

Rachel and Kevin were graduating next weekend. I was thrilled to have her coming back home too, I missed her terribly. She and Kevin made the trip back when I was having Harlee. She knew I didn't have anyone to watch the kids, so they stayed at her mom's and she played momma for a day or two. This also gave her an excuse for them to do some house hunting while they were here. I gave birth, alone, in a hospital room, with a nurse by my side, holding my hand. I didn't mind, at least he drove me to the hospital. I had forgotten what it felt like to be special to someone; just to have them hold my hand or tell me I was doing a good job at something when I would think I was doing awful. I forgot what it felt like to know that someone was dependable and faithful. I was the steadfast one daily—alone. What it would be like to have a partner that shared that, I would never find out.

I turned away from the window and looked down at my sleeping angel. She would never know the truth, how damaged her momma was. She was my gratification from the violence that was her making. I lowered myself to lay a gentle kiss to her head, to smell that scent that brought me comfort and tranquility. I walked out of the nursery with a slight close of the door.

I headed downstairs with thoughts heavy on my mind. My dreams had started up again while I had been pregnant. Not every night, but frequently. He'd show up here and there sometimes, just passing me on a street. Sometimes he would speak to me and sometimes he wouldn't. I blamed it on the hormones flowing throughout my body. I checked dinner and saw that it still had some time left for cooking. I started a pot of coffee and went to sit down at the table.

I remembered a time.

It was early summer. Junior year when we went to the local mud hole where everyone in McIntosh County could be found. Down off a dirt road through a grouping of pine trees, was the swampy earth that every teen flocked to. The sheriff had to know that we hung out there but he didn't seem to bother us, there were no homes around us and we didn't cause any trouble. We were all friends who were there to drink, laugh, and possibly drive out in the woods to get laid.

We'd run TJ's truck through the pit of wet clay. Sometimes we'd get stuck, sometimes we'd run, and go straight through, splashing mud up on whoever was standing too close. We met up with Bear and Rach, Lilly and Curt. I jumped out of the cab and headed to the back of the truck. TJ was already up there where he had moved the cooler from inside to the back where we'd sit and drink. He grabbed my hands and pulled me up into the truck bed, then guided my hips with his hands to his toolbox where he jumped up, hefting me up on his lap.

Curt and Lilly were on the other side. We sat there cheering on the drivers as they attempted their runs. We'd laugh our asses off when trucks would get stuck and every guy out there would jump out of the truck beds to try and get them out, that was the fun part.

"Hey, Elle, let's you and I go wrestle in the pit. Maybe our men would have fun cleaning us off," Rachel teased.

I looked at her and laughed. Bear thought he'd chime in with his encouragement as he wrapped her up in his arms and rolled his hips against hers. "Baby, you just made my dick

347

hard! Yeehaw! My old lady's gonna get down and dirty for me!" he screamed as he got up on the toolbox in the back of the truck. I heard more laughing and two echoed, "Holy shit!" coming from Curt and TJ. I rolled in hysterics.

We sat there in our spot for a while, chatting and teasing with our friends. All of the trucks had their radio stations tuned to the same channels so it sounded as if we were at a concert. Going into my third beer, TJ leaned into me and whispered in my ear, "Let's go get lost, baby." I knew what that meant. I felt all bubbly inside. I nodded and jumped off his lap so he could get up and I grabbed his hand. As we walked toward the woods, we'd yell greetings to those we knew. "Strawberry Wine" by Deana Carter was blasting on the radios. I turned to face TJ and put my hands around his neck. "We're heading to the woods, what are your plans with me once we get there? You do know that Jason only comes and kills teenagers making out in the woods, don't ya?" I said jokingly as I got up on my toes to plant a kiss on his lips. He smiled as I kissed him and told me that Jason ain't man enough to come 'round here. We entered the woods. I could still hear the music from the trucks off in the distance until we came to an opening that was bare from trees and clay. Darkness surrounded us. I couldn't see much but it looked like a meadow.

He let go of my hand and began walking around this huge field that looked neglected and lifeless. The grass was high and brown, there were thorns growing in areas, and I was kind of concerned that snakes were slithering around in it. I didn't even know what we were doing here until he began talking.

"I used to come here when I was a kid with my daddy, huntin'. We used to cross over this field to get into that shot of woods over there. This field, don't look like much now but come weeks from now, babe, this will be full of daisies. The sun's rays shine straight down on this here pasture. Everything that the sun possesses, the daises get. Not just the warmth, not *just the light, not just the nutrients—they get it all, Elle. See the woods over there? The rays don't go in the trees, their branches interrupt the beams. The light travels in 'em, but they don't get everything. The flowers never grow past this field. It's as if they know if they leave, they leave everything behind, and they die. These flowers have a perfect spot to the light...to life. This is where they're meant to be, Elle."*

I heard what he was saying. I began walking toward him, he turned around from looking at the trees when he heard me trampling over the knee-high grass. Reaching him, I put my arms around his waist and laid my head on his chest. Staying there for a few moments, I listened to the sound of his breathing and beating heart. "This is where I need to be, Elle. You are my perfect spot. This is why I brought you here. This is us, baby. If we pull away from each other, we die. But, if we stay right here, together, connected, we are alive and thriving."

I looked up at him and didn't have to say a word, he knew I was with him. I leaned up and kissed him softly. "I love you so much, Trevor. I'm here, baby...right here in the light with you. Always will be." He kissed me and smiled. "Elle, I don't want to hear you say how much you love me, I want you to show me how much you love me"

For some reason, I felt nervous. It's not like I haven't done it with him before, he took my virginity for Christ sake. I was apprehensive because this was me wanting to show him as best as I could that I loved him, for him to see how true and how deep. Words weren't enough for him, so my actions had to be.

"TJ—"

"No, Elle, no words." He started to unbutton his shirt, his eyes never leaving mine. Getting to the last button, he took it off and laid it on the ground. He came to standing straight again and didn't move. I took my one finger and ran it down his tight stomach muscles, feeling him reflexively clench. "No words, Elle. Just touch. Show me that I'm your sun." I flew to

him and slammed my mouth down on his. I kissed him deep. It was uncoordinated and messy, but I didn't care. This wasn't about how well I performed and how sexy I looked doing it, this was serious. This was concerning my life. He didn't seem to mind because he was right there with me. He untucked my shirt and I broke the kiss long enough for him to lift it over my head and throw it to the ground. I was fussing with my belt, never letting my lips leave his. I didn't want to break the connection between us. I finally got my pants off. Standing there in the middle of this pasture, grass knee-high, snakes possibly at my feet, nothing else mattered to me except this man in front of me. He broke the kiss to get his pants off and he laid down on the clothes that covered the ground. He went into his boxers to take himself out, that was when I stopped him.

"Don't."

He stopped and I knelt down next to him. He had a concerned look on his face. I looked over his silhouette under the moonlight and just imagined what he looked like laying sprawled out in front of me—just for me.

Silently, I whispered, "I know you said no words, but I feel like I just need to say this." I smiled, though I knew he couldn't see. "TJ, I'm going to attempt to show you how much I love you, baby, but speaking the words and physically showing you won't be enough. I gave you my innocence...no one else will have that. No one else will ever touch me, never feel me, like you will and it still isn't enough to show you how deep my love is for you, baby. So just know..." I was losing my battle with the tears, so I just barely squeaked out, "I can't show you enough." He reached up, grabbed my face, and put his mouth over mine again. Stroking my tongue lovingly, explicating that he understood what I was saying. I reached into his boxers and began stroking him. He broke the kiss and lowered his eyes to watch my actions. He reached down, completely removed his boxers, and continued watching me.

"That's it, baby. Up and down," TJ lustfully urged me on. I stopped for a moment and took off my panties. I straddled

him and bent down to kiss him as he positioned himself at my entrance.

"Another man will never be where I am with you right now. You get me, Elle?" I got him. I didn't want any other man there. I lowered myself down on him and closed my eyes. "Trevor," I whimpered. I was more alive than I had ever been. My senses felt heightened. I could hear things, see things, more clearly. I looked up at the moon. I could literally feel the heat absorbing into my skin from it. This was life, just like the flowers. I wasn't going to be leaving this. I couldn't.

"Elleny..."

A man's voice brought me back to my reality. A man's soft voice in my house. I stood up quickly, turned around, and saw Lilly and Curt standing in my kitchen.

Curt was in his uniform and Lilly's eyes were red from crying. Something was wrong.

Curt's voice brought me back to him again.

"Elle, honey, you might want to sit back down. Where are the kids?"

"Umm…" I didn't know what to say. Was it Bear? Had he been hurt? Shit, Rachel. Oh motherfucker, something's happened to TJ and they were there to tell me. Oh my god, I'm going to have a heart attack right here and die.

"Elleny," he yelled a little louder.

"Twins at school. Baby upstairs." That's all I could get out.

"Lils, go check on the baby real quick, please," he said to Lilly. She touched his shoulder as to reiterate something. What, I had no clue. She ran by me and went up the stairs. She disappeared as I sat down.

"Cups?" *He was going to drink coffee right now?* I pointed, I couldn't talk. I didn't want to ask because I couldn't stand to hear if it was about Trevor.

I got up and walked around the table to where Curtis was pouring himself a cup of coffee and I just stared at him. He poured his cup, turned to walk to me, and found me staring at him.

"I don't have a will." That really just came out of my mouth.

"And, with regards to my kids, I don't have anything written down legally as to where they would go. I know that Bear wouldn't want them. He's not even listed on JoJo and Luc's birth certificate."

He was looking at me like I had lost my mind.

"Uh, Elle, why are you telling me this?" I didn't know what he was going to say but I wanted him to know, just in case. If what he had to tell me had to do with Trevor, I wouldn't be able to go on.

Tears began to pool in my eyes. I didn't think I could get any words out of my mouth. Out of the corner of my eye, I saw Lilly walk back into the kitchen and come up behind me, putting her hand around my waist. Yep, this was it, this was how I was leaving this earth. I would never see my kids grow up.

"If you've come to tell me that something has happened to Trevor, I'm going to drop dead right here at your feet." His eyes went up to Lilly and stayed there.

"No, Elle, nothing's happened to Trevor. Honey, let's go have a seat, okay?"

Lilly led me back to the table and all three of us sat down. They both looked at each other. I looked between them like this was a tennis match and I wanted it to be over with.

"Just fucking tell me, Curt!" I yelled.

"Honey, your daddy and Mona are gone."

I thought for a moment, I knew the look on my face had to be strange. They weren't gone, they just got back. Then, it hit me. Gone… as in… dead. Dead.

I could sense they knew when it hit me. My facial expression had to have changed to… nothing. I was utterly and completely alone. I had no one. My daddy, the other half of my heart, was gone. What was I going to do? He was my strength now that TJ wasn't around. He was my pillar of power, my unshakable advocate. Who was I going to turn to now? I sure as shit wasn't going to go spend my fucking Sunday afternoons talking to a shitty ass headstone! I needed my daddy here, with me. I needed him here…with me!

I stood up, both sets of eyes on me. I didn't say a word, I couldn't. I was numb. I opened the sliding glass door to my back yard and heard the legs from the chairs scratch on the floor from where they were getting up slowly to see what I was going to do. I went down the stairs to the back porch. I put my bare feet in the grass, it was so soft. Some of the pieces I didn't step on tickled the tops of my feet. I just looked at my feet. No crying, no swearing, I just kept walking in a circle. Lilly came up to me and grabbed me by my shoulders, turning me to her.

"Elle, honey, talk to me." Tears were flowing down her cheeks and I said everything I could say to her.

"I'm being punished, Lilly. God is punishing me for what I did. I took my babies away from their daddy, thinking that I was doing the right thing. I wanted him to have a life out of Richland. I made an agreement with Bear, did you know that? Yeah, he would raise these babies as his own and TJ could go on with his life and be happy. Not be tied down to the likes of me. I'm being punished for doing what I thought was right. I gave up college, I gave up everything." At this point I was becoming more aware of what happened. "I gave up everything, Lilly! For him! And, I lost him too!" I began crying as she tried to pull me into her. I couldn't do it, she was too good to comfort me. I was nothing, I was an orphan in this world. I pushed away from her, screaming at the top of my lungs.

"No, Lilly! Can't you see? God hates me! I can't be near you, I love you too much to lose you, too! I can't take another loss!" I just fell to my knees and looked up at the sky and screamed with everything that was in me. No words, just screamed every emotion I felt rolling through me.

353

There was nothing left of my voice. I rolled myself up into a ball and just sat there. I couldn't cry anymore tears. I couldn't think anymore thoughts. All I could do was sit there and stare at my friend. The love that I felt for her and Rachel was the greatest of my life, aside from my children.

"I'm alone, Lils," I squeaked out.

"No, you're not," she replied almost instantaneously.

I laid my cheek on my knee and wished with all that was within me that I could be as strong as her, but I didn't have it in me. I had wasted it all on fucking Bear.

"What do I do, where do I go?" I asked my surroundings, looking for someone to point me in a direction, in any direction that would take me to happiness. I had already been down the roads of pain and misery. They seemed like dead ends to me, roads that had no intersecting streets to leave.

"You go on with your life, Elle." I didn't have a life. My husband was an asshole and I couldn't leave him. My heart belonged to a man who probably didn't give a shit that he still had it and had more than likely given his to someone else. But, I couldn't tell her that. I just smiled at her.

I knew I had to pick my kids up from daycare, so I got up hugged and thanked both of them for coming over and telling me personally. They had a key to get in, they could find the door to leave out of. I think I was still in a little bit of shock. I went upstairs, got the baby in her carrier, grabbed my purse, then went to go get my twins.

My cell phone was ringing off the hook, I wasn't about to answer it. I just let it ring. I went in the daycare like every other normal day and greeted everyone with a warm smile. I hugged my children so tight, I didn't want to let go, but this wasn't the place to do this. I also knew they would want to know why Grammy and Papa wasn't going to come over anymore. How did you explain this to three year olds?

I drove back home and started dinner like usual. Luc sat on the floor playing with his cars and JoJo sat up in her highchair playing with her dolls. I asked them how their day was and gave them a little snack to hold them over until dinner. I finally got tired of hearing the chiming of my phone that was in my purse in the other room, so I turned it off.

We finished dinner just as usual. I fed Harlee, gave her a bath, and got her in bed. I did the same with the other two. I had the routine down pat now that I had three and I was doing it alone. I got the other two in bed and headed back downstairs. I went to the cabinet and got the bottle of whisky down. I needed a shot. I poured myself a shot and downed it. I began to refill the glass when I heard what sounded like full grown men attempting to knock down my front door. "Open this motherfucking door now, goddammit!"

Holy shit, that's Rachel. I ran to the door, unlocked the two locks, pushed in the code for the alarm, and opened the door. Her hair was a mess, her makeup all smeared, and she was breathing uncontrollably.

"Rach, what the fuck?"

She bolted at me and pulled me into her arms.

"Don't you ever not fucking answer your phone again! What the fuck is the matter with you? Don't you know people care about you?"

I knew what this was about. Lilly called Rachel and told her about my breakdown. She thought I was going to have another episode. Lilly was such a drama queen.

"Rachel, look—"

"No! You don't get to blow me off, Elleny Jean! I have been calling you all day and you didn't answer. You scared the shit outta Lilly and now you're trying to blow me the fuck off."

I took a breath. Knowing Rachel, she drove like a bat outta hell trying to get here.

"I'm sorry, Rach. Come in. Is Kevin with you?" She walked in and I shut the door, locking everything up again.

"No, I don't even know if he realizes I left. Lils called me and I called you three times. You didn't answer, so I left."

"Jesus, Rach! Call your fucking husband! He's probably freaking out."

I couldn't believe her. This was exactly what I didn't want. People around me dropping what they were doing to come and rescue me. They had lives of their own.

I guided her into my kitchen and sat her down at the table. I went over to pour her a glass of wine so that she would calm down and asked if she wanted anything to eat. She nodded once, I was taking that as a yes.

I heated up some leftover dinner for her and sat with her as she ate. She called Kevin, he said he was going to kill her when he saw her, but he understood.

"I'm not going back for graduation, Elle."

I almost spit out my coffee.

"The fuck you're not! That's not happening, Rachel! You're getting in your car tomorrow and going back!"

If she didn't go back, I'd never forgive myself. This was her payoff for all that she had done. My issues were not going to keep her from that.

"It's just me walking across a stage, lady. I did that four years ago, it's fine. I'm needed here, with you."

"Rach—"

"Shut up, Elle. This isn't up for discussion, now drink your coffee and let me eat."

I shut my mouth and did as she said.

"Everything been taken care of, babe?" Rachel asked me concerning my daddy and Mona's wishes. My daddy was a planner, he had everything done when I was born. When Momma died there was nothing that needed to be seen to.

"Yeah, the only thing I'm worried about is when. That reminds me, do I need to call her family?"

Holy shit, I didn't even think about that. Her side of the family, I didn't know them. I wouldn't even know who to contact.

"I think Curt talked to them. You just deal with your daddy's affairs."

That took a lot off of me, knowing that I didn't have to deal with that as well.

"Honey, I know you're upset, but can I ask you something?"

I took a sip of my coffee. "Of course."

"Can I try to call him? I know you need someone right now—" She was talking super-fast because she knew that I would interrupt her. And, I did.

"Don't you fucking dare! I can't have him here and you know it...that was the deal! Besides, if he brings his wife or girlfriend to my daddy's funeral, they'll have to bury me right beside him. I couldn't take seeing that, Rachel Harrington, and you know it!"

I knew she was only thinking of my best interest but I couldn't deal with that shit right now. If Trevor McHale showed up at my daddy's funeral, they'd have to put me away forever.

She nodded her head and went back to eating. I went over to the cabinet and poured myself another shot.

The next day, I thought maybe the rumor of my daddy and Mona's death would travel through town and Bear just might come home, but he didn't. I guess he couldn't even act like he cared about me in front of people coming and going to pay their respects and offer their condolences. Most brought over a covered dish of something. The viewing was going to be the next night and I didn't know how I was going to deal with that. Rachel stayed with me last night. In fact, she slept in my bed with me just like we used to do. I laid there with her back to me and I'd twist her long hair between my thumb and index finger. It seemed weird now, but back then, that was just us. I felt comforted knowing she was lying there, because I don't think I could've taken a night when Bear came in for some lovin'.

The day of the viewing, Lilly and Curt came over. Kevin flew in and he was leaving again tomorrow evening, so that he would be there for graduation. I totally appreciated him coming and I told Rachel I would reimburse him for the ticket. She told me her four famous words, "Shut the fuck up." We were all riding together in the same limo. I made sure it had plenty of room because I needed these two girls with me. I was sitting on the couch while Lilly and Rach went to go get the kid's dressed. "What happened?" I whispered to Curt. I was so messed up yesterday, I forgot to ask. He was across from me sitting in the large armchair that my daddy used to sit in as he bounced Luc and JoJo on his lap. It made me smile. He slowly got up and came to sit next to me. He took my hands and placed them in his. I had known Curtis Noland all my life. He had been my best friend's boyfriend since the second grade. He heard everything that I had said to Lilly that day but he had yet to bring it up. I respected Curt, he was a good man and loved Lilly with every bone in his body.

"Elle, honey, let's wait until after to discuss this. I promise, I will tell you everything after. Let's just get through this first, alright?" I shook my head because maybe he was right. I didn't want to know what took my daddy away from me right now. The limo came and picked our group up, hauling us all to the funeral home. I grew up with Mark Weatherford, his family owned this funeral home. It was called Weatherford and Sons Memorial Home, but it was only one son. Mr. and Mrs. Weatherford didn't have any more children.

Mark met me at the door with his hand extended. "Elleny, sweetie, I'm so sorry for your loss. Please, come in." I extended my hand to him and shook it as calmly as I could. "Thank you, Mark, I appreciate it." I didn't know how this was going to go, but I had seen in movies that the next of kin sat right in front. I wasn't sure I could deal with that. I wanted to sit somewhere close to a door or exit just in case I needed to have a fast getaway. Still holding Mark's hand, I brought myself into him. He tried to back away, but I didn't let him.

"Mark, look, here's the deal. If at all possible, I need to sit close to an exit or maybe a door that would lead to an office. I really don't care, but if I get panicky, like I'm going to throw up all over your beautiful carpet, I need to have that door to look at, to concentrate on, instead of my daddy who is up there in front of me in a coffin with no more human fluids in his body. You get me?" He looked down and I could see he was thinking. He looked back up at me and smiled. "Lemme see what I can do."

I was standing outside the room where my daddy was resting with my newborn baby in my arms that he only got to see one time. JoJo and Luc were in the stroller in front of me probably wondering what in the hell was going on. The family could go in there and say their final goodbyes in private. I wanted to do that but I didn't think I could go in and look at him lying there, so I asked Mark if he didn't mind letting everyone else go in before me so that he could shut the coffin. I didn't want to see him.

Rachel and Lilly came out with red eyes and tear stained cheeks. I just knew I was going to go in there and throw up everywhere, but I had to do this. I needed to do this. I handed Harlee off to Lilly and Rachel sat with the twins while I slowly walked toward the door. I kept wringing my hands together like that was going to make this nightmare go away.

I opened the door and saw the coffin sitting in front of me. At that moment, everything became so surreal. I had to sit down before I passed out. My daddy was in that coffin, in front of me, never to hold me again. I would never be able to put my face on his chest and breathe in his smell, that scent that made everything better. I had no more daddy-daughter days and no more talks about how I was half his heart. I wasn't anymore, was I? He didn't even have a heart.

"Daddy?"

I walked nervously up to the casket. I was afraid to do anything. Finally, I put my hands on the side of it and laid my cheek down on the top of it.

359

"Daddy, I can't do this by myself. You've left me, Daddy…who do I turn to now?" I could feel the tears making a puddle between my cheek and the wood. "How do I continue on? You took the other half of my heart away. How will I be able to endure without you here? I love you so much and I'm sorry if I didn't make you proud, Dad. I know I put you through a lot of shit and if I could rewind time, I swear to god I would. I would be a better daughter to you. I'd take away every amount of pain I caused you. I would only bring you happiness, so that you would overflow with gratification." I lifted my head up for a moment and wiped my face. I drew a heart in the puddle of tears that was now dripping down the side of the casket. This was my moment—my final moment with the only man who showed me unquestionable and genuine love. I began to run my finger over the smooth wood. "My babies are going to grow up with a wife beater as their only male role model. They're never gonna remember or know how wonderful you were." My voice was rising. "They're never gonna get the chance to know how great and beautiful you were, Daddy. They're never gonna be able to hear what brilliant advice you give. How the fuck am I gonna live up to that, because I can't! I am none of that! I'm just a twenty-one year old, no college havin' momma that now has three babies and a fucking douche as a husband. There's nothing in this world that makes me even worth breathing the same breath as you, Daddy. I can't live up to that!" I went to sit in the chair that Mark placed in the room for me. I put my head in my hands.

I was done. I couldn't do this anymore. I was not up to doing this viewing. I said my goodbyes or my rant full of self-pity, whatever the fuck you wanted to call it. I wasn't staying for the other bullshit that was all just for show. I went up to the coffin one last time. I laid my lips to where I pictured his head to be and gave him my final kiss. "I'll do my best." That was all I said. I walked to the door, opened it, and walked out.

I didn't sit in that chapel during the viewing, I sat out in the vestibule waiting for it to be over with. I didn't care what anyone thought. People coming in late would do a double take as if they were missing something, I just nodded once and went back to looking in my lap. I saw the side door open and saw Mrs. Mueller as she walked out. She looked like she was heading for the restroom.

"Elleny…"

I looked up like I hadn't noticed her heading my way.

"Mrs. Mueller."

She stopped beside me, "Nice turnout tonight. Your daddy was well loved in this town, sugar."

"Yes, ma'am, it's a wonderful turnout." And it was. People had been coming and going all evening.

I could hear her clicking her tongue. "Such a shame what happened. Who knew criminals would break in and do that to such a gentle man and woman."

My head popped up and I looked at her. Her eyes met with mine. She could now tell that she had informed me of something I was not aware of.

"Uh…Elleny…um…" She didn't have time to finish. I stood up as fast as I could and turned toward the table beside me and flung everything on that table straight into the wall. I was screaming at the top of my lungs, I didn't care who heard me. There was another large table across from that one with a large vase, I picked it up and threw it against another wall. I flung everything off that table as well. Mrs. Mueller was looking toward the chapel doors and screaming right along with me.

"Oh, child…Elleny, honey, I'm so sorry, please…"

I saw the chapel doors fly open and Curt came barging through them. "Fuck!" I heard Curt's voice. I didn't see what happened, I was still too busy throwing whatever I could find. I knew what this was about and I knew why.

Bear had either killed them or had some of his shithead friends do it. He'd always said he'd get my daddy back for the threats he made against him. He did. He killed my daddy, that's why he hadn't been home. I felt huge arms wrap around my arms and waist and I fought against him with all my strength. I needed to destroy shit, just like Bear had destroyed me.

"It's okay, Elle. Honey, stop, your babies are out here." I heard Curt's voice in the back of my head. I heard Rachel bitching out Mrs. Mueller for running her huge mouth and all I could do was scream because I knew I was married to my dad's murderer.

Chapter 20

Present Day

I was awakened by a slight pain in the side of my neck. I sat up to adjust my position. I opened my eyes and saw my screensaver flashing before me. On a dining room table full of papers and electronics, I laid my head down for a minute and fell asleep. A container of Veggie Lo Mein with a pair of chop sticks leaning against the side of it sat next to my head. I looked around to take in my surroundings. I found the clock. 1:05 a.m. I got up and headed to the kitchen for a glass of water and looked around again. Nothing looked out of place. I wondered if he was even here. I didn't feel like going and looking for him, so I headed toward my room and opened the door. Moving in the room, I noticed the light in the bathroom was on. I walked toward the door and opened it slowly, no one was there. I headed in and turned on the shower. With the day I had, I needed to wash it away. I bent down to splash water on my face and started thinking. The name Natasha sat hard on my chest.

Who the hell was she and why didn't he tell me about her? He made it so plain to me that he didn't have anyone serious in his life. He wasn't one to do long-term relationships, but Sara said they were getting ready to be engaged. I needed to find out what was going on. Thinking on this, I questioned myself. *Why would I need to find out what was going on?* His past was none of my business, it wasn't like we were in a monogamous relationship. Our time was done. I was married

363

and TJ was my boss, that was it. He didn't owe me shit and it really wasn't my place to care. But, I did.

I finished washing my face and undressed to get in the shower. I washed my hair and quickly scrubbed my body. I grabbed a towel and wrapped it around my body and then grabbed another one and wrapped it around my head. I finished by brushing my teeth and headed for the bedroom. As I walked in, the lights were on and TJ was sitting on the side of the bed. He had his head in his hands, his elbows resting on his knees. I didn't say a word. I went straight to my luggage and grabbed my t-shirt and sweats. He heard me come in, so he picked up his head.

"Hi," he said softly. I didn't respond. I put my clothes on and quickly used the towel to scrub my head. I had to walk past him so that I could hang up the towels up. He stood quickly and turned me toward him so we stood face to face. I could smell alcohol on him mixed with the faint smell of cigarettes and a woman's perfume...expensive perfume. He bent down to kiss me and I turned my head.

He disgusted me. I couldn't even look him in his eyes. He was just with another woman and didn't even bother to wash her taste from his mouth before he put his tongue in mine. I pulled out of his grip without saying anything and headed to the bathroom.

I came back into the room, sat on my side of the bed, turned out the light, and pulled the covers over the top of me. I put my back to him. I heard the shower come on. *At least he was going to wash her from his dick before he attempted to stick it in me.*

I heard the door open, so I closed my eyes and pretended to be asleep. The back of my eyes grew black as he turned off the lights and my back grew cold as he moved the covers back to get into bed. I felt his arm come around my waist. Feeling him pull me into him made me want to go turn over a land a quick kick to his balls. I didn't want to be within fifty feet of this man right now.

"I have a headache." I couldn't believe I used that cliché.

I felt him vibrating against me. He was laughing hard.

"And, so it begins," he said as he continued to laugh.

I quickly flipped over and looked at him. "So what beings, TJ?" He lifted himself up so that he was sitting with his back against the headboard as he sucked both of his lips in, trying to hide the smile that was conveniently making its way back out.

"The wifely duties of denying her husband."

I looked at him like he was insane. I knew he could see the dumbfounded look on my face, yet he continued to smile at me.

I shook my head as I quietly said, "I think you've consumed way too much alcohol tonight with whoever you were out with. If you were smart, you would turn over, close your eyes, and pass the fuck out. We have a huge day tomorrow." Once again, I turned over with my back to him.

He put his arm over my side to try and roll me back toward him. "Aww, do I detect a lil bit of jealous there, baby? You know I am only yours," he stated as he licked the shell of my ear. I sat straight up, making him begin again with the laughing. Now, I was pissed. Not at him, but at myself. I didn't want him to realize this, but he could see right through me. I was jealous. I was so jealous, I could taste the unpleasantness pushing its way up my throat from the pit of my stomach. I just got him back and now he was out with some hooker-bitch, probably spouting off to her the same lines he used on me. But, I didn't get him back, did I? He wasn't mine, nor would he ever be. He was doing exactly what I wanted him to do, he was moving on with his life. That little confession that he fucked out of me this morning didn't help my case of pushing him away, but I could mentally write that off as being coerced. God, maybe it was me that was so fucked up in the head!

I knew my face was hard. It was beginning to ache from being pulled so tight. I knew what I had to say was going to sting, but it was for his own good. "TJ, I'm not jealous, there's nothing to be jealous of. This," I pointed between me and him, "is nothing other than good reunion sex. That's it, hon. You are open to do whatever you would like with whomever you would like. This is not going any further than where it is. You're not mine and…" I stopped for a minute to swallow back the words I didn't want to say. "I'm definitely not yours."

The smile left his face. I did it. I hit him right where I needed it to. He needed to take in everything I had just said and plant it right in the front of his brain. Then, I threw the cherry on top. "The saying we used to say as kids to each other—we're bendable, not breakable—remember that? It's bullshit. We are breakable. Always have been, always will be."

He sat there staring at me, trying to read my face. I was trying to keep it blank, emotionless. It was taking everything that was within me not to grab him and push my lips to his. I had to end this now.

"Now, I suggest that you lay down and get some sleep. You have an appointment in the morning."

I laid back down and flipped my back to him again. I didn't feel him move. He was still sitting up against the headboard.

"You remember that first day of school, our second grade year? My momma walked me into our classroom and I looked around. I wasn't scared, I wasn't nervous. Hell, we knew everyone already. Then, gazin' across the kids, I saw you over in the corner with Rach and Lils." As he was talking, probably because of the alcohol, his accent was coming through. "I couldn't believe it, Elle. I gotcha in my class. I walked down each aisle of desks, prayin'…no, beggin' the Lord that my desk could be next to yours." I knew where he was going with this story. I couldn't breathe, so I closed my eyes and just listened. It killed me hearing every word he was saying.

Tears were attempting to pool in the corners of my eyes, but I wouldn't let him know that he was getting to me. I couldn't, we'd be right back where we were. I could feel him tracing the pattern of the bedspread with his finger on my hip. "I came to my desk, saw your nametag on the desk next to mine, and I knew then. Right at that fucking moment, Elleny, I knew it. So don't sit there and tell me we're breakable." I felt his strong arm come across me to roll me over. My eyes were still closed, but tears were dripping down the side of my head into my hair. "Open your eyes, Elle, and look at me!" I couldn't stop them, they opened and I saw him—really saw him. I saw him as that little boy chasing me around the field our second grade year. I saw him bringing me the cookie that his momma had packed for him in his lunch our third grade year. I saw him kick Mike Edward's ass in the eighth grade for coming up to me at my locker and pinching my ass. I saw him, our senior year of high school, slip an anchor ring on my left hand ring finger, the same ring that was attached to a chain he wore around his neck even now. Whether we were breakable or not, we were continuously anchored to each other from the time we walked into Ms. Wilde's second grade classroom. However bad we wanted to deny it, that bond would never be broken. That was what made us unbreakable. Our bond was what we were talking about being bendable, not breakable. That's exactly how he wanted me to see him.

"He'll run off with my kids, Trevor. He'll kidnap my babies and take them to those hillbilly fucks he calls family. They'll hide my kids from me. I can't risk it. I've lost everything in my life that meant something to me. I can't lose my kids."

"Is that why we can't be together? Is that the big reason? Shit, Elle, I thought it was something big. We can deal with that, baby."

Wait…what was happening? We were backtracking here. I thought that would help my case, it didn't. I couldn't tell him why, he wouldn't understand. I kept the reasoning that JoJo and Luc were his to myself. This couldn't be happening.

"No!" I yelled and jumped out of bed. "I'm not taking any chances with my kids! No man is worth that…trust me. I found that out the hard way." I walked to my luggage, grabbed a pair of jeans, and slipped them on.

"Wait, where are you going?"

I had no clue. All I knew was that I had to get out of here and think. The whole situation was a storm brewing and I was fixin' to let loose.

I just shook my head.

"Goddammit, Elle, at least tell me where you're going?"

"I don't know, for a walk maybe? I'll be back later. Just get some sleep."

I walked up and down the streets of Burlington. Feeling the chilled night air hit my face mentally and physically revived me. I was making a list of pros and cons of why and why not to tell him. If I told him, he'd be pissed off enough to leave me alone. But, he'd come back with a vengeance and want to see the kids. I was fucked if I did, fucked if I didn't. I made it back to the hotel room just in time for a shower and to get changed for our first meeting.

I still had no idea what my plan was going to be. I walked into the dark room quietly, I didn't want to wake TJ up just yet. I tried to find my way around to my luggage to grab something to put on when I got out of the shower. I had just gotten my sweats and shirt off when I heard him.

"Where the fuck have you been?" I've only heard that deep tone a few times in my life and I knew what it meant. Trevor was extremely pissed.

"I told you. I went for a walk."

He clicked on the light beside the bed and that was when I noticed him. He looked like shit. He probably hadn't slept all night. Add a hangover to that and he was not a happy camper.

"TJ, sweetie, we have to be in the office at nine. Let's get you a shower and some food. Then you'll be good to go."

"We're not going."

This was not happening. I was up working on that schedule all hours of the night and now he said that he wasn't going to follow it? That was not an option. We had to do as many as we could to get this project done so I could leave by Tuesday. I couldn't stay any longer. This was killing me.

"Trevor…that's not an option. I could possibly push it back until later in the evening, but they have to be done today."

He didn't say a word. He picked up his phone and hit a number—one number.

"Morning. Yeah, I'm sorry to call so early. Chris, I need a favor. Go into Ms. Barker's schedule, print out all of the appointments she had set for today and tomorrow, and email them to Sara Montgomery, please. She needs to call each one and revise the schedule for next week. I appreciate it. Thanks, you too."

"Did you really just fucking do what I think you just did?"

I know the color of my face had turned two shades redder than what it should've been.

"Yep," he popped off and laid back down.

I had my back to him and was mumbling shit under my breath without realizing that he had gotten out of bed and was standing right behind me. He picked me up around my waist and hurled me over his shoulder.

"What are you doing?" I shrieked. I'm not sure who he thought he was, but you couldn't just manhandle people this way. I was kicking my feet up and hitting him in his back, but he was not putting me down.

"You wanna stay out all night long and make me fucking worry about you?" He tossed me down on the bed, caged me in with his arms around my head, and did a pushup to get down in my face. "You wanna be selfish and not think of others with the stunts that you pull, Elleny?" I couldn't see anything but those big, beautiful eyes. "Honey, I know you're husband doesn't give a shit about you, but goddammit, I do! When are you going to realize that?" I put my hands up on his chest to push him away, but he barely budged.

"Really? You care so much for me, huh? Then who were you out with last night drinking at a bar with?" That got him to soften a bit. I pushed against him again, this time it worked. I stood up quickly and went to the other side of the room. "Yeah, you think I'm a fucking amateur at smelling liquor and perfume on a man? Trust me, I live with a professional, Trevor. You didn't just stumble upon a naive little girl who sucks up your bullshit as though it was liquid through a straw. Hmm, let me guess…" I put my index finger up to my lips and my eyes to the ceiling, "maybe, Sara? No, she's young enough to have a curfew. Her momma would have done ground her if she stepped in one minute after ten. Maybe some chick you picked up in the bar? Oh, even better, the bar downstairs. That would make it just perfect. The woman that you supposedly have been pining over for seventeen years upstairs, dreaming of her wedding gown and what color flowers she will carry down the aisle while you pump and prod the "Can't turn a whore into a housewife" chick." I made my hand into a fist and started jacking off air. "Or…maybe you met up with Natasha." His head spun around, his eyes catching mine and he knew I knew.

"Fucking Sara," TJ whispered as he closed his eyes.

"Why, I think I hit a sore spot with that one."

I started to grab my pants and shirt to head to the bathroom, I wasn't staying in here. I was hungry and tired.

"What did she say to you?"

I looked back at him. Was he serious? Did he really want to go down that road? Well, I didn't.

"She said enough. Oh, by the way, the seat for the next in line to have a nice royal fucking from you already has been taken. Make sure you spout off all that bullshit you've been spouting off to me, she will soak it up!"

I didn't think a man could move so fast. One minute he was standing near the bed, the next he had me pinned up against the wall. He flipped me around so my front was to the wall. This was not funny, he knew how bad I hated this. I felt his hand run down my back until he came to my bra strap.

"Where the fuck is the clasp!" his voice was shaky again. I pushed him too far this time.

"It's in the front." Just as I was finishing my statement, I heard the rip. He tore the back strap of my bra, then he worked his way down to my panties. I heard the shred from the side where he had ripped them too. He was paying for this shit, I didn't wear cheap intimates.

He chuckled by my ear as I felt his body push against mine. I closed my eyes. "I thought maybe, since I was tired from being up all night long worrying over you and having a pretty shitty hangover, I'd make love to you nice and easy this morning. Maybe work off the rest of the alcohol that was left in my system after pacing the floor. But, I see you had a different plan in mind." He ran his hand over my ass cheek and then gave it a quick slap. "Ouch!"

"Now, this is how this is gonna work. You get a choice. Either I'm gonna fuck you like this, until you realize that I'm not that fuckin' prick husband of yours and you blow your load all over me like you did the other mornin'. Or, I'm gonna fuck you like this until you realize that my feelings for you are bigger than the both of us and you stop denying it. You stop thinkin' that there is someone else that will be takin' your place, there never was and there never will be. Obviously, my words can't scream that loud enough for you, maybe my cock can. Now, what's it gonna be?"

Either way, I was going to be fucked up against this wall. I had two choices to pick from and neither one of them were worth considering, so I closed my eyes and didn't say a word.

"I'm waiting for your answer, Elleny." He rolled his hips against my back side. I could feel how hard he was against me.

I still didn't answer.

"Oh I see, when I want you to open your mouth, you wanna be tight lipped? Well, how 'bout I take away your choices and just fuck you for both reasons? That sound good to you? I'll take that as a yes."

He brushed his cheek against mine and I could feel his stubble rub against the soft skin of my cheek. It scratched a little, but I had a feeling that was nothing compared to what I was about to go through.

He lowered his face down to my neck and rubbed his nose up against me. "Your smell is an aphrodisiac to me." I heard him inhale long, breathing in my scent. Every inch of my skin he touched felt like it was on fire. His hands were still holding mine up against the wall, so all he had to caress me with was his nose. He ran it down the back of my neck, following the path of my spine. He was teasing me and he knew it. He made his way to the bottom of my back and stopped. He pulled away from me.

"Spread your legs, Elle." I didn't respond either verbally or physically. I just stood there. He wanted this, he was gonna have to work for it. He stood back up and put his face back up against my cheek. I could feel his hot breath coming quicker than before, he was turned on and he was about to lose control because of my actions.

"Did you hear what I said to you?" I didn't say anything.

"Okay, we can do this the hard way then. Whether you like it or not, Elleny, I'm breaking you. Do you understand that?" I didn't respond. "I'm going to remove my hand from yours. If you move it, I'll restrain you another way." Please tell me he's not into that. I was just about ready to run out of there naked, I didn't care. I felt his hand very slowly move away from mine and head down the same path he just went down with his nose. I got goose bumps as he softly touched the sensitive areas. His hand didn't stop at the top of my ass this time, it continued down the middle until he finally found what he was looking for.

TJ began to moan. "I see you like this little game as much as I do. You're sloppy wet, baby."

My body had betrayed me again.

I was trying my hardest to ignore his words, but I couldn't. His fingers continued their torture, running back and forth between my core and my clit. He eventually began circling me slowly, over and over. "This right here…" he began to circle around my clit faster, "this is what's going to give you away, Elle." His fingers felt so good against me. He was building me up and he knew that. All he had to do was get me to a certain point and I would do whatever he asked. *Bastard!*

Lightly running his fingers across the small bundle of nerves, I gasped. He had me right where he wanted me. "Spread your legs for me, baby," TJ whispered, and I immediately spread for him. His finger diverted back to where they first had come from and slowly he entered me.

"That's the spot right there. This is the spot that I'm speaking to." He pushed his finger in farther and I moaned. "You like that, don't you?" He was still whispering against my face. His breath was hot and the combination of all he was doing had my senses on overload. His laid his lips up on the side of my neck. His voice was still very low and quiet. "Answer me, Elleny." I didn't bother opening my eyes, I didn't want to see him. He would know that he had won and I couldn't have that. I breathed out, "Yes." He kissed my neck again, this time I felt his tongue touch my skin. "Good girl." His glorious fingers drew out, then plunged back in slowly. "I'm going to drop my other hand from yours and the same rule applies, you understand me?" I didn't answer again. I was finding this to be crueler than Bear's tactics. If I had just agreed with him, maybe he would've let me go.

373

Finally, I spoke. "Okay, you win, TJ. Let me go. I don't think that you're fucking around or whatever you said. And, if it bothers you that much, you can turn me backwards and fuck me. There, I said it. You can let me loose now."

I heard him chuckle. "Tsk, tsk, Elle, that's not what I asked you. I asked you if you understood me. I tried talking with you, that didn't work. Now, since you let me know with that little outburst how you really feel, I can see that this is working beautifully."

Shit! His finger was still working me, I could feel my wetness dripping down my leg, but he was mind-fucking me as well. "Oh, Elle, you're every man's fantasy, but I'm the only one who is able to experience it firsthand. You're pussy's so wet, it's dripping. You're beautiful body's up against a wall, spread open for me, if you could only see yourself." I felt his finger leave my body and I was empty. He took his hand and ran it up the inside of my leg, collecting my essence on his fingers. He brought it up to the side of my face and I watched as he put his fingers straight to his nose and inhaled. "Smells just as sweet today as it did the day you became mine." He then plunged his fingers in his mouth, closed his eyes, and moaned. "Tastes just as sweet, too."

I was getting ready to orgasm right there on the spot. He turned my head so that it was farther to the side and put his mouth over mine. Immediately, he forced his tongue in my mouth. I could taste myself on his tongue before he broke the kiss. "Taste that, Elleny? Taste how sweet you are? It's all mine." Suddenly, I felt him rub his naked skin against my back. "Do you feel that, Elle?" I didn't answer him. "Grab it, Elle. I need to feel your hand around me." I stood there a moment without moving. I felt his hand return between my legs, going straight back to my clit. He began to go around the now bulging bundle of nerves slowly attempting to build my orgasm back up. "You can't stand for me to be away from this part of you for too long, can you, baby? If you wanted me there, all you had to do was ask."

His fingers began to speed up and I was building yet again. Automatically, my hips began to roll, lending encouragement to his fingers as they helped me find what I was looking for. "Yes, that's it. You're so close. Grab my cock, Elle." I reached behind me and felt him in my hands. I heard him hiss against my face. I picked up my head and leaned it back, into him, needing to remove the space between us. "Who does my cock belong to, Elleny?" I began to stroke him slowly, then a bit faster, following the same rhythm he was using on me. TJ moved my hand away from him and grabbed himself as he positioned his throbbing shaft up against my entrance. I pushed my ass back, urging him to fill me up. "Answer me, Elleny, or you don't get it at all. I will stroke one off and you won't get my cock." I pushed against him again, trying to tease him as much as he had been teasing me. There was no way in hell he would've wasted that on his hand. "One more chance, Elleny. Who does it belong to?" I was quiet. I felt his hands leave me. I turned my head and I was shocked to see him standing behind me, stroking himself fast and hard. *Fuck, he was serious.* "Me!" I screamed. "It belongs to me!" At that moment, he entered me fast and hard. I screamed in pleasure, feeling so full of him. Trevor pounded against me hard. "Who does this pussy belong to, Elleny?" He thrust against me so hard, I was riding up the wall. "Say it, Elleny! Fucking tell me!"

"You!" I screamed. "It belongs to you!"

"Whose are you, Elleny?"

"I'm yours, Trevor!" I screamed just as loud. I felt my orgasm growing bigger and bigger. He took his hand around to the front of me and just barely laid his finger against me.

"And who are you going to spend the rest of your life with, Elleny?"

"You, goddammit! You" I said through sobs.

I broke over the edge and orgasmed. It was so strong, I had to let him hold me up. I felt his orgasm hit at almost the same time. He turned me around to look at him. Still attached, he walked us to the bed. He softly laid me down. Sweat mixed with tears were rolling down my face. I didn't know what I was going to do. He was bound and determined to make this work when I knew it wouldn't. He pushed my hair out of my face and wiped under my eyes. He looked up at me as though he was reading my mind.

"God, you're so beautiful. I love you so much, Elle. I hope you can see that. I won't be apart from you again. I hope you understand that." He leaned down and laid a gentle kiss against my lips. I could taste the sweat on his top lip, and that even tasted like him. I couldn't talk, I just nodded my head in acknowledgement.

"We're not doing anything this weekend other than spending it together," he informed me. "Whatever you want to do, it's completely up to you." I laid there with his weight on me as he stroked the hair out of my face. "I'd like a shower. I need to eat and I need to sleep." He laughed for a moment and then proceeded to inform me, "Done!"

Chapter 21

Present Day

The next few days flew by in a blur. Saturday, after we cleaned up, we went down to the restaurant and ate an amazing lunch. We traveled all over Burlington and now we were walking down the pier. As we walked along, we could see clear out into the distance over the enormous lake. Boats were approaching and departing and it made me wonder where they were off to and where they were coming from.

We ended the afternoon renting bikes and following a scenic path that took us through some of the most beautiful scenery. We journeyed past beaches, the perimeter of some woods, and even a park. It was so different up here than it was in Georgia. The humidity was gone, but the air seemed so clear... so clean. People-watching was also an exciting pastime for me. I loved to see the different cultures. In Georgia, most could be found in overalls and jeans. Here, the apparel was not even close to that. I found out that some people wore the most eccentric pieces of clothing I had ever seen.

We stopped by a café for a coffee and a snack as we made our way back to the hotel. We ended up talking about his travels and his home, which he was going to take me to before I left. It was situated on a lake and had the best view ever, so he said. The rest of the evening we laid in bed and ordered room service while we watched movies, which ended up in a make out session that lead to me being thoroughly fucked, more than once.

Here it was, Sunday. Sitting in my t-shirt and a pair of TJ's boxers with my bathrobe hanging over the back of my chair, I was busy attempting to rearrange some appointments for the upcoming week when I heard the doorbell ring. I saw TJ come around the corner as I looked up at him. "Expecting someone?" I asked in a condescending manner. He looked at me with his eyebrows lowered. He didn't have to say a word. I heard his room door shut as I raised my hands up and mouthed an, "Okay," to no one.

I got up from the table, flung my robe around me, and went to answer the door. Again, forgetting about the peephole. There, in front of me, stood Sam Fordham.

I didn't even get the door open all the way when he came barging through. "Morning, good lookin', I brought you some coffee." He was walking straight to the dining room table as he spoke. He laid the bag of whatever he brought and the cup holder with two coffees in it on the table and turned around. I didn't think his eyes could get that big, but they did. I looked down and realized I didn't have a chance to tie my robe. I quickly threw it together and wrapped the tie around me.

"Sam, this really isn't a good time. How did you find out what suite number I was in, anyway?" He laughed and went into the living room to sit down on the couch. "I told the front desk I was your boss and that I had some work to deliver to you. Bagel?" My eyes went around the room in a matter of seconds. How in the hell was I going to get this man out of here before TJ came back in here? It only took so long to put some clothes on. "Uh, no thanks. Sam, I don't think that was a real good idea. I'm really busy and I need to get back to work, I only have a couple more days here and then I'm leaving, so I have to make sure I get everything that Mr. McHale needs done, done." I started walking toward the table to grab his things when I felt him come up behind me. I stood up, becoming one big ball of tensed up muscles.

I could feel him against me. "Sam, look, I don't know if I gave you the wrong impression, but I am so not on the same page as you. Now, I'm beginning to feel uncomfortable. Please, step away from me. Now." I tried to step away from him, but he placed his hands on the chair back that was in front of me, caging me in.

"Sam, I'm not going to ask again."

"Come on, Elle, you seem really uptight. Can I help you relax a bit?"

His hands went up to my shoulders. I pushed off the chair with all my might which sent him stepping back a few steps.

"Come on, Elleny. You're a beautiful woman, you've known I was attracted to you, you had to know."

"See, that's where you're wrong, Sam. I don't have time for soap opera drama. I'm here to do a job and go. That's it. I don't know where you ever got the idea I was interested, but you are way off."

He started to walk back to the living area and I began praying that TJ did not walk out right now. Suddenly, he turned around and began to unbutton his pants. "Sam!" I squealed. "What the fuck are you doing?" Sam stopped for a moment. "Well, if that's not what you're interested in, then maybe we could fuck a few times and be done." I couldn't believe what I was hearing. I had to giggle a minute because it amazed me just how big this man's balls were. I walked to the door and opened it. "Get out, Sam," I said and it wasn't nice. He continued to stand there. "Did you hear what I said? I said get the fuck out!" I was at that point beginning to yell. He had humiliated and insulted me and I wanted him gone. "You don't mean that. Just wait until you see the size of my—"

"I think you heard what she said, Sam. Get your shit and get the fuck out!" TJ walked out and saw Sam digging in his pants while I stood at the door, trying to get him out.

"Trevor, what are you—" He didn't finish. He looked at Trevor then at me, he understood now. He quickly began buttoning up his pants. "Don't like soap opera drama, huh, Elleny? Well, you sure as fuck know how to pick them then.

He's the main character. Going through women like outfits. Don't worry, honey, by tomorrow you'll be yesterday's news and then you'll come running to me. Too bad it will be too late by then. He tell you about Natasha? See if he tells you about the only woman he's ever given his heart to." I just stood there, shocked and hurt. I couldn't respond.

"That's enough, Sam!" TJ demanded. I saw TJ looking at me and then looking back at Sam. "Sam, if you want to keep your job, I suggest you get the fuck out now. I will see you in my office first thing tomorrow morning to discuss your misconduct here today." Sam scurried by me as he walked out the door. I threw the door closed but still didn't move.

"Ell—"

"Don't you fucking dare," I said quietly. "I'm going over here to this table and we're going to pretend this…" I circled my finger around, "in addition to this whole fucking weekend, never happened. Oh, and if you ever feel the need to prop one of the other women that you supposedly love with all your heart up against the wall and fuck her until she says what you want to hear, use those same words. They'll be eating out of your hand in no time."

I walked back over to the table, grabbed my information, my laptop, and headed back into my room and locked the door.

What the hell was wrong with me? Why did I want to believe him so badly? Obviously, he wasn't the same TJ I had fallen in love with. I could've seen that if my eyes had been opened. But, no, I had to look through rose colored glasses and saw what I wanted to see.

I had to stop thinking about that. I got back to work, finished the scheduling, and had every client that had pending contracts with Mac-Gentry scheduled by Thursday. I then called my kids, put my mask in place, and told them I'd be home on Thursday evening. I finished up with them and slid into bed, never unlocking the door.

I slept like shit that night, tossing and turning without being able to get comfortable. Finally, I got up and jumped in the shower. I was completely ready by seven. I ended up sneaking out of the hotel suite and taking a cab to work, I wasn't in the mood to see anyone. I just wanted to do my job and get home. I got into my office, got situated, and sent Sara an email. It wasn't pleasant, but I wanted to get my point across without having to stir up anymore drama.

> *Sara,*
>
> *During this week I have devised a system that will make these presentations run smoothly and quickly. I will have the contracts and presentations for the day set up and ready for that specific appointment. Once the contract is signed by all involved, I will record it onto the memory stick, file the original document, and then place them in a box—organized. You will come and collect the box at the end of each day and file them away. This will be the system that we follow. If you do not want to get behind, I suggest you cooperate. The faster we can get this done, the faster I will be out of your hair.*
>
> *Sincerely,*
> *Elle*

I looked at my watch. 7:15. I sent Mary a much nicer email telling her what time our first client was going to be here and if she would make sure that the conference room was set up with breakfast items and coffee—lots of coffee. Our first presentation was at eight. I began printing off everything I needed and placing it in the company folders. I grabbed the memory stick for that client then moved onto the next presentation. I had all of them done by the time our first client arrived. I grabbed all that was needed for the presentation, locked my office door, and headed for the conference room. I walked by TJ's office and didn't even see if he was in there. I heard him call my name as I went by. I stopped outside the door, closed my eyes, and took a deep breath before I turned and headed in.

"Shut the door behind you, please."

I looked at my watch. "Sir, we don't have time. The first cl—"

"I don't give a fuck about the client!" he howled.

I quickly turned around and shut the door. He turned the glass opaque and turned the music on, but I had a feeling that was not going to cover up the sound of his voice.

"Sir…"

"Did you just call me sir?" I looked down at my papers, but didn't answer him.

"I just asked you a question, Elle."

"I think you heard what I called you, Mr. McHale. I don't feel comfortable calling you anything else."

He chuckled ominously. "You don't feel comfortable calling me anything else."

Starting at one side of his desk with his arm, he swiped the desktop completely clear as fast and as hard as he could. The laptop that was on his desk ended up hitting the wall and crystal pen holders crashed into other fragile items. I gasped in surprise as fear rolled over me.

"You feel comfortable now?"

I couldn't answer him. I was too busy trying to get a grip on all of this. Everything was falling apart in front of my eyes.

I held up my finger to him, telling him to hold on. I poked my head out of the door. Poor Mary looked like she had seen a ghost. I had to get this cluster-fuck under control.

I smiled at her. "Mary, honey, could you go make sure the clients have breakfast. Coffee, juice…anything. I need a couple of minutes with Mr. McHale. Thank you."

I didn't wait for her to answer. I had to get back in there with TJ before heads started to roll. Considering that the only heads in there were mine and his…well, I wasn't willing to take a chance.

I shut the door, set the file and stick down on the chair that was in front of his desk, and stood there for a minute. TJ's breathing was rapid, I could tell he was still angry but we were on a time crunch so it was now or never.

"You 'bout done?"

I figured if I went southern on him, he'd have to pay attention. When I made my accent come through, I wasn't office Elleny. I was lover Elleny and he knew this. His head came up as his eyes locked with mine.

"You 'bout done throwin' your fit?"

"Elle, I can't do this again. I can't have you turn your back on me again. You won't let me explain about Natasha and I feel like you're gonna walk away from me for no reason at all—again."

I closed my eyes. I couldn't take the pain in his voice. He was as scared as a little boy.

I walked over, stood in front of him, and raised my head to look him in his eyes.

"TJ, we will talk about this, okay, baby? Just, later. Honey, we gotta get through these signings so that you can get down to Richland. Take a deep breath and let's go in there and do this."

He nodded his head, grabbed my face, and barely touched his lips to mine. It was hard to be this close to him. I felt dizzy, so I grabbed onto his forearm to balance myself. "I love you so much, Ellie-bean. I won't make it without you this time," he informed me as he touched his lips to mine. I stayed close to his face for a moment and whispered, "Love you, too."

We got through the first signing. I did what I had to do and put the paperwork in the box as I had told Sara I would. We worked all afternoon like that. It went smoothly and quickly, just like I told her it would. By six-thirty, I was exhausted. I set up everything for the next couple of days the same way and locked my door behind me.

We went home and I ordered room service. A bottle of wine, three beers for him, and food. I had to set myself up because I knew that this conversation was going to happen. I tried to keep busy before dinner got there. Hearing the doorbell, I was relieved. Maybe he would eat and we'd go to bed. I'd even planned on giving him a blowjob just to keep him from talking.

"I'm ready to talk," he said as he opened up his first beer. I didn't think I was ready to hear.

I grabbed the bottle of wine, went into the living area, and had a seat on the couch. TJ sat in the chair across from me.

"I met Natasha two years ago. She was a buyer in my company. She was blonde, blue-eyed, extremely thin, and a cut-throat bitch. She was the total opposite of you in every way, shape, and form. She would continually flirt with me or ask me out. At first, I ignored her. I'd push her away, but she was persistent.

So, one night, I had to go to a cocktail party and I asked her to come along. We went. We danced and drank and things happened, we ended up sleeping together. We went out a couple of times after that but nothing really became of us because I wouldn't allow it. She wasn't you." I began to pour myself another glass of wine because I'd already finished off a full glass. He continued, "A year went by, we talked and still worked together but we never went out again. Until one night she asked me over to her house. She was having a small get together and wanted me to come, I did. I'm not gonna lie, Elle. I slept with women, but my heart wasn't in it."

Was that supposed to make me feel better? Because it sure the fuck didn't.

"I went and ended up spending the night with her just like the last time. I got up in the morning and went home. Monday morning, she showed up just like normal. Couple weeks go by and everything was fine, until one night after work. I stayed late, I had a meeting or something in the morning, I can't remember, but she stayed late as well. As soon as everyone left, she came into my office and told me that she was pregnant."

My whole world shattered around me. I didn't know how to process this. He seriously could not find out now.

"I didn't have any children and I felt bad for her, Elle. I didn't want her raising a baby, my baby, alone without me."

I felt the wine that I just emptied from my glass fighting to come back up.

"I told her to move in with me, to stop working. I wanted my child to be healthy. I explained to her that I didn't believe in marriage, but she could tell people we were engaged if she felt the need. I swear, I had no intention of ever marrying her, Elle. Months went by, doctor's visits were made, and I was never allowed to go to them. She said that she wanted to wait 'til we could hear the heartbeat before I showed up. Hell, I didn't know anything about pregnancy, I just agreed. She went out, bought herself a ring, and then began to start pressuring me into getting married. We'd fight over it, night after night. Then, about three months in, I came home early and she was downing a bottle of wine. I confronted her on it, told her I was no doctor, but common sense tells ya not to drink when you're pregnant. That's when she confessed that it was all a lie."

My world had just shattered.

"I told her that she needed to be out by the end of the day. I didn't care where she went, what she did, I was done. She thought if she pretended to be pregnant, I'd marry her and she'd be able to get to my money."

I was speechless. What did you say to that?

"I'm so sorry, honey, that you had to go through that."

"Elleny, I'm thirty-five years old. I'm getting up there and I don't have any children, that just got me thinking."

This conversation could not happen. Just then, the wine won the fight. I ran as fast as I could into the bathroom and planted my head in the toilet, the whole bottle of red wine coming back up. *What a waste. That was a good wine.*

"Honey, are you okay?" TJ asked as he handed me a wet washrag.

"Yeah, I think so. I think I just had a busy day and I'm tired."

I felt bad about the Natasha thing. I didn't want to talk about it anymore.

"I'm sorry, TJ…about not letting you explain and for how she treated you."

"It's okay, it's for the best. I just wanted you to know the truth about what happened."

I couldn't think about anything anymore. I couldn't think about Natasha. I couldn't think about what he had said about me knowing the truth, I just had to let it all go. I just wanted to crawl up and bed and close my eyes. So, that's what I did.

The next couple of days flew by. The signings were going well and the presentations were flawless. I was doing what I needed to do so that when they moved everything down to Richland, it would be arranged easily. Sara was doing her filing every night. I think that was because she wanted me gone. Today was Wednesday and I was scheduled to leave tomorrow evening on TJ's company plane. I decided to go home and video conference the kids to tell them I'd see them tomorrow. I stopped by TJ's office and told him I was going to take a taxi home and he told me that wouldn't be necessary, he was leaving as well. We went to the car and drove to the hotel. I ordered room service for us while he went to take a shower. I figured this was the best time to call the kids. I had set up my laptop at the table and dialed the kids.

Harlee answered with a big hello. She always made me feel so happy. My sweet, precious baby.

"Momma, I got an A on my spelling pre-test today."

"Well, hello, my sweets, that's amazing! Congratulations! I'm comin' home tomorrow. You missin' me as much as I'm missin' you?"

"Oh, Momma, we're havin' so much fun! Luc was playing football with Uncle Curt and Uncle Kevin and Uncle Kevin said he sprained something. Momma, he did a whole flip in the air! It was so funny."

That was funny, I could picture Kevin doing that.

"Well, honey, I can't talk long, let me say hey to your brother and sister. I love you and can't wait to see you!"

JoJo appeared first. I turned to make sure that TJ was still in his room.

"Hey there, my beautiful girl! How's school? Did Auntie Rachel take you to your last thing?"

I saw Luc had appeared in the corner and I waved while she talked.

"Yes, I'm done now. All I have to do is take my paperwork up to the courthouse to hand in and I'm free!"

"That's great! There's my handsome boy. How was your day…did you have practice?"

"Yeah, I did. It was good. Did Harlee tell you about Uncle Kevin?"

I heard glass hit the floor and I turned around quickly. There stood TJ over my shoulder, looking at my twins—his twins.

"Uh."

I didn't look back at the kids. I just quickly said, "JoJo, I'll call you back," and hung up.

"TJ, I can—"

"Who the fuck was that, Elleny?"

I could hear the panic in his voice. I knew he would notice it as soon as he saw them. JoJo even had his dimple and Luc's voice sounded just like TJ's when he was his age.

"I can explain, Trevor."

"Who the fuck was that?!" he screamed so loud, his body shook. His eyes looked like they were going to pop out of his head. I had no choice, I was caught. I had to tell him.

I whispered really low, "They're my kids, Trevor."

"The twins," he stated as if he wanted to be sure we were talking about the same kids.

I couldn't talk. I was already crying because I knew what was coming, so I just nodded my head.

"Bear's twins…right?"

He was either trying to be delicate with me because he could see that I was already falling apart or he was trying to keep a handle on his temper. I didn't answer him.

"I asked you a question. Bear's the father of your twins, right?" he asked, slower this time. I didn't answer again.

He came up, put his hands on my shoulders, and shook me as he yelled, "Who's the father of your son and daughter, Elleny?"

I screamed back, "You are! They're yours, Trevor!"

He let go. He took a step back and I fell to the floor, sobbing.

"How…old?" I looked up, he was just staring at the open screensaver on the computer.

I whispered, "Seventeen."

He didn't even have to do any math, he knew. He closed his eyes.

"The lake."

I knew his mind was trying to take this all in. "I wanna know now what the fuck you were thinking, Elle." His voice was low and raspy, that voice I hated to hear.

"The weekend of our going away party, I ended up in the hospital, remember?" He nodded once. I continued, "You interrupted a conversation between Rachel, Bear, and I." He didn't nod this time, so I didn't stop. "I had just found out I was pregnant, that's why I was so sick. I didn't plan on anyone finding out, I was just going to leave town and move away but then Bear and Rachel walked in and a nurse said something. I made them promise not to tell you. I knew you'd throw away your scholarship and all I could picture was you resenting me for making you give everything up. So, Bear made me a deal. He'd marry me and raise the baby as his own if I gave up full contact with you. What we weren't counting on were two babies. A boy and a girl. I ended up having them alone. Bear never showed up to the hospital, so when the lady came to fill out the birth certificate, I didn't put his name on it. I didn't put anyone's name on it. They have his last name, but he's not their legal father."

As soon as I stopped, I noticed he was sitting with his head in his hands and elbows to his knees.

"Names?"

I didn't want to tell him their names. He knew their nicknames, that was good enough. I didn't answer.

"Elleny!" he yelled louder from under his hands.

"JoJo's name is Jordan Taylor Jackson."

He chuckled. "My initials."

I didn't want to continue. He was going to lose it, I just knew it.

"Elle…"

"His name is Luc, Trevor."

He stood up before I could finish.

"Don't you bullshit me, tell me his name!" he howled as he looked down at me on the floor.

I whispered, hopeful that he wouldn't hear me, "Dylan Lucas Jackson."

He went over to the table, grabbed the laptop, and hurled it right through the television that sat in the living room. I covered my head with my hands.

He continued to throw things and scream, but I couldn't hear him. I was stuck on the ground with my head covered up, crying.

"Those were my babies, Elleny! I missed out on everything! You even had the nerve to name them names that I picked out. Those names were meant for me and you! Not

Bear!" I looked up at him. Suddenly, he stopped and it became quiet. He had tears streaming down his face.

"He's going to try and take my kids, isn't he?" I could see his jaw clenching and his anger rising. I sat up and told him. "He doesn't know that you know and I'm still not leaving him. They don't know any different, TJ. They don't know about you. They know Rachel is my best friend, but they don't know that she is their blood relative." He closed his eyes.

That's when he started…

"I couldn't make myself write your name to address this letter to you. Every time I'd start, I'd find myself shaking."

I looked up at Trevor. He was walking back over to me and kneeling down beside me. I couldn't believe what I was hearing. I attempted to cover my ears, but he uncovered them, making me listen to the words—my words. The words I wrote in the note I left him in the truck the day he left for college.

"I need you to think of three things when you think of me, baby." He grabbed my chin and made me look up at him. I closed my eyes and listened to him repeat every word that had come from within me.

"Remember today, the day you left for college. Us, standing together, as I looked you in the eyes and I vowed to you that no matter what, I was anchored to you forever and always. Honey, don't forget that. You give my life meaning. You are the reason I am who I am. I am with you always. Please, don't ever forget me, because you will continually be the only thought that runs through my mind. Remember that I love you. My love for you is like a river, it continually runs strong and never does it recede. Remember that throughout your lifetime. Everything that I have done, that I am doing and will do in my life, is because of my love for you. You were my first love, my only love, and my love on my dying day. Be happy, baby! I want you to find someone that will make you as happy as you have made me. Never will I be able to know that kind of happy again. You deserve everything you have set out for, my love. Go, be what you are destined to be—a shining light. The warmth of your heart, the strength that you possess and your keen knowledge, have been blessed to you for a reason, fulfill that purpose. I want you to find someone that you can grow old with, that can make all your pain subside and give you memories that will be treasured between the two of you until you pass. You carry with you half of my heart, my love. Whether you like it or not. Keep it locked tight, don't ever harm it and know that you are forever loved."

He had memorized the letter. Every line. I continued to cry silently. He had memorized that whole letter and still remembered it seventeen years later.

"Did you hear what I said? Every day…" he wiped his eyes, but it didn't help, "Every day for four years, I woke up and read that letter." He started to walk over to me until he was standing right in front of me. "For four years, I read that letter before I went to bed. It consumed me! I thought about what I did wrong, where we went wrong, why the fuck you would marry him." I looked up at him. I couldn't stand what I saw in front of me, what I had created.

"Trev—"

"No! You don't get to talk now! You're time to come clean has come and gone," he yelled and then became quiet again. "Every day was a continuous struggle to even take a breath, Elle. I lived my life hour to hour, not even day to day." He had to stop because he was trying not to lose his temper.

"I was eighteen, TJ. I thought that what I was doing was for the best. I wanted you to have everything—"

"I didn't have everything! I had my family!" he roared over me. I pulled back and hid my face. "You had no right to keep that from me, Elleny. You wanted me to go out and achieve all this shit that meant nothing to me. All this…" he looked around the huge hotel suite that I was huddled down on the floor in, "this means nothing to me. I would've been satisfied with you in a small house, attending community college. I would have gotten to see you…." he paused again, taking a breath, "pregnant with my babies. Being able to watch them walk. Teach Luc all about football. Not fucking Bear…me! If you had known me the way you say you had, you would've known that. All of this would never amount to what I would've had. Just being there would've been worth all of this…tenfold."

I looked up at him, tears were streaking my cheeks and I couldn't say anything, all I could do was nod.

There, everything was out in the open, all my cards were on the table. I had nothing else to hide. Seventeen years of secrets, lies, and duplicities were out for all to see. I should've felt like a weight had been lifted off my shoulders, but I didn't. I couldn't imagine how my children were going to take this news. Never had I thought that this would be an easy thing to discover, but I didn't know until it came out how devastating it was. I had lied to the three most important people in my life. It hit me then that the choice I had once made thinking it was in the best interest of another, ended up destroying the lives of three innocent people.

He got up and went into his hotel room. I heard the door lock. I got up from the floor went straight into my room, threw some jeans and a shirt on, crammed all my clothes in my suitcase and left Burlington Vermont.

Chapter 22

Present Day

Three weeks had passed since my trip to Burlington and I had not heard from nor seen Trevor McHale. I wasn't really expecting to. With the way we had left things, I couldn't really blame him.

When I got home, I met with Lilly and Rachel and told them everything. Even down to the nitty-gritty details. Rachel turned her face up as though she had eaten something sour while Lils planted her elbows on the table with her hands to her chin, hanging onto every word. I told them about the fight and how I had just packed up and left. I also told them how much I missed him. I was right back where I was seventeen years earlier, tending to a broken heart. But, my heart was nothing compared to what I could only imagine his looked like.

I went to work and continued on my daily routine. I saw Bear once or twice and then he was gone for a week. He'd come home, do what he had to do, and then was gone again. Whatever. It was the same as it was for the past seventeen years. One night when he did come home, he started talking about the rumors at work; how some big-wig had bought the factory and that they were trying to prepare everyone for the takeover. I just listened and nodded.

Work was good. Mr. Stevens had gotten his promotion and moved into a bigger office last week. I got the space right next door to his. I was thrilled to have my own area. It seemed that since Loren received his promotion, work had slowed down. That was why when I received an email from Rachel demanding we have lunch later this afternoon, I cringed. I wasn't really in the mood to see anyone—especially talk with anyone. I just wanted to go home and lick my wounds. So, I decided to call her and get a rain check.

I picked up my office phone and dialed her number. On the second ring, she answered.

"Hey, biatch!"

"Rach, I'm swamped. Can we do lunch another time?" I started rustling around papers making it sound like I was multi-tasking.

"Nope."

I stopped what I was doing and sat straight up. Why would she would say no? She never said no.

"Are you pregnant?"

"What the fuck, Elle! Shut your mouth!" Okay, so that wasn't it.

"What's wrong? Are you sick? Oh god, please don't tell me you're moving. Is that it? Just tell me now, Rach. Just get it over with."

I heard her laughed. "It's nothing bad. I just know you've been down about what happened with TJ and I wanna take you out for lunch...and maybe do a lil bit of shopping," she said, raising her voice there at the end. *Oh, shopping...who could ever turn that down.* I closed my eyes and exhaled loudly. "Fine, let me see if Loren has a problem with me taking the afternoon off. I'll call you right back."

"Yay! Okay, call me back."

"Bye."

I wrote Loren an email asking if he minded if I took the afternoon off and that I would stay later tomorrow evening to finish up everything that I needed to from today. He got back to me almost instantly. He didn't have a problem with that and told me to have a good afternoon. I loved my boss!

I called her back and told her I could. She told me she'd meet me out front of my office building at one and be ready to shop our butts off. *Yikes!*

The morning kind of lagged. I did some paperwork, filed some away, and cleaned out the storage room. Finally, it was time for me to meet Rach. I turned off my computer and stopped by Loren's office to tell him I was leaving. He had his back turned to me, but I could hear his voice.

"Of course, Mr. McHale...I completely understand. I will make sure she does. Not a problem, sir. Thank you, you do the same."

He turned around to hang up the phone and saw me standing there. "Hi," is what he said. He knew I was going to ask him about the phone call but he just shook his head. Knowing that he wasn't going to tell me, I let it go. I lifted my hand up without saying a word to tell him goodbye.

As I walked down the hallway to the elevators, I had come to the understanding that I had learned a few things about myself that I had never realized. I was a fighter. Since I was eighteen, I had to struggle to keep my head above water. I did what I had to do for TJ, I kept my children safe and content, and I fought for my own well-being. I did what Mona told me to do. Bear might've wanted my blood and my sweat, but he never got my tears. I didn't have to be in complete control to realize that all was well. It was nice giving it up from time to time; to allow myself to hear a song on the radio, throw my arms up in the air, and just be free. That was the most liberating feeling that I have ever encountered. I also came to the conclusion that just because I think I'm doing something in the best interest of somene, doesn't mean I have the right to make choices that will infinitely affect their life's outcome. There again, it came down to letting go of control of the situation at hand and just sitting back to relax.

I walked out the front of the building and saw Rachel sitting there in her Mustang, top rolled back. It made me smile—huge.

"Hey, sweets," I greeted. I loved my sisters. I couldn't imagine where I would've ended up without them.

"Hey, biatch!"

"Where we going for lunch? I am so ready to get my retail therapy on, baby girl!" I joked with her.

"You'll see." She smiled back. I couldn't see her eyes with those big sunglasses sitting on her face, but something wasn't right and I was getting anxious. I had never liked surprises.

"Anything?" she asked as she kept her eyes on the road. The smile left my face, I knew she was asking about TJ. She wanted to know if I had heard from him. I hadn't and I didn't try to call him, he was pretty pissed when I'd left him. I figured he moved on. I looked down at my hands in my lap and just shook my head. Whether or not she saw me, I didn't really care.

We pulled into the country club that she belonged to and I looked her way. She never looked back at me, I hated being here. It was always so snobby and she knew this.

"Rach, what the hell? I'm not dressed for this." She reached into her back seat, pulled out a bag, and handed it to me. Inside was a gorgeous, sandy brown dress with white polka dots. I looked at her and she shrugged as she got out. We walked to the entrance and into the foyer. She turned to look at me and smiled.

"You go to the ladies and do your thing. I'll meet you in the bar when you are ready, 'kay?"

I looked at her for a second and finally agreed. This wasn't going to take long at all. I went into the ladies room and locked the door behind me. I quickly changed my clothes and unlocked the door. I took down my hair from the quick, little messy bun I had placed in it this morning and let if fall over my shoulders. I refreshed my makeup, squirted perfume in the air, and walked through it. There, a complete transformation. I looked as snobby as the people I would be sitting with this afternoon.

I walked back out into the foyer and looked down the hall for the bar. Seeing the entrance was straight ahead, I walked slowly.

"Ms. Barker-Jackson?" I turned around, a little surprised.

"I'm sorry, ma'am, are you Ms. Barker-Jackson?" I smiled at the older gentleman.

"Yes, sir, that's me," I said politely with all my southern charm.

"Please, ma'am, follow me. I've already seated your guest."

I followed him through hallway after hallway. It seemed we were going to the back of the club, but that was fine with me. Rachel knew I didn't like to rub noses with all those snobs. We walked to a set of closed double doors. The waiter waited for me to come up in front of them.

"This is where you'll be dining this afternoon."

I smiled and nodded once in understanding. He opened the doors and my mouth completely dropped open.

There, in front of me, was the entire side of the club encased in glass. The view was nothing I had ever seen before. A lake as far as I could see, glistened in the sunlight. To the right, was a small pier that two or three members of the club were standing on, hanging a fishing pole over the side. To the left, was what looked like a medium sized outside deck that may have been built on stilts. The deck had four or five tables, all of them with large umbrellas unwrapped and blocking the sun for a light lunch over the water.

My eyes came back into the room and a cold rush of chills started at my toes and continued to the top of my head. There stood Trevor at a table. Dressed in a black suit, hair all groomed, totally different from the man I left behind in Vermont three weeks ago, he just stood there looking at me. I eventually remembered to take a breath and looked to the older waiter, nodding.

"Thank you for showing me to my table." There was no lunch and shopping, this was a set up. I made a mental note to kick Rachel's ass as soon as I saw her.

I headed toward the table without looking at TJ. I reached my chair and he pulled it out for me. I nodded and sat, placing my purse on the chair next to me. He pulled his chair up to the table, set his hands on his piece of china, and looked at me. I couldn't look at him.

"Elleny," he said in a soft, loving tone that made my head pop up without thinking.

My eyes met his and we just stared at each other. I was trying not to convey how much I missed him. His face was blank and I couldn't read him.

"We need to talk, Elle."

Chapter 23

Present Day

Fear and anxiety took over me. He didn't look happy, so I knew this wasn't something good.

"You wanna talk to me now? Three weeks ago I was practically begging you to talk to me, but that wasn't a good time for you, was it? Everything has to be done on your timetable, Trevor, and I'm sorry, but I don't work that way." I went to stand up when I heard his low voice.

"Please, sit. This isn't about us, this is about our children. I want to meet them, get to know them. I want to be a part of their lives. I've missed out on everything. Please, Elle, I don't want to miss out on anything else."

Did he not hear me when I told him that fuck-face would grab my children and run off with them? What was he not getting about this? Bear was serious, he had proven that in every way possible.

"I'm sorry, Trevor. I can't take that chance. Now, if you'll excuse me…" I went to stand up and he joined me.

"What if I'm not asking, Elleny. What if I'm telling you?" He laid two documents down on the piece of china that should've been where my lunch was. Two legal documents.

Two brand new copies of my children's birth certificates, completely filled out.

"I've made some friends in high places."

That motherfucker!

"You bastard! Do you know what you've just done? You've signed my death certificate. He's going to fuckin' kill me, Trevor, and he's gonna take my kids…our kids. No one will ever find them."

I went to walk away, but he grabbed my arm. "Elle, wait."

I pulled my arm out of his grasp. "Wait for what, Trevor? For you to come to my house and tell my kids that you're their father? Or wait for the guillotine to come down on top of me while I sleep? You do what you've gotta do, Trevor, because I'm gonna do what I've gotta do."

I walked out of the dining room and down the hall. I didn't know where I was going, I just had to get out of there. Finally, I recognized where I was. I walked quickly out the front door looking around. I forgot I came there with Rachel. I started looking through the parking lot, hoping she was just hiding out somewhere until we were done talking, but I didn't see her around. I grabbed my cell phone out of my purse. Just as I pulled it out, a large hand wrapped itself around mine.

"I want us to be together, Elle. I want us to be a family." I looked up at him and tears immediately filled my eyes. I placed my forehead against his chest. "I'm tired, Trevor," I cried. I felt his hand on the back of my head. "I know you are, honey." I wrapped my hands around his sides and clenched his shirt in my hands. "I'm so tired of always being strong." I could feel him rubbing his other hand down my back. "Baby, let me be strong for the both of us. I want to be your strength." I started sobbing, my body trembling. I was holding onto him because I couldn't stand without his help. "I'm tired of having to live a lie, Trevor." He reached under my chin and pulled my face up to look at him. "You're free, honey. You're not caged anymore. Spread your wings, baby." I cried for all the time that we had lost. The seventeen years we squandered away and would never be able to get back. I cried for hurting him, for lying to him, causing him to miss out on his babies growing up. I cried for the hurt I had caused my children, this was going to devastate them.

For the pain and heartache they had to go through growing up, not having a normal childhood. Always having to watch over their shoulders. I cried for joy. I wasn't caged anymore. I could let someone else be the strong one, give them some of the control. I was exhausted from trying to push Trevor away. I couldn't fight him anymore. I wrapped my arms around his waist and pulled myself close to him. If I could've, I would have jumped in his skin, that's how close I needed to be to him. I missed him. For seventeen years I had pined for him, wishing he would find a way back into my life. Here he was. The other half of my heart. Holding me, telling me he wanted to be a family.

"Nothing's gonna pull us apart this time, Elle. He's not gonna hurt you or my kids anymore."

There it was, what I always wanted. Someone to take some of the slack. He was going to help me carry the load. He wanted his kids, they weren't just "bastard children" to him. They were his kids. *His.* He loved my babies just as much as I did.

"I told you babe, anchored to you, forever and always. That doesn't mean when we fight, we go our separate ways. It means when we fight. We may pull away, but we're strong. We're supported by each other. You'll always be joined to me, babe. No getting away from me again, I can promise you that."

I giggled and looked up at him. "We're bendable, not breakable."

He pushed my hair off my face and mouthed, "That's right."

I pushed up on my tippy toes and gave his mouth a sweet, gentle kiss before breaking it off quickly. Grabbing his hand and pulling him toward the parking lot, he laughed.

"Where we goin'?"

I giggled back. "Don't ya wanna meet your kids?"

401

We drove to the school. On our way, I called Rachel to ask if she would pick up Harlee so that we could spend some time talking with the twins. She agreed, happily. So, there we were, parked out in the parking lot, waiting for me to go in and get them.

"You ready?" I asked TJ. He looked so nervous.

He cleared his throat. "I think so." I smiled at him and he smiled back at me. "It will be fine."

I went into the school and had the secretary call for the kids. I signed them out and waited impatiently for them in the hallway. As soon as they reached me, I gave them a hug and explained why I was there picking them up early.

"I had an old friend come into town, he's moving back here and I thought you two might like to join us. Kind of a skip day." They high-fived each other and we walked outside. We came to the car and TJ got out. He looked so nervous, I was attempting to mentally communicate with him so that he would take a breath. It didn't work.

"JoJo, Luc, this is my friend, Trevor. We call him TJ." He stuck out his hand, his eyes going back and forth between the children he was meeting for the very first time.

Luc spoke first. "Umm, nice to meet you, TJ."

Trevor couldn't talk yet, so he just nodded. After Luc spoke, JoJo thought it was safe for her to speak so she said the same exact thing. "Nice to meet you, TJ." As he shook her hand, TJ nodded again. "Well, let's go grab a cup of coffee."

We made it to the coffee shop and decided to grab a cup and head to a park where there weren't as many people. I didn't know how they were going to react to this news so I wanted less people around.

We got to the park and found a cozy little area. TJ had a small blanket in the back of his rental, so we took that and laid it down on the grass. We all sat down and looked at each other. I looked at TJ and nodded. I was going to start this.

"Before I get started, I just want to tell both of you how proud I am of you and how much I love you. Everything that I have ever done in my life has been for the benefit and well-being of all three of you. Even though, at the time, it seemed like the best way to go, down the line, it really wasn't. I've always thought about ya'll before myself." They both looked at each other and said, "Okay."

If I was going to explain this, I needed to go to the beginning, for the most part.

"I've known TJ since second grade. He is Auntie Rachel's cousin and he was my first boyfriend—my only boyfriend." Out of nowhere, JoJo chimed in, "Before Daddy, right?" I looked at TJ and his jaw tightened. I didn't respond.

"My senior year of high school something happened." They could see something wasn't right. "I got pregnant." Luc started to sit up, putting this puzzle together. I had to hurry up and finish this so they didn't freak out. "I didn't tell TJ that I was pregnant. He had just been offered a scholarship and he needed to go. Daddy was TJ's best friend, he knew about ya'll. We made a deal. He'd be your daddy if I never told TJ about ya'll."

Luc stood up and pulled his hands through his hair. "No, no, no, no…tell me this isn't happening."

I had to stay calm or else he was going to lose control. "Luc."

"No, Momma, you mean to tell me all those times that motherfucker had been shitty to you—"

"Dylan Lucas! What have I told you about that tongue!"

He dropped down to his knees and held his head in his hands. I could see his chest vibrating. He was quiet for a long while. "I used to pray every night, Momma. Every night, I'd ask God to make sure I didn't take after my daddy. I didn't want to be that kinda man."

I broke down. I couldn't see my son like this. He was my protector. He was my sweet, precious angel that got me through so much.

I hugged him. Crying with him, repeating over and over how sorry I was for lying to him. I reached over and took a crying JoJo into my arms, too. I held my seventeen year old babies in my arms, as though they were minutes old and continued to repeat how much I loved them and how I didn't mean to lie to them.

I pulled away and said, "Your daddy is a good man, Luc. You are your daddy's son, you're just like him." Luc looked at TJ and I could see TJ's eyes were shiny.

I heard Luc sniff. "So, you're my dad, huh?"

TJ smiled a small smile, he really didn't know what to do. "Yeah, Luc, I'm your dad."

Luc ran to him and hugged him. TJ closed his eyes and hugged him as hard as he could.

"I guess that means you're my daddy too, huh?" JoJo said. She always had to ruin a moment. We all laughed and I looked at my daughter and her father, those tiny dimples right under their eyes were a dead giveaway.

She jumped in the middle of the hug and I came up on the tail end. We squeezed together for a minute or two before breaking apart.

"So, what happens now?" JoJo asked.

That was when TJ spoke up. "Well, I think I've lost enough time with you kids, I don't wanna lose anymore. I'm movin' back to Richland. My company's headquarters will be here now. I want us to be a family. I wanna marry your momma. I've already had your birth certificates changed. Now, I grew up in this town, so I know there's gonna be a lot of talk. If you have any questions concerning anything, you come talk to me about it, got it? We're all just getting on the right track, I don't wanna derail when we're just building up speed, deal?" Everyone agreed. We continued talking for a while, TJ got to catch up with them and they got to know about him. Then, I had to tell them the big news.

"One more thing, Bear has threatened that he would run off with you guys, including Harlee, and take you down to the swamps in Louisiana if I ever have contact with TJ again or tried to divorce him. He said he would hide you and never let me see you again, so for now, we cannot talk about this meeting. Okay? Not even to Harlee. I didn't think it was right to make you suffer anymore. I knew that he has been wanting to meet you and I didn't want to lie to you anymore."

They agreed and we decided that we needed to go. I had to cook dinner and get Harlee from Rachel's. TJ and the twins exchanged cell numbers and he told them that if they ever needed him, day or night, to call. If they ever felt in danger call 911, then call him. He already had his lawyers working on some things. That must've been the phone call with Loren.

TJ drove us back to my office. We all hugged goodbye and I told him that I would talk with him later. We got in the car and drove to Rachel's.

That night seemed to be more energetic. The twins and I seemed to be on the same page whereas poor Harlee was looking at us as though we weren't her real family. I had forgotten that JoJo had a dentist appointment in the morning, so I texted Loren, telling him that I would be in as soon as I dropped her back off at school. I apologized profusely about today and needing tomorrow morning off as well. I promised that everything would be caught up by tomorrow evening.

Bear never came home that night which made the night so much better. The next morning, I got the kids up for school and made breakfast. It was nice not having to worry about Bear walking downstairs and starting in on us. I wrote a note for JoJo to take to the office saying to be I'd be picking her up and the kids caught the bus to school so that I could finish up the dishes and get dressed.

I went upstairs and began my normal routine. I turned on the shower and went to make the bed while the water was heating up. That was when I felt my skull break into pieces. I gasped and then everything went dark.

Tracy Lee

Chapter 24

Present Day
Trevor

I woke up in my hotel room immediately thinking of that meeting. I got to hold my children in my arms. Yeah, they may have been seventeen and almost grown adults, but to look at a different human being and see your face on him and her, made me catch my breath.

I had some errands to run and was planning to stop by Richland Manufacturing to drop off some paperwork to the main foreman. The construction crew was supposed to be there first thing Monday morning to begin demolition on the old offices, making a new and much needed office building.

It seemed I had a bunch of penned up energy, I felt like I could run twenty miles and still not be winded. I laid out my suit and headed for the shower. I turned on the water, let it get hot, and grabbed my toothbrush. Elle had a habit of brushing her teeth in the shower, but I couldn't seem to bring myself to try it.

I couldn't stop thinking about her. Everything that had happened lately seemed like a dream to me. Seventeen years, I waited to come back to Richland, and I was coming back with a vengeance. Bear took everything that had meant something to me and I was coming back to collect. He was going to have a shit fit when he found out that I owned the company that he worked for.

With that, I planned on taking his wife, his kids—all of them—he would be left with nothing. I was planning on adopting Harlee as well, but I was keeping that a secret from Elle. I was making it a wedding gift. As a matter of fact, I scheduled a meeting this morning with Loren Stevens to discuss the matters at hand. On behalf of Elle, I had him file for divorce with her receiving full custody of the children and a restraining order for her and all three of the kids. I also had the paperwork on hand to file a motion of adoption for Harlee and a name change for the other two.

I finished brushing my teeth and looked at the clock, I still had plenty of time. I hopped in the shower and begin washing my body. Reaching my stomach and hips, I continued to my lower extremities. I was rock hard and thinking of Elleny was not helping. I could still feel her on my skin, her hard nipples rubbing against my chest, her ass pushed up against me as I pressed her up against the wall. Plunging my finger inside of her as she dripped down my hand. She smelled and tasted so good on my tongue. I took myself in my fist and begin to stroke. I was so hard, the head of my cock was almost purple. Slow at first, just like she teased with her tongue, I started to speed up. I thought about how hot and wet her mouth was. She loved it when I fucked her mouth fast and hard. She would guide my hand up to the back of her head, allowing me to control her motions and how deep my cock would go. Her grip on my hand would grow tight, telling me to hold her there for a second. Her teeth barely nibbled on the head while she licked at the tip like it was an ice cream cone, getting every glistening drop of my pre-cum. I began stroking faster. I could feel my orgasm building. I felt the first jet of cum shoot out against my hand, then relief as more and more sprayed with the water surrounding me. I took a breath in relief and finished washing up. I got out, quickly shaved my face, splashed on some cologne, and went to get dressed.

I ran my errands. Now I was sitting in Loren Steven's office looking around, hoping to see Elle. I hadn't heard from her last night or today but she said she'd call me.

Stevens was going over all the paper work that had been filed and had set up court dates. I heard my phone ring. I looked at the caller ID and saw JoJo's name. I answered immediately.

"JoJo?"

Stevens turned around. It was quiet on the other end of the line.

"Honey, you there?"

"Um, Daddy?" There went my heart.

"Um, you told me to call you if I needed something or if something was wrong? Well, I can't get a hold of Momma. She was supposed to be here at 8:45 for my dentist appointment and she's not here. Have you heard from her?"

I looked at my watch, 9:35. I couldn't breathe. I felt like all the air had been sucked out of the room. The first thing that went through my mind was not to panic for JoJo's sake. My eyes went straight to Stevens.

"Uh, no, honey, I haven't talked to your mom this morning. But, I'm gonna find out where she is, okay? She probably fell back asleep." Stevens grabbed his phone and began dialing. I couldn't wait for him, I had to find her. Hanging up with JoJo, I ran down the hall through the fire escape. I ran through the parking lot, digging for my keys. I beeped the locks and started the car right away. Without hesitating, I threw the car in drive and didn't stop between her office and her house. Too much time had passed. She could be dea—

No, I wasn't going to think that.

I pulled up in her drive and got JoJo back on the phone. "Hey, honey, can you tell me if there's a window or something unlocked so I can get in your house?" She told me about that key under the rock and gave me the code to the alarm. I opened the door slowly, peeking in to see if anyone was in the front area. It was all clear. The house was silent. There were dishes in the sink and plates still on the table. Soft, grunting sounds came from upstairs and I moved in that direction.

"I told you, whore! You didn't listen to me. I bet you'll sure as shit take me seriously now. I told you no contact with that motherfucker! Let's see if he wants you anymore, now that you've been treated like the whore you are!"

I eased up the stair, taking two, maybe three, steps at a time. I could hear him clearly now and quickly moved in that direction. I burst through the door and couldn't believe what I saw. Elleny was tied to the headboard with barbed wire. Her wrists were bleeding freely and the barbs were burrowing into her skin. I could see the meat hanging around the wire. He had beat her so bad, she couldn't even open her eyes. Her nose was broken, leaning to the side, and she was bleeding profusely from her head. You could barely even tell who she was. Bear was standing on the side of the bed, plunging into her as she laid there unconscious.

"Motherfuck!" I screamed. "What the fuck is wrong with you, Bear! This is Elleny, you son of a bitch! What the fuck are you doing! She's your wife!"

He pushed himself off of her, shoving his dick back in his pants. He laid his hand next to Elle's head, picked up a gun, and started waving it around. "Well, well, if it ain't Mr. Big-Shit," he laughed, hysterically. "What a great fuckin' day for a reunion. It's really great to see ya again, brother." He stood beside Elle for a moment, looking down at her. "Did you enjoy my wife? She's pretty good isn't she?" He dropped his empty hand down and slid his dirty bloody fingers down her legs. "I know it's been awhile for the two of you, but I've done taught her a couple things here and there." He put his hand up on the side of his mouth as he lowered his voice to a harsh whisper, "She likes it rough now." He turned his eyes toward her and threw his hand out. "This…to her, this is just foreplay." I could feel my breakfast trying its hardest to come back up as I swallowed to keep it down. I quickly took a step toward Elleny just as he took a large step closer to me.

"She's never been my wife!" he yelled, closing his eyes for a moment. He took a deep breath to calm himself down. "She's been yours! You…you piece of shit! I couldn't do anything right to make her love me! I thought I could make her love me. I tried and tried, but she never would. Not as much as I loved her! It's always been you!" He stepped back over to her, grabbed her by the back of the head, forced her head back, and looked at her face. "Do you know how hard it is to come home every day, look at her lyin' next to you in bed, and feel your heart almost burst from the love you have for her? But, you can see it in her eyes that she don't feel shit for you…do you? No, I don't 'spose you do." He let go of her head and let it fall back forward. He walked beside the bed and headed for the window as he looked out into the yard. He was sobbing, covered in blood and sweat. Suddenly, he exploded, "I gave her all of me and she stepped on it, shit on it, and threw it back in my face!" Spittle and blood tinged sweat was flying all around him. He laughed maniacally. "I was supposed to be the hero. The one who cleaned up *your* fuckin' mess. Because of you, she fucked up my life for seventeen years. I've missed out on everything. Everything!"

He was screaming so loud, his body was shaking. He went to the dresser beside the closet door, pulled the top drawer open, and took out a long hunting knife. He put the gun in his back pocket and began running his finger down the edge of the blade. "Her daddy never did care for me. Always thought his daughter was too good for the likes of me. She started thinkin' that, too. Thought that she had a pussy made 'a gold. That daddy of hers was puttin' shit in her head so I had to shut them the fuck up! We wasn't plannin' on that bitch of his bein' home though. It sure wasn't as easy as it looked on those crime shows. That knife sure did get a workout!" He chuckled.

He put his index finger to the point of the knife and poked himself, drawing blood. I closed my eyes and prayed that Elleny was unconscious for that little confession. He squeezed it a minute and then stuck it in his mouth. "You don't know what I've had to deal with. Her bitchin', her fuckin' naggin', for years! It was so fuckin' annoying." In a nasal, mocking voice he continued, "Give me your paycheck, Bear. There's bills to pay, Bear. I need you to stop and get diapers for the baby, Bear. It was all bullshit!" He stopped at the foot of the bed on her side and I asked, "Why did you stay, Bear? No one would have thought less of you if you had left."

He laughed an evil laugh. He wasn't the Bear I knew in school, the one I played football with. This man was pure evil. "You think I'm gonna let her go without giving me some type of compensation for my losses? I told her if she'd have given me her momma's money, I'd go. She'd say something about it being for them bastard kids of hers, so now it looks like I'll get that…and her life insurance. Hot dayum! This days gettin' better and better!"

It was taking all that was within me not to break this motherfucker's neck. He was nothing but a piece of shit. A crazy one, at that. He started walking back over by the dresser next to where Elleny was. He set the knife on top of it and took the gun out of the back pocket. I instantly did the first thing that came to mind.

"You want money, Bear? I'll give you money. How much you want?" The smile left and he contorted his face. He was looking at me like he was trying to read me. The smile came back. Bear took the muzzle upside his head as though he was thinking. I prayed that it would accidently go off. I looked back over at Elleny and heard her softly moan. She was alive. *Thank God.*

"Put your fuckin' eyes back on me, shithead!" he roared. I had to do something quickly. He was getting worse but the minute.

"Here…" I dug in my back pocket and grabbed my checkbook. "Take it, it's yours. Take it all. I'll sign whatever you want." I threw the book down on the ground not far from my feet. He stood there looking at it. He brought his eyes back up to me. He wasn't smart, but he was not a fuckin' idiot either. He looked back down. "What's the catch? You lemme take that and you get to take her?" I nodded to him without saying a word. He watched me closely.

He slowly began to bend at the knees to go down, but his eyes were still on me. His arm slowly reached forward to grasp the book. As soon as he got it in his hand, I reared back and kicked it forward with all my might. He went flying and so did the gun. I heard a loud bang, the gun had gone off. I wasn't thinking about where the bullet had traveled, I just wanted to make sure he was unconscious so I could get to Elle and make sure she was alive. As fast as I could, I ran toward him. I wasn't sure if he was dead or alive, but I didn't really give a shit. I retrieved the gun from the floor and stuck it in my front pocket.

I turned around to check on Bear. He was still lying on the ground, completely still. I called 911 and gave the dispatcher the information. She informed me that both police and medical were on the way. I threw the phone down and ran over to the bed to check on Elle. There was so much blood, I didn't know how she was still alive. Her breathing was so shallow, I could barely see her chest moving up and down. I looked at her wrists and realized I wasn't going to be able to untangle the wire. I looked at her head; there was a large gash at the crown. He had bashed her over the head with something.

"Oh, Jesus, God, baby." My voice was trembling with fear—fear that I was going to lose Elle. I couldn't help her. "I'm gonna get you out of here, okay. Just hold on. Oh shit, honey… stay with me, baby." I went to the bathroom to grab a rag, thinking maybe I could at least hold something against her head to stop some of the bleeding. I got it wet with cool water as quickly as I could. I shut the water off and ran back out into the bedroom.

Bear stood next to her. He had her head pulled back by her hair with a knife at her throat.

"Better say your goodbyes now, motherfucker!" I looked at him and growled, "No, Bear...don't fucking do this!" I could see him putting pressure on the knife that he held right below her left ear. He slowly started dragging it across her skin. His eyes never left mine. "Tell her now, motherfucker! Confess your love to her. Let it be the last thing she hears before she bleeds out!" It looked like he was drawing a thin black line on her neck with a black pen. He was slowly killing her because he knew it was torture to me. On impulse, I remembered the gun in my pocket. I dropped the rag, reached in my pocket, and grabbed the gun. I raised it without saying a word, aimed, and pulled the trigger. Bear's head flung back just a bit like he'd been jolted. He stood there for a moment. His eyes still on mine with a small black hole between them. The knife that he was holding fell to the floor and he followed, crumbling down to the floor beside the bed. Right beside Elle.

It was done...he was dead.

Epilogue

Two Years Later

"Breathe, baby… breathe." TJ's voice was what was keeping me grounded. "You're doing so great. I love you so much." I just nodded.

"Elleny, I need you to take another deep breath and push." I exhaled what breath I had, pulled in deep again, and held it. "One…two… three…" I listened for the ten in my husband's voice to know that I needed to start again.

"Okay…don't push anymore, the head is out." I laid my head back against TJ's hand that was holding my head up. I needed to close my eyes for just a few minutes. Fourteen hours of labor would make anyone exhausted. I missed this before with the other babies.

I took this moment to think back on what all had happened to us in the last two years to get us to this point. After TJ killed Bear, the police investigated and determined that it was self-defense since he was in the process of slicing my throat. Charges were never filed.

Four months later, TJ and I got married. Along with a name changing ceremony on all three of my kids. TJ legally adopted Harlee. We were all family. We were a true family and we were right where we needed to be. The twins graduated from high school and were accepted into the same college. That was a stipulation for me, and that they had to live on campus. TJ and I got them all moved in to their dorms and we made sure that they didn't go far. We spent as much time as we could with them. I put my house up on the market and sold it a month later. I wasn't asking much for it. I just wanted out of it. There were too many bad memories there. We ended up moving in with TJ. He was renting a smaller home because we had decided to have a house built so we stayed there until it was finished.

I had to have several surgeries to repair both my wrists where Bear had wound my hands up with the barbed wire and my neck. He destroyed some tendons and muscles but they were repaired. The doctor's said I was lucky, my wounds were so deep. the wire almost hit my artery. My neck was a shallow cut, that was more of a cosmetic thing then a medical necessity but my husband—I love calling him that—tells me all the time, "Baby, when you look in the mirror and see that beautiful face, I don't want you to have any memories of that day or that life." The scars were healing nicely. It may take one or two more surgeries on my wrists to get back to what was normal for me, but other than that, all memories of that day were gone.

I wanted TJ to have a chance at what he missed the first time, so I talked with my female doctor and I went off the shot contraceptive. It took a while, but I got pregnant. TJ was thrilled.

He went to every doctor's appointment with me. We even took some classes that the hospital was offering so that he could learn how to put a diaper on or make a bottle, even how to breastfeed and pump.

At twenty-four weeks, we found out that I was having another set of twins. I thought TJ was going to pass out. I laughed hysterically, but this time, I wasn't surprised. I felt extremely blessed. Here I was, married to my soul mate after being separated for seventeen years, and not only had I had one set of twins with him, but two.

TJ's voice brought me out from my thoughts. "Okay, babe, let's do this." He pulled my head up as he lowered his to kiss my forehead.

"This should be the last push to get this baby out, Elleny." I grabbed a breath and pushed with all my might. I heard crying…newborn crying.

It's a boy!"

I threw my head back and hit pillow. I got a break. I heard TJ's voice.

"Oh my god, baby, he's so beautiful. That's my son— our son, Elle. He looks so much like you."

Right now, I didn't care if the baby looked like Dracula. I wanted to close my eyes and rest. I heard the nurses in the corner with the baby. TJ was snapping pictures with his camera phone to send to everyone. The doctor was doing something between my legs and I was just lying there.

"Okay, Elleny, are you ready? It's time for the next one."

"Shit, already? Can't I rest?"

"Come on, honey, almost done. You've done amazing."

Okay, I've had enough with his Lamaze video watching self, he needed to just shut up.

"Honey, I love you, but you need to shut the fuck up with the amazing shit. I'm tired and I want this kid out of me and you sitting there smiling at me like you're on a ride at Disney is not helping matters."

The smile left his face and he pulled back a minute as the doctor laughed hysterically. "I was wonderin' if you were going to hit that stage of labor or not. Looks like you did. Don't worry, son, it's perfectly normal. Now, Elleny. Push now." I smiled up at my husband, he smiled back, and I knew we were anchored together, right at this very moment. I pushed three pushes and my daughter was born.

Later that night, in my hospital room, I woke up to the sight of my husband holding my newborn daughter, Mona Elyse McHale. She looked just like her daddy. So beautiful. She had Luc's disposition. She was quiet, yet she knew what she wanted when she wanted it. She was going to be the leader of the two.

"Momma, I think she's hungry," TJ said, looking at Mona.

"Bring her here." I held my hands out for her. He placed her in my arms and I rearranged my nightgown so that she could feed. He sat there, watching me feed our daughter.

"I've never seen anything more beautiful, my love. You have given me a gift I could never find anything close enough to give to you in exchange."

As I sat feeding her, my newborn son began to cry. My husband went over to his crib, picked him up so gently, and held him up. "Mr. Ryder Maxwell McHale, you must want to eat, too." TJ walked around with Ryder while I finished with Mona and then we swapped babies. He hadn't left my side. He was staying up here, sleeping on a hard, lumpy couch just to be next to me.

If five years ago I'd have had a chance to look at where my life was now, I would've jumped in your face and called you a liar. Never would I have thought I'd have found such happiness and that I would let go of the mask that had become such a norm to me. But, once I dropped it on the ground, I knew I would never need it again.

I stepped on it and then stomped on it incessantly to make sure that I couldn't pick it up and shove it back in my pocket. These feelings were real, they weren't just something that was set in my mind and would make an appearance with a song or a mood. This was a permanent feeling and I couldn't have asked for it with a better person. I never thought I'd be able to feel such love again, but with the personal experiences I'd had, they taught me to take it and never let it go.

THE END

About The Author

Tracy lives with her husband and 4 children in a small town just outside Tulsa, Ok. Originally from Brandon, Florida she was a city girl at heart. Wanting a change of scenery, she packed her kids up and moved to Oklahoma where now she's seen snow, touched farm animals and has cows in her back yard.

Being a stay at home mom, an avid reader and part-time blogger; she decided to put the three of them together and try her hand at writing and fell in love. In between running kids from band practice to PTO meetings, she enjoys her "me time" working on a little bit of her next book. She thoroughly enjoys head-banging heavy metal and a kickass game of Black Ops.

Be sure to add her to keep updated on her upcoming books.

Tracy can be found at:
www.authortracylee.com

Made in the USA
San Bernardino, CA
28 July 2014